Dissonance

Jonathan Bruce Brown

For Suzanne
With every good
wish!
Jonathan Brown
November 14, 2019

Copyright © 2016 Jonathan Bruce Brown

All rights reserved.

ISBN-10:1530218098
ISBN-13:978-1530218097

DEDICATION

To Marcy, who has taught me so much about life and love.

ACKNOWLEDGMENTS

Many thanks to Ann Smith, who kept encouraging me to stay with this project, to Mark Smith, Earl (Bud) Poleski and Susan Sandell, who helped me with invaluable facts about firearms, ammunition and Michigan law, and to Marcy, Margaret, Diane and Betsy for their sharp eyesight.

CHAPTER ONE

The bullet interrupted the great symphonic masterpiece in the rudest possible way.

Henri Falcano couldn't know the last moments of his life had come, and excitement coursed through his body as he led the huge orchestra through the tumultuous finale of Mahler's second symphony. The explosive power of the music filled him with elation, despite his best efforts to keep his emotions in check.

Falcano cursed inwardly as plucking strings made a sluggish entrance, but he forced himself to look bold and confident as he made his gestures more precise. The musicians responded quickly, and Falcano felt his muscles relax as their twisting line began to flow with the buoyant strength he wanted.

He gave an appreciative nod and smiled inwardly at the knowing looks on several of their faces.

Falcano felt a special kinship with this monumental work, often referred to as the "Resurrection Symphony." Its theme celebrated personal vindication, not the events of Easter, and Falcano felt the deepest kind of admiration for Mahler's life-long fight for recognition.

He knew Mahler struggled courageously against vicious opposition throughout his career. Many people couldn't understand Mahler's unconventional genius, but many others would never accept a Jewish musician as one of the most important conductors in the world.

Near the end of the symphony the chorus would sing *Du wardst nicht umsonst geboren*, "You were not born in vain." These words filled Falcano with tremendous empathy for Mahler, and in the rehearsals this week, they had mirrored his own keen sense that his destiny had come to a critical turning point.

Maybe things were finally about to work out for him!

Falcano's gestures became much more gentle and sweeping when the low brass intoned a glorious, hymn-like passage that seemed to rise through the air like a glorious ray of light. He paced his energy carefully as all six trumpet players joined in a powerful crescendo that led to a fortissimo passage of wonderful majesty and power.

The music swirled around him like a mighty whirlwind, and Falcano exulted as his arms ripped through the air to elicit all the expressive power the orchestra could muster.

Sweat trickled into the corners of his eyes, but he ignored it and forced himself to keep breathing smoothly. He couldn't allow himself to get winded.

With a twinge of self-reproach, he sneaked a peek at the video camera recording his every movement and facial expression. He shouldn't have risked even the tiniest lapse in focus, but he had a thrilling sense the recording would really show him at his best.

He suddenly felt sure he could win that coveted guest conducting job in Paris. A fresh jolt of exhilaration coursed through his body. An opportunity like that could vault him onto the world stage. It might be his first step toward the big time.

If he played his cards right, all of his troubles might soon be over!

Two soloists, a soprano and an alto, sat primly at his side in elegant evening gowns. Their composed faces gave the audience no hint of the tension that coursed through their bodies as they braced themselves to join in the music making.

A choir of 133 singers sat in tidy rows at the back of the stage. Most of the singers tried to look unruffled as the orchestral musicians created a constantly-evolving torrent of extraordinary sounds right in front of them. It wouldn't do to look too stage-struck.

The choir had waited in patient silence for more than an hour, but soon they would rise for their surprising entrance, one of Falcano's favorite passages in all orchestral music. The singers would all lift their voices at the same instant, but in the quietest whisper imaginable.

The electrifying effect of that moment never failed to astonish an audience.

After that, the music would build, little by little, toward the symphony's euphoric conclusion. The men's voices would echo profoundly dramatic phrases heard earlier in the low brass, the women's voices would add warmer tones, and the two soloists would sing a glorious duet, their voices soaring to fill the concert hall with thrilling brightness.

Falcano's hands barely moved as most of the orchestra fell silent and a trombone solo became the center of attention. His eyes shone with appreciation as the trombonist's rich tone sang out like the voice of a powerful operatic tenor.

More than 1200 people in the audience looked on in various states of mind, depending on their individual temperaments and mood. Some sat with pleasant, blank expressions on their faces. Quite a few noticed a skinny, eccentric giant in the violin section bobbing around like a boxer. But despite their moods, most of the audience felt increasingly captivated by the rising power and surging energy of the music. Many of them who had heard a recording of this symphony realized once again how much more exciting and engrossing music can be in a live performance.

The orchestra members also felt a variety of distracting emotions. An oboist, frustrated with her reed, pulled it off impatiently during long rests and swiped at the edges with her carving knife. A young violist who recently joined the orchestra felt the music flying by like a galloping racehorse.

But like the audience, the musicians felt a common bond of deep involvement with the music. All of them knew this symphony intimately, and most of them respected it deeply. They considered this music holy ground and worked as hard as they could to perform it not only well, but passionately.

Falcano listened in awe as the music built up more and more strength and finally seemed to dive headlong into utter turmoil. His muscular gestures felt like sword strokes as a soaring, defiant theme erupted in the horns and trumpets.

He tried mightily to resist his rising emotions, but this passage affected him deeply despite all his efforts to remain cool and objective. He always felt it represented some of Mahler's deepest frustrations, and he marveled at the composer's power to capture in music the overwhelming emotions that can burn in the heart when life is at its worst.

After the sonic storm passed, the music settled into an eerie stillness, as if time itself had stopped moving.

Falcano couldn't imagine a more dramatic contrast.

A bass drum rumbled as a single horn player intoned a gently rising phrase. Then vivid, hushed flourishes echoed from offstage trumpets as the flutes and piccolos chirped haunting birdsongs from the middle of the orchestra.

Mahler called this moment *der grosse Appell*, "The Great Summons."

Falcano marveled at the music's vivid depiction of the world waiting in breathless excitement for a moment of tremendous importance.

Soon the chorus would sing *Aufersteh'n*, "rise again," in their barely audible whisper. Then the music would start to build inexorably toward its overwhelming, ecstatic climax, that thrilling moment when *Aufersteh'n* would thunder from their throats as orchestral sound pealed forth with almost overwhelming intensity.

The choir members rose silently to their feet, and Falcano looked up to engage their attention as the music became softer and softer. When the orchestra's sound dwindled into complete silence he would cue their wondrous entrance.

Then a fateful moment passed.

Invisible beams of light from two tiny, hidden devices converged on a single spot four feet and seven inches above the podium.

Delicate sensors detected something solid in their path.

At that moment, in that space, it could only be Falcano's body.

When the display on a digital timer reached 9:23 p.m., an electrical impulse coursed to a solenoid device that depressed the trigger of a .223 caliber rifle mounted in the dark recesses of the ceiling.

A rush of superheated gases forced a projectile out through rifle's barrel at just under 3300 feet per second, almost three times faster than the speed of sound.

A scientist may have noted the bullet spun at approximately 198,000 revolutions per minute and its tip traced a slight spiral. A myriad of physical forces affected the bullet's path, but for all intents and purposes, it traced a line as straight as a laser.

A shockingly loud sound exploded in the concert hall as the bullet sped to its target, taking just five hundredths of a second to travel 169 feet to the exact point marked by the crossed beams from the electric eyes.

The bullet slammed into the conductor's back with cruel efficiency. Its unique design made it create a tiny entry wound and burst violently into pieces inside Falcano's body, wreaking havoc on his heart and internal organs.

Falcano stood for a moment with a look of utter astonishment.

Then he fell abruptly into the small space between the assistant concertmaster and the principal second violinist.

The music continued raggedly for a couple of seconds until everyone realized what had happened.

A wild cacophony of screams and shouts replaced Mahler's sublime music as people ducked for cover, ran toward an exit or sat numbly in their seats. Several peered up into the balcony area, fearing more shots might come.

A small group gathered quickly around the stricken musician to see if he could be helped.

It didn't take them long to abandon hope.

CHAPTER TWO

At 5:45 a.m. Wil Walker admitted he wouldn't be able to sleep any longer and sat up on the side of the bed. The gruesome vision of Henri Falcano collapsing into the orchestra had spun through his head all night. He wasn't sure he'd slept at all.

How could such a thing happen?

Wil shuddered as the searing image burned in his brain again. He saw Henri, larger than life, standing on the podium. Then, in the next minute, his friend lay bleeding out on the stage.

He held his head in his hands. How could anyone do something so brutal and malicious?

The aging bedroom floor creaked in protest as he stepped across the threadbare carpet to his cramped bathroom.

Wil rinsed his hair in the bathtub, trying not to look at the rust streaks in the porcelain and the dark stains in the ceramic tile. As he stood to dry his hair, he surveyed the dismal bathroom in disgust. Everything looked so old and dingy. This color scheme had probably been popular fifty years ago!

He stared dully into the small, cracked mirror, wondering why anyone would even want to kill Henri? It made no sense! Henri seemed to get along fine with everyone. And he was a musician, an artist. What could he possibly do to provoke someone that much?

Henri's death made life seem so fragile, so fleeting. Wil wondered who would care if he died tomorrow? He had lived forty-two years. What did he have to show for it? This house? The old dump was falling to pieces!

He thought ruefully he should be grateful he owned the place. He inherited it when his parents died in a terrible car crash. Having no house payment allowed him to get by on his pitiful income, but he didn't even have enough money to keep the place up.

He had his cranky old pickup, a 1999 Ford F-250, but it could quit any day, and God help him the next time it needed a repair bigger than a brake job.

He used to have so many dreams!

A deep weight of realization pressed harder on him every day. The time had come to face the bitter truth. Most of those dreams would never come true.

He lived hand to mouth, surviving on freelance music jobs, part-time teaching gigs and whatever else he could find. Occasionally, he even painted a garage or built a deck around someone's pool. He hoped only his best friends knew about that.

He hated to think about health insurance and his nonexistent retirement plan!

On three different occasions, he had almost landed college teaching jobs that would have given him much more security, but he always lost out to someone a little more experienced, a little better suited to the job description.

No, face it! They were just better!

Wil trudged down the squeaky stairs, trying to ignore the piles of papers and junk on the steps. He chided himself for not keeping the house cleaner, but no amount of spit and polish would make the place look good.

He felt more weary about trying to keep up with it every day.

His queasy stomach rebelled at the thought of food, but he knew he should eat, so he put two slices of bread in his grimy toaster and set a skillet on the back burner of the stove.

The front two burners on the ancient, avocado-green range hadn't worked in years.

As he stirred his eggs, Wil looked dispiritedly at the disheveled pile of his musical scores next to his piano. What kind of fool wrote classical music nowadays?

He had devoted years of his life to pounding out ideas on the piano and poring over page after page of musical notes. And who cared? Everyone thought orchestra music was written by old dead guys.

And maybe they were right!

What had he written that he could hold up against the great masterworks of Beethoven and Mozart? And just to be real, how much money had he ever made writing music? He could probably have gotten a better hourly wage flipping burgers!

He hardly tasted his eggs as he wolfed them down.

Suddenly he couldn't stand the thought of sitting around in the decaying house feeling sorry for himself. He poured his coffee into a travel mug, picked up his toast and walked out to his old pickup.

Wil barely saw the thick groves of trees on either side as he drove down his quiet country road. At the junction with the state highway he turned right toward the expressway.

He had no real plan about where to go. As the road climbed toward higher ground he took another bite of toast and a drag on his coffee, staring stiffly at the roadway ahead.

He remained dimly unaware as the majestic blue glory of Lake Michigan swung into view on his left and filled the horizon with wonder.

CHAPTER THREE

Detective Peter Jones frowned as he looked at the scribbled notes on his yellow legal pad. Yesterday he had been on the glide path to retirement. He could almost feel it!

And now this.

He had a visceral ache to be at his cottage on Torch Lake. A short drive, three hours due North, would take him to his doorstep, and he could be in his boat by this afternoon, staring through the miraculously clear water at objects on the bottom, fifty feet below.

Nothing tasted better than a fish that had just been caught an hour ago.

Reluctantly, to say the least, he forced himself back to the realities of the moment.

What a bizarre case!

The press would descend on this like locusts. How could they resist? A conductor shot in the middle of an orchestra concert? And by some kind of automated booby trap!

He hoped they would lose interest quickly and leave him alone to do his work, but every instinct told him otherwise. The press loved the most sensational stuff, the weirdest things that happened.

This case certainly fit that description.

Jones hated the common misperception that real crime only happened in the big cities, but he had hoped he could spend his last couple of years investigating the low-profile stuff.

He could deal with the never-ending flood of drug dealing, petty robberies, and the unspeakable things people did to each other in their own homes. That's where things really got ugly. Every cop in every town had seen aspects of human nature no one wanted to admit existed.

But at least all of that stayed under the radar. Everybody would be paying attention to this case, looking over his shoulder, second guessing everything he did.

The very thought made his skin crawl.

Jones stood up and crossed his makeshift interview room in two strides.

He had set up shop in a cramped cubicle that normally served as a practice area. A well-aged upright piano with yellowed keys and chipped brown veneer took up most of the space. That left no room for a table, so he'd been writing on a dusty black music stand with "St. Cecile Symphony" stenciled on its back in faded yellow paint.

He had already interviewed several members of the orchestra.

They had all witnessed an incredible horror, their conductor dropping dead right in front of them, shot by a bullet that came out of nowhere, but no one knew anyone who would want to kill the guy or why.

The orchestra's administrative director, Prudence McDonough, had arranged to meet him here at the symphony's small office space and offered to send out an email inviting the orchestra players to come here for interviews.

He jumped at the chance. Dozens of people had left the symphony hall by the time the police arrived, and he had no desire to track them all down.

The conductor's death seemed to leave McDonough more or less in charge in the orchestra's fuzzy management system.

He had interviewed her first.

She asked to be called Pru and said she spent most of her time convincing well-heeled music lovers to write fat checks and seeking grants from wealthy foundations. You had to make grant proposals sound like sexy, exciting initiatives, she said, even though they were really just new ways of describing what an orchestra had to do to survive.

Jones opened the door of his makeshift office and stifled a wry smile as he looked around the anteroom. What a cast of characters! Apparently orchestra musicians came in all sizes and shapes, but they certainly didn't look like a dangerous bunch.

The office felt jammed with so many people in the space usually occupied by a few staffers.

Jones jabbed a finger at the next name on his list.

"Is Greta Schmidt here?"

A slightly plump woman in a brownish print dress rose quickly and hurried to his side.

"I'm Greta."

Her red sweaty face made it clear she'd been crying.

"Hello. Is it Miss Schmidt?'

"Just call me Greta. Everybody does."

She leaned close to speak in a conspiratorial whisper.

"Who did this Detective? Who could do something so … so horrible, so heartless?!"

Jones thought she might burst into tears again.

"I have no idea yet. That's what we have to find out."

He ushered her into the practice room, closed the door and tried to find a comfortable perch on the thin padding of his metal folding chair.

Greta sat on a similar chair, crossed her hands on her lap and sat primly with her knees touching. She looked calm, but seemed to have a hard time catching her breath. She told him she played bassoon, and anyone hearing her heavy accent would know in an instant she had grown up in Europe.

Jones asked her several questions, but she had nothing new to offer, so he thanked her for coming and let her go.

The next person on Jones' list, Jim Pearce, strode in with a loose-legged gait and a jaunty grin, looking like a man at a bar ready to order a cold long neck.

"Have you got it solved, Detective?"

Pearce stood over six feet tall, and his muscular bulk made the room seem even smaller. He sprawled into the chair across from Jones and rocked back and forth, crossing his legs with his ankle on his knee.

Jones studied Pearce in mild astonishment. He had never seen a pair of cowboy boots quite like the exotic pair on his feet.

"What kind of leather is that?"

"It's rattlesnake! Do you like it? I could get you some, but they ain't cheap!"

Pearce's deliberate attempt to sound like a rube took Jones by surprise.

"What's your role in the symphony, Mr. Pearce?"

"Mr. Pearce? Are you talking to my Daddy?"

Pearce laughed, a little too loudly.

Jones regarded him coolly and let the question hang in the air.

After an awkward moment, Pearce set the chair down on all four legs and leaned forward with his hands on his knees.

"I'm the trumpet player. The *first* trumpet player."

Jones tried not to react to the strange emphasis.

"How long have you been part of the orchestra?"

"Almost ten years. I'm one of the old timers."

"Do you know anyone who would want to kill Mr. Falcano?"

Pearce seemed to hesitate before he answered, but when he did, he sounded very glib.

"No, of course not! He was a prince. Everybody loved him."

Jones saw a hint of a smirk cross his face.

"Everybody?"

Pearce looked at him searchingly, then looked at his fingernails, as if they were suddenly interesting.

"Well, you might talk to Charlie Kim, he's the concertmaster."

"And that means what?"

"Oh, yeah, I forgot. You're not a musician, are you? The concertmaster is the principal violinist."

Jones smiled thinly. Pearce's country twang seemed to be fading.

"Why should I talk to him?"

"He and Falcano had been feuding lately. There are always little spats going on in the orchestra, know what I mean?"

Jones almost scowled as Pearce arched his eyebrows knowingly.

"Anybody else?"

"Let me see …"

Pearce seemed more wary all of a sudden.

"You might ask Wil Walker what he knows about electronics. That's how this was done, wasn't it? Some kind of fancy electronic booby trap?"

"What do you know about that?"

Pearce waved his arm dismissively and sat back in the chair, his grin once again firmly in place.

"Nothing! Nothing at all! Word travels fast in a small town, that's all. And even more so in the orchestra."

"Ok, I'll talk to Walker. Anybody else?"

"I can't think of a *soul*, Detective."

Pearce stood up abruptly.

"Are we done? I've got a lot to do today."

Jones didn't see any point in pressing harder at the moment, so he let Pearce go.

He did notice Pearce stomped across the room very quickly, without saying a word to any of his colleagues, and took a seat by himself in the far corner.

Jones scanned his list again. He'd been able to cross off about half of the names. He wanted to learn more about a couple of them, but most of these folks were going to be no help at all.

Oh well, that was police work!

He found the next name on his list and stepped to the door.

CHAPTER FOUR

Wil eyed the familiar, run-down buildings wearily as he drove absent-mindedly into the small business district of St. Cecile.

The city had been much more prosperous at one time. The French explorers that named St. Cecile, like most of the other cities in Michigan, found huge tracts filled with magnificent pine trees. Giant rafts of logs had floated down rivers to be milled into lumber in the state's golden age. Later, the railroad made St. Cecile an important crossroads and an industrial city.

Now the town survived mainly on a few small industries and a fickle tourist trade. Lots of summer travelers came to spend time near Lake Michigan, but winter in St. Cecile could be a very lonely time.

The quiet lifestyle near the lake did appeal to a colorful assortment of painters, potters, weavers and other artistic types, and that made for a very lively cultural scene.

But none of that crossed Wil's mind today.

Some mysterious pull made him drive by the symphony office. He couldn't have said why. No one would be there on a Sunday morning.

He sat up in surprise when he saw the parking lot full and quite a few cars parked on the side streets. Apparently many others had also felt the need to gather there after what happened last night.

Wil felt torn between an urge to commiserate with his friends and an equally-strong desire to be alone, but when he saw an empty parking space near the door, he took it and walked in.

He looked around in amazement as he stepped through the door. More than half of the orchestra players had gathered in the tiny room and stood around talking in small groups.

He started to walk toward the oboist Gail Rotenska, a good friend, but Greta Schmidt grabbed his arm with surprising force.

"Isn't it terrible Wil? I just can't believe it?"

Greta pulled Wil closer and whispered roughly in his ear.

"There's a detective in the next room!"

Wil felt the moisture of her breath on his cheek and instinctively started to back away, but she had an iron grip on his arm.

"He's asking everyone all kinds of questions!"

Wil softened a bit when he saw the real concern in her face.

"They have to do that, Greta. What would you expect?"

"Do they really think a member of the orchestra could do such a horrid thing? Besides, we were all busy playing the concert when he was shot!"

"They have to find out everything they can, Greta. Just relax and answer their questions. Have they talked with you yet?"

"Yes. I was terrified!"

Wil felt a tap on his shoulder and turned to find a middle-aged man with short, sandy gray hair and a very thick mustache standing very close behind him. The look on the guy's face came from either vexation or boredom, Wil couldn't decide which.

The man looked at his legal pad.

"Are you Robert Walker? Oh, excuse me, do people call you Wil?"

"Yeah, my middle name is William and my friends call me Wil."

Wil felt a bit sheepish.

"My parents started calling me by my middle name when I was little. Blame them."

The man looked at him without a trace of humor in his face.

"My name is Peter Jones, Mr. Walker. I'm a detective. Could I have a word with you?"

Greta looked at Wil with a horrified expression and turned away quickly, hoping the detective hadn't noticed.

Wil waved her off and followed the policeman, who had already moved several steps away.

The noise in the crowded room gave way to uncomfortable silence as they stepped into a practice room normally used for teaching private lessons.

Wil wondered why the detective wanted to see him as he studied the man's stocky frame and slightly rumpled clothes. He wouldn't expect a cop to have scuffed brown shoes, a shirt that wouldn't quite stay tucked in and glasses that kept slipping off the bridge of his nose

Jones settled into a folding chair near the back wall and waved a hand at a similar chair at the end of the piano.

"Please have a seat, Wil. Thanks for coming in. It saves us the trouble of looking you up."

"I didn't have much choice did I?"

The detective didn't react, so Wil tried another tack to lighten the mood.

"You seem like a pretty normal person. Watching TV you'd think all police officers are smart alecks."

The detective looked at him darkly.

"Watching TV you'd think all musicians are nut jobs."

Wil swallowed with a cottony mouth and decided to stop trying to be funny.

"They tell me you are a composer in residence with the symphony, Mr. Walker. What does that mean exactly?"

Wil leapt at the chance to talk about something more familiar and comfortable.

"There's no specific job description. I write pieces for the orchestra and arrange tunes for special concerts, but I also help with other things behind the scenes."

"Like what?"

"The conductor and I bat around ideas for upcoming concerts."

Wil reddened and looked at the floor.

"At least we used to."

"Is that all?"

Wil looked up to meet the detective's gaze. His blue eyes seemed to miss nothing.

"I also give talks before the concerts, background on the music, pictures of the composers, things like that."

"That sounds kind of dry. People come out for that?"

Wil tried not to look offended.

"Actually, a lot of people do. I work hard to make it interesting, and I think the sound of great orchestra music is incredible, miraculous. I really enjoy helping people see what I love about it."

As he said it, Wil realized he had taken very little joy in music lately.

Jones looked thoughtful, but far from convinced.

"Can you make a living doing that?"

Wil flinched unwittingly, swallowed and tried to sound more confident.

"No, not even close. I do it because I enjoy having a connection with the orchestra. It pays a few bills, that's about it."

"All these people in the orchestra, is this their full-time job?"

Wil fought back fresh irritation. Musicians found it harder and harder to make a living these days.

"Everyone gets paid something, but they all have day jobs."

"So who are they?"

"Some of them are teachers or free-lance musicians. Several are graduate students from the big universities. A lot of the players are just gifted amateurs who do something else for a living."

"Is that unusual?"

"The orchestra is excellent for a town this size. Put it that way."

Jones seemed lost in thought for a moment, so Wil decided to take the initiative.

"Aren't you going to ask me where I was when Henri was shot, because I was in my seat with dozens of wi…."

The detective looked up sharply.

"There's no point. He was killed by some kind of automated setup."

"What?"

Wil realized abruptly how much that changed things. No one could be ruled out as a suspect.

"What kind of automated setup?"

The detective's impassive face gave away nothing.

"We're keeping the details to ourselves. We've heard you have some background in electronics, is that true."

Wil's stomach did a flip flop.

"What?! Who told you that?"

"That doesn't matter right now. Is it true?"

Wil cleared his throat nervously.

"Yes it's true. I majored in electronics when I started college. I just decided I was really a musician at heart, so I changed my major."

He wished he could read the cop's mind.

"Are you saying I'm a suspect?"

"All we're trying to do now is gather some information, Mr. Walker."

His eyes narrowed.

"You're not upset, are you?"

"No, I uh ..."

Wil grasped for something to say, then spoke in a rush.

"I have nothing to hide! You can't think I had anything to do with it!"

Jones regarded him with a searching look,

"Right now we're just asking questions."

Wil felt his face flush deep crimson as the cop looked into his eyes.

"We'll need some information, Mr. Walker, your phone number, address, where we can reach you."

Wil's voice came out in a croak.

"Uh, sure. Look, I'll be happy to help you any way I can."

"If we need to talk to you, we'll call."

"I, Uhh, ... ok, of course... I only meant ..."

Jones looked at him dismissively.

Wil stumbled out of the room in a daze.

CHAPTER FIVE

Wil felt everyone in the room looking at him as he walked stiffly toward the door. Some stared openly, but most of them cast sideways glances, apparently thinking he wouldn't notice.

His tried to look calm despite his burning face.

The police officer's attitude baffled him. Did Jones really think he could have killed Henri? And who had brought up his study of electronics? That was years ago. Who even knew about it?

More than anything he wanted to get into his truck and drive away, to have some time to think!

Greta hurried to his side, and he fought to swallow his irritation.

"What did he ask you about?"

She stood too close again, and Wil turned his head instinctively to avoid the unwelcome intimacy.

"Nothing, really, just routine."

Pru McDonough bent close to them with a conspiratorial air.

"Are you ok?"

Greta pressed even more closely to his side.

"Come on, Wil! What did he say?!"

Suddenly, Jim Pearce's resonant voice boomed behind them.

"You look a little pale, Willie! Are you under arrest, hot shot?"

"Jim!"

Greta scowled, and Wil saw similar horrified looks on several faces.

Pearce, never one to be subtle, stepped closer in three large strides.

"Come on, I'm just trying to lighten things up a bit. It's not like one of us did it."

Wil had to look away from Pearce's bizarre, incongruous grin.

Ted Mason, one of Wil's best friends, spoke up from his spot near a cluttered worktable.

"The killer could be anybody! I heard the gun was a booby trap. No one had to be there when it went off."

Wil admired Ted's quiet, gentle spirit and always felt he could count on him for a favor. Ted played piano and percussion. Only a handful of people knew he was gay.

"What? That's insane! How is that even possible?"

The heavy Slavic accent belonged to Helen Rubinstein, who sat in a folding chair with her legs tightly crossed.

The severe set of her face accentuated her striking beauty, and she held one arm up in the air as if she had a cigarette in her hand. Her dark formal dress seemed oddly out of place.

"Surely someone had to be there to aim it!"

She looked very close to bursting into tears.

Ted looked at her earnestly.

"I don't know all the details, but somehow it would only fire when Henri would be hit."

Pearce scoffed dismissively.

"No way! That's impossible."

Greta spoke up with a voice full of irritation.

"We'll just have to wait and see, won't we?"

She turned back to Wil with a look of deep concern.

"Wil, what did the detective want to know?"

"Uhh... I'd rather not go into that right now."

Wil cleared his throat nervously and wondered how he could make a hasty exit. He could feel his nonchalant façade crumbling.

"I mean, you know, we'll just have to let this play out and see what the police come up with."

Helen's face had become a grim mask. She tossed back her head to shake her fine blond hair off her shoulders.

"We'll all have our turn."

Wil had no idea how to read her dark mood.

Helen had been a child prodigy in Russia, and her parents had brought her to America as a teenager, hoping she would become a famous concert violinist. Like many gifted performers, she learned the competition was extraordinary and the public, who would stand in line for tickets to hear a famous star, had little interest in lesser known artists.

Talent didn't seem to matter nearly as much as getting the right publicity.

Suddenly the door opened and Jones walked out into the room.

"That will be all for today folks. We have everyone's contact information, and we'll be in touch if we need to talk with any of you."

The musicians seemed in no hurry to leave.

"Is it true that the gun was fired by a booby trap?"

Greta's voice still sounded strained and reedy.

"I'm sure there will be some information in the papers. We're not releasing any details for the moment."

Jones guarded tone again revealed nothing.

Pearce laughed derisively.

"Maybe it was a terrorist, and he escaped before anyone could see him."

Greta's irritation boiled over.

"Stop it, Jim! How can you make jokes?"

Pearce glared at her and shoved his hands into his pockets.

Jones spoke mildly.

"I think it's best if everyone goes home. I'm pretty sure they want to lock up the office."

"Who even told you to come down here?"

Helen sounded imperious.

"Look folks, you've all had a bad shock. Why don't you all just go home. There's nothing more you can do here."

Greta looked at Jones with her eyes burning.

"Our music director's been killed! You can't expect us just to go on about our business! And who's going to lead the orchestra?"

Pru spoke up in a cool even voice

"Leave that to us, Greta. We've called an emergency meeting of the board tomorrow night. They'll decide what to do."

"My God! How can you all act so calm?"

Greta finally burst into tears.

Ted took her arm.

"We're all upset, Greta. Come on. I'll buy you a cup of coffee."

He looked at Wil, obviously hoping his friend would come along on his errand of mercy.

"I, uh ... I've got some things I have to attend to. I'll talk to you soon."

Wil looked at the floor, then touched Greta's shoulder.

"Don't worry. We'll get through this."

Greta brushed at the tears streaking down her face and nodded.

Pearce looked to Jones with one last smirk.

"I guess we're not supposed to leave town, huh? Isn't that the way it works, Detective?"

Jones looked at him with a dry expression, then turned and made his exit without responding.

Wil lingered for a moment, trying not to look too anxious to leave.

Helen stood up and stepped toward him, somehow involving her whole body in the motion.

"We all want to know what he asked you about, 'dahling.'"

She arched an eyebrow to stress the sarcasm.

Wil decided it would look worse to act like he had something to hide.

"He asked me about my background in electronics."

He tried to say it smoothly, but a nervous catch came through in his voice.

"I guess someone told him I had some experience in that area."

No one seemed to have anything else to say.

Wil decided he could finally make a break for the door, but he had only taken two steps when Pru touched his arm.

"Wil, can you come to the board meeting tomorrow night?"

"What? Why?"

"Just humor me, ok?"

"All right, I'll be there. When is it?"

"Seven o' clock, in the conference room here at the office."

"Ok. See you then"

Helen crossed over to his side.

"Can you give me a ride, Wil? I haven't got my car. The battery's dead or something. I got a lift from Greta this morning."

Wil stifled a sigh. He wouldn't have some time alone for a little while longer.

"Sure. Let's go."

"Thanks."

She grabbed her purse and tossed the long strap over her shoulder, walking toward the door without once looking back at Wil.

Ted shook his head with a mournful look.

"I guess something like this can happen anywhere, huh?"

Pearce headed for the door with one last jarring quip over his shoulder.

"Anywhere and everywhere."

Wil bolted toward the exit too. He couldn't wait to get far away from all these people and this unbelievable situation.

The whipsaw changes in emotion had his brain reeling.

Surely the policeman's questions just caught him off guard. The cops couldn't really consider him a suspect!

Could they?

CHAPTER SIX

Helen stood waiting by Wil's pickup with her hands at her waist, looking off into the distance.

Neither one spoke as Wil unlocked the truck and they both climbed in.

Helen's icy, confident demeanor evaporated as soon as Wil accelerated down the street. She sank into the seat with a look of utter desolation, lit a cigarette with trembling fingers and inhaled deeply.

Wil stifled his irritation as the cab filled with smoke. They drove for several uncomfortable minutes before Wil finally broke the silence.

"How did your battery get run down?"

"There's nothing wrong with my car. I wanted to talk to you."

Wil grimaced.

"How did you know I'd be at the symphony office?"

She looked at him with a cold smirk.

"Are you kidding? I knew you'd come down, just like everyone else!"

She looked away, her body stiff with tension.

"Besides, everyone is afraid of what will happen"

"You mean whether the orchestra will fall apart?"

"Musicians are such children sometimes."

Helen blew smoke toward her window and stared hard into the distance.

Wil studied Helen's stony face as he turned onto the highway along the lakeshore.

"What did you want to talk to me about?"

"You know what I want to talk about! Had Henri talked with Leontyne or not?"

Wil did know what she wanted to discuss, and he had no interest in dealing with that problem now. He put his right arm on top of the steering wheel and glanced at her quickly, then turned his attention back to the road ahead.

"I know he was thinking about it. He probably did say something to her."

"He's been thinking about it for-EV-er, and no, he probably never said a damn word to her!"

"He, uhh … he was very busy, Helen. He probably just couldn't get to it."

"That's crazy! He didn't want to. She's organizing a tour across Europe with her orchestra, and I would be the perfect soloist, but he couldn't be bothered to stick up for me. He couldn't care less!"

Wil squirmed.

He knew Henri thought it would be a waste of time to put any pressure on Leontyne Philips, the conductor of a fine chamber orchestra in Chicago. Conductors get calls every day from people telling them what to do and how to do it, and they learn to make up their minds early and grow thick skins.

Henri had tried, and tried hard, out of consideration for Helen, but as he expected, Leontyne had chosen her program and hired a soloist long ago.

Helen wouldn't get the starring role that might jump start her career.

Falcano had told Wil all about it, but he had asked him not to say anything to anyone, especially Helen. Apparently he thought a clear rejection would hurt her more than acting like he had never gotten around to calling.

Wil didn't see any point in breaking the confidence now.

"Look Helen, maybe it just wasn't meant to be."

"That's easy for you to say! You don't seem to care if you ever do anything outside this little hell-hole of a town!!"

The caustic taunt reignited all of Wil's frustrations, but he wasn't about to tell her that. He gripped the steering wheel tightly and stared hotly at the road ahead.

Helen turned toward him with wide eyes and a face tight with anger.

"All he had to do was pick up the phone, or maybe buy the woman lunch!!"

"What makes you think it would have been so easy? Conductors can be pretty stubborn, you know."

"Oh, gimme a break!"

He thought she'd picked up a lot of American slang for a woman who had spent the first decade of her life in Russia.

She sat back heavily and crossed her arms tightly over her chest.

"You know all he had to do was say the right word!'

"Maybe not."

"Oh, please! You don't care if I ever have a career either, do you? What do you think I should do, sit here in St. Cesspool twiddling my thumbs?"

Wil felt exasperation rising in his chest.

"No, I think you ought to play! Play all you can. Give it your best. Maybe at the right place and the right time someone ..."

"What ... some movie producer will hear me playing while he's having a cheeseburger at the diner? We're about a thousand miles from ANYBODY here, Wil! Don't you care about that?"

Her words cut Wil to the core.

"Of course I do! I care about that very much."

He desperately wanted recognition, a chance to be involved at a much wider level, to write music that people listened to and talked about. Just like her, he wanted to be on the stage, wanted to be noticed. He thought every artist wanted basically the same thing, the chance to do something wonderful and have people respond enthusiastically, to try to achieve something truly excellent, and to be able to give it everything they've got.

Wil thought bitterly about his own miserable attempts to promote himself. It seemed the harder you pushed, the tighter the doors slammed shut.

Helen just sputtered and reached into her purse for another cigarette.

Wil's anger softened quickly.

He had always found Helen's European mannerisms fascinating, and he felt strangely drawn to the deep sadness that always hovered just below the surface with her.

He had often heard Russians were sad and withdrawn, people of 'great souls,' but Helen's angst went beyond that. It seemed she carried a huge weight wherever she went, a dark, nagging pain that never completely left her alone.

The tires crunched on the gravel as the truck turned onto Helen's long driveway.

As they drove toward the house, bright sunshine reflected brilliantly off the deep-blue lake and provided a stark contrast to the sullen mood in the pickup.

Helen stared through the windshield with a hard look on her face.

Wil hated to leave things this way.

"Maybe you should write her yourself."

"Don't you think I've tried? I don't even think she opens her mail!"

Wil had no idea what to say.

"How the hell are you supposed to get people's attention, Wil? How do you get a chance to be heard?"

Wil wished he had an answer to that very good question.

Peter Jones racked his brain as he left the symphony office, trying to come up with some kind of insight about the killer's identity.

He went back to the concert hall, hoping to get some small inspiration by standing on the podium where Falcano died. He examined the spots where the electric eyes had been set, then he climbed up the catwalk to the place where the rifle had been mounted on a small bracket.

What kind of person would kill someone in the middle of a concert with a Rube Goldberg contraption like this? A whacko? Did the very public setting give the killer some bizarre thrill?

Could the perp have wanted to make some kind of statement? Maybe, but nothing pointed to any kind of message.

What could Falcano have been hiding that would drive someone to murder?

Jones shook his head and headed out to his car.

When he got back to the station, he went to the evidence room and spread out all the parts of the deadly booby trap on a table, trying to figure out what it would take to design and execute a thing like that.

None of it helped a bit.

Jones felt his body droop as he headed up to his desk, a gray metal box pushed up tight against a drab, cinder block wall.

A deep, weary sense of the futility seeped through him like a paralyzing drug. Had he ever really achieved anything in this job? He might as well try to empty the ocean with a teaspoon! This bizarre case took the cake, for sure, but he had seen it all, over and over again, senseless killing, fraud, thievery, assault. What good did it do to lock up a bad guy? Dozens more always seemed ready and willing to step in and take over.

The unfinished work stood in piles on his desk, and he longed to be somewhere else as he sagged into his threadbare chair.

Then he sat back in surprise.

Someone had left an envelope addressed to "Detective Jones" leaning against his computer.

He quickly checked with the duty sergeant, who said someone had slipped it under the front door without being seen.

Jones sat back down, slit open the envelope, and found a single sheet, printed in the same, strangely-ornate typeface as the envelope.

He frowned as he read it.

ASK WILL WALKER WHY HE WAS PUTTERING AROUND IN THE SYMPHONY HALL THE NIGHT BEFORE THE MURDER!

CHAPTER SEVEN

Wil swung too hard and watched with dismay as his golf ball curled off to the right in a weak slice.

Every winter, as February and March dragged on, he grew more and more desperate for a chance to get out on the links. Spring had finally come, and the first warmish days beckoned him outdoors with irresistible force.

He shook his head and teed up another range ball.

You know better!

He had loved golf since he took up the game as a young boy. He relished the challenge of trying to loft the ball over a sand trap or coax in a long putt, and he enjoyed the process of selecting the best club, picturing the perfect shot and trying to hit the ball with just the right power and trajectory.

Some people got angry and frustrated playing golf. Wil almost always found his time on the golf course wonderfully soothing, almost therapeutic. Golf usually helped him relax and unwind like nothing else could, and if he ever needed to focus and calm down, this was the time.

Wil knew he had been down lately. He just felt stuck in the mud. Everything he had ever tried to do seemed to be going nowhere!

Seeing Henri ambushed like that, in the middle of one of the greatest concerts he'd ever conducted, had shocked him to the core. He had never experienced that kind of loss before, and he literally ached when he thought about Henri being gone. Henri had been a very special friend. Wil had loved writing music for him to conduct, and Henri had always performed his music with great care and respect.

The edge in Detective Jones' questions had been the final insult. Did he talk to everyone that way? He really seemed to think Wil could be a suspect.

Wil felt like a giant steel spring, wound way too tight and ready to bust. He had never even imagined being the object of that kind of suspicion.

Hopefully, hitting some balls would help him put things in perspective.

It couldn't hurt!

He took another swing and huffed as the ball dribbled a few pitiful yards off the tee.

Some people found music and golf a strange combination, but Wil thought the part of his spirit that loved a soaring golf shot was the same one that savored a majestic melody in the violins. The rhythms of the sport helped him find his balance as he walked briskly between shots and tried to find the right tempo for a smooth swing.

Once he had come across a picture of George Gershwin hitting golf balls at a driving range just like this one. The caption said Gershwin adored golf and had a compact, efficient swing that reminded people of his precise style of piano playing.

With a sudden pang of regret, Wil wished he had bought the book so he could cut out the picture and frame it. The sharpness of his self-rebuke surprised him, but he also knew he felt too weary to make the effort to find it again.

The picture would remain one more 'what if' on the ever-growing pile of things he should have done or could have done.

Wil took a deep breath, tried to shake the tension out of his muscles, checked his stance, and started what he hoped would be a smoother swing. The ball sailed a little straighter, but quickly hooked off to the left.

"Ahhhh!"

Wil felt incredibly preoccupied and tense. He knew most of his swings today would be awful, but he decided to keep trying. He certainly had no desire to go home and stare at the wall thinking about his dead-end life and the detective's probing questions.

"Ahh-uhhhhnnn!"

He took another stab at the ball and watched it skitter off a few yards without ever getting airborne.

"Ok, concentrate!"

Wil shook out the stiffness in his arms, waggled the club gently over the ball, took his address and swung in a more coordinated rhythm.

Finally one of his shots sailed out long and true.

He exhaled gratefully, put another ball on the tee and took his stance again. He forced his mind to focus on the matter at hand … good upright posture … ball positioned straight out from a point just behind the left heel … the club shaft in a good perpendicular position ... take it back in one piece and swing through.

Another decent shot!

Wil breathed out slowly again and tried to coax his muscles into repeating the pattern with consistency and ease … good setup … good position …swing smoothly.

He finally felt himself starting to relax as his attention focused on the search for the perfect swing, that holy grail that all golfers seek with unshakable devotion, steadfastly refusing to admit they will never find it.

Jones watched through a grimy window as Wil Walker parked his car on the street, rubbed his hands nervously on his jeans and walked toward the police station.

He had called Walker in to talk about the strange, anonymous note.

The guy seemed too sensitive and honest to be a very likely suspect, but his name had come up for the second time, and Jones couldn't really rule him out. He seemed to have as much reason to kill Falcano as anybody else, meaning no reason at all!

Jones exhaled loudly as he sat back down at his desk to review his interview notes.

Everyone praised this conductor to the skies!

Jones could understand the loyalty, especially right after Falcano's bizarre death, but he had to find something to go on. Nobody could be as perfect as this conductor seemed, and Jones knew people like that often turned out to be anything but.

No one could come up with a single reason why anyone would want Falcano dead, but someone had set a lethal trap and killed him!

What kind of motive could there be for killing someone like him? Some power struggle behind the scenes? Maybe a jilted lover? Or a lover's jealous boyfriend?

Jones scratched his scalp above his right ear in frustration.

He had a lot of digging to do!

Then the elevator opened and Wil stepped out.

Jones watched impassively as he walked across the squad room like a wary cat and stood up when he got to his desk.

"Please sit down, Mr. Walker. Sorry about the mess around here. We don't have as many visitors as a big city police station."

Wil sat, but his sour look showed clearly he didn't want to settle in for a long chat.

"No problem, Detective. What can I do for you?"

"You want a cup of coffee or something?

"No thanks. I'm good."

Wil looked like he had a belly full of smoldering coals.

Jones exhaled deeply and got to the point.

"I need to ask you about another piece of information that's come to our attention."

Wil squirmed in the chair, looking like he hoped Jones hadn't noticed.

"Ok, shoot."

"Were you in the concert hall alone the night before the murder?"

Wil's face went white in an instant.

"What?! I … I, uhhhh …"

Jones felt a pang of empathy as he watched Wil struggle for control.

"I didn't go anywhere near the stage! I was setting up for a presentation in a room just off the lobby. I always give pre-concert lectures there."

"Why on Friday night? Did anybody see you there? Was anybody with you?"

"No … no … I can't believe this!! Who told you I was there?"

"Does it matter? Do you have something to hide?"

"No, nothing!! It was completely innocent Mr. Jones! I was Henri's friend. Why would I want to kill him?"

Jones heard Wil struggle to control his voice and decided he had pushed him far enough for the moment.

"That's what I'm trying to figure out. Just relax. We don't suspect anybody at this point."

Wil settled back into the chair, but his stricken face spoke volumes about his inner turmoil.

Jones decided to try a different tack.

'Awn-ree,' is that how he said his name?"

Jones watched his visitor struggle to look calm.

"Yes, as in French."

"It says here he was born in DeKalb, Illinois."

Wil smiled thinly.

"Well, yeah, that's not that uncommon in the music business. A foreign sounding name will get you much farther than a name like Jack or Bill."

"So he dropped the y, put in an i and went French?"

"I guess so."

The look of fear and distrust on Wil's face hadn't faded one iota.

"Falcano sounds Italian."

"It does, but people didn't seem to notice the mismatch. At least they never said much about it."

"Do you know why anybody would want him dead, Mr. Walker?"

"No! I've been wracking my brains. It doesn't make any sense!"

"Try again."

Wil seemed to struggle for breath.

"It won't help, detective. Everyone liked him. Besides, he was a musician not a loan shark. What could he do to hurt anybody?"

"That's what I'm trying to figure out. Did anybody else know you were going to the auditorium Friday night?"

Wil looked down at his hands.

"Just Pru. I borrowed her keys. I didn't even see anyone there."

Suddenly, his head shot up.

"Did Pru make a big deal out of this?"

Jones debated a moment, then set the paper on the edge of the desk.

"This was stuck under the door at the station earlier today. No one saw who dropped it off. Somebody seems to think you should be checked out."

Wil stared at the note in disbelief.

"This is crazy! Everybody knows me. I couldn't hurt a fly!"

Jones actually considered that a fair assessment. He usually trusted his instincts. Could Wil be putting up that good a front?

"Do you have any enemies, Mr. Walker?"

"Not that I know of!"

Wil pointed at the incriminating paper in disgust.

"Why would anybody do something like that?"

"Lots of reasons. Maybe someone is genuinely concerned. Maybe it's an effort to deflect attention. Hard to tell."

Wil looked down again and seemed to be searching for words. Finally he looked up.

"You have to believe me, Detective, I couldn't have done this. I was Henri's friend. I had no reason in the world to kill him."

"It seems like nobody did. That's the problem."

Wil stood up, looking thoroughly shell shocked.

"Is that all then?"

"For now, but be sure you're someplace where we can find you."

Wil bolted toward the elevator, slamming his thigh on the corner of a desk in his haste.

Jones watched with a combination of amusement and disbelief as Wil tried to act like nothing happened and limped out of the room.

He turned his attention back to the incriminating note with a weary sigh.

Could he believe Wil's explanation? The guy knew about electronics and he'd been in the right place at the right time to set the trap. Maybe his relationship with Falcano had been more complicated than he let on.

Jones had to admit he didn't really know much about William Walker.

CHAPTER EIGHT

Wil's foul mood darkened even further as he walked through the back door into his squalid kitchen. A pile of dirty dishes hid the sink, and he should have emptied the trash two or three days ago.

His disgust went through the roof when he saw a teeming trail of ants stretching from a crack below the counter to some irresistible bit of decaying food in the dirty dishes.

He turned on the hot water with a dejected sigh and started to dig into the mess in the sink. He could clean up the dishes and spray for ants, but the counter would still be cracked and stained, the floors would still be sagging, and there would still be lots of crevices where vermin could get in. The drafty old place might as well have a sign for insects and mice saying "Ya'll come."

He could never win the battle unless he could completely redo the place, and where would he get the money for that?

When he finished his chores he flopped heavily onto the couch, splayed his legs out in front of him and cradled his head in his hands.

His meeting with Detective Jones had been another brilliant performance! Did he have to make things worse by being such a klutz? Had it really been less than twenty four hours since Henri died? The whole situation seemed completely unreal.

Jones had to understand he hadn't killed Henri. When the investigation got rolling everyone would know he had nothing to do with it.

Wouldn't they?

They had to believe that!

He told himself to be patient and let things sort out, but he didn't feel patient at all at the moment. He wished he could do something, anything, to help prove he was innocent, but he had no idea where to even start.

At the very least he could try to find out more about Henri, about the orchestra, about anything that would help! He just couldn't sit around waiting for something to happen. Maybe he could find something the police had missed.

He had to try!

His body felt unbelievably tense and stiff. Any relaxation he had gotten from hitting golf balls had fled long ago. He stood up, rolled his head in lazy circles and dangled his arms at his sides, shaking them loosely in front of him as if they were soaking wet.

None of that seemed to help much.

What could he do to keep his swirling brain occupied? Maybe he could work on his composition. That usually made him forget anything and everything going on around him. He didn't think he would accomplish much in this awful frame of mind, but anything had to be better than sitting around going crazy!

He walked through a small archway into his music studio, swiveling his arms and shoulders as he went.

The small room hardly deserved the name 'music studio,' but it did hold one of his prize possessions, a baby grand piano. The old instrument didn't look like much, a network of hairline cracks covered every inch of its dulled lacquer finish, but Wil loved the rich sound it produced and spent countless hours at its keyboard.

He walked over to the large desk and sighed when he saw the clutter of papers, books and coffee cups he'd left in his way. He knew he should tidy up the rat's nest before he got started, but he scowled at the thought, stacked some of the junk out of his way and settled into his chair.

For more than a year he'd been working on a symphony, and he'd hit a terrible dead end, a huge wall of writer's block.

He'd written many pieces over the years, but writing a full, four-movement symphony would be a huge leap forward. Unfortunately, like many composers before him, he found the very idea of putting a piece out there as his "first symphony" throughly intimidating.

Did the paralysis come from fear of failure? A feeling of inadequacy? He didn't know, but the infuriating stagnation bothered him more than all the other factors in his deep funk combined.

On his worst days, he feared he might be finished for good.

He shook his head vigorously. He couldn't allow himself to think like that!

To make it all worse, he had finished the hardest work for three of the four movements. A large stack of papers on the corner of his desk contained the rough drafts for a bold opening allegro, a dancing scherzo, and an exuberant finale. He'd already begun working out the full scores for these three movements on the computer.

He only needed to write the slow second movement. He'd tried dozens of ideas, but none of them had clicked. Something always felt wrong.

Usually slow movements came the most easily for him, but he'd been stuck at this spot for weeks.

He gathered his sheaf of sketches and spread them out on the piano's music rack.

Two black wires snaked between the computer and the piano. This MIDI - 'Musical Instrument Digital Interface' - system still seemed like a miracle to Wil, especially when he remembered the hundreds of hours he'd spent writing manuscripts in messy black ink.

MIDI allowed the computer to faithfully record every nuance of music played on the piano. The recorded music could then be replayed on the piano at the push of a button. The music could also be heard through a synthesizer, which could make it sound like any combination of instruments imaginable.

The big payoff for Wil came when he printed perfect, professional copies of his works with a click of the mouse. MIDI made corrections simple, and even major changes, like transposing a whole piece into another key, took seconds instead of hours.

Wil loved the computer system for creating the final manuscripts, but he still preferred to do the nitty gritty work of composing by hand, in pencil.

He reached across the desk for a new, super-sharp pencil and turned his attention to the pages in front of him. Scribbles of notation covered almost every inch of the paper.

The way he drew the notes almost always provided a great barometer of his mood. Exuberant or bold music came out as big, dark notes. Light chicken scratches indicated softer sounds or tentative indecision.

The tiny, insecure notes on these pages showed only too well his frustrated lack of progress. He had crossed out extensive passages with dark slashes, and he realized that had been happening way too much.

He had to get past this wretched inability to get anywhere.

C'mon, try to focus!

He studied the page intently, then selected a spot that seemed promising and plunked it out on the piano.

Drat!

He had hoped he could build this idea into something worthwhile, but today it sounded unbelievably trite and predictable.

He rocked his head back and forth and tilted from side to side, trying to roll out some of the tension in his neck and shoulders. When he felt a little better he played a few chords.

Everything sounded unbelievably dry and dead!

He decided to try another tack and played some of his favorite music by Bach, then a little Mozart. That had often been a good way to get his creative juices flowing.

He returned to a blank page in the sheaf of sketches, but after several more minutes he had to admit nothing would come again today.

The failure added more fire to his thorough disgust.

He slammed his fist against the keys with a loud, discordant bang, and immediately regretted it. If he broke a hammer in the piano, he would pay dearly for his childish burst of frustration.

Thankfully, when he played a chromatic scale for several octaves, all of the keys seemed to respond fine.

He took a deep breath and emptied his lungs forcefully as he got up from the piano. He had plenty of detail work to do on the other movements, and it would be many hours before he felt tired enough to sleep after a day like this.

Wil dropped into the desk chair, pressed the button to fire up the computer and stared into the oversized monitor. He arched his back and shook his arms again, then clicked the mouse a few times to open the file for the last movement. After a few more clicks he found the passage he'd been working on, and he leaned forward to study the measures leading into it and the pencil drafts in his sketches.

A pleasant, familiar absorption gradually began to take over. The boisterous sounds of the music filled his imagination and pushed aside the messy details of the murder, his talk with the detective, even the oppressive feeling that his life had become a bottomless rut.

His mind focused on the hundreds of details he had to pull together to turn his concepts into a finished composition.

For a long time he would be lost in a world of his own.

A world he treasured.

A faded black Cadillac drove slowly down the dry gravel road, leaving twin trails of dust hanging in the air. The tires crunched as the car pulled into what had once been a driveway in front of a huge gray barn.

The old barn looked timeless. Its paint had chipped off badly, disguising the fact it had once been bright red. Long, broad swaths of rust streaked the metal roof, and the warped, uneven hardwood boards had pulled away from the frame at random angles here and there. A thick growth of last-year's weeds, looking utterly dry in the early spring sunlight, covered the ground on all sides. A row of ancient trees stretched off into the distance on the right.

A person dressed entirely in black climbed out of the car and carried a thin, oblong package across the overgrown yard. Rusty wheels squealed on a mangled track as the barn door slid open. Then the dark figure stepped through the doorway, and the door slid back shut.

Inside the barn it seemed as if time could actually stand still. A few rusted tools leaned against the wall or hung from square-shaped rusty nails. They looked like they could be twenty years old, or a hundred. Pungent smells of old straw, dust, leather and wood permeated the dark, cool air.

Gaps between the rough planks of the siding let in random shafts of sunlight that carved eerie shapes out of the darkness. The planes of light revealed hundreds of dust particles and short, hair-like filaments swirling slowly in the stagnant air.

The mysterious intruder focused on the items in the package and seemed to take no notice.

Bales of straw filled one side of the barn from floor to ceiling. In the dim light they formed an unbroken, honey-colored expanse that stretched up until it disappeared in the dark spaces near the roof.

The dark figure pulled out a set of large papers, mounted them on the straw by thrusting huge spikes through their corners, moved to the opposite wall and raised an arm toward the strange gallery.

A crudely-enlarged picture of Henri Falcano stared out from the first image in the exhibition. *Pum.* A crisp-edged hole appeared in Falcano's forehead. *Pum, pum.* Two more holes appeared, forming a tight triangle.

The shots came from a forty-five caliber, semi-automatic Heckler and Koch pistol with a sound suppressor screwed into the barrel. The large rounds from the forty-five pierced through the target as if it wasn't there and burrowed several bales deep into the straw.

Pictures of Helen Rubinstein and Wil Walker hung next to Falcano's likeness. *Pum ... pum.* Helen's eyes disappeared. *Pum ...pum, pum.* Three holes popped up in a small circle on the bridge of Wil's nose.

The gallery continued with a picture of a young girl from a high school year book. *Pum ... pum, pum, pum.* Her mouth became a misshapen line.

The next picture featured a woman about 25 years of age. A clip ejected from the pistol and thumped onto the dusty floor. A new one quickly took its place. *Pum, pum, pum, pum.* A line of holes started at the woman's throat and rose diagonally toward her left ear.

A brightly colored trifold hung in the next space, revealing an anonymous nude model with a wide-eyed look and a pose that left nothing to the imagination. *Pum ... pum ... pum, pum ...pum, pum, pum, pum.* Her nipples disappeared cleanly. Then a line of shots began at her abdomen and obliterated the wisp of hair between her legs.

An elderly couple smiled benignly as a half-dozen bullets from another new clip ripped into their faces.

In the final picture, an old-fashioned image of Jesus knelt with folded hands as a shaft of light shone down on his upturned face.

The arm lowered for a moment, then jerked quickly back up.

Pum. Pum. Pum, pum, pum, pum. ... Eject, thump, ching ...Pu-pu-pu-pu-pu-pum. Pu-pu-pu-pu-pu ...

The close air filled with smoke as clip after clip slammed into the gun and a long barrage of bullets reduced the row of pictures to an unrecognizable pulp.

The hammer clicked without firing several times before the shooter threw the gun with savage force against the shredded remnants of the strange picture gallery.

Then the sound of heavy, rapid breathing filled the sudden silence.

After a long time, the dark figure picked up the gun, the door slid open and shut once again, a hasp slammed roughly together, and a blow from a gloved hand slammed shut a large padlock.

Sturdy, tight-laced boots stamped off toward the black Cadillac, and the car drove off into the gathering darkness.

CHAPTER NINE

Wil walked briskly down Main Street, wishing the low, gray clouds and the icy wind would just go away. Cold weather always seemed doubly cruel after the first warm days of spring. He almost expected to see small, icy flakes of snow skittering across the sidewalk.

Wil shivered and wished he'd parked much closer to *Le Bon Temps,* St. Cecile's newest restaurant. His quest to learn more about Henri's murder had to start somewhere, so he'd called Helen and asked her to meet him for breakfast.

Why hadn't he worn a heavier coat? His useless cloth jacket just served as a painful reminder of how fickle early spring could be in Michigan.

When he got to the restaurant, he tugged open the door and gratefully stepped through to the aromatic warmth inside.

The size of the Monday-morning crowd surprised him. The upscale eatery seemed very popular, for now, but Wil guessed many of the customers would soon tire of the fancy prices and go back to their regular coffee shops and waffle houses.

He didn't see Helen anywhere, so he walked to a booth near the back, hung his jacket on a hook and slid onto the seat, rubbing his hands together for a little added warmth.

"Good Morning, *Monsieur*. My name is Jacques. How may I serve you this morning? Would you like to try one of our flavored coffees?

Wil looked up in amazement.

"Is that you, Jack? I've known you since you were in the third grade. What's with the Jacques business?"

Jack leaned forward with a conspiratorial whisper.

"I have to greet every customer that way, Wil. He's trying to create, you know, a certain atmosphere."

"Just bring some coffee."

"What flavor do you want?"

"I just want regular coffee!"

"We have hazelnut mocha, raspberry crème and Columbian French roast."

"Geez! Bring me the hazelnut, I guess. Just make it hot and quick. What's on the menu in here?"

"Oh, sorry!"

Jacques scurried away and came back with a fancy menu about six inches wide and twenty inches tall.

"I'll be right back with your coffee."

Wil read the English text with relief, grateful he didn't have to navigate French at the moment, but he couldn't find blueberry pancakes or hash browns anywhere. The menu offered crepes, brioche, steamed eggs, cheeses, croissants and muffins. He wondered how many people just ordered eggs with bacon and toast anyway.

He'd almost made up his mind when the owner, Winston Nicholas, breezed up to the table and took a seat across from him.

"Hey, hey! How do you like it Wil? What do you think of my little bistro?"

Wil tried not to stare. Winston always wore garish outfits, but today he'd chosen a weird shirt with chaotic colors and jagged designs that looked like an artist's palette gone mad. He'd also left the top two buttons open to display a shiny pendant on a gold chain and a several curly strands of chest hair.

Wil decided he must have spent some time in a tanning booth, too.

Winston held his hand against his cheek in a way that just happened to display a pinky ring made of a huge nugget of solid gold.

Wil forced himself to smile.

"It's great, Winston. How's business?"

"Booming, look around!"

Winston beamed approvingly as he looked himself.

Wil thought he'd probably been admiring his new enterprise since it opened.

"Here's your coffee, sir. Do you take cream and sugar?"

"Thanks, Jack, just a little cream."

"C'mon Wil, call him Jacques! Just go with it. We'll never get this little town on the map unless we have some culture around here."

"Fake names and play acting won't give this city culture, Winston. Culture has to come naturally."

"Yeah, whatever. What kind of culture are you talking about, farmer tans and pickup trucks?"

Wil regretted his sharp tone immediately as Winston looked distractedly toward the kitchen.

"No, look, I'm sorry. This place is cool. I'm just saying we don't need to call people by French names to enjoy it. Just let the food and atmosphere do the talking."

"Yeah, sure, I'll think about it."

Wil decided saying any more would just make things worse.

Winston checked the room again, then looked back at Wil with a strange expression.

"What about this murder, Wil? You got any theories?"

"No, nothing. I can't imagine why anyone would want to kill Henri, especially in such a bizarre way."

"I heard the police questioned you again."

Wil felt his cheeks redden, and he hoped Winston wouldn't notice. He desperately wanted to avoid getting caught up in the small town rumor mill!

"So? They just wanted to ask me a few questions."

"Oh, yeah? About what?"

"I don't really want to talk about it."

Winston stared at him searchingly, but he didn't press the point.

"Suit yourself."

He stood up to leave, but sank back into his seat as Helen walked up.

"Hi Winston. Morning Wil. Have I kept you waiting long?"

"No, I just got here."

She looked at the seating arrangement, then slid into the seat next to Wil.

Nicholas beamed as he gazed across the table.

"How are you, pretty lady? What brings you to my humble establishment this fine morning?"

"It's a miserable morning, Winston. Have you been outside?"

Winston grimaced.

"You know what I meant."

He turned and raised a pudgy arm.

"Hey, Jacques. Bring the lady some coffee."

"Jacques?"

Helen looked at the server, then at Wil with a puzzled expression.

"Don't ask," Wil whispered.

The waiter walked over, his demeanor full of solicitude.

"Would you like hazelnut mocha, raspberry crème or Columbian French roast, mademoiselle?"

"I'll take the raspberry, and cut the crap, Jackie."

Winston shook his head.

"And you people call yourself artists!"

He waved off Jacques with a little extra force, then looked at Helen.

"I was just asking Wil what he thought about the murder. Who do you think could have done it?"

Helen picked up a menu with a toss of her hair.

"A lot of people. I think Mr. Fancy Henri Falcano was not the person a lot of people thought he was."

Winston looked fascinated!

"What do you mean?"

"I mean he only thought about himself. He was a selfish jerk."

"Maybe you killed him."

Winston turned jovial as Helen scowled.

"Hey, c'mon. I'm just kidding!"

"Oh sure, I know how to set up a fancy booby trap. I'm just a stupid musician, remember?"

"What are you talking about?"

Winston looked genuinely baffled.

"Haven't you seen the paper this morning?"

She reached into her oversized purse and tossed a copy of the St. Cecile Daily News onto the table.

Winston craned his neck as Wil grabbed the paper and read the headline aloud.

"Maestro Murdered While Conducting Concert."

Helen sputtered.

"Nice alliteration, huh?"

"Shhhh!"

Winston looked transfixed and fluttered his hand at her.

"Go on Wil"

"Police are investigating the shocking murder Saturday night of Henri Falcano, the conductor of the St. Cecile Symphony. Falcano was leading the orchestra in its season finale, a performance of Mahler's *Second Symphony*, when a bullet cut him down in front of hundreds of concertgoers. Police sources said Sunday the fatal shot came from a rifle fired by an automated device. No details were provided."

"Police 'sources?' Who is Jeanette trying to kid?"

Helen's mood obviously hadn't improved since Wil had driven her home yesterday.

Wil had always liked Jeanette Fields, who had been the editor of the paper in St. Cecile as long as anyone could remember. Jeanette controlled every decision about stories and layout, even the advertising, and she often wrote the editorials herself. Many people in town found her feisty, opinionated style more than a little intimidating.

Winston waved his hand again and the huge ring glittered, even in the artificial light.

"Go on."

Wil found Winston's expression puzzling. He looked cool and aloof on the surface, but Wil could tell he wanted badly to hear every detail.

Did his interest go deeper than morbid curiosity?

"Police said they had no leads in the bizarre slaying, which has put the entire community of St. Cecile on edge…"

The article went on to say the investigation would be continuing and included a very thorough biography of Henri. The final paragraph said the orchestra had reached a new level of quality, and significantly increased its budget and endowment, during his three years as music director.

"So, he was born in Iowa? Isn't that interesting?"

Wil frowned. Nicholas sounded like a drooling old gossip! What difference did that make?

Helen looked like she couldn't care less.

The mood changed as Pru McDonough walked up to their table, looking very businesslike.

"Morning everyone. I see you've been reading the paper."

"Hi Pru. We were just chatting with Winston. Why don't you join us?"

Wil appreciated hearing some semblance of warmth in Helen's voice, but the cordiality sounded wooden and contrived.

"No thanks, I was just leaving. Don't forget that board meeting tonight, okay Wil?"

Wil tried to hide his surprise. He'd forgotten all about it!

"Oh, sure, thanks for the reminder. Seven o'clock, right?"

"Right. Try to come a few minutes early, will you? I'd like to talk with you for a minute before the meeting."

"I'll be glad to."

She breezed through her farewells and hurried away.

"I wonder what that's all about?"

Helen's cordiality had vanished as quickly as it had come.

Winston leaned toward Helen before Wil could decide how to reply.

"I think you're right, he was a selfish jerk."

The sudden heat in Winston's voice caught Wil by surprise.

Helen looked up darkly.

"I'm glad he didn't have *everyone* fooled. What did he do to you?"

"Oh nothing."

He looked away as if he actually had a lot to tell.

"I just don't think people are always what they appear."

With that, he shook his finger at one of the servers across the room.

"Hey, not like that!"

He slid out of his seat, turning back briefly before he scurried off to correct the offending soul, probably a Cherise or Muzette.

"Excuse me. I have to keep an eye on these people all the time!"

Helen kept her spot in the seat next to Wil, but he thought she stayed out of a lack of desire to move, not a strong wish to be there.

She looked at him dourly.

"What? You think I'm just being vicious, don't you? I wonder who it could be? The murderer, I mean."

Wil took a sip of his hazelnut mocha and liked it more than he expected to.

"Who knows?"

Helen stared off into the distance with a blank expression.

Jacques came back and they ordered breakfast.

Wil appreciated finding out he could get whole-wheat toast to accompany his steamed eggs with cheese and cauliflower.

Helen had a croissant and some fruit.

They sat stiffly as an awkward silence stretched on and on.

Neither one of them seemed interested in lots of conversation.

CHAPTER TEN

Jones drove down a narrow country road wondering why he had been summoned to this remote spot. The officer who called him said it would be hard to find.

He pulled his collar tighter around his neck and goosed up the heater as he admired the towering oak and maple trees lining the tarmac. He took heart in their fresh green buds, but if plants really did have feelings, the new shoots must have wished they could retreat into the dark branches until this wintry wind gave way to some real spring weather.

The cold, blustery day felt like an insult after the warm weather of the weekend.

About twelve miles from the city, he turned down a rutted gravel lane and proceeded carefully, trying to avoid damaging the bottom of his car. Three miles later he saw a patrol car parked in front of a badly weathered barn that still looked like it could withstand a hurricane.

A uniformed cop, Michael Fisk, stood impassively in the unkempt yard with his arms folded over his chest. He seemed to be listening halfheartedly to the man standing next to him, a barrel-chested guy wearing well-worn work clothes, a stained brown jacket and a hat that said 'America's Best Chew, Red Man Chewing Tobacco.'

Jones parked by the side of the road and walked over to the men through a thicket of dried up weeds and grass.

"What do we have here, Michael?"

The farmer jumped in before the cop could answer.

"Some jackass vandalized my barn! The straw is worthless, shot full of bullets, hundreds of em, I think!"

Michael gave Jones a sympathetic look.

"We thought this might have some bearing on your murder case, Detective. You've got to see what happened in here."

The farmer led the way as they stepped into the barn and found the floor littered with shell casings. Jones had been skeptical, but there really did seem to be two or three hundred of them. The air still reeked of gunpowder.

"These pictures were ripped to shreds, but you can still recognize a few features. I think this first picture is the vic in your murder case, isn't it?"

Jones stomach tightened as he peered at the tattered papers. The image in the first one did have Falcano's hair and the outlines of his face. The rest of the face had been obliterated. He didn't recognize all of the pictures, but the next two looked a lot like Wil Walker and Helen Rubinstein.

Jones frowned. He knew the cost of bullets. Someone had spent a small fortune making this mess! But why? This couldn't be a simple case of vandalism. There had to be some bizarre reason for putting up these pictures and shooting them to bits.

It couldn't be to scare anyone or make someone look bad. Who would see it out here?

He turned to the farmer.

"How did you find this? Do you come out here often?"

"Hell no! I just happened to need one of the tools in there. Good thing I did! People just don't care about anything anymore. Shooting up a man's barn on some wild prank. It's disgusting! Who's going to pay for all this damage?"

The man put his hands on his hips and spit into the weeds.

Jones felt real empathy for his plight.

"Do you have insurance?"

"Certainly not! Who carries insurance on an old barn? That's the craziest thing I ever heard."

He stuck out his jaw and looked fiercely into the distance.

The grizzled farmer wasn't about to be placated.

Jones didn't blame him.

He told the uniformed cop to collect whatever he could of the shredded pictures and have some of the shell casings tested. He doubted they would get an ID on the gun, but stranger things had happened.

Jones tried to make some sense of this latest piece of the puzzle as he climbed into his car and started back down the country road.

No one but the killer would shoot up a picture of Falcano, that would be too weird a coincidence, but the whole stunt made no sense. Could the perp be sending him some kind of sick message, 'catch me if you can?' Could it be some kind of warm up for revenge, a prelude to more killings? Revenge for what?

He couldn't see what the killer had to gain from a stunt like this, and he hadn't learned any more about who could be behind it all.

What about Wil Walker? Would he shoot up a picture of himself, along with the others, to deflect suspicion?

Jones didn't think so, but he didn't have a single clue leading to anyone else.

An all-too-familiar sinking feeling gripped his gut as he drove back toward the station. The time had come to be doing something else! This case had him baffled, and he wanted to solve it, but the thought of sitting at that desk day after day, waiting for trouble to come his way, seemed more and more unbearable.

He could be sipping coffee in a comfortable chair behind his cabin, savoring the breathtaking beauty of Torch Lake and planning a blissful day of fishing.

After that, he could enjoy a long nap.

He had more than enough money to do just that.

Why hadn't he already turned in his notice?

CHAPTER ELEVEN

Wil walked into the symphony office at three minutes before seven. Pru waved to him from one of the groups of chatting board members and hurried over as soon as he came in.

"Hi Wil. I hoped we'd have more time to talk before the meeting."

"Yeah, sorry. I meant to get here earlier, but I think I hit every red light coming through town."

She crossed her arms and grinned with mock reproach.

"C'mon, you're always five minutes late for everything."

Wil smiled ruefully.

"Yeah, I try to do one last thing when I should be heading out the door."

"Don't worry about it. I wanted to let you know I've been talking with some of the board members, and we want you to be the interim music director until we can find someone to take Henri's place."

Wil shook his head.

"Wow! I'm really flattered Pru, but you can't be serious. There's lots of time to get somebody. You have all summer."

"We really don't, Wil. A proper search takes months, even a couple of years, and we need a solid person to take the helm in the meantime. People need to know the symphony isn't going to fold up and blow away.

"There must others you should ask, Pru."

"People trust you, and they respect you as a musician, Wil, but frankly, it's even more important to have someone who can keep things on an even keel."

"And you think that's me?"

"Don't underestimate yourself, Wil. Sometimes I think others believe in you more than you believe in yourself!"

"I don't know. I'll have to think about it."

Actually, he'd already made up his mind. He thought he'd be a fool to take the position. The shock of Henri's murder could shake the symphony apart, and if he took over just before the orchestra folded, he would never get another job in the arts.

"There's no time, Wil. If our donors start pulling their support we're in very serious trouble."

Wil knew she had a very good point. Budgets in the arts always seemed to hover on a very thin line between success and disaster.

Guilt began to take root in his mind as he thought about how to say no. He did feel an obligation to help out, but he also heard alarm bells in his head. He had to pull himself together before he could take on a job with so much responsibility!

And what about the questions from the police? He seriously doubted Pru knew anything about that, and he thought her attitude might be quite different if she did.

Well, he wasn't going to be the one to tell her, and surely nothing would come of that. How could it? He had nothing to do with it!

"Naturally the salary won't be quite as generous as Henri's, but I think you'll find it satisfactory."

Wil hesitated at that thought. He hadn't considered the pay, and some solid income would really come in handy.

"It sounds like you've got it all worked out."

"Not at all, but we need to know you're willing before we can even discuss it."

Wil barely opened his mouth before Jim Pearce thumped him on the back.

"Hey, Walker! What are you doing here? Did you get the cops all straightened out the other day?"

Wil reddened and hoped Pru didn't make too much of Pearce's rude jab. Unfortunately, Pearce's trumpet playing tended to be as loud and overbearing as his personality.

No one threw a party when Pearce got elected to the board as a players' representative, but he made it clear he wanted the job badly. Most of the other musicians had no interest in attending another meeting, so no one stood in his way.

Wil didn't have a chance to say any more as Bill Evers, the chairman of the board, called the meeting to order.

For once, all the board members seemed to be in attendance.

The conversation started innocently enough, but it quickly degenerated into a heated discussion of the murder. Evers tried several times to get back to the printed agenda, but everyone there had plenty to say, and they weren't about to be denied.

Wild rumors had apparently sprung up everywhere and made the rounds in record time. Wil admired the way Pru tried to keep things focused on facts instead of speculation, but she clearly had a losing battle on her hands.

He could tell her patience had come to an end when she rose to her feet and looked around the room with fire in her eyes. A physician, Benjamin Roberts, had been pontificating about motives for murder. His comments trailed off as everyone looked at Pru, who stood at the head of the table glowering with unmistakable defiance.

Wil didn't remember her looking quite so tall before.

She let the silence linger for a moment before she spoke.

"We've all been shocked to the core by this horrible crime. That goes without saying. But we have to think about the welfare of the symphony, and I think we have to do it now!"

No one made a sound.

"Our orders for season tickets were slow already, and our donors are very nervous about the future. We have to name an interim music director to keep things moving forward, and it's absolutely critical to appoint someone people know and trust."

She glared around the room, daring anyone to contradict her.

"I'm nominating Wil Walker."

Jim Pearce erupted immediately.

"Walker? Why him … of all people?"

Pru turned to face him, and Pearce sank back in his chair with a sullen scowl.

"He's on good terms with everyone and people know he will be fair and evenhanded."

"We need a music director not a baby sitter. It has to be somebody dynamic!"

Pru didn't flinch.

"Wil's credentials are impeccable. He has a doctorate from one of the finest universities in the country, and people have a lot of admiration for the music he writes."

"That's not the same thing as being a conductor, Pru. You have to have someone who can take charge."

"Wil can take charge."

Everyone's eyes turned toward Gail Rotenska, the other player representative, as if they were shocked she had spoken up.

Gail flushed and seemed to wilt.

Pearce went on with new enthusiasm.

"He can take charge of putting notes on a piece of paper. You need someone that can project some power up there, some authority!"

Pru turned to Rotenska hopefully.

"Gail, what do you think the members of the orchestra would say?"

Gail's courage had apparently fled.

"I don't know, Pru. Do we have some time to ask them?"

Pru's brows knit in frustration.

"Not really. We need to make a decision tonight!"

Wil wondered if Pru had lined up any support at all. Evers seemed determined to stay quiet, at least for the time being, and everyone had been watching the exchange between Pru and Pearce with growing alarm.

Suddenly Wil wanted the job very much! Pearce's insinuations made him furious, and he wanted the chance to show all of them he wasn't a helpless jerk. Maybe this opportunity had come at a perfect time!

Pru turned to Pearce with a look of fresh determination.

"What's your problem with Wil, Jim? Are you trying to get the job for yourself?"

Pearce stared at her, just for a second, then his whole demeanor changed.

"Heck no. I don't have any problem with Wil personally."

He shrugged and looked at Evers.

"I was just trying to say what I thought would be good for the orchestra. Go ahead. Put him in. Who cares?"

Pearce sat back in his chair. His body language screamed that he cared very much, as he splayed his legs in front of him like a high school sophomore in detention.

Evers came to life and seemed eager to reassert his authority.

"That doesn't exactly sound like a ringing endorsement, Mr. Pearce. Do you really think the orchestra would be well served by putting Mr. Walker in charge?"

Pearce glanced quickly at Pru, then turned his attention to his fingernails.

"Sure. The main thing is to get the right person for the permanent gig."

"What about you Ms. Rotenska, do you think the orchestra would be satisfied with Mr. Walker?"

Gail looked at Pru, then turned to Evers and spoke in a firmer voice.

"Wil is a fine musician, Mr. Evers, and we've seen him conduct. He's more than competent. I think he'd do an excellent job."

She nodded as if to say 'so there' and avoided looking at Pearce.

The tension in the room lessened, but only slightly. Pearce seemed like a volcano ready to explode, and several of the board members stared at the wall or looked down at the table to avoid looking anyone in the eye.

Evers turned to Pru.

"What about you, Pru? Do you really think Walker is the best one for the job?"

"It's vital right now to have some stability. We've got to have an interim director that can work well with the orchestra, the staff and the public. Wil is well liked and he's a problem solver. He knows how to get things done without stepping on people's toes. I've seen him in action."

Wil wondered when Pru had seen him do anything like that, but he kept his mouth shut.

Evers looked around the table hopefully.

"So, is that our consensus?"

Jeanette Fields spoke up with a voice of quiet authority.

"We're not in any position to second guess Prudence, Mr. Evers, and we have to take decisive action. The public has to know the symphony isn't going to be paralyzed by this."

Pearce leaned forward and looked around the room for support.

"Falcano isn't even buried yet!"

He shrugged with an uneven smile when he saw the tide had turned.

"But you're right, we need to move on. Congratulations, Walker. Don't screw it up!"

Evers cleared his throat, looking every bit the stuffy bank president.

"Perhaps we should hear from our candidate now. What do you have to say Mr. Walker?"

Wil stared at him stupidly. Evers request had caught him completely off guard. He quickly thought he should stand up and stumbled to his feet.

"I, uhh … thank you for the opportunity to do this. There's no way I can fill Henri's shoes, but I'll try to keep things in good shape until we can find a full time, ahhh … a permanent conductor. Thanks again."

He almost tripped as he sat back down.

What eloquence!

Evers called for a vote, which proved to be a casual show of half-raised hands. At least no one dissented.

Wil felt like he'd been chosen by default.

Pearce left quickly when the meeting broke up. Evers, Pru and Gail Rotenska gathered around Wil to congratulate him.

With the meeting over, Pru seemed to be in an expansive mood, and she smiled broadly.

"You'll do fine Wil, trust me!"

"Wish me luck, I'll need it."

"No way! You're the best one for the job. Besides, Henri had scheduled the performance of your new symphony for the first concert. It'll be the most natural thing in the world to have you conducting."

Wil suddenly felt a heavy weight of responsibility sink onto his shoulders, and he hoped desperately he could finish his symphony in time.

"Um, under the circumstances, maybe we should hold off on my piece until later."

Gail put a hand on his arm.

"Nonsense, that will be the perfect way to start the year!"

She leaned closer.

"And I'm sorry I sounded so mealy mouthed. I know you'll do a great job!"

Evers shook Wil's hand with a surprisingly firm grip.

"Thank you for taking on this responsibility, young man. It will be a great help to the orchestra."

Pru stayed behind as the others left.

"Sorry about that, Wil. I knew there might be some questions, but I didn't expect anything like that from Jim. What do you think was bothering him?"

"Maybe he was just surprised. I don't suppose many people beside you are thinking that far ahead. They're still trying to deal with Henri's murder!"

"Of course, and so am I. Well, get some sleep Wil. We'll talk soon about getting started. At least we're entering the offseason. There's only the summer pops concert between now and next October."

"Are you sure about this Pru?"

"Absolutely!"

"Well, thanks for having confidence in me."

Wil walked to his truck with a new spring in his step, but somehow he knew standing on the podium and waving the stick would turn out to be the easy part.

He drove home about ten miles an hour under the speed limit, staring into the night and imagining all the things that could go wrong.

Michael Fisk groaned when his telephone rang at 1:08 a.m.

The burly man climbed out of bed and scurried into the kitchen to answer his land line. He cringed as his bare feet touched the cold linoleum.

This had better be good!

"Hullo?"

His irritation rose even further when the line remained silent.

"Hullo? Who is this?"

A muffled voice finally spoke.

"Is this Michael Fisk?"

"Yeah, who's this?"

"And you're a cop in St. Cecile?"

"Yeah."

"This is just a concerned citizen. I saw something you ought to know about, and I want to call it to your attention."

"Call what to my attention?"

"It relates to that murder, you know, the conductor who was shot? It's in the alley behind the symphony hall. You'll find it in a brown paper bag."

"I'll find what? Is this a crank call? Who is this?"

"I don't want to get involved, so I put it back where I found it. Tell them you just happened to spot it. You'll be a hero and everybody wins."

"Is this a joke?"

"No, just look and you'll see. You know what they say, seek and ye shall find."

"You better not be puttin' me on!"

"Just look. You won't regret it."

CHAPTER TWELVE

Peter Jones walked up to his desk at 7:44 Tuesday morning and glared with irritation when he saw his message light blinking.

He hated voice mail!

People leaving messages rambled on and on, and the mindless computer just kept on recording. In the good old days, callers had to try later or leave a message with the desk sergeant. Even his old answering machine had a time limit. People had an incentive to get to the point. Not anymore!

At least he'd gotten the report from the state forensic lab about the slug that killed Falcano, or at least the bits that remained of it.

Jones knew the .223 caliber bullets, 5.56 millimeters in diameter, were used in M-16 rifles by all branches of the American military. The small bullet in a relatively large casing delivered an extremely accurate, high-velocity shot.

Solid .223 rounds could easily punch straight through a human body.

This nastier bullet had a thin metal jacket and a polymer tip that caused it to burst into fragments immediately after impact, devastating the internal makeup of whatever, or whoever, it hit. Farmers and ranchers loved the V-Max, or Varmint Express, ammo for shooting prairie dogs and other nuisance animals. The bullet virtually guaranteed a quick kill if it found its target, and it hardly ever went on through the animal to hit something on the other side.

Jones looked through the grubby windows, grateful that yesterday's gloom had lifted a bit, leaving a scattering of grayish clouds moving swiftly across the sky.

It would be a beautiful spring day at Torch Lake! He could be clearing away the effects of winter, raking the small, scraggly yard and picking up dead branches. Or he could just be sitting out behind the cabin as long as he wanted to, soaking up the sunshine, watching Canada geese fly overhead in their wondrous V-shaped formations, and savoring the chance to be near the water.

Somehow, being near the lake loosened the knots of stress in his body. He felt sure every day spent by the lake added a day to the end of his lifespan.

He turned back to his desk reluctantly and punched in his voicemail code.

"You have eight messages."

Oh great!

He pulled a note pad across the desk, hoping he could get any useful information down the first time and avoid having to repeat any of the messages.

A gravelly bubba voice blamed Falcano's murder on a terrorist plot. Had the area been searched for 'stinkin' A-rabs?'

Jones deleted that one in disgust.

A whispery, older-sounding voice suggested that Falcano had set the whole thing up himself.

"Some people will do anything for notoriety! I'm tellin' ya!"

Somehow Jones doubted the fame would be very satisfying for a dead man.

A man on a cell phone, almost inaudible through the static, suggested the government had to be behind it.

"Anyone who knows too much has to watch his butt in this country. You mark my words! They'll come for you too if you find out what Volcano knew."

The caller didn't say what amazing government secrets a musician in Michigan might have stumbled across. At least Jones got a laugh when the guy mangled Falcano's name.

The other calls were routine stuff, and he disposed of them quickly.

Jones started to reach for his backlog of files just as Michael Fisk, the patrolman from the barn, walked up to his desk.

"Hey, Detective. Look what turned up in the alley behind the concert hall."

Fisk handed him a small paper bag and stood back looking like he'd just won the lottery.

"What are you so happy about?"

"Look inside! It was wadded up when I found it, but I opened it up and checked inside. Good thing."

The bag contained one item, a rumpled slip of paper that turned out to be a WalMart receipt for a box of twenty Hornady V-Max cartridges. The ammo cost $18.79, and the total charge, with tax, came to $19.92. The purchase had been made with a VISA card, and the receipt listed the last four digits of its number, 4398.

The scrawled signature looked like it said William Walker.

It couldn't be this easy, could it?

He looked up at Fisk.

"You found this in the alley, right behind the concert hall? What were you doing there?"

"I just had a hunch, you know. It was just across from that big door at the back, the one with the loading dock. A whole lot of papers and dead leaves were back there, blowin' around in the wind. This was stuck, though, kinda wedged up against the bank building."

A small warning bell went off in Jones' head. It sounded quite a bit too convenient for Fisk to just be poking around back there. And why hadn't this evidence turned up when they were investigating the scene?

But on the surface, it looked pretty damning!

"Well, Fisk, you might get the gold medal. Nice work."

"Thanks detective."

Fisk walked off with a playful strut.

"Oh yeah, catchin' the bad guys. Findin' the clues! Sometimes I love this job…"

Jones rolled his eyes as he reached for the phone to check on the credit card.

He had to jump through some hoops, but it didn't take long to confirm a VISA card with a number ending in 4398 had been issued to Robert William Walker.

Time to talk to Walker again!

CHAPTER THIRTEEN

Wil drummed absent-mindedly on his desk with a couple of pencils, trying mightily not to let the glorious sunshine seduce him away from his work.

The erasers hitting the wood didn't make a very exciting sound, but that really didn't matter. Drumming to work out an intricate rhythmic pattern might be useful. This mindless flailing had no point but burning excess energy.

He had to concentrate! He needed desperately to make some progress on the slow movement for his symphony, but he couldn't think!

An endless swirl of questions and worries circled again and again through his brain.

Why couldn't he make even the slightest bit of progress on this piece of music? He had written dozens of pieces, and he'd never been so stymied before!

What if he was finished as a composer? Maybe he'd lost it!

In his youth, he thought his music would be played by orchestras around the country, even around the world, by this time. Instead, here he sat, alone in this room, unable to write a note.

He suddenly felt much closer to death than to the day of his birth. Did anyone outside this backwoods town give a damn about a single thing he'd written, or even know about it?

What if he'd been kidding himself?

It seemed silly to worry about the cops and this murder business, but he couldn't stop thinking about it. Someone had sent a note trying to make him look bad, and if the cops didn't figure out the truth, why wouldn't they come after him?

Could someone really be trying to set him up?

Being innocent didn't mean he could prove anything! He saw stories all the time about people who spent years in prison before someone proved they were innocent.

He appreciated Pru's vote of confidence and his new role at the symphony, but all of that came with its own healthy dose of apprehension. What if taking the job had been a terrible mistake? The board meeting had been anything but a ringing endorsement, and what if other people objected to his appointment? If the orchestra musicians, especially, rejected his leadership, what could he really do to keep the orchestra from going under?

The change had certainly ramped up the pressure!

He worked closely enough with Henri to know leading the orchestra involved all kinds of nitty-gritty details. The public saw the polished musical presentation. Wil knew most of the conductor's time went to personnel issues, budget management, publicity, fundraising, and dozens of other small but essential matters.

He had to get his symphony finished, and quickly, so he could give his full attention to that responsibility. But knowing that didn't help him get his work done. It made the paralysis infinitely worse!

Wil had realized long ago he couldn't rush his creativity. A looming deadline sometimes helped him focus and finish a piece, but if the process wasn't working, he couldn't force it. It happened in its own time, and he had never found a way to make things move any faster.

Unfortunately, a lot of work remained to be done after he'd gotten a good idea and written out the melody, harmony and rhythm.

Wil always found the orchestration fascinating in its own way. He thought translating the notes into instrumental colors felt like painting on a canvas, but that slow, exhausting work also required tremendous concentration.

After that he would need to lay out print-ready copies of the score and parts. The computer made that work much easier than it used to be, but he would still need to proofread everything very carefully and make all the painstaking corrections. Small mistakes might not seem important, but if too many got by, they would destroy any hope of a good performance.

And if he felt the music needed revision somewhere along the way, as he usually did, the process started again at the beginning.

But none of that mattered at the moment. Everything he had tried for this second movement seemed hopelessly inadequate, and he couldn't make an iota of progress until he found something that felt right.

He remembered someone describing writer's block as a blank page taunting the author with its emptiness. The goal remained aggravatingly elusive, hovering just out of reach.

Wil just knew he found it incredibly infuriating!

He wished he could be somewhere else, anywhere but in this room!

Suddenly, in a fit of frustration, he lurched forward and shoved all the clutter on his desk onto the floor. Then he sank wearily back in his seat, well aware his little tantrum hadn't achieved a thing.

He just had one more tangled mess to clean up.

He sighed dejectedly as he turned to the baby grand to try some improvisation. He let his hands roam freely over the keys, hoping to hear some rich nugget of harmony or a strand of dancing melody that would fire his imagination, but all the sounds seemed jumbled and completely useless.

He produced plenty of bland, pleasant sounds, but nothing with the poignant beauty and intensity he needed for this part of his symphony.

Then he thought of something else to try. He set a large sheet of staff paper on his desk, found another sharp pencil, and began making up little bits of melody.

Like most trained musicians, he didn't need a piano to make up melodies and write them down. He didn't have perfect pitch, and he couldn't hear music perfectly in his head like Mozart or Beethoven, but working this way often seemed simpler and more direct.

Maybe writing away from the keyboard tapped into a different part of his consciousness, he didn't know, but that approach had definitely helped him get some good ideas rolling in the past.

The results of his sketching seemed almost promising at first, but after several minutes he looked at his work with disgust, crumpled the paper into a tight ball, and tossed it across the room at the overflowing trash can.

His frustration boiled over as he looked out the window and saw a robin pecking at something in the grass. The lawn had begun taking on the vivid, deep-green color that made the first, lush growth of the year so refreshing after the dullness of winter.

He suddenly had an overwhelming urge to get outside, and he didn't see any reason to resist it.

He made himself a peanut butter and jelly sandwich, picked up a banana, got a Diet Dr. Pepper out of the fridge, and carried all the food out to his pickup. Someday he'd have to stop eating meals on the run!

Was it too late for a man in his forties to grow up?

He made another quick trip to the house to get his golf clubs, then he started the truck and sped down the driveway.

His worries seemed to shrink into proportion as the sun warmed his body and he downed his lunch. For months he'd been patiently shoveling snow and chipping ice. In a few minutes he'd be playing golf.

When he got to the course, he paid his green fees and walked out to the first tee with a growing sense of anticipation.

He stretched and took a few practice swings until a man of about seventy walked over. A teenager in a Detroit Tigers hat soon followed, and they all joined forces to form an amiable threesome.

Wil didn't expect much, and his spirits lifted when he hit his first few shots cleanly and they rose high into the fresh spring air.

He thought ruefully the first round of the year often went well. He needed to remember he played better when he just tried to swing smoothly and hit the ball in the right general direction. His golfing troubles would mount when he tried to press for longer drives and hit perfect pitch shots.

The sunshine and the warmer air soothed Wil's jangled nerves as he savored the rhythms of walking and swinging the golf clubs. His tight muscles seemed enormously grateful for the opportunity to move and stretch.

He allowed himself the luxury of replaying a few errant shots, and he and his companions chatted easily as they made their way around the course.

On the last hole Wil hit a drive that sailed high in the air, curved gently toward the center of the fairway and landed with a nice roll that added a few extra yards of distance.

The shot felt great, especially for the beginning of the season!

When he got to his ball he studied the flagstick, which stood on the front corner of the large, undulating green.

He shook his arms to relax his muscles as he paced off the distance to a nearby marker and decided he needed to hit his next shot about 129 yards. He took out a nine iron and stood back to visualize how the ball would fly if he hit it perfectly.

He tried to stay loose as he took a couple of practice swings, stepped up to the ball and took his stance. His swing felt liquid and easy, and he watched expectantly as the ball arched gracefully through the sky and settled about twelve feet from the pin.

When his turn came to putt, he decided he needed to aim about five inches to the right of the cup and hit the ball firmly. He kept his head steady during his stroke and looked up to see the ball roll smoothly toward the hole and curl gently into the cup.

A birdie! What a great way to finish the first round of the year.

He shook hands with his playing partners, and everyone smiled as the trio started walking up the tree lined path leading back to the clubhouse.

Wil's expansive mood shattered in an instant when he saw the flashing lights of a police cruiser in the corner of the parking lot.

Two uniformed cops stood next to the car, leaning against the hood on either side.

Wil's heart leapt into his throat when he saw them both staring straight at him.

CHAPTER FOURTEEN

Wil looked around the bleak interrogation room in a white hot daze.

His friends who described him as easygoing wouldn't recognize him today!

He didn't even try to stifle the hard knot of anger in his gut as he fumed about the incredible emotional roller coaster he'd been riding. He'd seen his friend and colleague brutally murdered, the police had asked him pointed questions, someone had gone out of their way to cast suspicion on him, and he'd been thrust into a position of great responsibility at a time of crisis.

Now the police had arrested him in public like a common criminal!

Wil could only imagine what his golf partners must have thought.

Actually, the officers said he wasn't technically under arrest.

Then could he leave?

No, he had to accompany them back to the station.

Why?

He would find out when he got there. Did he want to call an attorney?

No. Did he need one?

The officers told him of course not, but he could call one if he wanted to.

They all made the short trip to the center of town in silence. Then the cops escorted him into this stifling room and told him Jones would be in shortly.

Wil decided he could learn to hate Detective Jones! His rage stoked higher and higher as he waited for Jones to show up.

His hands shook as he checked the time again and again, and he felt his blood pounding in his veins. Wil couldn't wait to tell Jones to drop his crazy crusade against him. The police had to figure out who really did this and leave him alone!

God, he had never been so frustrated!

Jones finally shuffled into the room, leaned back in the chair across from Wil and studied him with a deeply puzzled look on his face.

Wil suddenly felt too enraged to speak. His mouth had gone utterly dry, and a sharp pain throbbed between his temples. He felt like a stick of dynamite, needing only the tiniest spark to set it off.

Jones finally broke the silence.

"You wanna tell me about .223 ammunition?"

What?!

"A box of V-Max shells for a .223 rifle, polymer inserts at the tips to make the bullets especially lethal. Why don't you tell me all about it?"

"You tell me!! I have no idea what you're talking about!"

Wil felt the last shreds of his self-control collapse in a rush, and without realizing it, he started to rise from his chair.

"Sit down, Mr. Walker!"

Jones voice hit Wil like a physical force, and he fell back into the chair in a heap.

The cop's face looked hard as rock!

Wil hadn't seen this side of Jones before, and his eyes burned with outrage at the unfairness of it all.

He must be in much deeper trouble than he thought!

"I don't own any guns, I don't know anything about guns, and I've never bought a box of shells in my life. Why do you keep coming after ME? I can't believe this!"

Jones said nothing and continued to study him with eyes like lasers.

Wil felt like a laboratory specimen.

"Can't you just leave me alone? I don't know anything about the murder."

"It's about these pesky clues that keeping turning up, Mr. Walker. Why don't you just tell me what happened?"

Wil flashed hot again.

"There's NOTHING to tell. I don't know anything!"

Jones sighed, reached across the table and handed Wil a xerox copy of a receipt.

"What about this?"

Wil glanced at the paper and didn't see anything familiar.

"What about it? I've never seen it before."

"That's not a receipt for a box of bullets that you bought?"

Wil stared back at the receipt in confusion.

Why did they keep this room so hot? His mouth seemed to be full of cotton, and he couldn't quite manage to take a deep breath.

"Detective, I have no idea what this is. What makes you think it's mine?"

"That isn't your credit card number?"

Wil squinted the paper, trying to make out the fuzzy digits on the poor copy.

"How would I know? I don't have my credit cards numbers memorized."

How could it be?!

Wil knew his face had to be bright red, and cold sweat suddenly broke out all over his body.

Jones eyes hadn't budged.

"Do you have your credit cards here?"

Wil shot him a sarcastic look, then reached into this pocket to get out his wallet. When he found his VISA and American Express cards, he started to compare the numbers.

"Suppose you let me do that."

Wil gasped and threw his wallet and the cards across the table.

"Sure, why not? I'd fool you if I sit here and cheat, right?"

Wil saw the color rise in Jones' neck and cheeks.

"Calm down, Walker! You're in a world of trouble right now. Don't go out of your way to make it worse."

Wil sat back and watched as Jones checked the numbers.

Then the detective frowned.

"Do you have any other credit cards?"

"No, just those."

"We can check you know."

"Go ahead. I wish you would!"

Wil flushed again. That ought to be easy enough!

Jones stared at him.

"Either you're one of the best actors I've ever met, or you really are baffled by all of this."

Wil gaped at him and tried again to catch a breath.

"I am! Will you please enlighten me?!"

"This receipt turned up in a paper bag behind the concert hall. Your name is on the VISA account. Your full name, Robert William Walker. "

"What?!!"

Wil's stomach convulsed.

"These … unhh … are you saying those bullets killed Henri… and you think they're mine? It's a mistake! It's not me! Walker is a common name … I mean … uhh ..."

His voice trailed off as he realized the chances of such a coincidence were millions to one.

He had to think!

"You have to believe me, detective, it wasn't me! I don't know how that credit card got my name on it, but I didn't do it. I … I …"

It all finally became too much, and he felt hot tears start down his cheek. He swiped at them with his hands and looked away fiercely.

"This can't be happening. It's like the Twilight Zone!"

Jones regarded him in silence for a minute.

"You just don't seem like the type, Wil. Maybe if you were evasive, or claiming to have a good alibi … I don't know. But I can read your emotions like a book. Something just doesn't add up."

Wil couldn't answer.

"Falcano was killed with a rifle mounted on the ceiling and hooked up to a fancy device that fired when he stood in the beams of two electric eyes. The whole thing took quite a bit of knowledge and skill to build."

Wil's mind raced as he tried to picture what Jones described.

"Why are you telling me this?"

"Maybe I'm giving you some rope to hang yourself with."

"Two electric eyes? It was set to go off automatically?"

"The beams crisscrossed over the podium and completed a circuit when Falcano's body blocked the way."

"I thought electric eyes shut off when the light is interrupted."

“Turns out it’s fairly simple to reverse that. You said you studied electronics. Would you know how to do something like that?”

Wil suddenly felt utterly drained, and he fought to concentrate.

“I could probably find out, but I didn’t.”

How could he make Jones believe him?

“Look, Detective, I know this looks bad, but I didn’t have anything to do with this. I have no idea how my name got on that credit card, and I didn’t set up any booby trap to kill Henri. You have to believe me.”

Wil couldn't read Jones' thoughtful expression.

“I have to find out the truth, Wil. I probably should arrest you right now, just to be safe, but there’s something strange about all this evidence that keeps popping up I’m going to let you go home, but don’t even think about going out of town.”

“Could somebody put my name on a credit card?”

“Of course. Identity theft is going wild. Once the crooks get someone’s personal information, they open bogus credit card accounts, get mortgages. People have had their houses sold right out from under them in bogus deals. There were millions of cases last year.”

“Really?”

“We’ll check the address on the account, but I doubt that’ll get us anywhere. It’ll probably turn out to be a post office box or an abandoned house.”

“But why would someone want to charge the bullets in my name?”

The color drained from Wil’s face as he realized the obvious answer for himself.

“If someone wants to stay in the shadows, the best thing to do is put someone else in the spotlight. Do you have any enemies?”

“No, not that I … I can’t imagine…”

“Well start imagining. Think about it.”

Wil felt sick. The cooling of his fiery emotions had left him him numb and confused.

He needed some fresh air and time to think. Every time he thought things had gotten bad, they got much worse.

"Think about those electric eyes, Wil. Maybe you can tell me something that will help after all."

"And maybe I can incriminate myself?"

"Yeah, maybe. Stay where I can find you."

Wil didn't realize he'd left his pickup at the golf course, five miles away, until he stepped out onto the sidewalk.

CHAPTER FIFTEEN

Jones braced himself as he walked toward Police Chief Walter Manning's office.

He had absolutely no desire to talk to his boss right now!

The two men tolerated each other, just barely, but Manning kept demanding a progress report on the Falcano case, and Jones had finally run out of excuses for putting off a meeting.

Not that he had much to tell.

He had never faced a more vexing case! Jones had no hint of a motive for such a bizarre murder and no real suspects. Falcano had no enemies, at least none Jones could ferret out. The ingenious trap with the rifle left the killer's identity a complete mystery, and Jones hadn't learned anything by tracing any of its components.

He had sent out several inquiries about the gun. Maybe they would tell him something.

The thought of retiring had never sounded better! If he resigned now, he could be at his cottage by dark. Somebody else could clean up this mess!

Jones sighed as he opened the door to Manning's office. He knew he wouldn't quit. His puritan sense of duty wouldn't let him.

But he could dream, couldn't he?

His irritation mounted when he saw the mayor, Eldon Fitzhugh, waiting with the chief.

As usual, the much larger Manning sat in his chair, wringing his hands and leaning deferentially toward the mayor, who stood like a ramrod beside his desk.

Jones always called this tableau their Laurel-and-Hardy pose.

He thought Manning needed the guts to stand up to the mayor and force him to buy some new patrol cars and updated equipment. And if he found the courage to do that, maybe the chief could make some long-overdue changes and bring the department up to snuff.

Jones thought all of that would probably happen when Hell froze over!

Judging by Fitzhugh's crimson face, their conversation had begun several minutes earlier. Manning had probably already gotten his usual, minutely-detailed marching orders.

When he saw Jones come in, the chief grinned lopsidedly and pushed his heavy, dark glasses back onto the bridge of his nose.

Jones started to make a hasty retreat toward the hallway.

"I see you're busy, Walter, I can come back later."

"No, nonsense, come on in! Sit down."

Jones stayed on his feet. He hadn't expected this surprisingly expansive mood from the chief, and the mayor's tight, cold stare hardly invited conversation.

Jones always thought Fitzhugh's shirt collar looked two sizes too small. He almost wondered how Fitzhugh kept from choking to death when he lost his temper, which happened often.

"I'd rather discuss the case when we have some time to ourselves."

"No, don't worry! The mayor can hear anything we have to say. How's the case going? Tell us, what's the latest?"

Jones reluctantly plunged in. It didn't take him long to outline what he'd learned about the electric eyes and the rifle, explain the findings about the bullet and tell them about the receipt in the crumpled up bag.

Manning smiled again.

"Great, great! You were just questioning Walker right? So we have a suspect in custody?"

"No. I let him go home."

The mayor exploded.

"You what? You have a receipt with the man's credit card number on it, and you didn't arrest him? What are you waiting for, a video tape of him cocking the rifle?"

Jones didn't appreciate the sarcasm!

"I can't see Walker as the killer. He's the sensitive type, and you can read his emotions on his face like a neon sign. He wasn't covering up when I asked him about the bullets and the credit card. He had no clue what I was talking about."

Manning looked up thoughtfully.

"Well, have you tried …"

Fitzhugh interrupted as if the chief wasn't there.

"Do you have a master's degree in psychology or something? The guy was prowling around in the concert hall the night before the concert! It all adds up! What more do you need?"

Jones struggled to keep his voice even. He hadn't mentioned Walker being in the concert hall, and he had a big problem with the mayor poking his nose into the details of the case.

"The auditorium sits empty most of the time. Anyone could get in there. We'll be looking into everything we've got, but I just don't think Walker is the murderer."

"What about the receipt? That's crystal clear!"

"If someone's trying to make Walker look like the bad guy, it would be child's play to get a phony credit card, buy a box of shells and plant the receipt as phony evidence."

"By wadding it up and tossing it in the alley? What are the chances we'd find it? There was junk blowing all over out there."

Jones wondered why the chief bothered to stay in the room.

"That's the beauty of it. If we do find it, it looks too farfetched to be a plant. If we miss it, the killer could have another receipt that 'mysteriously' comes to light later, or some other way to implicate Walker. We found the bag wedged up against the wall where it wouldn't blow around. How do you suppose that happened?"

"I'm not supposing anything! There's a receipt with the man's credit card number on it. That's plain as day. The same man was alone in the building the night before. It's not a big mystery! He's guilty as sin!"

"I'm just not satisfied Walker did it."

Manning raised a sweaty hand.

"Well, Peter …"

Fitzhugh thrust out his jaw and brushed aside Manning's feeble attempt to reassert himself.

"Maybe you don't know he had a motive, too!"

Jones almost laughed.

"What's that?"

"The symphony board picked Walker to take over as the conductor of the orchestra last night! Sounds like a nice step up for a freelance … well, whatever he was … don't you think? No one seems to quite know how he made a living."

Jones flushed. He resented being pushed this way, and he hated being blindsided with such an important piece of information.

"How did you find that out?"

"I have my sources."

The mayor rocked on the balls of his feet with his hands behind his back.

Jones could hardly bear the insufferable, triumphant look on his face.

"Peter, maybe you ought to arrest Walker after all. What if he bolts?"

For once Manning got to finish his sentence.

"I'm sure he won't run. It's not in his character."

The mayor snorted.

"Not in his character? Maybe we should make Jones the department's shrink, Walter, he's doing psychoanalysis again!"

Jones wanted to tell the man to shut up, butt out and go to hell!

Actually, he wondered what held him back. He had no fear of being fired. If Manning sent him packing, he could be fishing in Torch Lake tomorrow.

With great effort, he forced himself to make a civil reply.

"Let me do what I think is best. I'll start checking out Walker's new position right now."

The mayor turned to the chief imperiously.

"Walter, tell this detective we want that man arrested and put in jail immediately!"

He spat the word 'detective.'

Manning dithered.

"Peter, I ..."

The mayor turned back to Jones with a sour scowl and shook his finger in his face.

"Did you hear me, Detective? We want him arrested *right now*?"

Jones turned his back on the mayor in disgust and pointedly addressed the chief.

"Walter, as long as I'm the lead detective, I'll make an arrest when I'm good and ready and not before. Do you understand? Let me know if you have a problem with that!"

He turned crisply and stalked out, almost hoping Manning would call him back immediately and ask for his badge.

He could still hear the mayor sputtering after he closed the door.

Wil sighed heavily as he parked the pickup in his driveway.

How could this be happening? One damn clue after another seemed to be pointing in his direction! No wonder Jones had him at the top of his list.

He walked up to the front door, thrust his key into the lock and walked inside, cringing as he slammed the door a little too hard.

A receipt for bullets, bought with a credit card in his name! What could he expect Jones to think?

Suddenly a cold fear gripped his stomach.

Someone had spent a great deal of time and effort trying to make him look guilty of Henri's murder! What if they succeeded? What if he spent the rest of his life in prison?

Who could be doing this, and why? And why had they chosen him?

Wil shuddered as he realized he had his hands clenched into fists.

Perspiration soaked his body in spite of the cool weather. He swiped at the beads of sweat on his forehead and rubbed his hands on the leg of his jeans, feeling like he needed an hour in the gym to work out some of the tension tying his body in knots.

He spread his fingers as wide as they would go, extended his arms high in the air and pushed his legs apart to stretch every muscle he could.

The amateur yoga helped a little, but not much.

Could he just wait helplessly while somebody framed him? He had to do something, but what?

He didn't have a clue!

Suddenly, he felt an overwhelming urge to be a small speck in a huge sea of music. He wanted to lose himself in a world of sound that could carry him far away from this shabby house and all his aggravating problems.

He walked over to the sound system and searched for a certain recording, an organ sonata by Paul Hindemith, that matched his dark frame of mind perfectly. He found the CD quickly and put it into his player with eager anticipation.

As the sinewy, twisting lines of the music filled the room, he closed his eyes and threw back his head, listening intently.

He loved listening to this piece when he felt tense and frustrated. The music had a dark, dissonant energy that seemed to flow from the core of the universe. In college, he had listened to an old vinyl recording of this sonata through headphones, with the volume turned way up, until he had practically worn the grooves off the record.

The music rose and fell in powerful waves as the angular melodies danced over and around each other to create spiky, intense harmonies. The insistent rhythms pushed forward relentlessly. The vivid tone colors of the organ pipes seemed to flow richly into his body, right through the skin.

He turned the volume even higher and lay down with his back on the carpet. He forced everything else out of his mind and let the music fill his consciousness, gratefully sinking into the safe universe the music created.

At least for a few minutes, he didn't have to deal with Detective Jones, murdered conductors and a world in which he felt like a feather tossed around wildly on the winds of chance.

When the music stopped he stayed on the floor, exhausted.

This will pass, he told himself.

You'll get through this.

You'll do a great job conducting the orchestra, and people will decide you should have the job permanently! You'll look back on this and laugh in a few years when your career is riding high!

Your music will catch on and you'll have enough money to do whatever you want. You'll get a better house, drive a decent car and all your troubles will be over!

He almost jumped out of his skin when he heard a sharp knock on the door.

CHAPTER SIXTEEN

Pru McDonough greeted Peter Jones warmly when he walked into the symphony office. She looked very prim and proper in a tangerine jacket, black slacks and a crisp white blouse. A tasteful gold necklace and classic black heels completed the effect.

"You look very nice, Ms. McDonough. Do you always dress up so well for quiet days at the office?"

Pru smiled playfully.

"You never know when someone important will be coming in, Detective, someone like yourself. This is a business, even though we're involved in the arts. You have to dress like you mean business."

Jones wondered if everyone at the symphony operated under those same rules as Pru led him into a modest office off the main anteroom.

Pru sat delicately on the front of her chair with her forearms resting lightly on her tidy antique desk. Jones admired her perfect posture as he settled awkwardly into the smallish chair across the way.

Her office seemed as tasteful, spare and efficient as her demeanor. The dark blue area rug matched the size of the room exactly. The only other furnishings were a pair of beige filing cabinets, and the spartan decor highlighted a striking blue-green print that filled the wall behind her chair.

Pru's eyes gleamed as she saw Jones admiring the print.

"Are you a fan of Monet, Mr. Jones?"

"I do like the Impressionists. I know a little more about art than I do about music."

She smiled warmly.

"We'll have to get you coming to the concerts and broaden your horizons. What can I do for you, Detective?"

"Things seem pretty quiet around here."

"That last concert was the end of our regular season. Normally this would be a time to relax a little bit. It's quite different this year, as I'm sure you can imagine."

"Of course. How are things going?"

"Fine. We have several things to attend to. Henri normally handled the musical side of things and personnel matters in the orchestra. He will be greatly missed, Detective, but the affairs of the symphony are in good shape. We'll be ready for next season in plenty of time."

"What can you tell me about Wil Walker?"

"Wil? He's easygoing, relaxed. He's very bright, and a good musician, too."

"Does he play in the orchestra?"

"Not usually. He's primarily a composer. He writes pieces for us and gives lectures before our concerts, writes program notes, things like that."

"Is it true you've made him the new music director?"

She spoke without a moment's hesitation.

"I didn't, the symphony's board of trustees did. It's a temporary post, until we can hold a search and name a permanent director."

"Why Walker?"

"Why not? If you ask him to take care of something you can usually count on it, and he's a good musician. He has a doctorate in music composition. One of the most important things to me is that he gets along well with everyone. No one really has anything against him."

"Do other people in the orchestra have enemies?"

"Don't you mean did Henri have any enemies?"

Jones noticed she had scarcely moved since they sat down. Could she be on her guard?

"Okay, sure."

"I can't imagine why anyone would want to kill, Henri, Mr. Jones. He had a strong personality, most conductors do, but I really don't think he had any enemies of the kind you're talking about."

"Apparently he did."

"All right, I'll grant you that, but I never heard about any serious problems between Henri and anyone in the orchestra."

"What about people outside in the orchestra?"

"Not that I knew of."

"Was Walker trying to get the job as conductor?"

"Are you asking if Wil was jealous of Henri?"

"Was he?"

"Not at all! He and Henri were very good friends. Wil supported everything the symphony did in a very positive way. He just seemed to like helping out."

A gentle smile lit up her face.

"I think I shocked him when I asked him to fill in. I thought at first he might say no. Why are you asking about this, Mr. Jones?"

Jones tried another tack.

"What was Falcano like?"

Pru noticed he had avoided the question, but she went on amiably.

"He was very down to earth as music directors go. He traveled here and there to guest conduct other orchestras, but most of the time he lived pretty quietly. He wasn't a very public person when he wasn't working."

"What about his personal life?"

"Nothing too remarkable. He enjoyed parties but was never the last one to leave. He liked to sail and kept a few horses at a stable north of town."

"I understand he was single. Did he date very often?"

"Occasionally."

"Was he gay?"

"Heaven's no!"

"Did the two of you ever date?"

She flushed almost imperceptibly.

"We went out a few times. We realized it was not a good idea to mix our personal lives with our work relationship."

Jones noticed again that McDonough kept her self control on a very tight rein.

Could she have wanted Falcano dead for some reason? No one could be ruled out at this point, but he had a hard time imagining her crawling around catwalks to rig a booby trap with a rifle and two electric eyes.

"Did Falcano have any business dealings, investments?

"I really don't know."

They spent a few more minutes talking, but Jones had given up on learning anything very helpful.

Falcano seemed like the last person anyone would want to murder!

He thanked her for her time and rose to his feet.

"Falcano must have had an office here, right? Do you mind if I have a look around?"

"Not at all."

Wil opened his door and found Helen standing on the porch with her arms crossed tightly over her chest.

"I've been standing out here for five minutes."

She brushed past him into the house and perched tightly against the armrest of the couch.

"You had that damn music so loud you couldn't hear me knocking!"

"Sorry, I had to give myself a little music therapy. It's been a rough week."

She didn't seem to hear as she pulled out a cigarette, crossed her legs and squeezed them together like a vise.

"What's going on? I heard you were arrested."

Wil stood awkwardly between the door and the couch, wondering whether he should sit down or offer to make some coffee.

"I wasn't arrested. That detective just wanted to talk with me again."

"Why? Does he think you did it?"

Wil wasn't about to mention all the incriminating evidence.

"I think he's just checking out everything as carefully as he can."

She looked up with a sarcastic gaze that cut right through him.

"Well, William, you're the only person he's checking out as far as I can tell."

He didn't need this, especially right now!

"How did you know he called me in?"

"Marissa Falls and her husband were just teeing off when the police whisked you away. She called me on her cell phone."

"Oh, that's great!"

Marissa played cello in the symphony. If you wanted to spread some news quickly, giving it to Marissa would be your best bet.

Helen's expression softened, ever so slightly.

"She said the policemen looked pretty serious. Are you sure that's all there is to it, Wil?"

Wil wondered if she might really be here to help him. It would actually be great to have someone he could confide in, someone to help him sort out all this trouble.

She inhaled a big lungful of smoke and blew it harshly toward the ceiling.

"If you're going to jail, I'll be completely on my own."

Oh! So much for sympathy!

Wil decided he had no interest in making coffee and looked away.

"I think he knows I couldn't kill Henri."

Her voice erupted in a sudden shout.

"Oh, you're so good, aren't you? Who do you think did do it? ME?! Rick Johnson?"

Wil felt his own temper rising. He couldn't imagine a milder person than Rick, a clarinetist in the orchestra. Rick would probably have trouble killing a cockroach.

Why had she come here? Just to berate him? Out of curiosity?

"Well it wasn't me! The police are just asking questions, that's all. I have no idea who could have done it."

Helen looked close to tears and seemed to take no notice of what he said.

"I'm going crazy in this place, Wil! I was counting on Henri to help me get my career back on track."

Wil couldn't tell if she felt sorrow over Henri's death, or just bitterness about what he hadn't done, but his attitude softened as he realized how fragile she had become.

"He thought the world of you, Helen. He admired your talent very much."

"Well, he didn't act like it! Talk is cheap, Wil."

She looked away and took another uneven pull on the cigarette.

Wil had never heard her voice sound so harsh and brittle. He shifted his weight nervously from one foot to the other.

"Look, do you want some coffee or something?"

She leaned back, propping her arm against the couch to hold the cigarette near her face.

"Tell me what happened at the police station. Are you a suspect or not?"

"It doesn't matter what the police think. I didn't do it, and they'll figure out who did."

"So they DO you think you were involved!"

"I didn't say that."

"You didn't have to."

She stood abruptly.

"You look terrible, Wil. It's not hard to guess what's bothering you."

She turned and walked toward the door.

"But I need some help, too, Wil! What am I going to do?"

She whirled out.

Wil watched her go with a puzzled frown.

What had they really been talking about?

Jones whistled as he stepped into the conductor's personal office. He'd give anything to work in a place like this!

Everything in the room seemed to be made of wood, and very high quality wood at that! Jones admired the way it all seemed to match beautifully, and he decided Falcano must have spent a fortune decorating the place.

The elegant cherry paneling set the spacious room apart dramatically from the cream-colored outer office.

A large oak desk ringed with tidy stacks of papers stood in front of the only window, and a computer and telephone sat on a small table between the desk and the wall.

An impressive set of built-in shelves, stretching from the floor to the ceiling on the opposite wall, held a few dozen well-worn books, some colorful curios and an elaborate sound system. The stereo speakers seemed to be centered on Falcano's desk and were angled carefully to face directly at his chair.

Several art works with musical motifs hung on the walls, along with some colorful posters that looked like mementos of performances Falcano had conducted. Diplomas from two universities flanked an ornate certificate of merit from a music conservatory in Paris.

Jones admired the conductor's taste, but he found the office oddly formal and impersonal. He couldn't find any personal or family photos, and the room didn't tell him much at all about the man behind the public persona.

A worktable held some large, oblong booklets, some of them bound with black plastic combs. Jones opened the first one and realized it had to be a piece of orchestral music. The page consisted of line after line of music staves with notes sprinkled across them in interesting, seemingly-random patterns.

A list of Italian words filled the left side of the page. Those had to be the names of the instruments! He recognized some of them fairly easily. *Flauto* had to be flute, and *Violino* clearly stood for violin. Some of the others baffled him, names like *Piatti* and *Fagotto.*

Jones had to admit again he didn't know much about music.

He sat in Falcano's oversized chair, which proved to be wonderfully comfortable, and scanned the office from the spot where Falcano would have spent most of his time.

The mystique created by this impressive sanctuary would be imposing, even a little intimidating, to visitors.

Jones opened the top drawer of the desk, which held a neat stock of pencils, pens and other mundane office items, including a small pile of letterhead stationary with the symphony's logo on top. The side drawers held files and a few other items that seemed perfectly logical for a conductor's desk.

One space held an impressive collection of conductor's batons, slender white sticks of various sizes with handles of wood, cork or plastic.

In the back of the bottom drawer, almost hidden behind a jumble of other papers, he came across a bulky envelope.

He pulled it out and began to examine the contents.

Now, this could prove interesting!

CHAPTER SEVENTEEN

As he hoped he would, Wil woke up with an idea. He decided to learn more about electric eyes, rifles and bullets. Maybe he could figure out something that would help solve this terrible puzzle.

Many times, especially in his composition, he'd been amazed when a simple solution to a hard problem popped into his head after a good night's sleep. The human brain always amazed him! Sometimes you just had to relax enough to get out of its way.

After a hasty breakfast of cereal and yogurt, he took a steaming mug of coffee into his studio, booted up the computer and logged onto the internet.

What had the detective said about the ammunition? He described it as a two-twenty-something, with some kind of plastic tip.

Wil had been too upset during the interview to get the details straight.

He decided to try another angle and typed in 'electric eye.'

After a few seconds the screen changed, and he saw he'd gotten more than 587,000 hits. Great!

He waded through a long list of 'Electric Eye' restaurants, boutiques, tattoo parlors and tanning salons, and also found many websites offering futuristic music, magazines, books and games.

Finally, he started seeing more technical sites referring to 'optoelectronic,' 'electro-optic' or 'optical/electrical' devices. He explored a few of those and added several of their URLs to his bookmark list so he could refer back to them later.

Some of the sites had baffling arrays of mathematical formulas and schematics that weren't going to help him very much. He had a much sketchier background than Jones thought! He had dropped out of electronics study quickly when he realized how much math and science he would have to master.

A link took him to a page that defined a photoelectric cell, or photocell, as "a device which varies in electrical characteristics such as current, resistance, voltage, etc. when struck by light."

Finally, he might be getting somewhere!

It turned out many different kinds of devices actually exhibited the 'photoelectric effect.' Older phototubes were basically a pair of electrodes inside a glass tube. Photomultiplier tubes were used in a variety of applications, including television cameras that could detect the light of stars too faint to be seen with the human eye. There were also photovoltaic cells that could generate current without an external power source.

The article ended by saying, “It is simple to use current from a photocell to operate switches or relays. They are commonly found in many kinds of door openers, intrusion alarms and automated counters. Photocells in these applications are often called electric eyes.”

Several sites offered electric eyes for sale. He found electronic finish lines for sporting events, many different types of alarms and sensors, and even children’s science projects.

Wil noted ruefully the science kits were recommended for anyone seven and above.

So much for trying to find the killer that way. Anybody could do this!

He tried web searches under ‘ballistics,’ ‘ammunition’ and ‘rifle’ and found a ton of information about firearms and ammunition. Writers on the web described every conceivable detail about firing mechanisms, barrel design, scopes and bullet construction, and Wil found dozens of detailed articles about bullet speeds, spin rates, trajectories, the distances bullets could carry and the physical forces affecting their flight.

Several sites discussed the analysis of bullet wounds in graphic detail. He clicked past the horrifying pictures quickly. It turned out tiny details could make all the difference in identifying the means of death, the murder weapon and the identity of the killer.

He’d never dreamed all of this could be so complex!

He also found many gun shops advertised. He learned purchasing a rifle in Michigan required positive identification and a background check, but anyone eighteen years old or older could buy ammunition without any real restrictions.

That meant the person who really bought that box of shells had been able to do it without attracting much attention or leaving much of a paper trail.

One more thought down the drain!

He typed in 'identity theft' and found page after page filled with chilling facts and statistics. As far back as 1997, the secret service estimated people lost more than 745 million dollars a year to identity-theft scams. Average victims spent over 175 hours, and more than 1000 dollars, to clear their names.

Wil pushed his chair back from the desk and rubbed his eyes.

He'd spent two hours searching, and he'd learned quite a bit about several subjects he hadn't cared about at all, until now, but he hadn't gotten one inch closer to figuring out who might have killed Henri!

He shut down the computer and walked toward the kitchen, stretching as he went.

Someone wanted to make Henri's killing look like his doing, and the effort had been pretty damn successful so far!

Worst of all, Wil knew more bogus evidence would be popping up soon.

He had to find some way to fight back!

But how?

Jones took the envelope back to the police station, planning to have a good look at the contents by himself before showing it to anyone else. He tried to look casual as he walked into the small interrogation room, locked the door and twisted the blinds shut.

The light-brown, nine-by-twelve envelope had no markings on the outside. It could have come from anywhere.

The contents shocked him!

The envelope contained several documents and a detailed set of plans for a development on Lake Michigan. Not a modest line of beach bungalows or a cozy seafood cafe, a real eye-popper!

A twenty-story hotel with a revolving restaurant on top dominated the scene. One of the two swimming pools curled around two sides of the hotel like a small lake. The grounds included sprawling shopping areas, a dozen tennis courts and even a landing pad for helicopters.

Two eighteen-hole golf courses hugged the lakeshore on either side, one stretching to the north, the other extending to the south. The design included the biggest driving range and practice area Jones had ever seen, as well as a dome for winter practice.

The fences marking off the large private beach looked imposing even on the drawings.

Jones shook his head as he looked at the audacious scope of the plans.

A serpentine network of streets and 'homesites' wove through the whole area. Jones guessed the property owners would have access to the golf courses and beach area, but would pay dearly for the privilege.

The papers in the envelope included a letter of agreement with a well-known golf-course architect, copies of deeds for four pieces of property, and a financing proposal from First National Security, a large bank in Chicago.

Jones eyebrows shot up when he saw the whole development would cost just under 200 million dollars!

The bank papers included spaces for signatures by Henry Falcano, Winston Nicholas and Eldon Fizhugh, along with senior officers of the bank.

Jones' mind raced as he tried to sort out the implications of all this new information. He'd never heard a word about this project! There'd been nothing in the papers, no idle chat around town. He couldn't imagine such a big idea being developed so quietly.

And how had the conductor gotten involved in such a thing with Nicholas and the mayor?

But Jones had no doubt about one thing. He'd found the key to solving Falcano's murder!

Suddenly the doorknob jiggled, then a key turned in the lock and the door started to swing open.

Jones rushed to scoop all the papers off the table. He did his best to look casual when Walter Manning stepped into the room.

"Oh hello, Peter. Did you lock this door? What's going on in here?"

"I was just looking over a few papers and wanted some privacy."

"Oh, sorry. I thought the door had just gotten locked by accident."

Manning peered at the drawings on the table with more than a little curiosity.

"What's that you're looking at? Some plans for an addition to that retirement cottage you're always talking about?"

Jones debated and made a quick decision as he folded the plans and stuffed everything back into the envelope.

"It's nothing, really."

"It looks like something, Peter."

"Trust me, Walter. I'll let you know if it's anything you need to see."

The chief looked very skeptical as he leaned onto the table.

"The mayor is really pushing on this murder case, Peter. He wants to know why we haven't arrested Walker yet."

"I'm nowhere near being satisfied he's the killer, Walter! Do you want me to arrest people I don't think are guilty?"

"The evidence is pretty damning, Peter. What's the problem?"

"I told you I think all that evidence was planted! It just doesn't make sense to me that Walker would have killed Falcano. I'm working on some other leads, and you'll be the first to know when I'm onto something."

"Do your leads have anything to do with that envelope?"

Jones flinched as Manning glanced at the package under his arm.

"You have to let me do this the way I see fit, Walter."

"People want this thing wrapped up quickly, Peter. Maybe you have some pet theories that are interfering with your best judgment."

"My judgment's just fine, Walter! Now if you'll excuse me I have work to do."

"Ok, but don't drag your heels on this thing. We can arrest Walker and move on with this case without you."

"Well, I'd retire that very minute, Walter. Is that what you want?"

"Don't make threats you can't back up, Peter."

"I'm serious. Now will you please let me get back to work?"

Jones thought he heard a grating voice in the next room.

The mayor!

CHAPTER EIGHTEEN

Wil and Pru McDonough chatted amiably as they walked the three blocks from the symphony office to *Le Bon Temps.*

Wil felt a little shabby next to the elegance of her stylish clothes and bright spring coat. He couldn't help noticing her flawless fingernails matched the color of her jacket exactly.

He might have to step up his wardrobe in this new job!

Wil had invited her to lunch, saying he wanted to discuss his new duties, but he actually wanted to pick her brains about Henri and the murder.

For once, he felt energized, almost buoyant.

A cool morning had given way to a delicious spring afternoon, the kind that made the long Michigan winters and all that lake-effect snow seem worthwhile. The sun, richly brilliant after its long winter in hiding, warmed his soul as much as his body. The crisp, fresh breeze from Lake Michigan seemed to flow right through him, and the sensation made his blackest fears ebb back to a much more bearable level.

But most of all, it felt great to be doing something proactive!

When they got to the restaurant they took a seat near the front door.

Their server, "François,' offered them water and tossed menus on the table before scurrying away.

Wil doubted Winston would have liked his lack of cordiality.

Pru looked at her menu approvingly.

"I'm going to get the chicken Caesar salad. What about you?"

"I think I'll have a salad and this grilled pork chop. The spices on it sound pretty exotic."

He wondered if the *frites* on the side would be normal fries, or something equally out of the ordinary.

François took their orders in a rush, and they both smiled wryly as the discussion turned to plans for the orchestra.

Pru told Wil that Jeanette Fields had agreed to run a full-page article in the newspaper and would be contacting Wil shortly for an interview. Pru had also prepared letters for donors and the orchestra players outlining the decisive steps she had in mind to help keep things rolling.

They also discussed some university professors and talented free lancers who might fill the openings in the orchestra.

"You've been a one-woman task force, Pru, and a darn good one!"

"That's my job."

She allowed herself just a hint of a smile, but Wil could tell she appreciated the compliment.

François brought their lunches, and Wil had to admit the food tasted excellent. Winston might be going overboard on the atmosphere, but so far, the food had lived up to the hype. Wil liked the *frites*, but he found he wanted to dip them in ketchup just like the fries from any diner.

Wil watched his companion take a bite of salad and decided he needed to improve his table manners as well as his attire.

"How are you holding up, Pru?"

"I'm fine. It's been quite a shock, but we were well organized before this happened. I think things are in good shape to move ahead."

"What about personally, how are you feeling?"

"I'm okay. Henri and I had a good working relationship, but we weren't exactly close. He kept to himself and I did the same."

"Didn't you go out with him for a while?"

She eyed him warily.

"That was a long time ago."

"Who did Henri spend time with, Pru?"

"I'm not kidding, Wil, I didn't know that much about his private life."

"Do you know if Henri had any enemies?"

"Now you sound like that detective."

He lowered his eyes to avoid her sharp gaze.

"Well ... did he come to talk to you? What did he want to know?"

"He asked about you for one thing!"

Wil groaned to himself.

"What did you tell him?"

"I said you were the man for the job. Was that a mistake?"

Wil was surprised how quickly irritation had risen in her voice.

"No! I mean, I hope not! What else?"

"He wanted to know who Henri associated with and socialized with. I told him there wasn't much to tell. He spent quite a bit of time looking around in Henri's office, too."

Wil knew he should drop the subject, but he couldn't help forging ahead.

"Do you know of anyone who had something against him? I can't figure out who would want to see him dead, can you?"

Her eyes narrowed.

"I have no idea, Wil. Why? Are you trying to solve the case too?"

He debated how much to tell her.

"I, uh … I'd like to help if I can. Besides, I'm curious, aren't you? It's baffling!"

"Of course I'm curious, who wouldn't be? I just don't have any ideas that I think will help."

He finally decided she should hear the bad news from him, not someone else.

"Detective Jones has been asking me some ... uhm ... difficult questions."

Her eyes opened wide, and she stared at him with a look of genuine alarm.

"What has he been asking?"

"Never mind, I'm sure it's just a misunderstanding."

"A misunderstanding? What is there to misunderstand?"

He wished he had never brought up the subject!

Nothing! I'm sure it's nothing! Let's forget it."

She held her hard stare a moment longer, then looked purposefully away from him toward the large plate glass windows.

That was the end of the conversation as Ted Mason and Ben Watanabe, a violinist in the orchestra, appeared over Pru's shoulder.

Ted slapped Wil on the shoulder with the familiarity of an old friend.

"I guess this is the place to be these days, huh? Is this a private party or can we join you?"

Pru seemed to gather herself, but her smile looked stiff.

"No, please do."

The host, who Winston called the *maitre'd,* had been leading them to another table. He nodded with a sour look on his face, bent awkwardly at the waist and stalked away.

Ted leaned toward the others with an air of conspiracy.

"He needs a musician to teach him how to bow. Go show him Ben!"

Ben laughed as they settled into the remaining chairs.

François came to the table and offered the newcomers some water and a pair of menus.

Ted beamed at Wil and Pru as Ben studied the menu.

"How do you like the place?"

Pru spoke first, and Wil thought he heard an icy undertone in her cheery words.

"It's nice. Is this your first time?"

"Yup, first time. How about you, Wil?"

Wil forced himself to smile.

"I tried some breakfast the other day. It was great. What are you up to?"

"I just wanted to get out of the house, maybe see some people. Ben said he wanted to check this place out, so we decided to give it a try."

They spent a few minutes asking each other about plans for the summer and trading vague descriptions in reply.

François reappeared, and Ted ordered a cheese omelet with shallots and potatoes. Ben opted for *Saumon griller*.

Wil thought he might as well take this opportunity to find out what he could from the two men.

"Do you have any theories about Henri's murder, Ted?"

He tried not to react as Pru shot him a dark look.

"No, it's unbelievable! I just can't imagine any reason for such a thing."

Ben agreed with the general disbelief.

Wil decided he had done enough damage and didn't ask any more questions. His upbeat mood seemed like a distant memory.

His feeble efforts as an amateur private eye had been an absolute disaster!

CHAPTER NINETEEN

The rough, gray boards of the old stairway creaked as the figure in black descended into the dark basement.

A lone, dusty light bulb hung from a grimy porcelain fixture above the top steps. It's feeble pool of yellowish light cast weird shadows against the large, flat stones of the damp cellar wall and the thin handrail made of old metal pipes.

At the bottom of the stairs, a switch that may have once been ivory-colored protruded at an odd angle from an open junction box full of twisted wires and loose coils of black tape.

A gloved hand flipped the switch, and more weak light seeped from four low-watt bulbs to reveal a ceiling of rough-milled timbers almost obscured by a jumble of slanted pipes, drooping wires, cobwebs and indistinct objects hanging from large rusty nails. The crumbling, uneven concrete of the floor had large stains that might have been there for decades.

A filthy, hulking furnace filled the space to the left of the steps.

The dark figure moved over to the far wall and struck matches to light an uneven hodgepodge of candles on a low table. A flickering glow soon rose to illuminate an eerie shrine, the same oversized picture of a teenage girl that had earlier hung in the old barn.

The girl's sweet smile formed a stark contrast to the oblong splotches where something caustic had almost eaten through the paper.

Suddenly, a metallic shape glinted in the dim light. Then a huge knife flashed through the air, turning end over end and landing with a loud thwack.

The large blade pierced the girl's throat and stuck fast in the hard oak boards behind the picture.

A gloved hand twisted out the knife and heavy boots thumped against the floor.

The knife flew through the air again, and its tip buried in her right eye, creating a wide gash through her eyelid.

The ritual repeated again and again, and dark slits appeared in a tight pattern on her face and throat.

The knife flew with unerring accuracy, always landing parallel to the floor with its point sinking deep into the hardwood.

Next to the makeshift shrine stood a small wall of straw bales that extended from the floor to the ceiling.

The person in black pulled out a sheaf of papers, and the gallery from the barn reappeared as the images were hung one by one with large rusty nails thrust through their margins.

Henry Falcano peered out with a sage look on his face. Wil and Helen Rubinstein joined him, smiling benignly. A smaller version of the picture from the yearbook followed, along with the twenty-something woman and a fresh centerfold. The older couple and the image of Jesus completed the set.

A single, swift thrust buried the knife to the hilt through the center of Falcano's face.

The gloved hand pulled the blade back quickly and stabbed it into the image again and again.

The pictures of Wil and Helen received similar treatment and were soon riddled with deep punctures.

The girl from the yearbook watched from the wall as the attacker battered her smaller self and the other two women with slashing blows.

The elderly pair got special treatment. The knife cut slowly into the picture and traced lines in various shapes across their unknowing faces. The razor-sharp blade cut the paper effortlessly, moving slowly at first, then gradually picking up speed.

When their pictures hung in tatters, the dark figure moved to stand before the depiction of Christ.

An arm slashed violently through the air, nearly cutting the picture in two. After two more strokes the picture hung in pieces, but the knife sliced again and again over the spot where it had been.

The dark shape moved back and forth through the lineup, slashing with furious energy, cutting the thin paper quickly with savage strokes and continuing to hack at the inert straw long after the shreds had fallen to the floor.

Finally the attacker whirled and threw the knife with brutal force into the very center of the smiling face on the wall. The blade vibrated where it landed just for an instant.

Then a cry of rage filled the dark basement.

Just as quickly, the voice stopped.

The figure stood mute for a moment, then bent over and blew out the candles with a long, fierce breath.

The knife remained where it was, a glaring contrast to the innocent, youthful face in the devastated picture, as the dark shape moved up the stairway and the light died away.

CHAPTER TWENTY

Peter Jones tapped three fingers of his right hand on his desk as his call to First National Security Bank bounced around in an automated answering system.

He hated wading through the layers of prompts on these things, but he really hoped he could find out what he needed to know on the phone. He certainly had no desire to make the three-hour drive to Chicago!

Jones sat up involuntarily when a smooth professional voice came on the line.

"Commercial Loan Department."

He'd gotten through to a human being!

"Yes, hello, I'm trying to reach George Benson. Is he available?"

"Who's calling please?"

"This is Peter Jones, I'm a detective in St. Cecile, Michigan."

"A detective? Can I tell Mr. Benson what this is about, Mr. Jones?"

"Sure, it's about a funding proposal he developed for three men here in St. Cecile, Michigan."

"I'll see if he's available. Please hold."

Click.

A gush of syrupy music came over the line, and Jones started drumming with his fingers again. He grimaced when the music dimmed and a dramatic voice intoned "Let First National Security Bank help you meet all your financial needs. Our loan officers are specially trained to provide in-depth, personal …"

Click.

The receptionist had come back sooner than he expected!

"I'm sorry Mr. Jones, Mr. Benson can't take your call right now. Is there a number where he can reach you?"

Jones sighed and gave her the number.

Nothing could be easy!

He started to examine the bank document more carefully and jumped when the phone bleated next to his ear.

There had to be a way to change that revolting ring tone into something more palatable! He made a mental note to check.

"Peter Jones."

"Hello, Mr. Jones, this is George Benson. What can I do for you?"

Apparently Benson hadn't been as busy as he thought!

Jones couldn't help noticing Benson's polished, cool voice sounded like a bad actor's impression of a banker.

"Hello, Mr. Benson, thanks for calling back so quickly. I have a few questions about a funding proposal you drafted for a project here in St. Cecile."

"How did you find out about this, Mr. Jones?"

All of a sudden Benson sounded a little less cordial.

"I don't think that's important. It's part of a murder investigation."

"What kind of murder investigation?"

Benson sounded surprised, or possibly evasive.

"Henri Falcano was one of the partners listed on the proposal. He was killed here last week. I thought you might have heard about it."

"We have lots of murders here in Chicago, Mr. Jones. We don't usually hear the local news from Michigan. How can I help you?"

Jones thought he heard a bit of sarcasm on the word 'local.'

"We're trying to find out if this planned development had any role in the murder, Mr. Benson. Can you tell me any more about it?"

"What would you like to know?"

"Was it a pipe dream or were they really trying to build it?"

"I'm afraid I don't know. You'd have to ask one of the partners."

Jones frowned. The man certainly wasn't volunteering anything!

"How did the men seem when they were talking with you? Did you think they were serious, or was it a fantasy?"

"I can't read people's minds Mr. Jones. They gave us some numbers and we wrote a proposal outlining how the project could be financed. That's all there was to it."

"Did you meet with them in person at all, or did they just send you the material?"

"It's been a long time, Mr. Jones. I really can't recall."

It had been less than a year according to the date on the document. Jones seriously doubted the man got that many requests for loans of 200 million dollars!

"Can you remember anything at all about the men involved, what they were planning or how they meant to go about it?"

"I'm terribly sorry, Mr. Jones, I really can't. Now if you'll excuse me, I have some pressing business."

"Ok, thanks for your time."

Jones hoped he hadn't sounded sarcastic himself, but he really didn't care.

"Thank you, Mr. Jones. Goodbye now."

Benson stressed the word 'you' with a patronizing tone that set Jones on edge. The banker's practiced air said 'may we be of service,' but Jones found his arrogant aloofness infuriating.

The man hadn't told him a single thing!

Jones leaned back in his chair. He could understand Benson being a little publicity shy, but he had dodged even the simplest questions.

Why would he be so obstinate?

Jones took the rest of the papers out of the envelope and spread them out on his desk.

He didn't have much to go on. The rest of the bank proposal just listed costs, interest rates and payment schedules, along with several pages of legal boilerplate to make sure nothing got left to chance.

The drawings laid out the grand scheme, but without a lot of details. Maybe the plans hadn't moved beyond conceptual stage after all.

The deeds showed two parcels of property had been purchased by Eldon Fitzhugh and two by Winston Nicholas. The total area of all four tracts seemed to be about 600 acres. He didn't recognize any of the seller's names. The prices were high, but they didn't seem out of line for good land near Lake Michigan.

Jones tried to think of a quick way to locate the property. The lengthy paragraphs of the legal descriptions would only make sense to a land attorney or a surveyor.

Wait a minute!

He looked back to the drawings. Sure enough, the lakeshore at that particular spot had a very distinctive contour with two small peninsulas reaching out into the lake. Between them, a rough semicircle of beach formed a natural harbor.

An elaborate system of docks at the southern end of the inlet had been labeled 'Yacht Marina' on the plans.

Jones dug through a stack of papers in his bottom desk drawer, came up with a map, spread it out next to the plan and spotted the unique bit of coastline quickly, about three miles southeast of the city.

A quick trip to the county land office would tell him who owned the rest of the land.

Wait, he had a better idea!

He jotted down the names on the deeds, pulled his sports jacket off the back of his chair and walked out to his car.

He welcomed the chance to be away from the office as he pulled onto a country road about half a mile inland from the lakeshore.

Minutes later, he found what he had been looking for and pulled into a well-kept asphalt driveway leading to a tidy farmhouse surrounded by large shade trees. Behind the house stood a cluster of sturdy buildings: a large, bright-red barn, a tall circular silo and several smaller structures. He could only guess what their purpose might be.

Jones felt a deep ache of nostalgia as he remembered the farm where he had worked as a young boy. He had actually been too young to be strictly legal. Mr. Bitner had told him with a smile that if someone from the 'gub'ment' came by, he should just say he was a member of the family.

They had walked down row after row of beans, chopping out the weeds and sharpening their long hoes every few laps. The farmer could clean up four rows for every one of Peter's, but after some practice, Jones could handle two.

A few years later they had toiled from dawn to dusk stacking bales of hay and straw on large wagons to take them back to the barn. The first few bales seemed light. After several hours in the punishing heat, they became unbelievably heavy!

He had crawled into bed night after night with aching muscles and tender, sunburned skin.

Jones knew those days were gone for good. Chemical sprays had eliminated the need for hoeing beans, and nowadays, most of the hay and straw went into large round bales, like giant jelly rolls, designed to be lifted by a machine.

Mr. Bitner had taken him home for 'dinner' every day at noon. The Bitners called the three meals of the day 'breakfast, dinner and supper,' and Jones still remembered the incredible food! Every meal had a main course of fried chicken, roast beef or pork and included fresh vegetables, homemade bread and a huge cake or pie.

After they ate, Peter got to knock around in the yard while Mr. Bitner took a short nap. Then they returned to the fields for several more hours of toil.

Jones recalled the backbreaking work fondly and seemed to recall he never slept more soundly in his life.

Mrs. Bitner had been remarkable too!

One time he got to watch her slaughter chickens for an upcoming gathering of the Bitner clan.

She had the birds trussed up in a stack next to her, and chatted away as she lifted them one by one onto an old stump she used as a chopping block. The chickens clucked calmly as she took firm hold of their legs in her left fist, placed their heads on the flat surface, and gently stretched out their necks with a sharp machete.

In one swift motion she lopped off the chicken's head and grabbed the neck, holding on tight as the wings flapped wildly. When the involuntary movement slowed, she tossed the headless body into a large basket and casually reached for the next bird.

Jones often heard her say she could wash a car 'as clean as a whistle with one pail of water!' That wasn't a boast, just a statement of fact, and once Peter got a chance to see her perform this miracle of frugality and efficiency. She soaped down the whole surface with one rag, then rinsed the car with a second cloth and toweled it dry. When she had the car sparkling clean, she poured a few remaining drops from the bucket and smiled knowingly.

The process wasn't so difficult if you thought about it, but Jones wondered how many gallons of water went down the drain in the average carwash.

He suddenly longed to be back there! In those days the world seemed like a cornucopia overflowing with possibilities.

He'd probably never been in better shape, and his problems were simple. Life had been easy, and good!

Now he would settle for a little peace and quiet.

His mind jerked back to the present as he parked near the back of the house, walked over to the porch and gave three quick taps on the door.

"Hello, young man, what can I do for ya?"

Jones couldn't believe his eyes. A modern-day Mrs. Bitner stood before him! She had greeted him, a perfect stranger, like a long lost friend. And calling him young had been a great bonus!

"I'm trying to find out who owns some property in this area, and I wondered if you could help me."

"You'd better ask my husband about that. He's out back by the barn, help yourself."

She scurried on about her business with a refreshing lack of curiosity about his intentions.

Jones walked back by the barn, shouting an occasional "Hello?"

"Just a minute, I'll be right out,"

A hearty voice had boomed from an open doorway in one of the outbuildings, and Jones heard some mysterious clanking and shuffling before a round old gentleman in faded overalls and a flannel shirt ambled out to meet him.

"Gotta get some parts for my tractor. I thought I had some spares but I'm gonna haf' to run into town."

The man's wide smile seemed to hide nothing, and Jones liked him immediately.

"How do ya do, young fella, whatcha need?"

Young fella? Jones decided he would have to come here more often!

He had met many farmers. Some were dour and sullen, acting like life was an endless chore. Some were rude and brusque. They never had time to talk to you and always seemed to have something much more important to do.

He could tell these folks were different. They had an obvious zest for life, and he had a strong feeling their days were full of laughter and genial companionship.

"I'm hoping you can tell me who owns, or used to own, a few parcels of property near here. I'm a police officer."

He thought he ought to identify himself and hoped that didn't change things.

"Why shore, I'll be glad to. It's no secret who owns a piece of property. You know what, it's time for dinner. You look like you could do with a good feed. C'mon in."

The farmer headed toward the house with a rolling gait, apparently never doubting that his guest would take him up on his offer.

Jones had no intention of turning it down.

A feast of wonderful smells met them as they walked into the kitchen. Jones hungrily eyed the table set with roast beef, steaming bowls of boiled potatoes and green beans, fresh-sliced tomatoes and cucumbers and a blackberry pie. A huge loaf of freshly-baked bread stood on a cutting board waiting to be sliced.

Jones smiled when he saw three place settings.

The woman's eyes gleamed when she saw the delight on his face.

"I thought Harold might bring you in for dinner. I'm Betty Zimmer, and this is Harold. I'm sure he never thought to tell you his name."

"Thank you for inviting me folks, I'm overwhelmed."

"Well, it's time to eat and there's plenty. Dig right in."

Jones ate with great relish, as more poignant memories from his childhood surfaced one after another. He knew time had burnished his recollections into rosy half-truths, but he wasn't in a mood to be too analytical.

They talked animatedly about all kinds of 'important' topics, the weather, the changing times and, as Harold put it, "them crazy politicians in Warshington."

After the meal Mrs. Zimmer bustled about, clearing the table and cleaning up.

Jones offered to help, but she refused with a laugh and a casual wave of her arm.

"You men talk about your business. I can take care o' this stuff."

She leaned over and whispered to Jones with a twinkle in her eye.

"I'll make him do the dishes next time!"

Her husband just smiled.

Jones pulled out the map and showed Harold the small harbor.

"Can you tell me who owned this property? It's just over that way."

"I know where it is, young fella. I've lived here 65 years!"

Jones feared he had insulted him, but Mr. Zimmer showed no signs of taking offense as he hooked his thumbs in the straps of his overalls.

"Most of that property used to be owned by the McKinley family. They owned a couple thousand acres, right on the lake. Some of the prettiest land you're ever gonna see."

"How can I get in touch with them?"

"Ya can't! They're all dead. Some foreign folks bought the land. I think their name was Frankenstein."

Mrs. Zimmer laughed over by the sink. She put them on her hips, yellow gloves and all, and turned to face them.

"It wasn't Frankenstein, Harold, it was Rubinstein! They died too. They had a daughter that lives there now, all by herself. She wishes she could sell the place."

CHAPTER TWENTY-ONE

Jones admired the high ceiling and ornate décor as he stepped into the lobby at the St. Cecile Daily News. He remembered well the buzz of activity that used to fill the grand old building.

The place had become a relic from an earlier time, in more ways than one. A lonely receptionist sat behind a large counter near the front door, and two more employees sat idly at large desks near the back of the cavernous space.

Jones thought any customers straggling in to buy a want ad or drop off an obituary would have plenty of personal attention!

He wondered how long the paper could survive. The Daily News still published a print edition, but now it relied heavily on its barely-profitable online operation.

Jeanette Fields kept the Daily News alive almost single-handedly, and Jones knew she could tell him more about those resort plans if anyone could. She seemed to know everything that happened all the time.

He decided to avoid the cramped elevator and took two stairs at a time as he climbed up to the third floor.

Jeanette greeted him cheerfully as he stepped up to her door.

As they shook hands, Jones admired the colorful rings on her fingers and wondered how her hands could seem so unencumbered in spite of them.

She seemed to thrive on being busy at an age well beyond the time when many would have retired. Jones always thought she moved with the supple ease of a woman many years younger, and her stylish black dress and tastefully understated makeup made her look fresh and vital.

Jones appreciated her design skills as he settled into a chair across from her ornate desk. Her office combined the efficiency of a busy workspace with the luxury of a comfortable hideaway. Everything looked immaculately clean.

The room held an impressive assortment of furniture and memorabilia, but in a tasteful arrangement that seemed uncluttered and very natural. Dozens of photos on the walls depicted historical happenings in St. Cecile, and several showed Jeanette with world famous politicians and business leaders.

He knew she had a lot of connections, but he had no idea the list included this many movers and shakers!

Jones wondered how to approach the subject of Falcano's plans without giving too much away.

"Mrs. Fields, what can you tell me about a proposal for a resort development near here?"

"Well, there are nice resorts all along the Lake Michigan. There are some world-famous ones up near Traverse City. I'm not sure what you're asking."

"I was thinking closer to home, right here in St. Cecile."

Her eyes narrowed.

"You'd better be more direct, Mr. Jones. What's this all about?"

He sighed.

"Can we talk in confidence, Mrs. Fields?"

"Of course, off the record, as they say. But I must warn you, if you're talking about a big story, and I get the slightest inkling of it from another source, I'll go after it with all I've got."

He decided to trust her.

"I don't know if it's a big story or not. Maybe it's nothing. I was looking around in Henri Falcano's office, and I came across a very ambitious set of plans for a large resort on Lake Michigan, just outside the city."

"You don't say."

He seemed to have her complete attention, and in spite of the situation, he enjoyed seeing the dancing light in her eyes.

"The key piece of property used to belong to a family named McKinley. Now it's owned by a young woman named Helen Rubinstein. She's a member of the orchestra. That's about all I know about her so far."

"Go on."

"The most surprising thing is a loan proposal from a big bank in Chicago listing three partners, Henri Falcano, Winston Nicholas and Eldon Fitzhugh."

Her eyebrows arched as her lips curled into a sly smile.

"My, that's a set of strange bedfellows!"

"Yes, and I hoped you could tell me more."

"I wish I could, Mr. Jones, but I don't know a thing about it, and I do find that more than a little bit strange!"

"They had already purchased some property, but they were asking the bank for 200 million dollars."

"My goodness!"

"There was also an elaborate set of drawings of the whole layout - a large hotel, two huge swimming pools, tennis courts, two golf courses, a yacht marina, a whole bunch of building lots, even a helipad. I hadn't heard a word about it either, but I thought maybe I was just out of the loop."

She sat very straight, with her eyebrows raised.

"You'd think they would be talking it up everywhere. A project like that requires lots of spadework. They'd need permits, zoning exceptions, plans for sewer and water lines, road improvements, the lot."

"That's pretty much what I thought. So why the secrecy?"

She leaned forward and nested her hands together.

"I can't imagine, Mr. Jones. What do you think?"

"I don't know, but it makes me think something very strange is going on. Did you ever hear of those three being business partners?"

Her eyes widened, and Jones felt again the keen intelligence behind her calm professional bearing.

"Not at all, in fact, it's downright odd."

"Can you think of anything that would pull them together?"

"Not a thing, but you can bet I'll be thinking about that now!"

"What about this young woman, Helen Rubinstein, do you know anything about her?"

"Rubinstein, Rubinstein…"

She put a hand on her cheek.

"I remember an older couple named Rubinstein buying property out on the lake a few years ago. You're saying a young woman?"

"I think her parents bought the land originally, and now they've passed away. She's inherited it."

"Oh yes, that makes sense. We did a feature article on them a few years ago. I can get a copy of it for you. They emigrated from Russia and wanted to build some kind of home-away-from-home for Russians living in the U. S. It wasn't anything fancy, a few houses, a community building, maybe a restaurant. I don't think they had it all figured out."

"But nothing like the plans we've just been talking about."

"Heavens, no!"

"What else can you tell me about Falcano, Nicholas or Fitzhugh?"

"Henri Falcano wasn't in the news much, except as the conductor of the orchestra. He was doing an outstanding job as far as I could tell. Nicholas is a wheeler dealer. He always wanted free publicity for his restaurants, but we are pretty good at avoiding that kind of thing."

Jones appreciated the amusement in her shining eyes.

"What about the mayor"

"You mean beside the fact he's a pompous ass?"

Jones looked down, trying to hide his smile.

"Go ahead, laugh! It's no secret to anyone who's ever been around him. He's a control freak, and he's complained about our coverage so many times I've lost count. I just throw his letters in the trash."

"Did you ever hear of him being involved in a business deal this size?"

"No, and I didn't think he had enough money to even think about something this big. For that matter, neither did Falcano or Nicholas. That's the strangest part about this whole thing. How did they plan to pull it off?"

"Well, maybe it was all a pipe dream. Maybe they got a wild idea, asked the bank how much it would cost, and that was the end of it. That's what I'm trying to find out."

"Do you think it might have something to do with Falcano's murder?"

"That's the fifty-thousand dollar question, isn't it? He's murdered for no apparent reason, and here's a big secret plan that no one knew anything about. It's hard for me to imagine there's no connection."

"I'm inclined to agree. How can I help you, Mr. Jones?"

She leaned forward in her chair, and Jones could feel her interest in being involved. All of a sudden he wondered if that was such a good idea.

"Well, it has to be kept quiet for the time being."

"Of course! But when the story breaks, you'll give the paper an exclusive in-depth interview, right?"

"Sure, why not?

He thought for a moment.

"I would appreciate it if you can find that article about the Rubinsteins for me, along with any information you have about the daughter and our three amigos."

"I'll be happy to. I'll get some eager-beaver intern working on it, and we'll find every scrap we've ever written about them."

"And this is just between us, at least for now, right?"

"Believe it or not, Mr. Jones, I do know when to speak and when to keep my mouth shut."

As he turned to leave, he hoped he could believe it.

"Thank you very much, Mrs. Fields, you've been a big help.

"Please, it's Jeanette!"

She waved an arm dismissively over her head.

"I'm not that old, you know!"

She stood up as he walked toward the door.

"I'm the one that should be thanking you, Mr. Jones."

"If I'm going to call you Jeanette, you'd better call me Peter."

"Keep me posted Peter, and don't worry. We won't print a word until the time comes."

Jones replayed their conversation in his head as he walked the five blocks back to the police station. It hadn't seemed worthwhile to get in the car for such a short distance, and he certainly wasn't in any hurry to get back! The walk would do him good and give him some time to think.

Had he told her too much?

He had to confide in her if he expected to get something in return, but giving information to the press always made him nervous.

The national media still hadn't gotten wind of this bizarre story, but a juicy online article about it might catch their eye, and they could descend on him like a cloud of locusts!

He made a mental note to think twice before telling Jeanette anything else.

When he got back to the office he found a note on his desk asking him to call Pru McDonough at the symphony office.

He dialed the number and sat back in his chair distractedly. His mind had already begun drifting to other things when the line clicked.

"Pru McDonough."

"Hello, Ms. McDonough, it's Peter Jones."

"Thanks for calling back so quickly. Mr. Jones. I've found something I think you'd better see right away."

"What is it?"

"It was lying on Henri's desk. I don't know how we missed it before. It's a threatening letter to Henri."

He sat up with a jerk. "What?"

"And it's from Wil Walker."

CHAPTER TWENTY-TWO

Wil berated himself as he peeked timorously into the lecture hall full of gray hair and bald heads. Why had he come here today? He felt utterly unprepared to talk about anything intelligent in front of such a large group of people.

A month ago, his friend Alex Wotila had invited him to visit his Elderhostel class so they could meet a composer who wasn't an old dead guy, just a picture on a book.

Even then, Wil had deep reservations.

He used to love talking about his music writing, but his bitter funk had begun to make him question his deepest convictions. How could he persuade these people to see composing as a calling worthy of commitment and sacrifice? He barely felt that way himself.

And what if they knew he might be charged with murder? What would they think if they heard him talk about lofty ideals of music composition tonight and saw his picture on the front page of the newspaper tomorrow?

Wil had tried to gather his thoughts, but the swirl of worries and regrets in his brain pushed everything else out of his head.

His feeble efforts to help with the investigation had gotten nowhere! He shuddered as he remembered the disastrous breakfast with Pru. Why had he told her anything? He should have known she would panic at the very thought of more terrible publicity for the symphony.

A fresh wave of anxiety convinced Wil he couldn't possibly go through with the lecture. He would just have to bolt and make his apologies later!

He turned to leave just as Alex stepped up behind him, grabbed his hand and pumped his arm enthusiastically.

"Hiya Wil, thanks for coming!

Wil wilted as he realized he'd missed his chance to escape and managed a lopsided grin.

"Hey, it's my pleasure. Sorry I'm a little late."

"No sweat, it's just now time to start. Let me warn you though, this is a tough class to reach, and they're highly opinionated. You may be in for some pointed questions today."

"That's okay. I always like good questions."

"Well, some of these folks may take it a little farther than that."

"What do you mean?"

Alex just grinned.

"You'll see. Don't worry, you'll be great!"

With that, Alex swirled off to start the class, and Wil made up his mind to try his best.

Wil cringed as Alex gave him a glowing introduction. If only his friend knew how unworthy he felt right now!

Suddenly Alex looked right at him, and Wil's attention snapped back to his friend's voice.

" … I have known Wil for many years, and I find his music very rich, uniquely fresh and always honest. It is truly moving to hear. He's not writing to impress the authors of textbooks, he's composing music that comes from the core of his being. His music is beautiful, it's compelling, and it has a power born of deep authenticity. I give you my friend, Wil Walker."

With that, Alex stepped aside, and the class welcomed Wil with a timid round of applause.

Wil felt incredibly touched by his friend's words. He tried to draw encouragement from them as he started talking, but everything he said seemed to fall flat.

He couldn't ignore an older man glowering at him in the front row, and he could see others in the back looking out the windows or struggling to stay awake. He tried to focus on friendlier faces, but his heart sank as he felt his last shreds of concentration slipping away.

Later, he tried to play recordings of a couple of his compositions, but that bombed too when the sound equipment wouldn't work.

Alex apologized profusely, but he couldn't get it going.

The whole session had become a complete disaster!

Finally, with about ten minutes left to go, Wil decided to ask the class if they had any questions.

The man in the front row shot up his arm immediately.

Alex nodded in the guy's direction.

"Go ahead Bert."

Bert sat up in his chair eagerly.

"Look, Mr. Walker, we appreciate your coming in to talk with us, but we have some questions about all this modern music. We love the Tchaikovsky and Beethoven we studied, but all this modern music seems like crap. It's so weird! Is that the kind of stuff you write?"

The man set his jaw and sat back with a challenging stare.

Wil had no idea what to say after an attack like that. He certainly wasn't going to defend all modern music. He found some of it crazy, too

"Well, that's a very broad question. There's so much …"

His antagonist interrupted with an upraised hand.

"A lot of the, quote, *classical,* unquote, music from the last hundred years really turned a lot of people off, you know."

Wil saw Alex grinning ruefully at the man's rudeness and sarcastic tone, but the people in the back had started perking up. Apparently they thought things were finally getting interesting.

Oddly enough, Wil felt something deep inside him stirring, and he realized with surprise he wanted to take the man's challenge head on.

"A tremendous variety of music was written in the the past century. There's really something for everyone. The music of Gershwin, Copland and Rachmaninov is enormously popular. People may have a hard time understanding some of the more adventurous music at first, but it's had a tremendous influence on movie music and all kinds of music we hear every day."

Bert jumped back in.

"Yeah, but some of this stuff we studied in class is so strange. Why would anybody write music like that?"

More hands went up, and Wil felt his passions coming to life in very unexpected ways as he told the class about some of his favorite composers and musical experiences. The conversation grew more and more animated, and Wil hoped his listeners began to understand why he relished the wonderful diversity of music so much.

In the end, the discussion seemed to focus on the question of why some music had so much dissonance.

Wil had definitely warmed to the task.

"Almost all music is a balance of dissonance and consonance. What matters is how they complement each other and how the music speaks to us on a deep level. I've heard some very dissonant music that was wonderful, even awe inspiring."

Bert clearly disagreed!

"Like what?"

"I once heard a piece by a man whose forty-year old daughter had died of cancer. The powerful dissonance in the music made it an anguished cry of the soul, and I found the whole thing very moving. But every piece of music shouldn't be like that. Some music should be harsh and dark, and some should be bright and joyous. Music should reflect the full spectrum of our emotions."

A woman in the back spoke up hopefully.

"So where does music go from here?"

Wil suddenly felt enormously grateful he had come here today. The conversation had helped him recover something significant, even vital, a reassuring strength in his spirit. He hadn't lost his deep convictions about music, he had just let them slip out of sight and out of mind.

"I think composers need to write music they really feel and strongly believe in. They have to write rich, deep music that is exciting and beautiful. If they do that, I think audiences will get excited about composers and new music again."

Bert scoffed.

"And you really think that can happen."

Wil almost felt elated.

"I do Bert, I really do. If I didn't, I wouldn't spend untold hours writing music, and I wouldn't be here talking about it with you."

Alex looked thrilled with the way things had gone.

"What do you think needs to happen, Wil?"

"Orchestral music is wonderful, it's magnificent, but it will become a dead art if we only play music that's hundreds of years old. Music needs new composers, and not a few, lots of them, but I believe the composers need to reach out to the audience, too. We have to TRY to compete for the hearts and minds of people out there."

Bert scowled, but Wil smiled with satisfaction.

Alex thanked Wil for coming, and several in the room applauded as the class got up to leave.

Wil savored the feeling he had at least given them something to think about.

He shook his friend's hand again when everyone had gone.

"Do you really believe what you said about my music, Alex?"

"You know I do, Wil. It was such a shame you couldn't play any of your pieces today. You would have shown them you write music everyday folks can appreciate as much as experts. You are a significant voice, Wil. Don't ever forget that."

Wil felt a deep welling of gratitude.

"You don't know how much that means to me, Alex."

"Is everything ok, Wil?"

Wil looked up.

"Maybe not so much, Alex, but things will sort out. It'll just take some time."

"Well, give me a call if you need someone to talk to."

"Thanks Alex, I appreciate that very much!"

Wil trudged out to his truck deep in thought.

He would write that slow movement for his symphony, and it would be wonderful! He would be an excellent music director for the symphony, whether he stayed for a short time or longer.

And he would help the police figure out who really killed Henri.

He wouldn't accept failure as an option!

Pru spoke firmly, but Jones noticed her hands shaking as she pushed the letter across the desk to him.

"I had to go into Henri's office to look for some information. I started looking through a stack of papers, and I found this near the top."

Jones found that puzzling, but he decided not to say anything.

He turned the letter over to see if anything had been written on the back.

"Is this the way you found it? Was there an envelope or anything?"

"No, nothing. It was just like that."

“You did the right thing, Ms. McDonough. Thank you for calling this to our attention.”

“Calling it to your attention? My God! I think it’s pretty damning, don’t you?”

It certainly did look that way!

CHAPTER TWENTY-THREE

Jones stared across Walter Manning's desk in growing disbelief as the chief wheedled and prodded. Manning seemed intent on ignoring everything he said!

"Chief, this letter is completely bogus! I searched that office myself, and this letter wasn't there. Somebody's been trying to pin this thing on Walker all along, and this essentially proves it. It's the clumsiest thing I've ever seen."

Jones tried not to think of the beautiful cottage on Torch Lake, his comfortable chair, the peaceful deep woods and the lake teeming with fish, just waiting to bite his hook and volunteer to be his dinner.

Manning dithered and pursed his lips, studying the letter like an archeologist with a rare artifact.

"Peter, be reasonable. Isn't it possible you just missed it before?"

Jones fought to keep his voice even.

"No, I was looking specifically for anything pertinent to the case. I do have a little expertise in this field you know!"

"Of course, of course. I just mean anybody can make a mistake. Maybe it was under something else, or you didn't notice what it said."

The chief looked at Jones with a condescending air of concern that made him even madder!

"Stranger things have happened, Peter."

"Walter, I'm telling you, I looked through everything on that desk and this wasn't there. Someone came in and planted it. There's no doubt in my mind! And why would Walker be stupid enough to write a letter like this if he was going to kill Falcano?"

"Why does any criminal do something stupid, Peter? Crime isn't logical. He wrote a letter and now he probably wishes he hadn't, it's that simple."

Jones found it simple alright, simply infuriating!

"Chief, the whole thing is typed, including the signature. Anybody could have written it. A good defense attorney would get this thrown out in two seconds."

"We've got a whole pattern of evidence, Peter. We know he had opportunity and a motive, we have a receipt for the bullets found at the scene, and now we have this. Why are you so intent on ignoring the obvious?"

Jones wondered, not for the first time, if somebody behind the scenes could be calling the shots and telling Manning what to do.

"Because it's *too* obvious, Chief. It's a setup and a very clumsy one at that. Somebody's trying to toss Walker our way, and when I find out who that is, *then* we'll have the murderer. This letter convinces me even more that Walker is innocent."

"Oh come on, Peter. I think you've been reading too many murder mysteries. Walker killed Falcano so he could take over as the head of the orchestra. He dropped the bag with the receipt as he was leaving, or maybe on the way in. Fortunately for us it didn't blow away. Now we find this letter on the conductor's desk, and you want to make up some big conspiracy theory. Make sense, man!"

Suddenly the door flew open and Eldon Fitzhugh stormed into the room.

"What's going on in here?"

Talk about the last straw! Jones wondered if the mayor ever thought to knock.

Jones fumed as Manning showed Fitzhugh the letter. How could the chief encourage him to interfere?

Fitzhugh pronounced judgment with a snarky tone that made Jones even more furious.

"Well, this is pretty clear. So we have this man Walker in custody, right?"

"Not yet, Eldon, that's what Peter and I were just discussing."

"Discussing?! What's the problem?"

"Peter believes Walker is innocent and someone is trying to frame him."

Jones hated being talked about like he wasn't there.

"That's the craziest thing I've ever heard! Unless I'm mistaken Detective Jones works for you. Isn't that right, Chief? Order him to arrest this man now! If he refuses, fire him and give the job to someone who will. Stop messing around with this!"

Manning suddenly looked ready to assert himself, if only a little.

"Now just a minute, Mr. Mayor. Peter is an excellent detective, the best I've got. I was just explaining to him that we have to be reasonable, and Walker is the logical suspect."

"Reasonable? All we have to do is act like we've got some brains! Walker did it, and it's time to get him behind bars. I don't see why we're standing around here talking."

Why are YOU here at all, Mr. Mayor!

Manning turned to Jones with a pleading look.

"Peter, why don't you arrest Walker, just to be safe? If you feel there are other things to investigate, you go right ahead, but he'll be safely in custody. What's wrong with that?"

The mayor looked like a fish gasping for breath!

"I'll make an arrest when I believe I have the guilty party, Chief. This evidence does more to clear Walker than to make him look guilty. I'm not going to do exactly the opposite of what I believe is right."

"Walter, tell him he's being crazy!"

Manning had the air of a referee who couldn't control a prize fight.

"Ok, Peter. You do what you think is best for now, but we'll be watching you like a hawk."

Manning waved a finger at Jones like a scolding third grade teacher.

"If it turns out Walker is guilty, and he leaves for Mexico or something, you're going to be in a world of trouble!"

Fitzhugh erupted like a bursting volcano.

"What? That's it?! Walter, are you going crazy too? Get this man arrested!"

Jones decided he'd been dismissed and fled the room.

He could see people all over the squad room sneaking a glance in his direction.

No wonder.

The sound of the mayor pontificating, and Manning trying to placate him, carried through the glass door as if it wasn't there.

Jones felt a desperate need to find the real killer before the mayor and Manning ran over him like a steamroller.

He needed time, and a very big break!

Jones pored over the letter and tried to concentrate. There had to be some way to figure out who planted it, and he needed to do that soon, very soon.

The mayor had finally stomped out. Manning seemed to be leaving him alone, for now, but Jones read his impatience loud and clear. The chief hated loose ends and conflict, and he could decide to force Peter's hand any minute.

Jones couldn't believe Manning could fall for a preposterous sham like this planted letter, but then, he'd hardly even glanced at it.

Fitzhugh hadn't either.

But why? Jones thought that question really needed to be answered. If the mayor pushed this hard out in the open, had he put on even more pressure behind the scenes?

Jones read through the letter one more time.

> Dear Mr. Falcano, You should know someone out there doesn't like you very much. You love strutting around on the stage and telling all those people what to do, don't you? Maybe you should watch out, watch your back. You never can tell when someone might do something drastic.
>
> Will Walker

This had to be the handiwork of the real killer, and Wil Walker certainly hadn't written it. Nothing about it sounded like his work! The crude, even clumsy, style didn't sound like him at all.

The simple block of text looked like a letter written by a kid. The note could have been printed on any computer, and the lack of a date seemed way too convenient.

'*Dear Mr. Falcano*'

That sounded oddly formal. Could it be some kind of sick mockery?

'*You love strutting around on the stage and telling all those people what to do, don't you?*'

That seemed like jealousy! Did conductors really have that much power over people? He'd have to ask Pru and some of the others, and he needed to press harder to find out if Falcano had any enemies.

'Maybe you should watch out, watch your back.'

Could the killer be someone who took perverse pleasure in ambushing someone? Only cowards shot someone in the back; ask any Hollywood director!

'You should know someone out there doesn't like you very much.'

That had a childish quality too, like a playground taunt.

And why the typed signature? The killer had to know that wouldn't be very convincing. A forged signature might give the deception away, but the typed signature made the whole thing seem pretty flimsy, just lazy!

Maybe the killer had improvised it in a hurry. Why the rush?

Jones sighed and tucked the letter into a file folder.

Suddenly the phone gave an asthmatic bleat. The startled detective jumped in his chair and had to laugh at himself.

"Hello, this is Peter Jones."

"Mr. Jones, this is Jeanette Fields. Is there something I should know?"

"I don't think so, why?"

"The mayor is marching up the stairs to my office right now, and he looks like he has smoke coming out of his ears."

CHAPTER TWENTY-FOUR

Wil stared at the keyboard in frustration. Why couldn't he get anywhere? He had never had so much trouble writing anything, and the harder he pushed, the more paralyzed he felt!

What could be wrong?

Well, he knew at least one answer to that. How could he expect to concentrate and write beautiful music with this suspicion hanging over his head?

But he needed to keep trying!

He kept plugging despite the nagging fear he might never get this piece off the ground.

When he heard three sharp raps on the door, he knew Helen had come to pay another call. He got up from the piano reluctantly and trudged through the living room in his stocking feet to open the door.

She looked out of sorts as he let her in, just the way she had every time he'd seen her for the past few days, ever since the murder, in fact.

She brushed past him with hardly a look in his direction, walked stiffly across the room and let her body drop into her accustomed place on the couch.

"What was that music you were just playing?"

"I was just trying out some ideas for the slow movement of my symphony. I can't seem to get any ideas going."

"I don't know why you spend so much time and effort writing music, Wil. You'll never make any money at it, you know."

"Oh no, not you too!"

"What's that supposed to mean."

"I got an earful of that kind of talk from Alex Wotila's class today."

She looked at a spot on the far wall as she talked, as if her mind was a thousand miles away.

"Well maybe they had a point. Don't you know nobody cares about composers writing classical music anymore?"

"Maybe, maybe not."

She turned back toward him with fierce intensity.

"Face reality Wil! Go to Amazon and look around! It's all hip hop, country and rock and roll. You might even find some jazz. But you'd have to search high and low to find any new classical stuff!"

The heat in her voice caught Wil by surprise.

"A lot of people love classical music."

"Oh sure, and if they want Beethoven or Mozart they have hundreds of recordings to pick from. Why are they going to buy some new thing by a composer they've never even heard of, Robert William something-or-other?"

Her stinging words lanced deep into Wil's gut.

"They haven't heard of me *yet.*"

He wished he hadn't put so much emphasis on the word 'yet,' but his talk with the Elderhostel students had helped him remember what he cared about most, and he had no desire to let Helen tear all that down.

"They're never GOING to Wil! People avoid new classical pieces like the plague!"

Wil felt his ire rising.

"It doesn't have to be that way! Why should all the new stuff be rock or pop? You know as well as I do a lot of that music could be written by third graders. I don't see why people can't be interested in new orchestra pieces, too, as long as they're fresh and exciting."

"Well why isn't it happening, Wil? You tell me."

He wondered if Russians had a special talent for sounding world-weary and sardonic.

"I do think people will be interested if the composers write music that's good enough."

"I doubt that very seriously, Wil, nobody's even paying any attention."

"Well, you've heard my music. What do you think?"

Their eyes met and her voice softened.

"You know I love your music, Wil. It really is beautiful. The colors are bright and fresh. It can sing and it can cry. Sometimes it makes me remember things that happened when I was a child."

She'd given him a great compliment, but she looked away fiercely.

"I just think our culture has gone to hell! I don't think people really understand the language of music anymore, and they don't really want to. They flock to the latest commercial gimmick like lemmings, and they'd all go over the same cliff together if the right marketing scheme led them on. You're dreaming Wil. The days when composers like Liszt and Verdi were treated like gods will never come again."

"I'm not asking to be treated like a god, Helen. I just want some people to listen, and I'll always try to make it worth their while. That's all I want, to have a voice, maybe to be a positive influence in this great cultural train wreck we're living in."

It sounded very noble to talk that way. He wondered if the music he wrote really lived up to the fine words!

She sighed.

"Well dream on, mister. I think you're kidding yourself."

"Well, maybe I am. I guess I'm just too stubborn and dumb to quit."

Helen seemed not to hear as she stared into the distance. Then she covered her face with her hands and burst into tears.

Wil stood next to her feeling helpless and foolish as her slender body shook with sobs. He'd been going on and on about music, and she obviously had something else, something overwhelming, on her mind.

She suddenly looked very much like a scared little girl.

After a few minutes, she wiped her eyes and pulled out a tissue to blow her nose.

"Oh Wil, I'm just in such terrible trouble. I don't know what I'm going to do."

Wil hesitated.

"Tell me what's going on."

"I can't, it's just not that simple!"

"Well, tell me what you can."

"I told you I can't talk about it."

She looked into his face with eyes full of overwhelming sadness.

He had a sudden, powerful urge to take her in his arms and kiss her, but he let the feeling pass. She seemed so vulnerable and fragile. It wasn't the right time, and she probably would have been horrified.

Wil turned away feeling confused and a little bit hurt. Something terrible had gone very wrong! Why couldn't she tell him about it?

He stepped to the window, trying to think of what to say next, just as Detective Jones' car pulled into the driveway.

Oh no! What now?

CHAPTER TWENTY-FIVE

Wil felt the stress rising in his body as Jones' unmarked police car pulled in behind Helen's beige BMW convertible. The detective studied Helen's car for a moment before he walked down the narrow sidewalk to the front door.

Wil opened the door before Jones could knock.

"Come in, Detective Jones, what can I do for you?"

The sharp ache in the pit of Wil's stomach came back with a vengeance. The detective couldn't be here to give him good news.

"Um, you know Helen Rubinstein, right?

"So charmed to see you again, Detective."

Her face had become a hard, brittle mask. Only the haunted look in her eyes hinted at the deep emotion she had just been going through.

"I was just leaving."

"Ms. Rubinstein! I'm glad you're here, I need to ask you a few questions too."

Her eyes widened and the color drained from her face.

"Me? What can you possibly want to ask me?"

"It's about your property on Lake Michigan. You do own land there, right?"

"Yes, of course."

She backed over to the couch, perched on one edge and lit a cigarette.

"Is this a bad time, Ms. Rubinstein."

"No, no, go ahead!"

She gave a wave of her hand, trying to appear casual, but her body looked rigid with tension. Wil knew the detective could see that as easily as he could.

"Have you been approached by someone about buying the land?"

"No, I'm trying to sell it. Do you want to buy it?"

Jones didn't react to her mocking tone.

"Henri Falcano never asked you about it?"

Wil hadn't thought any more color could drain from her face, but he'd been wrong.

"Henri?! Are you trying to imply I might be connected with the murder? My God!"

"I'm just asking if he made any inquiries about your property."

Her laser stare hadn't budged from Jones face.

"Of course not! Why would he be interested in buying real estate?"

"That's what I'm trying to find out. Do you know if he had any plans for a development project, maybe with some partners?"

"On my land? You've got to be joking! Anyway, he's dead. How can any of this possibly matter now?"

She looked furtively toward her car and took a deep pull on the cigarette.

"So no one, Falcano or anyone else, asked you about buying your land for some kind of big development?"

"I already told you, no! I wish to God someone would. Maybe I could move out of this hellhole!"

Wil looked away. Unfortunately, he had seen this caustic look on her face before.

Helen stood as a painfully awkward silence hung in the air.

"May I go now, Detective? Is there anything else?"

Jones hesitated.

"No, that's it. Is there a telephone number where I can reach you?"

She gave him the number and hurried out the door.

Wil heard her maneuver back and forth several times to get out of her parking space. He knew she would do anything to avoid asking Jones to move his car. When she got clear, she backed up the entire length of the driveway and sped off.

The scene with Helen had certainly done nothing to calm Wil's nerves.

"What do you need from me, Detective?"

Jones sighed and handed him a xerox copy of the letter.

"This suddenly showed up in Henri's desk. Do you recognize it?"

A freezing shudder passed through Wil's body as he read the note, again and again, in growing disbelief.

"You have to believe me, Mr. Jones. I didn't write this. I've never seen it before. I have no idea where it could have come from. I know this looks bad but I, uhh, I …"

"I believe you, Wil, and I don't think you wrote it."

Relief flooded over Wil like a huge wave.

"Oh, thank God! But who, how …"

"Unfortunately, there are some others at the police station who think you should be arrested right away."

"Oh, great!"

Wil's tension returned and gripped him like a giant, cold fist.

"Do you know anything about a development plan for Helen's property?"

Wil jumped at the chance to talk about something other than his own guilt or innocence.

"No, nothing! And for what it's worth, I think she was just as surprised as I was when you asked about it."

"But something's bothering her, right?"

Wil wondered how much he should say.

"Yeah, it sure seems that way."

"You don't know what it is?"

"No, I just tried to ask her about it, but she wouldn't tell me anything."

"How close are the two of you?"

"We've known each other for a couple of years."

"What's her story?"

"Her parents died just after she moved here. She wants to be a concert violinist and feels trapped here in St. Cecile, so far away from all the big cultural centers."

"What's a concert violinist?"

"Someone who makes a living performing as a soloist with orchestras."

"Can she do that, or could she if she lived somewhere else?"

"The top artists are famous. Do you recognize names like Itzhak Perlman and Van Cliburn?

"Sure."

"A lot of outstanding performers don't make anywhere near the kind of money they do. Then there are a whole bunch of good players, like Helen, who teach or play in an orchestra to make ends meet. She had a promising start, but she's afraid her career is fizzling out."

"Is it?"

"Maybe. It's awfully hard for someone like Helen to get noticed."

"How good is she?"

"Very good! She has excellent technique and there's great passion and drama in her playing. Maybe it's that Russian angst. The trouble is, a lot of talented performers never quite get their big break."

"What about you, are you looking for a big break?"

Wil flushed.

"Maybe. But I don't lay awake nights thinking about it."

Wil wondered if cops could always detect a lie.

"You mostly write music, right? Are you a performer too?"

"I don't play anything nearly as well as Helen plays the violin. I like to work behind the scenes, putting together music for other people to play."

"Is it a big step up in your career to become the interim conductor of the orchestra?"

Wil grimaced.

"Do you mean did I want it bad enough to kill for it?"

"Ok, sure. It's got to be asked."

"No way! I'm flattered the symphony asked me to do it for a while, but I never craved the job, and I certainly wouldn't kill Henri to get it!"

"Sorry, I didn't mean to get you worked up."

Wil took a deep breath and exhaled loudly.

"This whole thing has me very worked up, Detective."

Jones looked at him, but Wil couldn't tell if he had sympathy or suspicion in his eyes.

"What about this letter. Does the way it's written remind you of anyone?"

Wil read it several times, desperate for some flash of inspiration.

"No, it makes no sense! It just gives me the creeps to think someone murdered Henri and now, obviously, is trying to make it look like I did it! It's crazy!"

He felt a surge of panic and looked at the detective with tears stinging his eyes.

"You have to believe me, Mr. Jones! It wasn't me!"

"I hate to say it, Wil, but the important thing is not what I believe, it's whether or not we can prove it."

Wil felt very small.

"So some people really do believe I'm guilty?"

"There's pressure to solve the case quickly. That's all I'd better say for now."

"But there's more, right? You said some people already want me arrested!"

"Maybe it's better if you don't know."

"I have to know!"

"That's going to have to do for now. I'm sorry, Wil."

Wil stared back at the poisonous note.

"Wait, Detective, here's one thing. I sign my name "Wil,' with one 'l.' Whoever wrote this signed it like the word 'will,' with two 'ls.'"

"Hmm, I'd looked at it a dozen times and hadn't noticed that. I guess it's one of the words you look at but don't really see."

Jones started toward the door.

"Well at least that's a start. You wouldn't be too likely to spell your own name wrong. Do you see anything else that might shed some light?"

"No, that's it. It's infuriating!"

They both looked up at the sound of tires crunching on the gravel.

A black and white patrol car pulled into the drive, then another, then another. Half a dozen cars assembled in front of the house, and a small army of uniformed officers walked purposefully toward the door.

"Just stay calm, Wil, I'll find out what's going on."

Wil pulled open the door when he heard a heavy knock. His knees felt watery.

A tall, beefy cop at the head of the line spoke first.

"Are you Robert Walker?"

"Yes."

"We have a search warrant, Mr. Walker, please step aside."

Jones stepped closer with his anger plain on his red face and in his wide eyes.

"What's this all about Miles?"

"You'll have to ask the chief, Peter."

Jones reluctantly gave way as the officers streamed into the house.

"I'll do that as soon as …"

He glared incredulously as the chief and the mayor stepped up to the door.

"What the hell's going on here, Walter?"

"Just relax, Peter, it just seems prudent …"

The mayor interjected in a harsh voice.

"What are you doing here, Jones? Maybe that's what we ought to be asking!"

"I'm a police officer doing my job. I'd certainly like to know what *you're* doing here!"

Fitzhugh pointed a bony finger in Jones' face and turned to Manning.

"Are you going to let him talk to me that way?! That's insubordination!"

"I answer to the chief, *Mister* Mayor, and it's completely out of line for a civilian to be involved in serving a warrant."

"Technically he's right Eldon, maybe you'd better …"

"Don't you stick up for him, Walter! He's mishandled this whole investigation from the beginning. I want to know what you're going to do about it."

Jones ignored the mayor and turned to Manning.

"I thought I was handling this investigation, Walter. Who authorized this search warrant?"

"I did Peter. It seemed wise to check things out. The evidence is …"

The mayor chimed in with a bright red face.

"Somebody has to get this investigation into high gear! You seem to be in no hurry, and now we find you hobnobbing with the chief suspect. How do you explain that?"

Jones felt his self-control slipping dangerously.

"How do *I* explain it, how do you explain …"

"Chief, I think you'd better see this."

A uniformed officer gestured from the music studio.

"I've been checking his web browser. He's got a whole slew of bookmarks for sites about electronic gadgets and firearms."

The mayor crowed like a gamecock.

"You see? I told you! I told you so!"

Jones wilted and put a hand on Wil's arm.

"Is that true?"

Wil sputtered and fought to catch his breath.

"I was just, it was …"

One of the uniformed cops grabbed Wil roughly and pulled his hands behind his back.

Jones stepped back with a stricken look on his face.

"Don't panic, Wil, we'll sort this out."

The cop called Miles started the familiar litany.

"You have the right to remain silent …"

CHAPTER TWENTY-SIX

Jones seethed as he followed the mini-fleet of police cars back to the police station.

Manning's galling interference had definitely reached a new low. The chief should never have allowed the mayor to steamroll a search warrant, and Jones hated having any connection with the ham-handed arrest he'd just witnessed.

He felt more like a bystander than the lead detective, and he didn't like the feeling one bit!

When they got to the station, Fitzhugh hovered nearby until Jones issued a scathing ultimatum. The mayor insisted he had every right to stay, but he finally strutted out with a smug look of triumph that made Jones want to punch him in the face.

Jones stayed by Wil's side during the humiliating booking procedures. Wil looked utterly stunned as the cops took his fingerprints and snapped a mugshot.

After that, he took Wil into an interview room and took great care questioning him, knowing Manning would be watching through the one-way glass. Jones threw in several softball questions designed to let Wil protest his innocence, but he knew Manning only heard what he wanted to hear.

His approach baffled the other detective in the room, Joe Walsh, but when Jones gave Walsh a stealthy pleading look, the veteran cop let him have a free hand. Jones thanked his colleague, and they shared a knowing nod, when they finally called it a night and sent Wil to his cell.

Jones felt all of his thirty years on the force as he plodded wearily out to his car. He had to admit things had taken a dramatic turn. Wil insisted he only looked up the websites to help the investigation, but this latest bit of incriminating information had Jones worried.

Could he have been wrong about Wil?

If Walker had killed Falcano, he was by far the best actor Jones had ever seen, but stranger things had happened!

Walker had the opportunity, the skill, and even a possible motive. People had committed murder for all kinds of ridiculous, petty reasons, and a new job, a fresh start in life, just might be enough incentive to make him want to eliminate the competition.

Jones had to find out what really happened before things spun completely out of control!

A good night's sleep did Jones a world of good, and he felt a renewed sense of resolve as he drove to Greta Schmidt's downtown apartment. Pru had given him a list of key people to interview, and Greta had answered her phone on the first ring.

The knots in his shoulders seemed to soften a bit as he settled gratefully onto Greta's overstuffed couch.

She fussed over a pot of tea for several minutes, and Jones found her quaint formality oddly touching as she set down an elegant tray of flowery china and a small plate of sugar cookies. With everything in place, she settled into her cozy chair and smoothed her hair with a nervous wave of her hand.

"Thank you for agreeing to see me, Ms. Schmidt."

"Of course, Mr. Jones, this whole thing has been so terrible. I can't believe it's really happening."

The tiny, cluttered apartment made Jones feel a bit claustrophobic, but he had to admit he found it homey. Bits of furniture and luxuriant plants filled every available nook and cranny. The ruffled fabric on the couch crowded his legs as he tucked his feet under the low coffee table.

Greta's bassoon rested on a special stand next to an ornately carved piano, but Jones wondered how she got close enough to play either one. Several piles of dog-eared sheet music covered the floor all around.

Books and mementos jammed the incredible number of shelves lining the walls. Jones hoped they were fastened more securely than they appeared to be! A wildly eclectic mix of posters, photographs and paintings filled every inch of the remaining wall space.

A small, plump dog with curly brown hair tore breathlessly back and forth in the cramped space next to Jones feet, and the dog's enthusiastic energy showed no signs of flagging.

Greta crossed her hands over her chest.

"That's Muffin, Mr. Jones. Isn't she adorable?"

Jones wondered how Muffin managed to maneuver among all the obstacles, but she seemed to know the terrain very well.

"Muffin, lie down and leave the nice man alone!"

Greta's mild exhortation had absolutely no effect, so she laughed merrily and swept the dog into her arms.

"She won't bother you, Mr. Jones. Will you Precious?"

She snuggled Muffin with a flurry of affection, burying her face in the fluffy fur of the dog's belly and shaking her head playfully.

When Greta set Muffin down, the dog settled near Jones' feet, laid a moist jowl on his knee and looked up at him imploringly. She seemed intent on climbing onto his lap, but Jones knew he'd be licked thoroughly if he allowed that to happen.

He tried to prod her away without being too obvious.

"Muffin, you lie down and behave yourself!"

Greta sounded more amused than stern.

The dog backed a foot away, then crept about eleven inches back.

Jones took a drink of tea and settled deeper into the marshmallow-soft couch.

"What can you tell me about Henri Falcano, Ms. Schmidt?"

"Please, call me Greta."

"Sure, thank you, Greta, but what about Henri? Was he well liked? Did he have any enemies?"

She teared up instantly.

"Everybody loved him! Well, I guess you can't say loved, but everybody got along with him fine. He never did anything to hurt anybody, Mr. Jones. This whole thing is just horrifying!"

"Did you know him well?"

"I didn't socialize with him, Mr. Jones. Not many people in the orchestra did. He kept to himself. Once in a while he would tell us about a trip he was making or something, just to lighten things up, but it was all very breezy, nothing too close to home."

"Can you think of any reason why anyone would want to kill him?"

"No, none at all!"

"What about people in the symphony? Was there friction between Falcano and any of the players or staff?

"Well, you know, there are always complainers."

"Like who?"

"I'm sure it had nothing to do with the murder!"

"I just need to get a feel for Henri's life, how he got along with people. Please tell me."

She looked at him reluctantly.

"Well, ok, but I'm sure it's nothing. Some people, like Jim Pearce, always wanted to argue about everything. Jim would say the music was going too fast, and five minutes later, he'd gripe that it was too slow. He'd raise the roof if the rehearsal ran five minutes long. It didn't seem to matter what really happened, he just liked to complain."

"But you don't think he could be the killer?"

She blanched.

"No, no way! He's just a loudmouth. No one would commit a murder over something like that, would they? I don't want to make trouble for anybody, Mr. Jones."

"Please, don't worry. I'm not trying to bust someone for raising a ruckus in rehearsal. You're just helping me understand the dynamics in the orchestra. You're being very helpful."

Greta smoothed her skirt and looked at him earnestly.

"Do you really think it could be someone from the symphony?"

"We don't know. That's what we're trying to find out. Did anyone leave the orchestra in a huff?"

"People come and go, but no, nothing like that."

"Were there any other significant conflicts that you know about? Did anyone have some kind of longstanding grudge?"

"Orchestras are like big families, Mr. Jones, complete with all the dysfunctions! There are all kinds of cross currents, people getting bent out of shape about who said what, who gets to play a certain solo, petty disputes, you name it! It can get very ugly, but I can't imagine anything that would make someone kill Henri."

"Sure, that makes sense. But if there's anything that seems out of the ordinary, I'd like to know about it."

"There is one thing, it almost seems too silly to mention."

"Please, go ahead."

"I heard a terrible shouting match going on in the symphony hall one night. It was coming from Henri's office, and the other voice could have been Jim Pearce's. I just don't know!

That's why I didn't want to mention it. I hate to say something terrible about someone when I'm not even sure that's who it was!"

"Do you remember when it happened?"

"No, not exactly. See! It's useless! I didn't even want to bring it up."

"Everything is potentially useful Ms. Schmidt."

"You keep forgetting to call me Greta."

Jones hesitated. "What about Wil Walker?"

"What about him?"

She apparently hadn't heard about his arrest. Could the rumor mill be that quiet?

"Can you think of any reason why Wil Walker would want to kill Mr. Falcano?"

"Wil?! You've got to be joking! Why would you even ask such a thing?"

"Did he work closely with Mr. Falcano?"

"They were friends. I don't know if they were close, but they worked together often on the things Wil did for the symphony. They always got along fine as far as I could tell."

"Did Wil get along well with everybody else?"

"Of course! Everybody likes Wil, Mr. Jones. Surely you can't think he had anything to do with it!"

And, actually, he didn't, not that his opinion mattered much right now!

Jones tried to make the next question sound routine.

"Do you know anything about Mr. Falcano's business dealings?"

"Business dealings? All I knew about was his work with the symphony. He was one of the most private people I've ever met, Mr. Jones. He never talked about things like that."

"Did you ever see him associating with Winston Nicholas or Eldon Fitzhugh?"

"You mean the owner of *La Bon Temps* and the mayor? They probably knew each other from fund-raising events, things like that. But that's not what you mean is it?"

"No, did you ever hear about them working together as business partners?"

"No, I never even saw them together."

"Can you think of anything at all that might be behind this?"

"No, that's what makes it so weird!"

She looked ready to cry again.

"Well, thank you very much, Ms. Schmidt?"

"Greta."

"Right, sorry Greta. Can you suggest anyone else who might be able to tell me more about the real Henri Falcano?"

"Well, Pru McDonough worked closely with him in the office. You've probably already talked with her. Bill Evers is president of the symphony board of trustees. You might try him. He's the president of American Eagle Bank."

Jones wondered if the chairman of the board could be miffed because the partners passed over his bank for a big real estate loan.

"Anyone else?"

"Jeremy Rice sometimes works as an associate conductor. He's a trombonist in the orchestra and runs a music store on Second Street. He might be a good person to talk to."

"Thank you very much, Ms. Schmidt, you've been very helpful."

"I don't see how. I wish there *was* something I could do. This is such a terrible thing. I still can't believe it really happened."

Jones wondered what she would think when she heard the interim music director had been arrested and thrown in jail!

"There's one more thing that might be worth mentioning, Mr. Jones, even though I think it's the opposite of what you're looking for."

"What is it? I'm looking for anything that helps me understand."

"Helen Rubinstein. She was in love with Henri. You could see it in her eyes when she looked at him."

Jones let that sink in for a minute.

"Was he in love with her?"

"I don't know. He thought she was special, you could tell that. But I never saw them together or heard anything about them dating. Maybe it was all one sided."

Jones thanked her for her trouble and asked her to call him if she thought of anything else.

Henri and Helen?

He had one more thing to add to his list!

CHAPTER TWENTY-SEVEN

Jones felt the relaxation from Greta's apartment melt away as he sat in Bill Evers' office. If you wanted a movie set to look like a cliche of a banker's workplace, this cavernous, dark room would be perfect.

The nameplate on the door said 'William J. Evers, III.'

Evers' gleaming wooden desk held only the bare essentials: a phone, a pen holder, a large blotter and the obligatory photo that had to be a picture of his wife. No children. Grown perhaps?

The only pictures on the wall, two oversized portraits, appeared to be earlier executives of the bank. Two tidy chairs sat in front of the huge desk at opposing angles that could have been set by a mathematician. A small settee across the room looked like no one had ever sat in it.

Evers eyed him from behind the desk and seemed, strangely, to be sitting at attention in his massive chair.

Jones found Evers remarkably tight lipped, even for a banker. He hadn't yet said three words if two would do. He'd already said he didn't know any reason why someone would kill Falcano, he didn't know Falcano or any members of the orchestra all that well, he just knew Pru McDonough on a professional basis, and he'd just met Wil Walker when he'd been nominated as the interim music director.

Jones had only been here five minutes, and this interview had already run out of gas!

"Were you ever approached by Mr. Falcano, Winston Nicholas and Eldon Fitzhugh about financing for a big resort development they wanted to build on Lake Michigan?"

"Together?"

"Yes, the three of them working together, or any one of them acting alone."

"No."

Jones thought Evers ought to be more curious about something like that, but the man's inscrutable face revealed no emotion at all.

"Could they have developed a project like that without you knowing about it?"

"Of course. I can't know everything, Detective."

Jones fought to stay patient.

"Do you think they might have come up with a plan and sought financing elsewhere?"

Evers' face finally reddened, ever so slightly.

"In the first place, those three would never work together. But if they did, Eldon would certainly have consulted me first about financing. Winston and Henri, too. They would never have gone behind my back."

"Are you sure about that?"

"Of course, we've worked together for years."

Jones thought he must have hit a nerve. Evers had finally started talking, but he certainly had no imagination.

Evers hid behind rules of confidentiality when Jones probed for details about his dealings with the three men, and Jones found the stonewalling infuriating!

"Can you suggest anyone else I should talk to?"

Evers pursed his lips and studied the sparse contents of his desktop for a moment.

"I'm sorry, Mr. Jones, there's no one. Now if that's all, I'm afraid I must let you go. Please don't hesitate to contact me again if I can be of further assistance."

He made no move to stand or offer a handshake.

Jones rose to go with a sour feeling in his stomach.

"Thank you very much, Mr. Evers. I appreciate your time."

Further assistance? There'd been no assistance at all! Jones had no doubt Evers knew more than he had let on, but the banker had no intention of telling him anything.

Why would Evers be so tight lipped?

Who could he be protecting, and why?

The profusion of musical gear in Jeremy Rice's tiny music shop brought back a flood of vivid memories for Jones. He had loved music as a boy, but he chafed at the hours of practice required to get any good at it.

His mother had forced him to take piano lessons, and he would give anything to go back and tell his young, smart-aleck self to quit bellyaching and stick with it!

He had joined the school band too, but he quit before he learned much of anything.

He took up guitar as a teenager, and he and some high-school friends started a rock band. They took over his Dad's garage and loved annoying the neighbors by turning up their amps way too loud. The band never made any money, but Jones had loved the thrill of filling the air with their cacophonous improvisations. The music made them feel immortal!

Every bit of space in Rice's store held pianos, electronic keyboards, band instruments, sheet music and musical bric-a-brac that Jones never dreamed existed. Guitars of every shape and description filled display racks and hung from hooks in the ceiling. A large selection of electrical cords, connectors and box-shaped speakers stood ready to amplify the sounds to modern decibel levels.

Rice had devoted a large corner area entirely to drum sets. The drums came in a variety of flashy colors, but high-gloss black seemed to be the most popular offering. A profusion of golden cymbals hung one above the other in displays that looked like uneven stacks of plates.

A large rack held wooden sticks, some as thin as a pencil, some thicker than Jones' thumb, with dozens of sizes in between. Next to that stood an incredible selection of thin rods tipped with colorful balls of plastic, rubber, metal and wound yarn. Those seemed to be for playing instruments like xylophones.

Many of the other items on display looked like they might be shaken, struck or scraped to make musical sounds.

Jones shook his head as Rice walked up behind him.

The musician proved friendly and talkative. Jones asked about some of the instruments and equipment, and Rice seemed completely at ease with all of it, but unfortunately, he didn't seem to know any more than the others about possible motives for the murder.

It turned out the title of associate conductor made him little more than a slightly-glorified errand boy. He had conducted a couple of pieces with the orchestra, but he really didn't get many chances to be on the podium. He sometimes helped with chores like mailings, sorting the player's music and setting up chairs and stands.

He hadn't worked especially closely with Falcano, and he certainly wasn't privy to the conductor's personal life or business dealings.

Jones felt his frustration mounting. This agonizingly slow process had gotten him nowhere! He told Rice he wished there was a way to gather the people in the orchestra together and talk to them all at the same time.

"Oh, we could do that. No problem! I'm sure they'd love a chance to sit down with you and hear how things are going in the investigation."

Oh great! He'd have to downplay that part.

"Would it be hard to get everyone?"

"No, I'll call Pru. We have an email list that we use whenever we need to get information out quickly. We'll set up a meeting for tomorrow night. Would that be ok?"

"That would be perfect. Where?"

"We can all cram into the symphony office when we need to. I don't imagine everybody will be able to make it, but people are hungry for information. You'll probably have a great turnout."

And I'll tell them as little as possible!

"What time?"

"Say seven o' clock?"

"That should work fine. Thank you Mr. Rice."

"No, thank you. I certainly hope you find out who did this, and soon. Everyone in the orchestra is feeling traumatized. Have you made much progress yet?"

"Not yet."

Quite the opposite.

The meeting might be a big help, if it didn't turn into a protest demonstration over Walker's arrest!

CHAPTER TWENTY-EIGHT

Wil looked around the jail cell for the hundredth time.

This couldn't be happening!

Rage, fear, frustration, hope and despair took turns swirling through his brain at breakneck speed, and he had never felt such an excruciating sense of unreality. He had done nothing, but he felt utterly powerless to stop this trap from closing in on him with relentless force.

His heart raced constantly, and every few minutes his body shook uncontrollably. Sweat drenched his hands. He wiped them over and over again on the legs of his jeans, but he couldn't get them dry. Everyone else he saw seemed to find the air comfortable, but he felt rigid with cold.

He had always pictured jails as dark, gloomy places, probably because of clichés in the movies. This one had plenty of light, but the cheerless yellow-white glare, completely devoid of any warmth, made him feel like an insect in a canning jar.

The sickly beige paint on the bars and walls had peeled in several places, leaving uneven splotches of creamy yellow, blue and brown. The painting seemed to be frequent, but far from permanent.

The barren cell contained nothing but two beds, a grimy sink and a tiny, disgusting toilet.

At least no one had come in to take the other bed.

The night had been the longest Wil could ever remember. He'd dozed and snapped awake dozens of times. All told, he'd probably slept less than an hour.

It seemed he hadn't slept at all!

Every sound in the hallway made him look to the door instantly, hoping to see Jones coming to release him.

Surely this nightmare would end soon. They had to realize he couldn't be guilty!

What a luxury it would be to face the mundane problems of a normal day. He had always taken for granted the right to walk out of any room and go where he pleased. Now that seemed like the most precious gift imaginable. He longed desperately to bolt through the door at the end of the hallway and find his way out into the sunshine.

Agghh! Let me out of here!!!

Jones had given him a lawyer's phone number and told him to call as soon as possible. Wil refused to believe he needed one, at least at first, but when the reality of his situation sank in, he called the number and left a message.

Fresh worry clutched at his innards. Why hadn't the lawyer come?

And how could he pay for a lawyer anyway?

Wil strained to see as he heard a shuffle at the end of the hall.

He sank back wearily onto the bed when he saw a deputy walking past the corridor.

Oh God!

Prisoners on TV and in the movies always looked blasé or just depressed. Wil knew he could have a panic attack at any moment, and he thought he understood exactly how a caged animal felt.

Only one thing mattered, getting out!

Mr. Jones, where are you?! Where's my lawyer?! Somebody stop this insanity!!

He slumped on the bunk and pressed his hands against his face.

Jones walked into the symphony office and saw an impressive number of people had shown up for the meeting. Most of the musicians ignored the rows of folding chairs and stood between them in clusters of animated conversation.

Pru McDonough saw him come in and hurried over.

"Thank you for doing this, Detective. It's a great idea. I'm sure there will be dozens of questions."

"I'd actually prefer to be the one asking questions, Ms. McDonough."

"You can let them know in general terms what's going on, can't you? Everyone is so upset. They want to know what's happening."

They won't like what they're going to hear.

"I'll do what I can, but I need to hear from them. We've got to get a break in this investigation."

"Of course, of course. Please wait over here, Mr. Jones, I'll get things started."

Pru walked to the front of the room and asked everyone to sit down.

The firm authority in her voice caught Jones by surprise, and the crowd complied much more quickly than he expected them to.

Pru smiled wanly.

"Hello everyone. Thank you so much for coming on such short notice. I'm sure you are all curious, but mainly we're here to help the police with their investigation. This is Detective Peter Jones. I'm sure you all know who he is. Please be patient and let Mr. Jones run things the way he thinks best."

She walked toward the end of the front row, sat primly on one of the chairs and turned to face in his direction.

Jones gave her a nod of appreciation for setting the tone so adroitly and wondered where to begin.

The facial expressions in the room ran the gamut from expectancy to disbelief. He recognized a few of the people, but not many. It seemed clear most of them expected him to be a miracle worker, but he didn't feel like he had any miracles in his pocket.

"Thank you for coming, folks. I'm not really accustomed to speaking in front of large groups of people, so please bear with me. And please tell me your name if I call on you for a question or a comment. Ok. I'm sure you're all wondering what's been going on so far. We're really looking for answers at the moment."

Better get the hard part out of the way.

"There's a certain amount of circumstantial evidence ..."

He abruptly realized he couldn't bring himself to say Wil had been arrested.

"We've taken Wil Walker into custody for questioning."

He heard an audible gasp. Then everyone started talking at once.

Jones held up his hands and pleaded for quiet.

"Please, please, folks. This is only a very preliminary stage in the investigation. We have to explore every possibility."

The murmuring died away slowly, but he could hear about five people directing questions at him. He pointed to a woman in the front row.

"Go ahead ma'am. Would you tell me your name, please?"

She stood with an incredulous face and put her hands on her hips.

"My name is Janelle Parks. I'm a violinist. Are you trying to tell us Wil Walker is a suspect? There's no way Wil could have done it!"

She stayed on her feet, daring him to contradict her.

Jeez, this is off to a great start!

"Please be patient folks, we're just getting started. What I need from you is information that will help me figure out what actually happened."

"You can't believe Wil did it!"

The voice belonged to Greta. She looked shocked to the core, and Jones saw with keen regret, more than a little betrayed.

"We're exploring a lot of possibilities, and I'm afraid that's all I can really say right now. I'd like to ask a few questions if I may."

Jim Pearce stood suddenly in the back.

"Look people. The police know what they're doing. We have to stay out of their way and let them do their jobs. If they say Walker is a suspect, who are we to question it?"

"Mr. Pearce, I'm not saying Walker is a suspect and I'm not saying he isn't. You would have heard soon enough he's in custody. I thought it best you heard it from me."

Jones turned back toward the assembled group and swallowed nervously.

He'd blundered badly, and the mood had taken a significant turn for the worse. Most of the musicians looked shocked and resentful, and they'd be afraid to say anything. He'd become the enemy, someone attacking one of their own.

And he couldn't say he believed in Walker's innocence. He had to keep an impartial stance, and they wouldn't believe it for a second.

Way to go, idiot!

Jeremy Rice rose cautiously, looking a bit bewildered.

"I talked with the detective yesterday, folks. It was my idea to have this meeting. I think you'll find he's reasonable and fair. Let's try to give him some help."

He sat down slowly and glared at Jones with a look that said 'make this right, and the sooner the better.'

Jones tried to keep his tone cool and professional.

"Thank you Mr. Rice. Can anybody tell me what Mr. Falcano did when he wasn't working?"

"He kept to himself, detective."

A plump, balding man on the right stood hesitantly.

"He didn't socialize much with members of the orchestra, and we really didn't know much about what he did in his spare time."

"What's your name sir?"

The man looked embarrassed.

"I'm Felix Bartleby. I'm a French horn player."

Everyone seemed to take their identity from the instrument they played.

"Thank you Mr. Bartleby. Anyone else?"

Several people looked tentatively around the room.

A woman near the front spoke from her seat.

"He was always friendly enough in rehearsals and such. He could put on the charm for donors and season ticket holders, but none of us got very close to him. I guess we never thought much about his social life. He kept his private affairs to himself."

"Does anyone know more about his life away from the orchestra?"

No one offered anything. Either they really didn't know, or they weren't about to tell him squat. Maybe some of each.

"What about business dealings. Does anybody know anything about that?"

More silence.

He tried to ask the same basic questions a few different ways, but the response didn't change at all.

The mood finally softened a bit when Jones asked what Falcano had been like as a musician. The room filled with laughter and tears as people rose one after another to share vivid stories about memorable performances and funny things that happened in rehearsals. Jones learned a lot as he listened to the poignant conversation, but not much that would help with the investigation.

The meeting had turned into a chance for people to comfort each other and celebrate the past.

Soon all pretense of talking with Jones had disappeared. He felt like an intruder at a family gathering, and he knew when to step back and let things take their own course.

He hesitated to break in, but when he finally did, he asked about Wil Walker.

The spirit in the room changed instantly from reminiscence to zealous defense.

Hands shot up all over the room, and everyone described Wil as a gentle, positive man who genuinely loved helping people get excited about music and had a special talent for writing beautiful compositions. Several spoke of small kindnesses Wil had offered, seemingly expecting nothing in return.

One woman, a violist, fiercely described him as a peacemaker, a friend you could count on, and many in the room nodded in agreement.

If anyone disagreed, they kept their mouth shut.

Jones felt a sharp burning sensation in his gut. Who wanted to frame this guy, and why? Nothing in this whole scenario made any sense!

When the discussion started to wind down, everyone looked at him to see if he had more to add.

He'd have given anything to say he wanted Walker freed as badly as they did. Instead he thanked them for their time and gave them his phone numbers and email address, inviting anyone who thought of something else to contact him.

As the meeting broke up, the musicians returned to their small groups and resumed their animated conversation. No one looked anxious to leave.

Jones decided to hang around in case someone wanted a private word, and he chatted with Pru and a couple of the others until people finally started to straggle out.

Pru asked about Wil's arrest with a face that seemed to be set in stone.

"You have no idea how damaging this could be for the symphony, Detective. No idea at all!"

Jones thought he had a very good idea. The publicity would be devastating! But he didn't press the point.

Jones was just about to leave when someone tapped him on the shoulder.

"There are a couple of things you need to know that didn't come out in that meeting."

CHAPTER TWENTY-NINE

Jones turned to see Helen Rubinstein staring at him with a steely expression, her crossed arms pressed tightly against her body.

"What's that Ms. Rubinstein?"

"Henri was a liar. I know none of those people wanted to face that and ruin their little lovefest, but it's true."

Pru looked truly shocked.

"What are you talking about Helen?"

"I know you don't want to admit it either."

Helen turned back to Jones.

"But you couldn't rely on his promises. Maybe that will give you a clue about why he was killed."

If she wanted to get his attention, she had succeeded brilliantly.

"What do you mean, Ms. Rubinstein? What did he promise you?"

"You wouldn't understand. Just take my word for it. He couldn't be trusted."

She looked like that was obvious and he was a fool for asking.

Pru made no effort to hide the outrage on her face.

"Helen, that's unbelievably cruel! I can't imagine what you're talking about. Detective, I always took Henri at his word and I never had a problem."

She whirled back to Helen with eyes full of fury.

"What are you playing at Helen?"

"I'm not playing, and I'm not making it up, either!"

She gaped at Pru for a moment longer, then stormed out of the room with a final glare at both of them.

They both watched in stunned silence as she slammed the door of her car and sped off.

Pru drew back and shook her head in amazement.

"That's unbelievable. I wonder what's bothering her?"

"That's something I'm going to have to find out, Ms. McDonough."

As Jones walked to his car, he bitterly admitted he hadn't budged from square one.

He knew a lot more peripheral stuff about Falcano and the symphony, but the meeting had gotten him nowhere.

Helen seemed very eager to make some kind of point, but somehow, Jones knew he would have to spend a lot of time and effort to get it out of her.

He decided to interview Nicholas and Fitzhugh before he tried to talk with her again.

After what seemed like an eternity, a guard took Wil to a small, dingy conference room and said his attorney would be right in.

Wil would have given anything to know what time it was. The police had taken his watch, he hadn't seen the sun since the day before, and it seemed like it could be any time from midnight to noon.

Time had never seemed to move more slowly.

Finally the door opened, and a middle aged man with a ragged shock of graying hair shuffled in and introduced himself as James Winningham.

Wil wondered if Jones had picked the first name in the book. The lawyer's thick mustache needed a trim badly, his tie drooped at a weird angle, scuff marks covered the toes of his brown shoes and a streak of chalky dust ran up the leg of his pants.

But Wil didn't seem to be in a position to quibble, so he decided to trust Jones and hoped Winningham cared more about his work than looking the part.

Wil asked about the time, and Winningham looked at his watch.

"It's 9:37."

"A.M. or P.M.?"

Winningham looked at him quizzically.

"It's morning. Peter Jones tells me you're in serious trouble, Mr. Walker. Why don't you tell me about it?"

Winningham sat back in his chair with a reassuring look of complete concentration.

Wil started hesitantly, but before long, he could hardly speak fast enough to say everything on his mind. His emotions ran the gamut from rage to terror, and he struggled to fight back tears as he insisted on his innocence. The infuriating sense of unfairness filled his gut with fire.

"How in the world can I prove I didn't do it, Mr. Winningham?"

"That's the 50,000-dollar question, Wil. The best way would be to find some proof someone else did it. I think Peter Jones believes you're innocent. That's the main thing on your side at the moment."

"He said some others weren't so sure. Do you know who he's talking about?"

"Not really, but that's the least of our worries for the moment. Right now we have to concentrate on getting you out on bail and putting together a defense. Let's review the facts. The bullet came from an automated device hidden in the concert hall. Is it true you were there alone the night before the murder?"

Wil glowered with resentment.

"Are you asking me if I killed him?!"

"No, Wil. Look, I know this is difficult, but you need to calm down. I need to know as much as I can about what happened, okay?"

"Aw'right. I'm sorry. I'm just so upset I can't function."

"I know. Tell me what you were doing there, okay? That was on Friday, right?"

"Yeah, I was checking on the setup for a lecture I had to give before the concert the next day. It's something I always do. I usually check things out just before I get started, but I had a busy day Saturday, so I borrowed a key from Pru and went over on Friday."

"Who's Pru?"

"Prudence McDonough is the orchestra's administrative director. She runs the business end of things, keeps the budget in line, that sort of thing."

"Okay, so you borrowed her key and went to the concert hall. Then what happened?"

"Nothing! I made sure everything was set in the lecture room, then left. I was only there ten or twenty minutes. I never went near the auditorium!"

"Did you see or hear anything unusual?"

"No, I wasn't really paying attention. I was just doing some very routine stuff."

"Is there any way we can prove this evidence is being planted?"

Wil reddened.

"There should be! The first time I talked with Jones someone had gone out of their way to tell him I'd once studied electronics. Then he got a note saying I'd been at the concert hall."

"Is that all?"

"No, then a receipt turned up with a fake credit card number under my name. That's when I knew for sure someone was working hard to make me look like the bad guy. I had to fight back!"

"What about the incriminating stuff on your computer?"

"I thought if I could find some information, I might be able to help Jones figure out what happened. That sure backfired, didn't it? I gave whoever is framing me more help than he could ever ask for. What a mess!"

"That's for sure."

"There's one more thing. Jones showed me a threatening letter that showed up on Henri's desk. It was typed, not handwritten, but it was supposed to look like it came from me. I think Jones was very skeptical about it even before I saw my name misspelled with two 'l's instead of one."

"Hmmm. You wouldn't be too likely to spell your own name wrong, would you? But that wouldn't carry much weight against all this other stuff in court. A good prosecutor would blame the typo on autocorrect or something."

"What can I do?!"

"One step at a time, Wil."

"One step at a time? That's easy for you to say. My life is going down the toilet!"

Winningham sighed.

"Look, I wish I could tell you not to worry, but I think you know how serious this is. It doesn't look good. Peter believes someone is planting this stuff, but it all looks very convincing. You were alone in the concert hall the night before, the credit card number on the receipt is in your name, and your new job makes it look like you had a perfect motive."

"I never wanted to take over Henri's job!"

"I know, but we're talking about how things look. The computer links make it look like you researched the subject, and along with your background in electronics, boom, it all ties up with a neat little bow."

"This just *can't* be happening!"

"Is there anything that can help us here, anything that gives you an alibi?"

"No, I was alone Friday night, there's no way around that. Saturday I was running all over the place. No one would have seen me for more than a few minutes at a time. I can't prove I didn't do it, and I have no idea how to find out who did!"

"That's Peter's job and he's giving it all he's got."

"It hasn't helped so far."

Wil knew how childish that sounded as Winningham let it slide.

"Do you know anybody who hated Falcano, or who might have some reason to want him dead?"

"No, that's what's making me crazy."

"Ok, Wil, let's see if we can get you out on bail, then we'll take it from there. Is there anybody you'd like me to call, or anything you need?"

Wil looked at the floor dejectedly.

"Mr, Winningham, I don't have any money. I don't know how I'm going to pay you for this."

"Don't worry about that for now. Think about who could have done this, and why. I'll be in touch soon."

Wil slogged back to his cell feeling defeated and utterly alone.

The guard watched impassively as he walked into the cubicle.

Then the door slammed shut.

The loud metallic clank sounded to Wil like the gates of hell closing forever.

CHAPTER THIRTY

Jones went to *Le Bon Temps* in the early afternoon and found the place almost empty. Small groups at three tables lingered over one more drink, but most of the lunch crowd had left.

A teenager in a ruffled shirt hurried over to greet him.

"I beg your pardon, sir. May I help you? I'm the *maitre'd*, Pierre."

"Pierre?"

Jones grinned as a sour look crossed the kid's face.

"It's Pete. Don't ask."

"Okay, Pierre, I'm looking for Winston Nicholas. Is he here?"

"Sure, just a minute, I'll get him."

"You don't need to do that. Just point me in the right direction and I'll find him."

"I don't mind at all, sir."

"It's fine. I'm with the police and I'm here on business."

"Oh ... okay."

Pierre suddenly looked a lot more cautious. He drew back a little, then turned and scanned the rear of the restaurant. He pointed to a man in tight slacks, an open-necked shirt and gaudy neck chains that looked vaguely Caribbean.

"There he is, over there, checking a few things in the bar."

"Thanks."

"My pleasure."

Jones walked through a small archway into the bar and found Nicholas lecturing the bartender, telling him he needed to 'project the proper air of class and European charm.'

The smattering of patrons made an effort to look the other way without being too conspicuous.

Jones took the opportunity to study Nicholas.

His shiny white shoes seemed jarringly out of style, but then, so did his gold jewelry, oversized watch and the rest of his gaudy outfit.

His toupee looked almost convincing.

Nicholas finished berating his employee and looked pleased with himself as he strolled around the room chatting with the customers in a loud, boisterous voice. Jones noticed he always got around to asking people how they liked the restaurant. Most of them mumbled something nondescript and quickly turned back to their drinks and conversation.

An older man in the corner waved Nicholas over as if he wanted to share a secret. He tried to speak quietly, but his thick, slurred voice carried easily across the room.

"I heard how you had to come down hard on your man over there. Wouldn't it be nice if you didn't have to watch your employees every second?"

"You got it, man. It's so hard to find good help these days."

Nicholas' voice had the same conspiratorial tone, and he concealed it just as poorly.

Very original, Jones thought. He wondered what kind of luck Nicholas had keeping his employees on the payroll.

He waited patiently and sure enough, when Nicholas finished with the bar patrons, he made a beeline in his direction.

"Good afternoon, sir, do you need a table?"

"Actually I came in to talk with you, Mr. Nicholas."

"Great! Have you been in the restaurant before? How do you like the place?"

"This is my first time, and I have to admit your restaurant looks very nice. My name is Peter Jones. I'm a detective with the St. Cecile Police."

"A detective?"

The lack of surprise on Nicholas' face told Jones his visit had been expected, but he did notice a flicker of caution in Nicholas' eyes.

"Yes, I need to ask you a few questions."

"Go for it."

"Is there a place where we can get a little more privacy?"

"Yeah, I have an office in the back. Follow me."

He led the way through a swinging door into a bright kitchen jammed with massive stainless steel ranges, a walk-in freezer, several refrigerators and an enormous dishwasher. An incredible assortment of cooking utensils and pots and pans cluttered the work tables and hung in orderly rows on large racks.

Nicholas scowled when he saw a knot of cooks and waiters lounging in a corner near a massive sink.

"Let's get busy in here!"

A grizzled man in a white hat spoke for the group without looking up.

"It's our break time."

Nicholas continued on his way as if nothing had happened, stepped into a short hallway, and opened an unmarked door with a key from the jumbled ring on his belt. He pointed to an empty chair as they walked in.

"Make yourself comfortable. I'm sorry, what was your name again?"

Jones thought he probably knew exactly who he was.

"Peter Jones."

"Right, right! Have a seat Mr. Jones."

Piles of papers, file folders and boxes of supplies filled every corner of the small office, but there were also many personal touches. Autographed pictures of Nicholas posing with celebrities covered the walls. Jones didn't recognize most of them, but a few were household names. He wondered how Nicholas had gotten so many of them to sign 'To my dear Friend Winston…' Mementos from vacation spots all over the world filled the top of a small table next to the cluttered desk.

"You like my collection of knick knacks? I always like to pick up a little something when I travel. It helps me remember where I've been, and that's no small thing when you get to be *our* age, eh Detective?"

Jones didn't appreciate the clumsy attempt at familiarity, but he found it interesting Nicholas had tried it. Something in his nature seemed to crave approval from everybody except, obviously, the people who worked for him. Maybe them too, in his own strange way.

"I'm investigating Henri Falcano's murder, Mr. Nicholas."

"I figured as much. How's it going?"

"Not too bad, we're still in the early stages."

"I heard you've arrested Wil Walker."

Jones wondered how Nicholas felt about that, but his expression gave away nothing.

"Who told you about that?"

"I own a restaurant, Mr, Jones. This is a good place to keep up on what's happening."

"I guess so. Have you heard any good theories about what happened?"

"No way! I'd never have guessed it was Walker, though. He hardly seems like the type."

Jones sat up. He hadn't expected that.

"What do you mean?"

"You've talked with him. He's the sensitive type, never seems to hold a grudge against anybody. What makes you think he did it?"

"I can't really discuss that, Mr. Nicholas, but I appreciate your thoughts. Does anyone else strike you as a possible suspect?"

Nicholas smiled indulgently.

"No, the whole thing is a stumper. I can't imagine why anybody would want to kill Henri in the first place. He never hurt anybody. He was one of the good guys."

Jones looked Winston straight in the eye.

"What can you tell me about a resort plan he was developing."

"What?"

Nicholas' eyes narrowed, and he looked up warily.

"We found some drawings and information about an ambitious project in the planning stages. The papers had your name listed as one of the partners."

"Oh, that!"

Jones almost congratulated him for his fast recovery.

"That was just a pipe dream. We talked about it for a while, had some plans drawn up, but it just sort of fizzled out. There's no way it had anything to do with the murder."

Something on the corner of the desk seemed to catch Nicholas' eye.

"Are you sure he wasn't going ahead, maybe without you?"

"Boy, you've been doing some homework on this."

Nicholas chuckled hoarsely, then cleared his throat.

"I'm telling you nothing happened. It was ancient history. You'd be a lot better off spending your time on other things."

"There were copies of deeds for two pieces of property you purchased, Mr. Nicholas. That sounds like something to me."

Nicholas shrugged and gestured toward the dining room of the restaurant.

"I invest in lots of things, Detective. That's my business, in case you couldn't tell. Buying property on Lake Michigan is a great way to make money. The market rises and falls, but good property on the lake is always in high demand."

"Did you invest any more money in the project, Mr. Nicholas?"

"No way! I've got most of my money tied up in this place."

Nicholas slumped back in his chair, trying to look casual.

"I'm tellin' ya, the whole idea was just pie in the sky. We talked about it for a while, and I'm not really sure what happened to tell you the truth. We just kinda lost interest, I guess."

"You're sure?"

Winston suddenly looked much more serene.

"Of course, it never amounted to anything! Not to change the subject, but who do you think did it?"

Like I'd tell you.

"We're just trying to develop as many leads as we can. Is there anybody else you think I should talk to?"

"No, not really. It's all a big mystery as far as I'm concerned."

"Well, if you think of anything I should know, give me a call, ok?"

Nicholas laughed with an unwelcome air of familiarity.

"Of course, of course! I mean, that's one of our most important duties as a citizen, don't you think? We have to do our part to help out when we can."

Jones mumbled in half-hearted agreement, thanked him for his time and threaded his way back out to the street.

Nicholas would be anxious to help, as long as it didn't mean telling him anything!

A multi-million dollar deal gone bad could certainly create hard feelings, but Jones wasn't one step closer to figuring out how and why it could be a motive for murder.

Nicholas knew more than he let on, but what?

Jones had nothing tying him to the murder except for his name on that bank document.

He needed to figure out what really happened with that land development scheme, but he would certainly keep an eye on Nicholas in the meantime!

An old-fashioned phone jangled on the severely-meticulous antique desk.

"Eldon Fitzhugh."

"It's Winston. That detective has a line on the plans for the lake development."

The mayor bolted upright and stiffened into a ramrod.

"What?! How did that happen? What did you tell him?"

Fitzhugh's face turned crimson as he herded his chair closer to the desk and put his fist up against his chin.

"Nothing, nothing, calm down. I just wanted to give you a heads up. He's been asking around about it, and he'll probably talk to you soon."

"How did he get wind of it?"

"I asked but he didn't say. There's nothing he can really find out, is there? Just play dumb when he asks you about it."

"You were supposed to keep the whole thing quiet. He should have never found a thing."

"Don't yell at me! He knows, and that's that. What's done is done. Just keep cool. As long as we stay mum, he's got nothing."

"Just see that it stays that way."

"Hey, I need to keep this quiet as much as you do"

"Okay, okay, you just rattled me a little bit."

"You think I wasn't rattled? Just keep your mouth shut and I'll do the same."

"You better!"

The line clicked dead.

Fitzhugh pressed his lips into a thin line as he hung up the receiver.

Then he pushed his chair back with a ragged sound somewhere between a sigh and a snort, stared blankly at the window, and shook his head with a tight grimace of disbelief.

CHAPTER THIRTY-ONE

Wil held onto a tiny, desperate hope for vindication as a uniformed cop escorted him into the courtroom for his arraignment.

His surging emotions had given way to an eerie numbness, and his guts felt completely hollow. He could tell his face looked stony and blank. To the people in the courtroom he probably looked sullen and heartless, like a guilty man getting exactly what he deserved.

When he settled into a chair behind the defense table, he felt his small sliver of optimism melting away. An overwhelming sense of dread and unreality mounted inside him as his nightmare became all too real and started to seem inexorable.

He looked down with revulsion at his orange jailhouse coveralls and felt his old life melting away forever.

Somebody, please, stop this insanity!

Wil jumped as he felt a hand on his arm. He hadn't heard Winningham join him at the table.

"Are you ready, Wil?"

Wil wondered if he could throw up with nothing in his stomach.

"Please, get me out of this!"

"I'm going to try my damnedest. Are you okay?"

"I don't think so. I can't believe this is real."

"Try to look natural."

"Sure, that's easy for you to say!"

Winningham peered at him over his thick glasses and let the sarcasm slide.

Wil looked at the D.A. with a mix of fear and unreasoning hatred. The man looked about thirty-five. The crisp lines of his blue, pinstriped suit fit his wiry body with tailored precision, and his black shoes gleamed like mirrors.

Somehow Wil knew the prosecutor planned to make a major score today. His face had the eager look of a rookie pitcher in his major league debut.

Wil turned to Winningham, hoping for some shred of reassurance. "What's going to happen today?"

Winningham exhaled slowly and shot a glance at the DA.

"They're going to explain the charges against you, make sure you understand your rights, and hopefully, set bail."

"How in the world am I going to come up with money for bail?"

"Let's take it one step at a time, Wil."

Wil had no idea what to say.

At that moment, a clerk told everyone to rise, and a rotund judge in an enormous black robe swept into the room and planted his ample girth behind the bench.

Wil's senses seemed unnaturally acute, but in a tunnel-vision sort of way. He had no idea what kind of weather lay outside the window, or who might be seated behind him, but he saw the judge in a weird kind of heightened perception. Wil almost thought he could count the white hairs on his balding scalp.

He stared a the judge's pudgy face, hoping for some sign of understanding and compassion, but the man's expression remained stiff and inscrutable.

He hadn't looked a Wil once, and that didn't seem like a good sign.

After a few preliminaries, the D.A. stood, tweaked his silky tie with a bony hand, and charged Wil with one count of open murder.

The judge spoke, without looking up, and explained that the open murder charge would allow conviction either for first-degree murder or for a lesser charge.

Wil's heart jumped when the judge finally looked right at him and called his name.

Winningham rose quickly, and Wil lurched to his feet, trying not to look shaky.

The judge's stare bored into Wil like a laser.

"Mr. Walker, do you understand the charges against you?"

Wil gasped. He had to talk now!

"I do, Your Honor."

Wil's voice sounded weird in his own ears. Where did that croak come from?

He had no doubt that a carefully-constructed booby trap proved premeditation. It would be first degree murder all right.

He wanted to shout 'But I'm not the killer!'

"How do you plead, Mr. Walker?"

"We plead not guilty, Your Honor."

Wil took absurd pleasure in hearing Winningham speak with such a firm, clear voice.

The D.A. cleared his throat harshly and spoke with equal force.

"We request bail be set at one million dollars Your Honor. We believe the defendant is a flight risk."

"That's ridiculous, Your Honor!"

Wil had no idea Winningham could sound so animated and emphatic.

"My client absolutely maintains his innocence, and he intends to remain here to prove he had nothing to do with this terrible crime."

The judge paused for a brief moment.

"Bail is set at five hundred thousand dollars."

The prosecutor smiled with smug satisfaction.

Winningham's mouth set in a terse line.

"The trial will begin on July seventeenth at 8:30 sharp. Does anyone have a problem with that?"

The judge glared at the two attorneys, daring them to object, and they both assented quickly.

"Are there any further questions?"

"None, Your Honor."

"No sir."

The judge rapped his gavel and stood up to leave.

The trial would start in about two months.

Wil still felt small and fragile, but the cushion of time seemed to open up possibilities. The process began to feel less like a roller coaster and more like an opportunity for sanity to prevail.

He turned to Winningham.

"What do I do now?"

"First we'll try to arrange for your bail. Do you know anyone who could help with that?"

Wil shook his head.

"I have a few ideas. Hopefully we'll have you out in a few hours. Don't panic Wil. We have a lot of tools at our disposal and there's a long way to go."

A bailiff took Wil's arm.

Everything in Wil's spirit protested as he turned and started the long trek back to his cell. But somehow, in that moment, he knew something fundamental had changed in his mind and heart.

He would never again allow himself to feel so helpless and timid. He wouldn't stand by meekly and allow himself to be convicted of something he didn't do.

At least he would go down fighting!

He had allies and resources. Jones would try to find the real killer, and Winningham would fight for him.

Wil had a new peace born of inner conviction and resolve.

Some of his oldest, most cherished hopes had died, and he had to let them go, but a quieter, deeper strength had taken their place.

CHAPTER THIRTY-TWO

Jones fantasized about writing a letter of resignation as he sat down heavily at his desk.

He could be flowery and formal, or he could just say "I hereby resign my position as detective … effective immediately." It would be fun to take a few swipes at Manning and the mayor. This would be his last chance!

No, that would be petty.

He decided he should keep it as simple as possible.

Then he sighed, knowing he wasn't writing any letter at the moment, and turned his attention to the pile of waiting mail.

The report on the rifle used in Falcano's murder had arrived, and he hurried to open it. Apparently the gun had been stolen from a place called Mort's Quality Firearms in Grapevine, Texas.

Texas? Why did that sound familiar? And how did a rifle from Texas end up as a murder weapon in St. Cecile Michigan?

"Peter, can you come into my office for a minute?"

Jones recognized Manning's reedy voice, and he looked up to see the chief peering across the room at him with a no-nonsense look on his face.

"Yeah, sure."

What now?

Manning disappeared into his office as Jones approached.

When Jones eased into the room and closed the door, Manning leaned back slightly in his chair and stared straight at him.

Jones looked back at the chief impassively. One side of Manning's collar stuck up at a comical angle, but Jones stifled the urge to mention it.

"What's up?"

"Sit down, Peter."

"I'd rather not."

He still had hopes for a quick exit.

"Please, sit down."

Manning sounded ominously brusque.

Jones wondered what had set him off, but he slouched into the chair, trying to look casual.

"Do you want to tell me why you were questioning Winston Nicholas, Peter?"

Jones stared at the chief incredulously.

"I have to question anybody who can help shed some light on this thing. What's the beef?"

"I just got a call from the mayor ..."

"The mayor? Is he running this office, or are you, Walter?"

"I work for the mayor, Peter, and so do you."

Jones sat up a little straighter.

"Yeah, but I don't let him run me like a puppet on a string."

"And you're saying I do?"

Jones knew he should back off, but he couldn't make himself do it.

"You're the one who seems to jump every time he calls."

Manning's face darkened.

"Look, Peter, the simple fact is we have a man in custody, and all the evidence points to his guilt."

"It *seems* to point that way!"

"Okay, seems to, but your little crusade is starting to look a bit ridiculous. The evidence is convincing, and I don't really see any reason to doubt it."

"Well I do."

"We've been over this and over it, Peter. What did you think you could find out from Winston Nicholas, anyway?"

Jones sighed. Time to lay his cards on the table.

"I was looking in Falcano's desk and found a set of plans for a huge real estate development on Lake Michigan. There was also a financing offer from First National Security Bank for two hundred million bucks. The partners listed were Falcano, Nicholas and Mayor Fitzhugh."

"Eldon?"

"Yes, Eldon!"

Jones tried to keep the sarcasm out of his voice, but he knew he hadn't succeeded.

"Well, even so, what makes you think that has anything to do with the murder? You can't suspect Mayor Fitzhugh!"

"Why not? Just because he's the mayor?"

That came out stronger than Jones intended, too.

"No, not *just* because he's the mayor, but he *is* the elected leader of this city, and you have no real reason to suspect he did anything wrong."

"I have a duty to look into all the possibilities, Walter."

Jones fought the urge to stand up and edge closer to the door.

"Why is everyone hell bent on pinning this thing on Walker and looking the other way? What ever happened to good old fashioned police work?"

"What ever happened to accepting reality, Peter? The truth is staring you in the face, and you refuse to accept it!"

Jones looked out the window and tried to reign in his temper. They were both getting way too worked up.

"Look Walter, Wil is in custody, and there's no harm in exploring all the possibilities. What if he didn't do it?"

"Is he a friend of yours now, Peter?"

"No, but I do feel for him. I think he's being framed, and he probably feels like he's being flushed down the toilet."

"What if he's guilty, and he just feels like he's getting caught?"

"Just let me keep looking. If it turns out he did it, so be it."

The chief mulled over that idea with a sour face.

"Well, OK. But while you're doing that, don't aggravate the mayor and innocent citizens."

Just that quickly Jones flashed hot again.

"We don't know who is innocent, Walter, that's why I have to do my job."

"Just do it without stepping on people's toes."

Jones didn't know how to do that, but he had run out of things to say.

The chief suddenly seemed to relax, and he tilted back in his overstuffed chair with a condescending smile.

"So tell me, did you learn anything valuable from Winston Nicholas?"

Jones had no desire to discuss it, but he didn't see any good way to refuse.

"Nothing much. He said he, Falcano and Fitzhugh talked about building a development on the lake, but they just let it fizzle out. He denied it had anything to do with the murder."

"And doesn't that make sense?"

"The plan involved two hundred million dollars, Walter. That's a lot better motive for murder than anything we've supposedly got on Walker. I think we have to get to the bottom of it."

"Did he try to accuse the mayor of anything?"

Jones looked at the chief dryly.

"He said none of them had gotten very serious about any of it. I just don't think that makes much sense."

"Why not?"

"Because it's a lot of money, and Nicholas and Fitzhugh had already purchased some land. The biggest parcel they still needed is owned by a woman named Helen Rubinstein."

"Isn't that Walker's girlfriend?"

"They're friends. I think that's about it."

"Funny how his name pops up no matter how you look at this."

Jones decided to leave well enough alone.

"Is that all?"

"What else have you found out?"

"I just now learned the rifle used in the booby trap was stolen from a gun shop in Texas, some town called Grapevine."

"Grapevine? I know that area. It's just North of Dallas and Fort Worth. Didn't Walker go to school near there?"

Jones felt a jolt of realization and cursed himself for not realizing what had jogged his memory!

He kept his voice even to hide his chagrin.

"He has a doctorate from the University of North Texas in Denton."

"That's very close, Peter. They're about thirty minutes apart."

Manning's face lit up, but his broad smile had a nasty edge.

"Like I said, Peter, isn't it funny how everything seems to point back to Walker?"

CHAPTER THIRTY-THREE

Exhaustion took over when Wil got back to his cell. His brain and his body felt completely disconnected from each other as he flopped onto his bunk.

He had almost fallen asleep when a guard stopped outside his cell and shouted a number. A loud buzz sounded at the end of the hall, and the lock opened with a metallic clunk.

"Walker, you've made bail."

He popped up eagerly as the deputy swung open the door. The thought of stepping out of this bleak cage into sunshine and fresh air had revived him more quickly than he would have believed anything could.

The guard walked him through a second door that opened after a loud buzz, and they stopped at a counter where Wil got his watch, wallet, keys and loose change in a plastic bag.

After one more security checkpoint, Wil stepped out of the jail onto a grimy sidewalk with an unexpected spring in his step.

The sky hung low with slate gray clouds, but who cared.

It felt great to be out!

Then Wil saw Peter Jones standing on the sidewalk in front of a large black car, and his brightening mood evaporated in a flash. He hadn't even had one minute of freedom. Did he have to face more pressure already?

"Hello Wil."

"Hello. What are you doing here?"

"I thought you could use a ride home for one thing."

"Gee, thanks."

The bitterness in his own voice surprised him.

"Look, Wil, I know you think I'm the enemy, but I'm not. I still don't think you did it, and I want to find out who did. That may not seem like much help, but I'm afraid it's all I have to offer at the moment."

Wil looked at him warily.

"No, that actually means a lot. But if you think I'm innocent, why was I arrested and charged?"

"I'm only one man, Wil. There are lots of people involved in the process. Some of them, let's just say they're very short on imagination."

"What do you mean?"

"The person who's trying to pin this on you has set a nasty trap, but it's clumsy. There are obvious holes in it. Some people can't seem to figure that out."

"Why not?"

"I don't know. Maybe it's easier to stick with the obvious. I hate to say this, Wil, but it may be impossible to straighten this out until we find the real killer."

"How are you going to do that?"

"I honestly don't know. Hop in."

Wil climbed into the passenger side and sat stiffly with his hands on his knees.

Jones pulled out into the street and headed toward the edge of town.

"Have you ever seen this much traffic on St. Cecile on a weekday afternoon?"

Wil had barely noticed.

"No, I guess not."

Every stoplight seemed to turn red as they approached, and it took several minutes to get out of the downtown area.

Neither one said a word for a while.

Wil stared out the window, wishing he had some time to unwind and think things over. Dark, gloomy weather almost always dampened his spirits, and he didn't really think he should talk very freely with Detective Jones. He hoped Jones meant what he said about helping exonerate him, but he couldn't trust blindly in his good will.

Jones seemed to be lost in his own thoughts too.

Wil finally broke the silence.

"Do you know how Winningham arranged for bail?"

Jones smiled.

"Yeah, the symphony came through for you. Pru McDonough wasn't on board at first, but she came around and agreed to make a few calls. Some of your friends put up enough money for the bond."

Wil flushed crimson. He hadn't thought he could feel any deeper shame. The thought of his friends coming up with their own money to bail him out made him feel infinitely worse.

"That's terrible. This is bad enough without dragging them into it, too."

"No, Wil, that's great. You have friends who believe in you and care about you."

Wil stared at the floor.

"Who, do you know?"

"Greta Schmidt, Ted Mason, a few of the others. No one person. They all seemed happy to help, so don't worry about it. They'll get their money back when you're cleared."

Wil studied Jones' face, trying to decide whether he meant that or was just trying to make him feel better.

He couldn't tell.

Jones looked across at him.

"Do you know anything about a place called Mort's Quality Firearms in Grapevine, Texas?"

"Grapevine? I used to play golf there when I was in graduate school. That was years ago. I don't remember that much about the place. Why?"

"The rifle used to kill Falcano was apparently stolen from there earlier this year."

A fresh, electric shock lanced through Wil's body.

"And you think I might have gone there and stolen it, then brought it back here and killed Henri. Is that what you're saying?!"

A flash of irritation crossed Jones face.

"I'm trying to figure out what happened Wil, that's my job!"

"Well I haven't been there in years. That ought to be easy enough to prove."

"Actually, it's virtually impossible to prove someone *hasn't* gone somewhere, especially if you're talking about a long enough span of time."

"Well, I'm telling you that I haven't been there, or anywhere near there, in years. If you think I'm innocent, why are you asking me all these questions."

"I have to go where the truth takes me Wil, but I have to dig. The Texas connection doesn't prove a thing, but I have to know what it means. If someone spent a long time planning to frame you, they could certainly steal a rifle from a place where you used to live."

Wil hadn't thought of it that way.

Suddenly, all the tension and emotion of the past few days caught up with Wil. His body shuddered as tears filled his eyes.

He hated to lose it in front of Jones, but he couldn't stifle the depth and intensity of his reaction. His battered nervous system was purging itself the only way it knew how.

He ruefully rubbed his face with his hands. He cleared his choked throat nervously and wished he had a Kleenex for his runny nose.

"I guess men aren't supposed to cry, huh?"

"Don't worry about it."

Jones face softened with compassion as he looked at him.

"Do you need anything?"

"No, I just want to get home and be alone for a while."

"Are you sure that's the best thing right now?"

"Yeah, I need some space and some time to think."

Jones pulled into Walker's driveway, and his car crunched to a stop near the walk to the front door.

"Call me if you think of anything I need to know, okay?"

"Yeah, sure. Thanks for the ride, Detective."

CHAPTER THIRTY-FOUR

Jones ached as he watched Wil trudge slowly to the door and fish out his keys. Wil looked like anything but a murderer as he put a hand up to his neck and stretched, trying to work out the stiffness in his back.

Finally the door swung open and Wil stepped inside.

Jones reached into the glove compartment for his bottle of Pepto Bismol as he backed out of the drive and started slowly back toward St. Cecile.

God, what a mess!

He took a healthy swig, chucked the bottle back into the rats' nest of papers in the glove box, and slammed the door shut.

Jones knew strong displays of emotion didn't prove innocence. He had seen murderers, rapists and wife beaters weep bitterly. But this seemed different.

Wil's emotion wasn't the guilt-ridden catharsis of confession. Jones could feel his excruciating frustration at being unfairly accused. A terrible cycle of events had snatched him out of his comfortable life and now threatened to crush him. And to make it all that much worse, a ruthless killer had singled him out for evil betrayal.

That double shock would be difficult for anyone to handle!

Jones ground his teeth and struggled to hang on to his professional demeanor. It wouldn't do to become too friendly with Walker, but his heart went out to him.

He had to find some thread that would start leading him toward the truth.

Maybe he should start by finding out what happened in Grapevine Texas.

Wil stumbled through the living room into the kitchen and tossed his keys and wallet onto the table.

For once, he paid no attention to the cracking linoleum and stained walls.

He wished he hadn't broken down in front of Jones, but he realized he really didn't care. The emotional roller coaster of the past two days had drained him completely. He had never experienced a deeper weariness. His limbs seemed inert, feeling nothing and doing nothing, but his mind buzzed with a strange mix of agitation and dread. His body craved sleep desperately, but he doubted his brain would cooperate, at least anytime soon.

He had to do something to unwind, and he looked gratefully toward the safe refuge of his piano.

He walked slowly, almost in a daze, into his studio and sat down at the keyboard, hoping a few minutes of playing would help soothe his teeming emotions. He let his hands randomly explore the keys, operating more on the level of instinct than of thought and intention.

The sounds filling the air came out as a disorganized jumble, but they resonated deeply with his battered psyche. Some part of his mind felt the chilling sensation that sometimes washed over him when dark chords filled his body and matched his hurt perfectly.

His conscious mind receded farther and farther into quietness, as deeper levels of his spirit communed with the instrument.

After a time something stirred in his awareness, and he listened more closely to what he had just been playing. He realized dimly he had found exactly the music he needed to start the slow movement of his symphony.

He came fully awake as he played the aching music again and again.

Heartbreaking poignancy throbbed in the rich, low chords, and a melancholy tune moved gently in their midst. Somehow the music spoke of an unbreakable, defiant will to endure, whatever the cost.

Tears filled Wil's eyes again, but this time they came from a quiet, deep emotion at the very core of his being.

He played the passage several more times, memorizing it, watching where his hands flowed across the keys, learning how the music rose and fell, how it moved and where it led.

The next few minutes would be critical. He often found the magical process of inspiration mysterious, and it sometimes filled him with awe, but he also knew it could be very fragile. The wonderful, keen insight of his dream-like state could quickly dissipate and be lost.

He needed to get the music written down as completely as he could before it faded from his consciousness.

He hurriedly got a sheet of staff paper, set it on the piano bench and played the passage again. His hands darted to the paper, scratching notes and rhythms onto the page as fast as he could write. Then he quickly moved back to the keyboard, rehearsing the phrases one more time.

Back and forth, again and again.

Whenever he had written a passage of the notes correctly, he moved on to the next sequence, and wrote it down as rapidly as he could.

The opening phrases of an orchestral movement emerged in full flower in his mind. He knew exactly how it should go, how all the chords and melodies should flow together and what shades of instrumental color would bring it all to life.

He worked feverishly, a quiet excitement gripping him despite all that had happened.

Then the doorbell rang.

Not now!

His fingers traced a resonant sonority in the low register and he raced back to the paper to record it.

Ding-dong. Ding-dong.

Not now!

CHAPTER THIRTY-FIVE

Jones turned from one back road to another after he left Wil's house.

He wanted some time to mull things over, and frankly, he just wanted some time alone. He certainly had no desire to hurry back to the station.

That seemed to be a recurring pattern lately!

Manning wouldn't look him in the eye, even if their paths crossed, and the other officers at the station seemed to be avoiding him at all costs. Maybe they all thought he had gone crazy. He really didn't care what they thought, but he had no desire to go there and feel like an outcast.

He realized suddenly this would be an ideal time to talk with Helen. He had her address, and the trip there would take him down several more quiet country roads.

With any luck, he wouldn't have to go back to the office at all!

On the way, his thoughts returned to Walker.

Wil had looked like a whipped puppy! Time in jail affected people in many different ways, but it clearly had devastated Wil's sensitive nature. Jones wondered how Wil would adapt if he actually had to spend time in prison. The harsh environment could kill his spirit, and if that happened, his body might soon follow.

Jones felt his cheeks flushing hot as he thought about Manning falling for the absurd trail of phony clues.

Why would someone insist on remaining anonymous to report Wil's trip to the symphony hall? Did they think he would order a hit on them or something?

And how would a bag holding a credit card receipt get stuck in a brick wall unless someone stuffed it in there?

Why would Walker get a new credit card in his own name to buy the rifle shells? He could easily have concealed his identity by using cash. Someone had gone to great lengths to get that fake credit card, and Jones thought that proved someone wanted the name on the card to be discovered.

How could the job at the symphony be held against him? The orchestra came up with that idea, not Wil.

And Walker's story about the websites made perfect sense. Jones had no doubt Wil would try to help by looking up information about the case. The bookmarks looked damning because of the way they turned up.

Jones wondered if a good techie could figure out when a bookmark had been created.

The letter on Falcano's desk had been the clumsiest plant of all. Jones knew it hadn't been there when he looked the first time.

Manning had bought the whole business way too willingly. But why?

Jones could easily picture the mayor applying tremendous pressure behind the scenes. Fitzhugh's role in all of this might be the key to unlocking the whole mess!

Then the car topped a rise, and the glorious, blue-gray expanse of Lake Michigan appeared on his right.

Jones drank in the vista gratefully. Even in the dismal light, the magnificent sight filled his senses and tugged at his heart.

The ever-changing motion of the water held a special fascination for him. He loved the wild energy of powerful waves beating against the shore, the peaceful strength of gentle swells stirring placid water, and the bracing sight of thousands of ripples glistening in brilliant sunshine.

The water seemed like a female force to him, and she always urged him to come closer, to stand on her beach and feel her cool, damp air on his skin, to let her waves break over his feet and swirl around his ankles, to gaze out to the horizon and let her deep blue depths fill his senses.

The water had something to tell him, and she would never blurt it out. He was supposed to spend eternity pondering it in her gentle caress.

He lingered for several minutes and only moved on reluctantly.

When Helen's land came into view, he stopped the car at the top of another hill and got out for a better look.

What a fantastic spot! No artist could create a better layout.

Two arms of land reached out to embrace the lake on either side. The gently curving beach between them formed a wondrously inviting inlet. Beautiful raised bluffs overlooked the water on each side, and their high ground gave way to gentle slopes easing gradually down to the beach. The proportions were perfect.

It was a picture post card waiting to be photographed! No wonder the Rubinsteins saw it as an ideal place to build a safe haven for their fellow exiles.

Jones could easily picture the massive hotel, a green carpet of golf fairways, and a flourishing development of beautiful homes on this land.

The only surprise might be why no one had thought of it before.

Jones got back into the car and drove at a leisurely pace toward Helen's house. Fruit orchards and squares of woodland alternated with gently-rolling swaths of grassy meadowland on both sides of the narrow road.

The sun broke through the clouds as he pulled into the driveway, and golden sunlight added a storybook quality to everything in sight.

The whole place had a wonderfully refreshing air of spaciousness and peace.

Jones rounded a wooded curve in the lane, and a large Victorian house came into view. Dormers jutted out at a variety of imaginative angles from the house's roof, and an ornate cupola sat atop the structure like the centerpiece on a wedding cake.

Jones wanted desperately to go up there. The cupola's windows had to offer a spectacular view of the shoreline.

The place must have been stunning at one time, but it needed painting badly, the narrow, wooden siding had sagged out of alignment in several places, and the deteriorating windows looked far from airtight.

The house sat in a copse of huge oaks at the top of a rounded hill, and the ground sloped away from it on all sides. A badly overgrown lawn in the back extended several hundred yards down to the lake.

Jones admired the prosperous souls who built the place, no telling how many years ago. They certainly had exquisite taste in land!

Helen had parked her BMW at a careless angle near the back door.

Jones walked up to the front of the house through a thicket of overgrown shrubs, climbed the steps, and tried to choose a safe path through the badly rotted floorboards on the porch.

Small glass panes next to the imposing door revealed a dark hallway inside.

He couldn't find the doorbell.

Jones knocked several times with no response. He was about to leave when he heard footsteps approaching from the back of the house.

Helen appeared in the hallway and pulled open the tall door. Her wary, inscrutable eyes and sullen scowl made it abundantly clear how she felt about seeing him.

"Oh, hello, Mr. Jones. What can I do for you?"

Jones could hardly believe the contrast with the last time he'd seen her. She hadn't put on makeup, she'd pulled her hair up loosely, and she had on a baggy Detroit Tigers sweatshirt over tight black stretch pants.

"Don't pay attention to my shirt, Mr. Jones, I'm not a sports fan. I bought it at a yard sale."

Jones noticed a dark callous on her neck that marred her otherwise classic features.

She caught him looking at the blemish and touched it lightly with her fingers.

"It's an occupational hazard for violinists, Mr. Jones. If you see a violin player without one of these, they don't spend much time practicing."

"May I come in?"

"I suppose."

She swirled away with a ragged, irritated sigh.

"I was just having some tea. Would you like some?"

"Thank you."

"We can sit in the kitchen if you don't mind."

"That'll be fine."

Jones recoiled from the oppressive atmosphere of decay as he followed Helen through the long hall toward the back of the house. The dust-covered furnishings in the adjoining rooms looked ancient and untouched.

He wondered if Helen spent most of her time in another part of the house.

When they got to the kitchen, Helen pointed vaguely to a heavy chair next to the massive table in the center of the room.

Jones eyed the cavernous room uneasily.

Smoky residue obscured the high ceiling, the white cupboards had aged into a sickly yellowish shade, and the long gray counter held nothing but a large sink with deep rusty stains. The stove and small refrigerator looked like relics from the 1930s.

The kitchen was tidy and well swept, but in every other way, the old place looked like an abandoned building. It seemed to Jones Helen lived here like a ghost, making no impression at all on her surroundings.

The house provided shelter, but it certainly didn't feel like Helen's home.

Helen poured the tea into delicate, china cups and settled into the chair across from him.

Jones decided not to press too hard at first.

"This is a beautiful old house."

"I suppose. I hate it! Everything is rotting. It needs to be completely rebuilt … or else burned to the ground."

The acid in her voice made Jones hesitate. Did she always sound this bitter about everything?

"What did your parents plan to do with it?

"They adored the Victorian charm, but when my father died, my mother had no way to fix it up. Their dreams all crashed and burned here, Mr. Jones. No wonder I love it so much, huh?"

He wasn't sure how to continue.

"What would you like to do with the place?"

"I have it for sale. Do you want to buy it?"

She gave him a withering look.

"I didn't think so. Buyers aren't exactly lining up, Mr. Jones."

"That seems surprising. The land is very beautiful."

"I suppose so. I spend most of my time inside."

She lifted her teacup with incongruous daintiness and took a long sip.

"Henri was helping me with the arrangements. He said the market was depressed."

Jones tried not to stare as he let that bit of news sink in.

So, Henri had been 'helping' her sell the place. Fat chance! More like he stalled her until he could close a deal with his cronies.

Jones looked at Helen with fresh compassion.

"The cupola on your roof is very impressive. Do you suppose we could go up there and take a look?"

She glared for a second, then gave him a resigned look.

"I don't see why not. It's this way."

She pointed toward a door that lead into the interior of the house, drained her teacup and stood up.

"I hope you don't mind tight spaces."

"Not at all."

He followed her into another dark hallway. Jones glimpsed a jumble of bright colors and satiny fabrics through a partly open door. Her sanctuary?

They walked up a broad staircase, which Jones thought could have been gorgeous if someone cleaned the accumulated grime from the woodwork. The stairway led to a landing dominated by a large window that probably hadn't been washed in a decade or more.

They continued on to the right.

Helen opened a door near the end of an upstairs hallway to reveal a steep spiraling staircase with triangular treads. The steps looked ancient, but they were beautifully crafted.

"Lead the way, Mr. Jones."

Jones instinctively ducked his head and looked up as he started climbing the steps, which made one full revolution before coming to a stop below a trap door.

When Jones got to the top, he pushed open the door, climbed through, and held the door for Helen.

He could hardly believe his eyes!

CHAPTER THIRTY-SIX

Wil felt like ignoring the doorbell, but it kept ringing insistently every few seconds.

He finally slammed the heel of his fist against the piano bench and bolted toward the door.

"Ok, ok ... I'm coming!"

He frowned when he jerked back the door and saw no one standing there. Someone had pressed the doorbell repeatedly until a couple of seconds ago, and now the porch stood empty. He didn't see anyone on the sidewalk or driveway, either.

Then he saw a thin package lying on the mat.

Maybe the mail carrier had dropped it off, and Wil hadn't realized how long it had been since the last ring.

He shrugged, picked up the parcel, and tossed it onto the couch, locking the door behind him.

At least the interruption had been brief!

Several minutes later he looked with satisfaction at the music he'd written.

He played through the passage once more, just to savor it, knowing he could develop the music in any number of ways from this promising start. A rough outline of the whole movement had already started to grow in his mind.

He almost had the music memorized, but writing it down preserved all the small but critical details that made it complete and distinctive.

He thought it had come out perfect, but it would take time to be sure. Ideas that seemed thrilling at first sometimes left him cold when he came back to build on them.

He had learned the hard way not to be overconfident!

A lot of work remained to be done, but he had finished the hardest part. The challenge now would be to coax out transformations that were already implied in the opening phrases, then shape all the music into a pleasing whole.

He set the staff paper on his desk and stretched luxuriantly to relax the kinks in his arms and legs. His weariness returned with a vengeance, and this time he had no doubt he could sleep. He'd probably be comatose before his head hit the pillow.

He made it halfway to the bedroom when he remembered the package

It could certainly wait until morning, but curiosity got the best of him, and he turned back to the living room to retrieve it.

A figure in dark clothing knelt silently in a brushy thicket about 200 yards away.

The dense tangle of shrubbery provided excellent cover, even though its leaves were just starting to fill out. The barrel of a high caliber rifle poked out through an opening in the thick screen of branches.

From this vantage point, large windows provided an almost unrestricted view into Wil's isolated house.

A powerful scope tracked Wil every step of the way as he carried the parcel into the kitchen.

Wil sliced open the manila envelope with a steak knife.

His stomach lurched as he pulled out the contents.

With a shaking hand, he held up the first page, a copy of Henri Falcano's publicity photo.

The picture had been savagely disfigured with angry red marks. Jagged crimson lines cut across Henri's face in every direction, and ragged holes riddled the paper. The pen must been used like a dagger to stab the page again and again.

Henri's eyes had been completely obliterated.

In the distance, the rifle barrel followed Wil's every move.

The stealthy observer wore gloves of exquisitely thin black leather that provided an excellent tactile connection with the rifle.

The fingers of the right hand rested lightly on the outside of the trigger guard.

The left hand cradled the barrel very gently, holding it extremely still, except when tiny, precise adjustments were needed.

A picture of Wil came next in the pile. It looked like an enlargement from a symphony program. His image had suffered the same horrifying treatment. The cluster of holes in his throat looked like they had been made with furious force.

Will tried to swallow, but his tongue felt like a big piece of dry, rotted wood.

He flipped quickly to the next page, a picture of Helen with similar holes all over her face.

A picture of a teenage girl followed.

Wil didn't know her, but he doubted anyone could have recognized her through the angry red marks obliterating her face and the hornet's nest of holes around her eyes.

The remaining pictures were a foldout from a girlie magazine with the genitals mutilated, an elderly couple with their faces destroyed, and an old fashioned picture of Jesus that practically hung in tatters.

A note scrawled with the same red ink completed the grisly stack. Crude capital letters spelled out its brutally simple message:

WALKER YOU ARE GOING
DOWN DOWN DOWN!!!!

Wil felt nauseated and sick at heart. The mutilated pictures in his hands came from pure rage. He had a malevolent enemy, a monster willing to kill with brutal force. And the sadistic jerk wanted to make him look like Henri's killer.

What had he done to earn this kind of hatred? And how could he protect himself?

A violent shudder shook his body.

He called the police station and asked for Detective Jones. He didn't think he could trust anyone else there.

A deep, droning voice told him Jones had left for the day and could probably be reached in the morning.

Wil sank back into his chair.

He knew he'd never sleep now, despite his bone-numbing fatigue.

A muted laugh erupted in the thick brush as the crosshairs of the scope settled a few inches below Wil's left shoulder.

A shot in that spot would be a quick kill to the heart.

The hunched figure stayed in place for several more minutes as Wil sat motionless in the chair.

Then the dark shape rose and backed away without making a sound.

CHAPTER THIRTY-SEVEN

The view from the cupola literally took Jones' breath away.

He had considered that only a saying until this very moment.

The windows certainly needed cleaning, but an astonishing panorama lay at his feet, and he drank it in greedily.

The glorious lake stretched across the horizon in stunning beauty, and the bare limbs of budding trees traced starkly beautiful shapes against the water and the adjoining landscape. Dramatic shafts of light from the lowering sun cascaded majestically through the dissipating clouds, and the luminous beams lanced through the misty air in subtle shades of shifting color.

When he could speak he turned to Helen, who seemed utterly unmoved by the splendor in front of them.

She lived in paradise and treated it like a mausoleum!

"What did your parents have in mind for this place?"

"They were such dreamers! They thought people would flock here. 'If you build it they will come?' Hah! Well, they couldn't build anything. It took all their money just to buy the place, and then they were stuck here."

He phrased his next question carefully.

"Are you sure no one ever talked with you about building something else on this land?"

Her face revealed no obvious reaction.

"No, I only wish someone had!"

She looked around the small space and gazed out over the water.

"Do you know what this is, Mr. Jones? It's called a widow's walk. The name came from desperate wives who watched and waited for ships that never came."

Jones saw the muscles of her jaw working on the grim mask of her face.

He hesitated for a moment.

"You have to tell me, Helen, what did Henri promise you? Something he did hurt you very badly, what was it?"

"You have to know everything, huh?"

She looked very close to tears.

"Just because he's dead you think you can ask anything, pry anywhere. People are entitled to some privacy, you know."

He went on gently.

"Someone is trying to make it look like Wil Walker killed Henri. I have to find out what happened."

She paled.

"Wil? You think Wil might have done it?"

"I don't, but a lot of evidence has turned up. Some people think it makes him look guilty as sin. I think it has been planted to make things look that way."

"What?"

Jones barely heard her, even in the tiny space.

"I shouldn't have told you that, but I'm trusting you, and I'm asking you to trust me. Please, tell me what Henri promised you."

A look of agonized indecision hovered on her face.

"You really think it could have something to do with the murder?"

"I have to understand Henri's character, Helen. What he did away from the office is a complete mystery. I won't reveal anything I don't have to."

She seemed to struggle for a moment longer, then she started trembling and the dam burst.

"He asked me to marry him, all right? Are you happy now? He said he loved me! He made me keep our engagement secret for some insane reason, but he said we'd be married when the time was right. He had money, connections. I loved him Mr. Jones, but marrying him also meant I had a future."

She crossed her arms tightly against her body and looked at him with a face full of misery.

"Everyone who ever cared about me has died. I'm all alone in this God-forsaken corner of hell, and I have no idea what I'm going to do!"

The intensity of her outburst seemed to leave her helpless. She burst into tears and fell against his body.

Jones held her awkwardly as her slender frame shook with sobs. He barely felt her small, fragile shoulders against his chest.

He waited patiently until she started to regain control.

Finally, she stood back and swiped at her face with fierce embarrassment. She rubbed her hands against her sweatshirt and looked to one side ruefully.

"I'm sorry, Mr. Jones, I get overwhelmed sometimes."

Suddenly, she fixed Jones in a stare of scathing intensity.

"You can't think Wil killed Henri, that's just impossible!"

"I don't, Helen, but I have to find out who did."

He thought a moment.

"Do you know if Henri made promises to anyone else?"

"He was a complicated man, Mr. Jones. We spent a lot of time together, but it was always in private, away from everyone else. He never told me much about the rest of his life, and I didn't pry. I guess I was a fool."

"I don't think so. Do you have any reason to believe he wouldn't go through with it, marry you?"

"I guess not, but if people knew, at least I'd be the bereaved fiancé. I'd sound like a raving lunatic if I said anything now. Who would believe me? I'm right back where I started, broke and alone."

"I need to ask you one more time, did you know anything about a plan to develop this land into some kind of resort?"

She gave him a searching look.

"My parents wanted to build a haven for their Russian friends. That's all I ever heard about. Are you saying there was something else?

"I'm not sure, maybe yes, maybe no."

"And Henri was involved?"

"I'd rather not say."

She turned away in disgust.

"So much for all your talk about trust."

"Okay, but anything I say has to be kept in absolute confidence, all right?"

He hesitated again before plunging in.

"I was searching Henri's desk, and I found a set of plans for a large development on this land, a hotel, two big golf courses, a housing development, the works."

He decided not to mention the other partners.

She clutched at her stomach with a look of horror.

"Are you saying Henri wanted to marry me to get control of the land?"

Jones felt a deep stab of regret. Why had he told her that?

"I have no idea, Helen. I didn't know marriage was even in the picture. I'm trying to piece it all together."

"That's terrible, it's just absolutely horrible ..."

Jones racked his brains for something reassuring to say.

"Don't torture yourself, Helen. Right now, we have no idea what happened. Maybe he was just dreaming about your future together."

"Somehow I don't think so."

She reached into a pocket and took out a cigarette. Her hands shook badly as she reached up to light it.

Jones wanted to kick himself!

"Maybe we'll never know exactly what happened. He said he loved you. Hold on to that."

"Sure."

Why had he told her anything? He'd let his feelings get the best of him, and he'd gone way over the line. She seemed to make him feel more like a counselor than a detective.

Awkward silence filled the air as they made their way down.

Jones asked her to call him if she thought of anything else he should know.

She coolly said she'd keep it in mind.

As Jones drove away, the clouds broke up even further in the gathering dusk. The lake became a dark, brooding presence just out of sight.

Had Falcano really loved her, or had he been scheming to get control of the land?

Who stood to gain by his death? With such a big deal in the works, wouldn't his partners want him alive? If he lied to Helen, maybe he'd lied to them, too. What if they found out about that?

Was he a fanatic for secrecy, or just a very private person? His life seemed to be a patchwork of secret, leak-proof compartments.

Jones had to find some way to learn more about the mysterious Mr. Falcano!

Wil woke up sweaty and exhausted.

A relentless swirl of terrifying questions and vague fears had swirled through his brain all night long, and nightmares haunted the brief snatches of sleep he did manage to get.

At one point he dreamed he was locked in a tiny black box, spinning slowly and sinking into an infinite sea of tarry blackness. He tried desperately to scream, but he couldn't make a sound to break the overwhelming silence of the terrible void.

Later he dreamt a terrified group of people pleaded for mercy under a furious assault. Blood streamed down their faces, and they waved their arms frantically, in a vain attempt to ward off an enormous, razor-sharp blade that slashed at them again and again.

Wil couldn't see who or what controlled the weapon.

He saw himself in the group, but he felt separated from his body, and an impotent feeling of panic ripped at his bowels as he viewed the scene from a distance.

The group of victims included the mute image of Christ, and his face filled with infinite sadness as the violence raged on and on.

Another time Wil felt as if his arms and legs were bound by tight coils of thick rope, and he struggled with feverish panic against the restraints.

He startled into wakefulness again and again and struggled to find some comfortable position for sleep, as he groaned and tried to banish the hideous images and unanswerable thoughts from his mind.

The sun hadn't risen when he sat up on the edge of the bed and held his head in his hands. He wasn't getting a bit of rest. He might as well get up.

He lurched, stiff-legged into the bathroom and turned on the shower to let the water warm up. His haggard face stared at him from the mottled mirror. Dark puffy circles outlined his red eyes, but he appreciated the look of bitter determination he saw in them.

First things first! He needed to tell Jones about the bizarre package he'd received as soon as possible.

After his shower, he brushed his teeth and shaved distractedly, then he walked into the kitchen and put on a pot of coffee.

He tried calling the police station again, and a crisp, efficient voice told him Detective Jones usually came in at around eight o'clock.

He looked at the frumpy kitchen clock his mother had bought decades earlier.

Six twenty-seven.

He couldn't just sit here! He decided to kill some time with a drive along the beach. Maybe the cool spring air and some time near the water would help clear his head. He'd try to meet Jones when he got to work.

He toasted a bagel, smeared it with cream cheese, filled a thermos with steaming, milky coffee, and juggled his breakfast in his arms as he pushed through the back door.

Someday he'd give up the bad habit of eating while he drove, but not today.

The old pickup protested as he cranked the starter, but after a couple of gasps and misfires, the balky engine shuddered to life and began running relatively smoothly.

Most days Wil didn't mind the old relic, but someday it might be nice to have a vehicle that didn't look one step from the junkyard.

He took a bite of the bagel, sipped the hot coffee carefully, and started backing out the driveway.

Suddenly, he felt like an idiot. He'd left the packet of mutilated pictures sitting on the table! He slammed the pickup into drive, pulled up to the front of the house and scurried inside.

Jones needed to see these pictures! Maybe they would give him some ammunition to convince people someone else had done all this.

As he scooped up the package, he felt a powerful urge to be sure all the doors and windows were locked up tight.

With that done, he went out through the front door. The neglected dead bolt protested as he turned the key, but after a short struggle, it shot into place with a satisfying thunk.

He put the pickup in reverse again, backed out to the narrow road, and turned west toward the old winding highway that ran along the lakeshore.

As Wil's pickup receded in the distance, the dusty black Cadillac emerged from the woods and paused briefly at the edge of the road.

The car turned smoothly, then it accelerated quickly in the same direction.

A hunting rifle with a huge scope rested under a light blanket behind the front seat.

CHAPTER THIRTY-EIGHT

Wil's mind eased a bit as he drove along the old highway.

His tires hit the tarry dividers in the concrete with a rhythmic '*chunk, chunk, chunk*' that had an almost hypnotic effect on his frazzled brain.

The rising sun warmed his face, but the real balm to his spirits came as the brightening light unveiled the placid, silvery beauty of Lake Michigan on his left. The awakening lake seemed to play hide and seek behind sand dunes and stands of trees as the truck sped along.

About ten minutes from his house, Wil turned down a gravel lane toward one of his favorite spots, a bluff with a spectacular view.

He loved the dramatic beauty of the place and always felt it lowered his blood pressure a few points just to visit there.

The spot provided a perfect vantage point for viewing freighters trundling by in the distance. He had a used copy of the boat-watching guidebook, several years out of date, but he got a thrill when he could identify one of the big boats by its distinctive shape and markings.

He kept a pair of binoculars on the floorboard to help him get a closer view, and he even enjoyed the eerie visual distortion they created when he looked out over the water.

He parked in a small gravel lot, slung the strap of the binoculars over his shoulder and walked through the sand for several hundred yards to the highest point on the dunes.

When he reached the top, he stood with his legs wide apart and drank in the scene eagerly. The sunlight had grown stronger, and the rising cool breeze gently ruffled his hair and clothing. He took in lungful after lungful of the fresh moist air and felt himself gradually unwinding.

Gentle waves washed up on the beach and quietly fell back far below him. The only souls on the beach were a few early risers out for a morning walk.

He spotted a couple of ships near the horizon, but they were too far away for good viewing.

He couldn't escape the terrible weight of his problems, but out here he could start to put things in better perspective. He had a battle on his hands, and he had to find the strength to see it through to the end.

He did believe he could trust Jones, but in the long run, he couldn't depend on the detective or anyone else to clear his name.

He had to find a way to take care of himself!

Far below his feet, a tall guy in jeans and a baggy sweatshirt tossed a stick into the blue-green water. A small, gold-colored dog dove into the water like a torpedo, swam for all it was worth, snatched the stick with his teeth and headed back to the shore.

From Wil's high perch they seemed to be living in another time and space.

He smiled as the little dog popped out of the water like a cork, dropped the stick at the man's feet, shook himself violently and begged for another throw.

Wil would have given anything for their carefree spirit!

Finally, with a deep breath of resignation, he turned and walked back to his truck. His head and his stomach both felt more trustworthy.

Time to find Jones and show him the package.

Wil didn't even notice the dusty black Cadillac in the far corner of the parking lot, much less the driver, whose face hid behind the brim of a large, dark cowboy hat.

Jones dawdled his way down Main Street, wishing with all his heart he could just stay out in the cool, crisp air.

He had absolutely no desire to make this trip to City Hall, so he took his time, savoring every last second of the bright morning sun.

Why wasn't he in shorts and a tee shirt at his house up North, gassing up his boat and checking his gear before a day of basking in the sun and pretending to catch fish?

His stomach tightened a bit as he braced himself for his meeting with the mayor.

The man's abrupt manner always got under his skin, and Jones knew Fitzhugh would push him to crucify Walker.

He'd made up his mind to stand his ground and keep his cool, no matter what the mayor said. At least he'd try.

All too soon, he stood in front of the St. Cecile's classic limestone Government Offices Building.

Jones pushed through the ancient revolving door and admired its smooth operation and large brass crosspieces. They didn't make doors like this anymore.

He debated briefly whether to wait for the elevator, then started briskly up the staircase, stepping deliberately into the shallow indentations thousands of footsteps had worn in the terrazzo. The thick brass handrail, shiny from decades of use, felt wonderfully substantial under his hands.

Suddenly, Jones remembered coming here as a boy. That must have been fifty years ago! The place had seemed enormous, and the trappings had looked magnificent.

Somehow, now, it all seemed a little cramped and shabby.

Jones had to force himself to step into Fitzhugh's office.

The tall door, made of pebbled, greenish glass, seemed like a relic of another time, and the large block letters saying 'Office of the Mayor' had yellowed with age.

The frosty receptionist said the mayor would be available in a few minutes and told Jones to take seat.

Jones fumed as he sat down.

Eight o' clock in the morning. He had to be the first one here! Could the mayor be making him wait as some kind of weird power trip, a way to put him in his place?

He took a deep breath, reminded himself of his plan to stay cool, and tried to swallow his pride.

He wondered if he could focus his mind by rehearsing what he would ask. Then he had to laugh. He'd thought about little else since he woke up this morning!

Then the mayor opened the door to the inner office and stepped through.

"Good morning, Mr. Jones. How nice to see you. Please come in."

Jones cringed at the mayor's odd formality and heard no trace of warmth or cordiality in his seemingly polite words.

"Good morning, Mr. Fitzhugh. Thanks for seeing me."

"Of course, of course. Please sit down."

Jones couldn't begin to read Fitzhugh's blank face as they stepped into his sanctuary.

The mayor fussed like a nervous hen as he brushed his clothing, settled stiffly into his chair and fixed Jones in a tight stare.

"What can I do for you?"

Another seemingly polite phrase, but as usual, the mayor had gotten right to business. No preliminaries or chit chat.

Jones sank onto the hard, formal chair in front of the mayor's huge desk and noticed Fitzhugh's gleaming leather chair looked almost as stiff and uncomfortable as his.

Jones scanned the bizarre décor in the mayor's office and thought everything should be ripped out and replaced.

Behind Fitzhugh, an imposing mass of thick, maroon drapes stretched from the floor to the ceiling and blocked the light completely. Jones almost shuddered. You could spend the whole day in here and never once see the glorious day outside!

The enormous desk held only a few papers and even fewer personal items, an antiquated pen and pencil holder, some photos in fussy, mismatched frames and an old black telephone.

The three flowery pictures on the wall seemed oddly out of place. Jones remembered seeing television ads offering these prints for sale like dish soap or vegetable choppers. 'Only three payments of $39.99!' The brightly colored pictures looked pleasant enough, but Jones thought art should be about something other than mass marketing.

Jones turned his attention to Fitzhugh, who stared at him with eerie intensity behind his giant bunker of a desk.

The mayor looked even more fidgety and ill at ease than he had earlier. His body seemed to be oozing pent up tension.

But then Jones always thought he looked that way.

"I'm trying to find out more about Henri Falcano, Mr. Mayor. Did you know him very well?"

The mayor eyed him with cold detachment.

"We saw each other from time to time. I wouldn't call him a close friend."

"Do you know who his close friends were?"

"Not really."

Jones returned the dry stare. *Don't offer any more than you have to!*

"What kind of contacts did you have with him?"

"The symphony plays a very important role of the cultural life of this city, Mr. Jones. We often discussed matters pertaining to that. I would see him occasionally at social gatherings and such."

Fitzhugh pursed his lips prissily.

Jones squirmed, wishing he could wipe the smug, patronizing look off the mayor's face. He warned himself again to stay focused.

"Who would he spend time with at events like that?"

"He had excellent social skills and knew how to make a positive impression on important people in the city. I guess he'd usually make the rounds, have a good chat with some of the movers and shakers, then make an early exit. I don't think I know much that can help you, Mr. Jones."

Fitzhugh gave a wan smile with his lips, but the rest of his face remained oddly stiff.

"So your only contacts were through social events and cultural affairs?"

"Oh, we discussed a few business dealings, nothing significant, I can assure you of that."

Jones felt a red flag go up and fought to keep his face noncommittal. That last comment had been rehearsed. Fitzhugh knew what he planned to ask!

Jones decided to dive right in.

"I found a set of plans for a very ambitious project in Mr. Falcano's office, Mr. Mayor. The partners listed were Falcano, Winston Nicholas and you."

"Oh that!"

The mayor laughed dryly.

"Nothing ever came of it, Mr. Jones, it's as simple as that."

More rehearsed material! Jones knew his skepticism had to be obvious.

"Are you sure?"

"Of course I'm sure. It was nothing."

The mayor cleared his throat roughly and looked at his watch. His smile suddenly looked even more forced.

"Is that all you wanted to ask me about?"

"Who was behind it, Mr. Fitzhugh. How did the idea get started? What happened to stop it?"

Fitzhugh's look turned even colder.

"I already told you it was nothing."

Jones tried to keep his voice even.

"There was an elaborate set of drawings, and a big bank in Chicago offered to loan you two hundred million dollars. That sounds like something to me, Mr. Mayor."

The mayor pressed his fingertips together and glared.

"It was just an idea that went nowhere. That's all there was to it."

"Was it Falcano's brainchild, or did you or Nicholas come up with it? Who paid for the drawings? Who contacted the bank?"

Abruptly, the mayor sat back in his chair with a condescending smile.

"I already told you, that was quite some time ago."

Fitzhugh seemed to be trying to look nonchalant, but Jones thought he failed miserably.

"I know, but surely you can remember who … "

"It was just talk, we've covered all that. Now leave it alone! I can't see why you want to pry into all of this anyway. It's really none of your business."

Jones enjoyed watching the mayor's phony self-control melt away.

"It's none of my business?! A murdered man was involved in a huge land deal, and you're saying it's none of my business?"

"That's *exactly* what I'm saying. It was nothing."

The heat in Fitzhugh's voice just fueled Jones' frustration as their conversation circled pointlessly. Jones felt his temper getting away from him.

Time to cut to the heart of the matter.

"If it's nothing why are you so afraid to talk about it?"

Fitzhugh stared at Jones with real fire in his eyes, and color started rising in his cheeks.

"Are you questioning my integrity? I assure you, I never let anyone call me a liar. I take great pride in that!"

"I never said you were lying. I'm asking how the plan got started and why it never got off the ground."

Fitzhugh's face reddened even more, and he gripped the corner of his desk with white knuckles.

"I told you to drop it! What else did you want to ask me about? I'm a very busy man, you know!"

"I want to talk about this, Mr. Mayor. I think it has something to do with the murder, and I need to get to the bottom of it."

"What are you implying, Mr. Jones?"

Jones felt something let go in his own self-control.

"What are you hiding, Mr. Mayor?"

The mayor's mouth worked like a fish gasping for breath.

"Who do you think you are? You can't talk to me like that!"

"I'm a detective investigating a murder, *Mister* Mayor! I'd like to think I'd get cooperation from a city official like yourself!"

It probably hadn't helped to say the word 'mister' in such a sarcastic tone!

"Why you insolent, insubordinate … I'll have you fired before the day is out!"

Jones' anger burned cold now. He knew anything he said would just make things worse, but he couldn't hold back.

"I guess I've really touched a nerve, huh?"

The mayor sputtered and jumped to his feet. He grabbed for the phone, and the headset dropped and clattered noisily against the desk. He finally got hold of it and thrust it against his ear.

"Get me Walter Manning!"

He cradled the phone against his shoulder and shook a bent, bony finger at Jones.

"You'll regret the day you ever lipped off to me, Detective!"

Jones enjoyed the spectacle of Fitzhugh's fury, but he knew immediately he shouldn't have.

The mayor waited in a white heat of impatience, moving the phone from one hand to the other and shifting his weight abruptly. His body practically vibrated with rage.

Jones let the scene sink in for a minute, then he dropped ruefully back into his chair.

Now he'd done it!

He wouldn't care if he lost his job, but he didn't want to be kicked off this case now, not with Walker indicted and the real killer walking around free.

"I'm sorry, Mr. Mayor, I didn't mean to …"

"It's too late for that now!"

Fitzhugh turned abruptly and shouted into the phone.

"Walter, get over here right now!"

Jones tried to catch his eye.

"Please, let me …"

Fitzhugh ignored him.

"Don't tell me to calm down, Walter! I want you here in five minutes. I want this son of a bitch fired *right now*! Do you hear me? I want him gone *now*!"

CHAPTER THIRTY-NINE

Wil had been sitting by Jones desk for almost forty-five minutes when he saw the detective walk stiffly into the room.

The chief of police towered over him, matching him step for step, and gesturing energetically with his hands.

Wil averted his gaze as they stepped closer.

"He's my boss, Peter! I got him to let you stay on, but just barely. I've never seen him so angry. What did you say to him?"

"I asked him some questions, Walter, the kind of questions I would ask anyone involved in a murder investigation."

Wil looked up just in time to see the chief give Jones a look that said 'Oh yeah?'

"Look, Walter, I appreciate you going to bat for me, but I'm investigating a murder, and I can't treat people with kid gloves."

"It's no secret you don't respect him, Peter, but please, try not to throw gas on the fire, will you?"

"If I ask him some questions, he needs to cooperate. He's an elected official, not the king of the world."

"He's a good man to have as a friend and a bad one to have as an enemy."

"I'll leave that to you, Walter. I can't play that game."

"What were you ..."

They both saw Wil at the same time.

The chief's mouth hung open for a second. Then he caught himself and closed it abruptly.

"Hello, Mr. Walker. What are you doing here?"

"I need to show something to Mr. Jones."

"What is it? Let's have a look."

The detective rubbed his forehead with his hand.

"Please Walter, let us talk in private, will you? I'll give you a full report."

Manning looked offended, but he backed off.

"All right, but see that you do."

He waved a finger at Jones, looking oddly awkward in the process.

"I'll be keeping a close eye on you, Peter."

"Yeah, I know. That's great."

Jones looked at Wil to emphasize his sarcasm.

Wil found the surreptitious confidence surprising and strangely gratifying.

The chief scowled and walked away, and Jones herded Wil into the cramped conference room.

"How you doin', Wil?"

"Terrible! What would you expect?"

"Just that, I guess. What's going on?"

"Somebody dropped this off at my house last night."

Jones gave a low whistle as he spread out the mutilated pictures and the cryptic message on the table.

"How bizarre. This is the same set of images we found shot to pieces in an old barn. The note is a new wrinkle."

Wil had no idea what to say to that bit of news.

Jones studied the faces intently.

"I recognize Falcano, you and Helen. Do you know who the rest of these people are?"

"I have no idea. The whole thing has to be some kind of weird message from Henri's murderer."

"Yes, but what's the point?"

"Good question."

"This centerfold is from a magazine. Anybody could pick that up, but the rest of these pictures seem to be personal. And why the picture of Jesus?"

Wil found that equally baffling.

Without warning, the door burst open and Walter Manning stomped in.

"Let's see what you've got!"

Wil thought the room seemed way too small all of a sudden.

Jones jumped to his feet, his hands balling into fists at his side.

"I told you I'd brief you when we got finished."

Jones' look of outrage caught Wil by surprise. What was going on between these two?

The chief looked like a miffed child reclaiming a lost toy on the playground.

"I decided I don't want you closeted in here with a murder suspect examining evidence."

"What? I've been a detective here for twenty-five years! Are you saying I'd tamper with evidence?"

"Maybe I'm questioning your objectivity, Peter. I think you're getting a little too close to this one."

This time his look said 'so there!'

"You're overstepping your authority, Walter! If you think I'm not competent to handle this case, I will quit, but I promise you that won't be the end of it!"

"Calm down, Peter, and just show me what you've got. I am still the chief of police, remember?"

Jones scowled, but he turned his attention to the stack of papers on the table and pointed with a flippant wave of his hand.

"Someone left these at Wil's house last night."

"Or so he says."

Wil felt his stomach lurch again, and he stared at the chief incredulously.

"Are you saying he did this?! Someone broke into a barn the other day and made a makeshift shooting gallery out of the same set of pictures."

Jones almost spat the words.

"I'm saying what does it prove? Walker could have done this as easily as anyone else."

"Oh sure, and he brought these to us just for laughs?"

"He's trying to deflect blame from himself. Maybe he thought this would throw us off the scent."

Wil wished he could leave the room. They were talking as if he wasn't there.

Suddenly his own anger boiled over.

"Somebody left these sick pictures on my front porch, Mr. Manning. Some sadistic creep murdered Henri Falcano, and he wants you to believe I did it. I'm not a murderer, and I don't take out my frustrations by mutilating pictures."

Manning looked at Wil like a scientist eyeing a laboratory specimen.

The rest of Wil's frustration came out in a rush.

"I thought, just maybe, these pictures could help you figure out who really did it. I guess I should have saved myself the aggravation."

Wil thought he saw a hint of a smile on Jones face. Maybe he was glad Wil finally showed some backbone!

"These pictures prove nothing, Mr. Walker."

Manning's matter of fact voice cut like a knife.

Jones suddenly turned all business.

"Not by themselves, chief. I'll have them dusted for prints."

He turned to Wil.

"Could anyone have seen who dropped them off?"

"You've been to my place. It's in the middle of nowhere."

Manning looked on with a scowl of disapproval.

"Suit yourself, Peter, but I doubt you'll find anything. There's no proof this nonsense has anything to do with the murder, anyway. It's just a set of pictures someone has been scribbling on."

"Scribbling?! Look how jagged and rough these lines are, Chief. You can almost feel the anger. Look how the holes were punched through. It's as if someone attacked the paper with a vengeance. They just happened to be holding a pen instead of a knife. And what about this?" Jones held up the paper threatening that Wil would be going 'down, down, down.' That's pretty clear, wouldn't you say?"

"It proves nothing, Peter. Like I said, Walker could have done all of this as a smokescreen."

"Oh my God! What about your objectivity, Walter? You've made up your mind Walker did it, and you refuse to consider any other possibility!"

"Why make such a stretch, Peter. We don't have one shred of evidence implicating anyone else. Everything we do have points to Walker."

"The evidence we have would blow away like a pile of dust in the hands of any competent defense attorney."

"Maybe, maybe not. Walker has been indicted for the murder, and I'm considering him the prime suspect until there's a good reason to believe otherwise. I suggest you don't allow your personal feelings to get in your way."

"I know what I believe, Walter. My feelings have nothing to do with it."

"Whatever you say, Peter, but don't mess up. And don't rile up the mayor any more, or we'll all be in deep trouble."

"I'll do what I have to do to find out what really happened!"

"Just watch your step."

Wil felt like a hapless referee at a heavyweight fight.

Manning turned on his heel and bustled out of the room, leaving the door open.

Jones took a deep breath.

"I'm sorry you had to hear that, Wil. It wasn't a very professional conversation to hold in front of …"

He paused awkwardly.

"In front of a suspect?"

"Well, yeah … sorry. In front of any civilian, really."

"So he's the one who thinks I did it."

"Don't worry about that, Wil. I have to find the real bad guy, then all of this will go away."

Wil looked at his hands.

"You don't believe I made these, do you?"

"No, I think the killer is showing off. He had no reason to give you these except to grandstand a little bit. Maybe he's getting some kind of weird thrill out of shaking you up. Maybe that's his first big mistake."

"But it won't help unless you can find him, right?"

"Let's worry about that when the time comes."

CHAPTER FORTY

Helen sat very still in a small wooden chair in the cupola, staring through the windows but seeing nothing in particular.

Her beautifully made chair fit the contours of her body perfectly. An antique dealer would have drooled over it, but that thought couldn't have been farther from Helen's mind.

A large bottle of liquor sat on the floor to her right. People seemed to think all Russians loved vodka, but Helen preferred the tangy bite of tequila.

She'd also brought along a small bowl of lime slices and a finely etched shot glass.

The ornate glass seemed a little out of place, but she liked to do things with a touch of elegance.

She sucked some lime juice after each stinging gulp of the booze, but soon the sour green wedges were all used up.

She kept filling the glass and draining it anyway.

After one more drink, she looked out the streaky window and shuddered.

Henri had said her land was contaminated, useless. It made her skin crawl. Someone had even fouled the earth beneath her feet!

No one would ever buy the place now. How could things be any more hopeless?

Everything she ever had was useless, gone!

She filled the shot glass again and drained it in a single gulp.

A small handgun with a full clip of ammunition sat on her lap.

She bought the Glock so some slimeball couldn't corner her in a parking lot and rape her. She never doubted she could shoot someone, even shoot to kill, in the right circumstances.

But she never imagined she'd be doing this … sitting alone, with the gun on her lap, trying to make sense out of questions that had no answers.

Widow's walk, what an ironic name! Could you qualify as a widow if you'd never been married, only asked?

She filled the glass again, tossed the pungent liquid into the back of her throat and grimaced as it burned its way down to her stomach.

Henri said he had a plan to fix the land. Hah!

How was that even possible? And why wouldn't he tell her about it? He said he had to find out if it would work first. He didn't want to get her hopes up.

The man had so many secrets, so much to hide! What was he so afraid of?

It was enough to drive you mad!

No ship was coming in to save her. No prince in shining armor would be coming to her rescue.

She picked up the Glock and admired its simplicity. Every feature had a function. The pebbled handle held it securely in her palm. Her fingers fit perfectly into the small indentations below the trigger.

The gun could take her to a place of oblivion. Maybe there she could have some peace.

She took another shot of tequila and tossed her hair back as she swallowed it.

Maybe today she would put the Glock in her mouth and pull the trigger.

Henri had said he loved her, but she didn't know what to believe. How could you ask someone to marry you and not even be willing to tell anyone you were together?

He said his mother had some kind of phobia about Russians. Not something normal, an irrational fear, and he was afraid the shock would kill her. If anyone knew in town, he said, she would find out, and it would be too much.

Helen wondered bitterly how could she have fallen for such a load of crap!

He said he had figured out a way to break things to his mother gently, that they would be able to announce their plans soon.

It was all so infuriating!

And now it was too late.

The next shot of tequila slid down her throat much more easily, so she followed it with another.

Henri's death had ripped her heart out! There had been other men, but she couldn't turn to anyone else now. Maybe she never could!

Wil had taken her out a few times, a long time ago, but he was so quiet and shy. When he stopped calling, she hadn't really minded.

The thought that he had been charged with Henri's murder horrified her. It couldn't be true!

But what if it was?

Pearce had tried to ask her out several times, but she always told him to drop dead. He only cared about one person, and that was Jim Pearce. He was exhausting to be around.

And then there were the trolls.

Winston Nicholas practically drooled whenever he was around her. What a repulsive toad!

Even the mayor. He had come by the house asking to look at her property. The way he stared at her made her feel naked. She pitied the man's poor wife.

He said he knew someone who would buy the place and had her sign some papers. Fat chance! The buyers would run when they found out the land was fouled.

She had never felt so utterly alone. Her family was gone, and she had no real friends. Not one she could really talk to.

All the things she loved had turned to dust.

She hardly ever listened to music anymore.

As a girl, she'd been delirious when spring finally came.

She stared at the buds opening on the trees, the bright yellow swatches of daffodils popping up in the yard, and the bright green color of the fresh grass.

And she felt nothing.

Her fingers caressed the rounded edges of the gun. The craftsmanship was really quite excellent. She was beginning to understand how guns could hold such a fascination for so many people.

Maybe if she waited one more day things would get better.

Better how? Wise up you fool, things aren't going to get better!

She took a swig of tequila from the bottle and hardly noticed as it slid down her throat, so she took another one.

Some part of her watched in horror as the wretched, desolate fears in her head merged into a single hideous cloud of pessimism and grief.

She didn't feel the tears that appeared at the corners of her eyes and began streaming down her cheeks as she sat, stone still, in the unyielding chair.

She picked up the gun, caring not at all about its exquisite balance.

It lay in her hand like a friendly serpent.

Maybe I'll do it today.

CHAPTER FORTY-ONE

Wil cursed himself for staring at the television like a zombie.

He'd been clicking the remote mindlessly all evening, and every new channel he saw seemed more ridiculous than the last.

He tilted his head from side to side and stretched his cramped arms and legs. His stomach felt like a black hole, and a dull ache had been spreading from his head down into his shoulders.

He'd give anything to have his old life back. The problems he used to have seemed so trivial compared to this bizarre, overwhelming sea of trouble!

The scrap between Jones and the police chief baffled him. Did the chief really believe Wil had killed Henri? Could Manning be protecting someone else?

Wil wondered who he could really trust.

He thought Jones believed him but how far would the detective stick his neck out to help him?

And would the people at the symphony stick with him, or would they start to believe he must be the killer?

Wil looked around the tattered living room in disgust.

He'd been at home doing nothing most of the day. He'd gotten some groceries and cleaned the house a little bit, but he felt like a powder keg of nervous energy. Every random sound made him jump, and he found it impossible to concentrate on anything for more than a few minutes at a time.

He tried to find a comfortable seating position and pointed the remote back at the TV.

Click … "book your getaway now to the sun drenched island of … *click* … "This kid is showing tremendous promise in the big leagues, Miguel! …

Wil scowled. Who would be watching a game between the New York Mets and the Atlanta Braves here in Michigan?

Click … and now, the fifty-thousand dollar question - wild cheering - ARE YOU READY? … *CLICK*!

He almost threw the remote at the television, then tossed it on the couch, feeling foolish.

What could he do to sort out this mess? He had to do something!

He saw no point in bugging Jones.

Helen had come to tell him something just before his arrest. Maybe he should find out what had been on her mind.

He walked into the kitchen, wondering where he'd left his phone, found it in an unopened pile of junk mail, found her number, and sent through the call.

After five rings, the tinny sound of her voicemail came on.

He decided not to leave a message and angrily jammed the phone in his pocket.

He looked at the clock. He decided he shouldn't call anyone this late, even if he could think of someone, so he started flipping off the lights and headed up to bed.

He had stayed up late, hoping that would make him tired enough to sleep, but once again, he found himself tossing and turning late into the night.

His hyperactive brain doggedly refused to settle down.

The same questions circled endlessly through his head. Who really did this? Why had the monster chosen him as the sacrificial lamb? Why wouldn't the cops, except for Jones, believe him?

He had no answers for any of it, but that didn't stop him from rehashing his fears and worries again and again until he became thoroughly exhausted and frustrated.

Whenever he did manage to doze off, he jerked awake with a start. After what seemed like the fiftieth time, he punched his pillow in irritation and lurched over onto his left side, only to toss back onto his right side a few seconds later.

A few hours before dawn, he finally lapsed into a deep, almost comatose, slumber.

When the morning sun roused him, he looked around the room in a daze until the whole mess suddenly flooded back into his mind.

He groaned and pulled the covers over his head, wanting desperately to return to the sweet oblivion of sleep, but he knew he couldn't. The waking process had progressed too far, and he'd be better off getting up.

After a hasty wash up, he had a quick breakfast of coffee, a few bites of bagel and some fruit and sat staring out the window.

He had to do something - almost anything - to either help with his problems or take his mind off them!

He tried to call Helen again, but she still didn't answer.

She always seemed to answer quickly when she wanted to. Maybe she just didn't want to be bothered.

Finally, almost in desperation, he plodded into his studio to try to work on his composition.

Writing music often provided a soothing balm for his soul that nothing else could equal. He loved immersing himself in the work, and when things went well, nothing existed but the wondrous patterns of sound he worked to create. He'd get lost in a world he loved, a magical place where he could shape and polish the gentle arcs of melody and bold tapestries of rhythm any way he wanted to.

The notes stayed where he put them. They weren't like people. They didn't argue with him, and they didn't refuse to take his calls! The world of tones and rhythms had no deceptions and no nasty surprises, and it certainly didn't have anything like murders to tie his life in knots!

He took out the passage of music he'd written two nights earlier and set the paper on the piano. He almost had to force himself to play it. More than once he'd written something that seemed like spun gold at first, but sounded pathetic when he came back to play it a day or two later.

He pressed the keys very tentatively at first.

Thank God! The music seemed just a vivid and alive as it had when he'd first come up with it.

He played through it several more times, letting the feel and flow of the music fill his consciousness. He experimented with a few changes, but decided he had it right just the way he'd written it down.

A thrilling, familiar feeling - a deeply gratifying sense of satisfaction - surged through his body, but now the hard work of composition really began. He could already imagine dozens of possibilities for developing and transforming the theme to shape the rest of the piece. At this stage he needed to brainstorm, gathering ideas and writing out bits of melody and harmony like an artist's sketches. Later he would need to select the ones that were exactly right, refine them, and put them in a sequence that had just the right phrasing and flow.

The music needed passages of great strength and moments of deep intimacy. At some point it needed to build to an intense climax. He also needed to decide whether the movement would end peacefully or with a powerful crescendo.

He played though several possible variations and wrote some of them down with quick, precise strokes.

He loved very sharp pencils for this kind of work and kept a large collection close by in a pewter mug. When one got the slightest bit dull, he wanted to toss it down and grab a fresh one. Sharpening the blunt point might risk breaking his concentration. His pencil fetish might be a weird quirk, he'd freely admit that, but it worked well for him, and he wasn't about to change it.

All too soon his mind wandered back to the trouble besetting him, and he found it harder and harder to concentrate.

He knew he'd been fortunate to get as much done as he had. He had finally broken through his writer's block! He loved the sound of the music he'd written, and he had a very good idea how he wanted the music to develop from this promising start.

Not bad, especially under the circumstances.

He stretched and walked toward the kitchen. His appetite seemed a bit stronger now.

His brain felt energized, and he tried to focus that positive energy on figuring out how to prove his innocence.

There had to be a pattern. How could he find it?

Who would want to kill Henri, and why?

If he didn't figure it out, maybe no one would!

A raspy bleat erupted from the phone on Jones' desk.

He had chosen a new option from his menu of ringtones, but he hated this one as much as the one he'd replaced!

He eyed the phone with disgust and picked up the call.

"Hello."

"Hello, Mr. Jones, this is Jeanette Fields. How are you?"

"Just peachy, Mrs. Fields. What's on your mind?"

"Peachy? I haven't heard that one in a while."

"Sorry, just kidding around."

"Oh, sure, don't be sorry."

She laughed politely, and Jones regretted his weak attempt at humor.

"What can I do for you?"

"I was just wondering how things are going with the Falcano investigation."

Jones hesitated. She seemed very sympathetic, but he knew very well anything he said now could appear in print.

She had sent him a large envelope jammed with information about Helen's parents, Mayor Fitzhugh, Winston Nicholas and Henri Falcano. Helen had received far less coverage in the paper, but there was a glowing review of a solo performance she'd given with the symphony. Jones hadn't found any major revelations in the clippings, but they had given him lots of helpful background information.

Jeanette's offer of discreet help seemed genuine, but Jones decided to be cautious.

"We're exploring a number of leads."

"You can cut the crap with me, Peter, what's really happening."

"I'm not anxious to see my innermost thoughts in the paper, Mrs. Fields."

"I told you to call me Jeanette, and I'm not calling for the paper. This is strictly between us."

"Okay, if you say so."

"Trust me, Peter. I'm not after a story, certainly not one that's meddling in your investigation. I'd dearly love to break a story frying some of the big fish around here, but we'll worry about that when the time comes, okay? I'm calling because I think I have an idea that might help you, but first I need to know how things stand. Our reporter is filing a flood of stories about Wil Walker being arrested and charged. What's going on?"

Jones sighed. The news had to come out sometime.

He decided to confide in her and hoped he wasn't making a big mistake.

"The chief is falling for the circumstantial evidence that makes Walker look like the bad guy. The arrest was none of my doing."

"So you don't think he's the killer?"

He sighed heavily.

"I really don't. It just doesn't make sense."

"Okay, thank you. And don't worry, you won't see that in print tomorrow. Are you still pursuing that business about the land development on Lake Michigan?"

"I'm trying to. It's been one dead end after another so far."

"Well, that's why I'm calling. You know Falcano kept horses, right?"

"Yeah. Thanks to all the information you sent."

"Well, he boarded them at a small stable about an hour south of here. The owner is an old friend of mine, Thomas Salisbury. Maybe Henri let his hair down a bit when he was out in the fresh air with his horses. It wouldn't hurt to ask."

Jones skipped a breath.

"That's a great idea, Mrs. Fields. How do I find this place?"

"I mean it, call me Jeanette."

"Okay Jeanette. How do I get in touch with him?"

Jones jotted down the information and hung up the phone thoughtfully.

A trip to a horse farm sounded much more appealing than sitting around the station avoiding Manning.

He felt more than ready for a little drive.

CHAPTER FORTY-TWO

Wil looked in disgust at the turkey sandwich he'd made for lunch.

It tasted like cardboard, but everything did lately. His appetite had been miserable.

He racked his brain as he ate. The questions about who killed Henri wouldn't leave him alone. What could he DO to figure out who did it and why?

He had tried to call Helen again just before lunch.

She still didn't answer.

Who else could he talk to? Could someone at the symphony tell him more? Who else did Henri spend time with? Where did he go when he wasn't working?

Wil choked down the last few bites of his sandwich with an air of resignation, finished his Coke and set his dishes by the sink.

He needed a plan, but he couldn't even figure out a good place to start!

For lack of a better idea, he decided to mow the lawn.

The fresh emerald grass grew like crazy for the first few weeks of spring, and he knew there'd be trouble if he let it get much longer.

Normally, he liked mowing. He usually enjoyed transforming a ragged expanse of grass into a manicured carpet, and he seldom refused any good excuse to get outdoors, especially this time of year, when the world came to life after a long winter.

Today, though, the repetitive work seemed like an onerous chore.

He pulled the cranky old mower out of his ramshackle shed, and his irritation mounted as he pulled the starter cord again and again with no sign of life from the engine.

He had almost reached the point of giving up when he heard a tiny cough.

After three more strenuous pulls, the mower came stuttering to life and surrounded him with a dense cloud of acrid blue smoke.

The sound gradually settled into a better rhythm, and he listlessly started to walk the machine back and forth across the lawn.

He heaved a sigh of relief when he finished the job, and he put the mower away without even looking back for the stray tufts of grass he would normally have gone back to tidy up.

After a quick shower, he poured himself a large glass of ice water and flopped onto the couch with nervous energy still coursing through his body. He started to turn on the television, but the idea of flipping through the channels again made his skin crawl.

The questions about the murder pushed insistently back into his consciousness. What could he do? Who could he talk to?

He stared out the window, hoping to think of a strategy, but nothing would come.

The sun streamed in through the windows, and Wil realized he would usually be dying to play golf on a gorgeous spring day like this.

Why not?

It would get him out of the house and hopefully, help him relax. Maybe he could come up with some ideas if he could calm down a bit. He put on some slacks and a loose shirt, locked up the house and threw his golf bag into the bed of the pickup.

His spirits started to lift a little when he got close to Five Oaks Golf Course. The grand old clubhouse had once been a Victorian mansion, and it radiated an air of quiet dignity. The long green fairways stretched like peaceful gardens all around it.

When he saw the jammed parking lot, he almost turned around to go home.

He had hoped the crowds would be thinning out by this time in the afternoon. He'd been picturing a quiet practice round by himself, with time to think and even hit a few extra shots for practice. When he paid his green fees, the starter told him the other two courses in town were closed for a college tournament and a corporate outing.

Drat!

The course would be packed with three times the usual number of golfers, and they would all be competing for the same space. Hopefully he could find some enjoyable playing partners.

Wil stepped outside and saw a welcome sight. By some miracle, the first tee seemed to be empty.

He hurried over.

His tense, stiff muscles resisted his hasty efforts to loosen up, but he wanted to get going quickly. Maybe he could still manage to get some space to himself!

Wil teed up a shiny new ball and tried to visualize a perfect drive. Then he took his stance. When everything felt right, he took a swing, but the awkward, sloppy swipe he produced had none of the smoothness and grace he'd been hoping for.

The shot curved wildly to the right and flew out of bounds into a thick stand of trees.

Wil cursed. What a lousy start! In a competitive round, he would have to hit his third stroke from right here.

He teed up another new ball impatiently.

The next swing felt smoother, but the shot took off in the same direction and landed in some tall dead grass just short of the tree line. After an agitated walk, and several minutes of searching, he found the ball in a terrible lie.

He slashed fiercely at the next shot, trying to cut through the thick rough, and he watched in dismay as the ball squirted weakly off to the right and followed its predecessor into the woods.

Great! With the penalties, he already had five strokes on the hole, and he still hadn't hit one decent shot!

Wil dropped another ball and managed to slap it out onto the fairway.

He hit the next shot near the front of the green, chipped on, and somehow made the putt for an ugly nine.

Wil shook his head. He never played this badly! Playing like an idiot wouldn't soothe his ragged nerves. Quite the opposite.

He resolved to do better on the next hole.

A short path led through some trees to the next tee, and Wil rounded the corner to see two groups already waiting there.

He looked back and saw a foursome rapidly approaching from behind.

Damn it!

He briefly considered heading home, but he had come out to play, and that's what he intended to do.

The twosome ahead of him showed no signs of inviting him to join them. Things would flow better for everyone if they did.

Wil didn't try to wear stylish clothes on the golf course, but these two had on clashing outfits that made it look like they dressed in the dark. One of the big men belched loudly, and the other, not to be outdone, lifted his rear and answered with a long burst of flatulence.

Wil reluctantly stepped closer and asked if he could play with them.

The two large men puffed on their thick cigars with looks of mild annoyance as they considered his question, but they could see the holdup as well as he could.

"Why not?" the taller one said, "I'm Frank, and this is Herb."

They didn't mention their last names, and neither one seemed to pay much attention when Wil told them his.

Frank and Herb needled each other relentlessly as they waited for the tee to clear. The banter seemed almost playful, but Wil felt a mean-spirited edge just below the surface.

He waited dejectedly as the foursome ahead of them pranked each other during their backswings, laughed at their poor shots, and casually hit new drives if the first one went awry. The group finally scooted down the fairway, playing chicken with their carts and splashing each other with their cans of beer as they went.

Wil wished he hadn't come. So much for his plan for some calming time outdoors!

When their turn finally came, Frank took a couple of waggles, with the big cigar still dangling from his mouth, and made a vicious cut at his ball.

His shot flew halfheartedly down the fairway and dove into the right rough.

Herb went through a similar routine and hit a shot that lodged in slightly thicker rough on the opposite side.

"Go ahead, Bill."

Frank mumbled the words halfheartedly as he and Herb sauntered over to their golf cart and swung heavily into their seats.

Wil decided not to bother correcting his name.

Frank and Herb continued their conversation in a loud semi-whisper as Wil tried to gather his concentration.

He made another rushed swing and stared in disbelief as the ball took off on a low trajectory and hooked sharply toward the out-of-bounds stakes on the left.

"Tough luck, Billy! I don't think you're gonna find that one."

They both laughed as Herb gunned the cart and they took off.

Wil's slow burn rose a couple more notches toward complete disgust.

The rules called for him to take a penalty stroke and play his next shot from the tee, but he couldn't do that now, unless he wanted to take a chance on braining one of them. That thought had a certain appeal, but he picked up his golf bag and trudged down the fairway fuming.

When he reached Frank and Herb, they had already hit their second shots. Their body language radiated impatience as they waited for Wil to play.

Wil tossed down a ball and hit a shot that curved left and disappeared under the branches of a thick pine tree.

Frank and Herb zipped off in their cart immediately.

Wil's latest ball had found an unplayable lie, so he took a drop, mentally counted another penalty stroke, and chipped weakly onto the green. In a practice round like this he wasn't really keeping score, but he hated playing like such a hack!

Frank and Herb had shorter putts than his, but they hit theirs first as if he wasn't there.

When they finally acknowledged his presence, Wil hunched over his putt, trying to concentrate.

He took the putter back smoothly, but a loud, choking cough erupted behind him on his downstroke. He lurched, and the putt trickled weakly toward the hole and stopped well short and to the left.

Frank whacked Herb's back with an open palm.

Herb reddened and coughed again into a balled fist.

"Sorry Bill, I must've gotten something down the wrong pipe."

They both seemed to find the whole thing hilarious as they ambled back to their cart.

Frank loudly asked Herb what stocks he liked this week as they raced off toward the next tee.

Wil's frustration boiled over. He considered golf a game of courtesy and manners. He hardly ever felt like leaving the course in the middle of a round, but really didn't need this aggravation.

He had already come a long way from the clubhouse, but maybe he should just walk to his pickup and go home.

His plan to help him to relax and think more clearly had backfired badly!

He had no idea that four hundred yards away, well hidden in the trees, a figure dressed in camouflage had the scope of a high powered rifle aimed directly at the back of his head.

The crosshairs traced a line down the back of Wil's neck and settled on a spot right between his shoulder blades.

A soft voice hissed a weird imitation of a rifle firing.

CHAPTER FORTY-THREE

Jones felt almost free driving down the two-lane highway in the bright sunshine.

The budding tree branches contrasted beautifully with the freshly plowed fields, and the greening countryside seemed fresh and new. Jones relished the promise of warmer weather and longed for the relaxation that came with the summer months.

It always seemed to him the world slept fitfully during the winter, keeping its guard up in order to survive. In the summer everything could rest and grow in peace.

Unfortunately, he knew all too well that summer brought out creatures that could sting and bite, and in nature, like human society, there were always enemies ready to devour the innocent and unsuspecting.

The countryside seemed more remote with each turn, and he enjoyed the feeling of exploring far from his usual haunts. A beautiful checkerboard of fruit orchards, pastureland and woods unfolded in the landscape around him. Green spikes of winter wheat poked up in many fields, sprouting from seeds that had been in the soil all winter, waiting for the spring thaw.

The parcels of land varied in size and shape, but the boundary lines always ran in perpendicular lines unless they followed a stream bed or natural obstruction. Jones thought to himself with satisfaction that farmers were a very orderly sort.

When he came to the address Jeanette had given him, he saw an elegantly understated sign that said 'Salisbury Stables, Fine Thoroughbred Horses, Est. 1894.' Two gleaming white posts supported the sign in a freshly cultivated bed of daffodils and crocuses.

A long driveway led from the road to a classic house surrounded by a tidy collection of white barns, stables and storage buildings. Jones' tires seemed to hum as he turned from the rough surface of the country road to the smooth blacktop of the driveway.

As he drove into the yard, he couldn't see a chip of loose paint or an unkempt shrub anywhere. Sparkling white fences outlined generous sections of pasture, and a dozen magnificent horses stood in one of them with the stately, aloof expressions only they possessed. Jones knew horses had relatively small brains, but he always thought they seemed to ponder the world from a special, lofty position of omnipotence and insight.

He parked near the stately house, and a tall gentleman in khaki slacks, sturdy leather boots and a dark brown jacket walked toward him from one of the outbuildings.

The man's unhurried gait and relaxed bearing couldn't hide an unmistakable impression of great physical strength. Everything about his demeanor communicated an air of prosperous competence and the ease born of a lifetime of experience.

"What can I do for you, sir?"

The man spoke quietly and waited placidly for an answer, but Jones noticed his eyes never stood still. He seemed to be continually looking for a scrap of paper that needed to be picked up, a weed that needed to be pulled or a nail that needed to be pounded in.

"You must be Thomas Salisbury. My name is Peter Jones. I'm a policeman from St. Cecile."

"Yes, I know. Jenny told me you'd be coming."

"Jenny?"

He laughed dryly.

"Are you surprised to hear she has a nickname? We go way back."

Jones savored the fertile smell of the air as he admired the gently rolling land and the impeccable farm.

"You have a gorgeous place here."

"Thank you. Would you like to see the horses?"

"It's that obvious, huh?"

They spent several minutes in amiable conversation as Salisbury showed Jones the well-kept stables, his stores of feed and straw, a room filled with gleaming saddles and an impressive spread of exercise areas, corrals and lush pastures.

They stopped near a fence, and a light brown horse with a dark mane strolled over, stretched its neck over the fence, and nudged Salisbury's shoulder with its snout.

"Most thoroughbreds aren't this tame. Maggie's Girl is like a pet, aren't ya?"

He reached up and stroked the horse's neck affectionately.

"This is one of Jenny's horses."

Jones couldn't hide his surprise.

"Really? I didn't know Jeanette owned horses."

"There's probably a lot about Jenny you don't know."

Salisbury's eyes twinkled with amusement as he pulled a piece of carrot from his pocket and let her munch it.

"Maggie had quite a future in racing at one time, but she got injured before she had a chance to really show what she could do. When she got better, she was getting too old. She's had some promising foals, but things never quite came together for you, did they, Maggie?"

Maggie whinnied, tossed her head playfully and trotted back into the pasture.

"Are Falcano's horses still here?

"Yeah, we're still trying to sort out who's supposed to get them. His mother is elderly, and I don't think he has any other family to speak of. It'll all be sorted out in the courts, I imagine."

"Which ones are they?"

"That's one of them there, and that's another one next to that tree."

The two horses he pointed out seemed remarkable, even in this collection of beautiful animals. The first one, jet black in color, seemed to stand several inches taller than any of the other horses around. The second horse had a stockier build and a mottled back that looked as if someone had dripped multi-colored paint all over it.

Jones' eyes widened as he saw the horse's muscles ripple like those of a powerful Olympic athlete or a professional football player.

"That one looks like a powerhouse."

"You better believe it. That's Cherokee Warrior. He won several races and everybody thought he'd make a fortune when we put him out to stud. If he sired any colts with his strength and a little more size, they'd have been unbeatable. His previous owners were heartbroken when he turned out to be sterile."

"Was that Falcano's interest, making money?"

"Not really. He bought several horses relatively cheap because they were past their prime or had no real future, like Cherokee. I guess he just admired them. He'd come out here and spend hours, just hanging around, riding once in a while. He'd pitch in and shovel manure with the best of them."

"Did the two of you talk much?"

"Not an awful lot. We mostly talked about horses."

"Did he say much about his work?"

"I knew he was a musician, the conductor of the orchestra up in St. Cecile. I love music, but I don't get out to concerts much. I spend most of my time right here or traveling with the horses."

"Did he talk about his personal life?"

Salisbury hesitated.

"Not usually. He did tell me one thing in strict confidence. There's not much point in keeping it to myself now, is there?"

"What was that?"

"He wanted to get married. There was a young woman in the orchestra, her name was Ellen, something like that."

"Helen?"

"Yeah, that was it. I think he was crazy about her, but he said people in the orchestra might not like him dating another one of the players."

"That doesn't make sense."

Salisbury hesitated before going on.

"Actually there was more to it than that. She was from Russia."

"So?"

"He told me once his father had been a soldier during the war."

"World War Two?"

"Yeah. After the war he'd gotten into intelligence work, very secret stuff. He was killed mysteriously and Henri's mother always blamed the Russians. She hated them. It was off the charts, some kind of phobia with her. Henri said she'd go ballistic if he married someone who had been born there."

"Did he really believe that?"

"He said she'd gone a little crazy after his father died and was completely irrational about it. If anybody even mentioned Russia she'd just get hysterical. She was getting very old. He said it couldn't be too much longer before she died or went completely senile. Then her objections wouldn't be an issue any more."

"And he thought she'd try to stop him if he planned to marry Helen?"

"He thought it would kill her, or the next thing to it. I asked him why he didn't just marry the girl and keep it a secret from his mother. He said he could never do that. Holidays would be a problem, you know, things like that. He was stubborn enough. I'll say one thing for him, he always did things his own way."

"Why keep it a secret from everybody else?"

"I guess he was afraid his mother would get wind of it. She used to call him at his office all the time. He seemed to think she'd lose it if she found out he got engaged without telling her. I don't know. It was a big mess."

"Well, it seems strange, but it does explain a few things. Did he ever say anything about any business plans?"

Salisbury scratched his cheek.

"Well, maybe so. He did say he wanted to build a big hotel or something like that. He even had a place in mind, but there was some kind of a snag that kept him from going ahead with it."

"A snag?"

"Yeah, some kind of a problem. He wouldn't say what it was. But he said if he could pull this off it would solve all of his problems, getting married, money, all of it. He seemed to think it could ruin everything if folks knew too much about it."

"Did he mention any partners?"

"He just said it was going to be huge, very fancy. There was just that one problem he had to get solved, then he said it would all come together."

"But he didn't give you any idea what that problem it was? Something personal, financial maybe?"

"Not a clue, sorry."

"Well, you've been very helpful, Mr. Salisbury, thank you very much for your time."

Jones didn't rush to leave.

The warm sunshine, the open air and the regal horses made it easy to imagine why Falcano found this a great place to get away from it all.

Finally, reluctantly, he walked to his car and pulled open the door.

Salisbury seemed to sense his feelings.

"Come on out any time, detective. Any friend of Jenny's is a friend of mine. She's one of the great ones, you know."

Jones was starting to understand that.

On the way back he decided to stop by Helen's.

He had some news she might really love to hear. Henri had told Salisbury he loved her and planned to marry her. Maybe his plans for the property really were about their future, not a land grab. All the secrecy still seemed odd, but maybe he had good reasons for what he did.

But Jones had one other reason for stopping by. He wanted to push harder to find out how much she actually knew about the development plans.

The sky had darkened considerably by the time he arrived at her house.

She didn't answer the door, so he walked around her BMW to the back. He could see a glimmer of light burning somewhere, but his knock still went unanswered. He shook the knob, but the rickety old door held surprisingly firm.

He walked slowly back to the car and gave one more look toward the house before he got in.

He'd have to get in touch with her tomorrow.

CHAPTER FORTY-FOUR

Jones drove almost two miles before he decided to go back.

He just had a hunch she was in that house. Helen had been isolating herself, and she certainly hadn't seemed eager to see him in the first place.

He wouldn't be surprised at all if she just hadn't bothered to answer the door.

The house looked utterly deserted when he crunched to a stop in the driveway.

The twilight had given way to a complete, stifling darkness. No more lights had been turned on, and he had trouble finding the walk to the front porch, but he had come this far, and he wasn't leaving without trying to talk with her.

He made his way up to the door and knocked insistently. It had to be hard to hear in that huge house.

After several tries, he beat on the door as loudly as he could with the heel of his fist.

Nothing.

He went around to the back door and went through the same routine there.

She certainly should have heard him by now.

He cupped his hands over his mouth.

"Helen? This is Peter Jones. I need to talk with you."

He hesitated, then circled back as close as he could to the house, wondering if he could find another entrance.

A thick barrier of gangly, overgrown shrubs made it difficult to see anything inside, but the only glimmer of light seemed to be coming from the upstairs hallway.

When he got back to the front door, he twisted the wobbly old knob with more force and the door popped open.

"Ms. Rubinstein? It's Detective Jones. Are you home?"

A mausoleum couldn't have been any quieter.

He would have a very hard time explaining this if Helen wanted to make a stink, but he wasn't about to turn back now.

"I'm coming in."

No one answered.

He walked through the dark hallway to the kitchen and flipped on a switch. Weak, yellowish light seeped into the room.

The kitchen looked exactly as it had the other day, except for a large knife and a few slices of lime on a cutting board.

"Helen? Can you hear me?"

If she just wanted to avoid him, she had taken things a little too far.

He walked back toward her bedroom. The door stood open, but he couldn't see anything in the enveloping darkness.

The light from the upstairs hallway cast a faint glow in the living room, and he quickened his step as soon as he could see a little better.

"Hello! Helen, are you here? It's Detective Jones."

He reached the top of the stairs and turned toward the entrance to the cupola.

The door to the spiral staircase hung slightly ajar, releasing a thin sliver of light into the gloom.

"Ms. Rubinstein? Hello?"

He hurried down the hallway, pulled open the door, and immediately recoiled in shocked surprise.

Spatters of dark blood covered the steps and the floor.

When he looked up, another drip landed on his cheek.

He swiped it away with a shudder.

"Helen?!"

He ran up the stairs in a panic.

A horrifying stench of vomit hit him as pushed open the door and climbed into the cupola.

He found Helen's body crumpled at an improbable angle next to an overturned chair. An appalling pool of bile and blood spread in all directions. Shards of broken glass littered the floor under her head.

Jones' blood froze in his veins when he saw a forty-five caliber Glock on the floor near her hand.

He reached for her neck and breathed a sigh of relief when he felt a faint pulse.

With a shake of his head, he pulled out his cell phone to call for an ambulance.

Wil ran more than walked as he hurried into the surgical wing of St. Cecile Memorial Hospital.

The jarring sound of a television sitcom filled the waiting room, and he looked around in irritation to see a large family staring with rapt attention at the glowing screen.

Apparently they were waiting for someone in a more routine surgery!

Wil saw Jones talking quietly with Pru and hurried over. Greta, Ted and Gayle Rotenska looked on with deep concern.

As Wil got closer, he heard Pru ask Jones about Helen's condition, and the others bent their heads closer to listen.

"I'm not sure."

Jones' matter of fact delivery couldn't hide the distinct undertone of concern in his voice.

"She's in surgery now. I was promised a report about twenty minutes ago, but I haven't heard anything."

Jones turned toward Wil and gave him a rueful look.

"Hi Wil."

Pru raised an eyebrow at their obvious familiarity.

"I didn't really expect to see you here, Wil."

"What do you mean?"

"Well, with the charges against you and all, I figured you'd have your hands full."

Wil flushed.

"You don't think I did it, do you?"

"I don't know what to think. I know it doesn't look good."

Pru's frosty attitude hit Wil in the gut like a fist. Did she mean it didn't look good for him, or for the symphony?

He turned back to Jones.

"What happened?

"I found her unconscious in the cupola at her house. There was a forty-five handgun on the floor. We'll have to wait and see what the doctors tell us about what happened."

Pru's wide eyes stood out in sharp contrast to her ashen face.

"What were you doing there?"

"I stopped by to talk with her. The house looked empty, but her car was there, and I thought I saw a light inside the house. The front door came open when I tried it, so I went in. Good thing I did."

Greta spoke in a shaky voice.

"How long had she been lying there?"

"I don't know that either."

Jim Pearce suddenly appeared in the doorway.

"I heard there was a fuss going on. What's up?"

Pearce jammed his hands in his pockets and stared intently at Jones. He looked genuinely stricken.

Pru answered first.

"Helen had some kind of an accident at home."

"What kind of accident?"

Wil had never heard Pearce sound so distressed.

Before they could say anything else, a youngish man in surgical garb approached.

"I need to speak with Detective Jones?"

"I'm Jones.

"I'm Dr. Mark Janson. Were you the one who brought in Helen Rubinstein?"

"Yes. How is she?"

"I really can't discuss that with anyone but the police and her next of kin."

Pru jumped in emphatically.

"She has no family, at least for thousands of miles. The rest of these people work closely with Helen. We're as close to family as you're going to get."

Janson looked skeptical, but he apparently decided to forge ahead.

"She's in pretty bad shape. She had some nasty cuts and lost a lot of blood. We're giving her intravenous fluids now. We may have to give her a transfusion."

Jones spoke first.

"What happened? How did she hurt herself?"

"She apparently had been drinking heavily. She had a close call with alcohol poisoning."

"Alcohol poisoning, is that serious?"

"It can be very dangerous, even fatal. She passed out from drinking way too much, way too fast. In that situation the bloodstream continues to absorb alcohol at a very rapid rate. Her brain told her body to get rid of the booze and she started to vomit, even though she was unconscious."

Greta put her hand over her mouth and looked shaken to the core.

Janson looked at her darkly and went on.

"Victims of alcohol poisoning sometimes choke to death on their own bile. She could have anesthetized her brain to the point where her breathing would just shut down. She'd never have woken up."

Jones face looked as haggard as the others

"But Helen's case wasn't that bad?"

"It was bad enough. She apparently fell in a position where she was able to vomit without asphyxiating herself, which could also have killed her. Her fall apparently broke the bottle she'd been drinking from, and she got some deep cuts in her scalp. We had to put in about fifty stitches."

"Could she still die?"

"We'll have to keep a very close watch on her for the next twenty-four hours or so. If she pulls through that, she should be doing much better in a few days. She'll have to take it easy for a while. Is there someone who can help her since she has no family nearby?"

"She can come to my place until she's feeling better!"

Emotion choked Greta's voice to the point where she could barely speak.

"Let us know what help you need Greta. We'll all bring in meals and such, won't we?"

Ted assumed he spoke for everyone and looked around for affirmation.

Pru spoke sharply, sounding like she wanted to shoo everyone out of the room.

"Of course we will. Will there be anything else doctor?"

"I need a contact person, someone we can call in case something happens."

"I'm the administrator at the symphony office. Will that do?"

"I'd prefer a relative. You're sure there's no one."

"No, there's no one."

"In that case, please come with me. We'll need your contact information."

Pearce turned without a word and made a beeline for the exit.

Wil turned to the others, but they all seemed to avoid looking directly at him.

"How did everybody hear about this so fast?"

Greta spoke up.

"Pru called and asked a few of us to come down for moral support. Didn't she call you?"

"No, I got a call from the detective. He thought I might want to be here."

Jones said nothing.

Wil looked awkwardly at the group, unsure of what to say. They all seemed to feel as uncomfortable as he did.

Ted made an effort to smile.

"Well, I guess there's not much else we can do for now. Give us a call when you get Helen home, Greta."

Ted reached a hand toward Wil.

"Good luck with your situation Wil. We're all pulling for you."

The others quickly agreed, but the chorus of timid support evaporated all too quickly.

Wil could see they had no idea what to believe. Maybe he would feel the same way in their position.

The whole situation filled him with shame and frustration. The trap that had been set for him was destroying his life all too successfully.

The group broke up and everyone left quickly.

Jones gave Wil a quick slap on the back as he turned to go, but Wil found his facial expression impossible to read.

Wil waited around until Pru came walking back down the hallway.

She stopped in her tracks when she saw him, but she couldn't avoid him completely without doing a U-turn.

"Oh, you're still here?"

She certainly didn't sound happy about it.

"It wasn't me, Pru. You've got to believe that."

The desperation in his own voice took Wil by surprise.

"That all has to be worked out in court, Wil. In the meantime, I think we'll have to reconsider your position as interim music director."

"What?"

Wil hadn't thought about the job in days, but this caught him completely by surprise.

"I'm innocent, Pru."

"I have to think about the symphony first, Wil. I'm sure you can understand that."

"Sure, that makes sense. I, uh …"

He had no idea what else to say. Her mind seemed to be made up.

"Is there any more news about Helen?"

"She's resting now. We'll just have to wait and see how she does."

CHAPTER FORTY-FIVE

Wil slept poorly again and woke up feeling groggy and drained of energy.

He thought wearily he'd give anything for a peaceful night of deep, healing sleep as he plodded to the bathroom. The thought of Helen hovering near death added another agonizing layer of dread and anxiety to his troubled mind.

Why hadn't he gone to check on her when she didn't answer his calls? Maybe that was asking too much, but the hollow ache in his heart made him wish he had at least tried to find out if she was ok.

He called Ted and Greta to ask about her progress, but neither of them knew anything more.

The hospital switchboard connected him to a nurse on Helen's floor, but the woman's icy voice made it clear she wasn't about to tell him anything. She dismissively said no information about a patient's condition could be released except to family members, and the line clicked dead.

Wil suddenly remembered it was Sunday morning, and he felt a keen longing to go to his church.

He would be the first to admit he didn't devote enough time and energy to nurturing his faith, but he considered belief an important part of his life.

His parents' senseless death at the hands of a drunk driver had shattered the simplistic faith of his childhood. He struggled to believe anything for a long time after that, but over time he came to a deeper, more personal faith.

He believed people's lives moved inexorably in one direction or the other, either upward, toward the light of God's purposes, or downward, into the abyss of darkness.

He couldn't accept the view of good and evil as armies, battling for supremacy. He considered darkness a lack, the absence of light, but he also knew evil and ignorance could stubbornly cling to their death grip on emptiness.

His life only felt meaningful when he tried to move toward the light.

Part of him wished he could serenely believe God would deliver him - and Helen - from all this trouble, but he believed God worked in much more mysterious ways, prodding and leading as people grew through difficulties and trials, not rescuing them, untouched, with magic carpets.

He considered the church a very imperfect part of that dynamic, but he valued the connection it offered with others who sought to grow and learn, and he knew he wanted to be there today.

When he arrived at All Saints Presbyterian he checked his watch. The choir would already be warming up, but he walked slowly to the back door, lingering long enough to savor the bright colors of the daffodils and crocuses lining the sidewalk.

He found it a little difficult to abandon the clean, cool morning air and step into the stale dry confines of the towering building.

The entryway led into a bright basement area where folks gathered to drink coffee and chat before the service. As Wil walked through, people seemed to stare for a second and quickly turn away.

He put his head down and plodded on. Were they really gawking at him? He told himself not to be overly sensitive.

He quickened his step when he got to the rehearsal room, where he could hear Bill Willoughby, the organist and choir director, leading the choir through the morning's anthem.

Willoughby exhorted the singers to pronounce the words clearly and emphasize the dynamic contrasts in the music as Wil pulled on his choir robe, grabbed his folder of sheet music and slipped into his place with the other baritones.

A moment later, Willoughby urged the choir to sing with warm, blending tone and pronounced the anthem ready to go.

The room seemed strangely quiet. An undertone of chatter and laughter usually bubbled up whenever the choir stopped singing, but today everyone seemed to have their heads down.

Wil wondered if he could be the cause. Did everybody know?

He felt his face and neck turning crimson, but it would be very awkward to leave now!

The time for the service had almost come, and the singers quickly filed out toward the sanctuary. Willoughby started to play a stirring prelude, and bright notes surged from the pipe organ in energetic bursts as the choir assembled in the back of the sanctuary.

Wil found the talent of organists like Willoughby thoroughly amazing. He loved to watch their feet flying across the pedals as their hands danced on the keys. Occasionally a toe or finger would dart out to touch a knob on the console, and the organ would shift to an entirely different palette of wondrous tone colors.

When Willoughby accompanied the choir, he often urged the singers onward with a raised arm or a nod of his head, and he always accomplished this magic without the slightest interruption in the music.

Wil took a moment to savor the ornate, dignified décor of the sanctuary. He loved the way the carved stone walls rose in magnificent arches toward the ceiling. The tall stained-glass windows glowed with dazzling colors in the bright morning light, and the dark wood of the pews contrasted dramatically with the red carpet in the aisles.

He scanned the congregation, looking for familiar faces. As usual, quite a few people had come, but there were also lots of empty seats.

Wil knew many churches were more popular. Some he saw on television had huge congregations, but he often felt their approach seemed more like entertainment than a church service. He'd never been particularly comfortable in a setting like that.

He liked the richness and depth of the services here.

After some opening words from the minister, Willoughby filled the air with the opening strains of the first hymn. As the congregational singing began, the choir flowed through the aisles and filed into the chancel area behind the pulpit. They settled into their seats when the hymn ended.

Wil found his attention wandering through most of the service. He usually found the familiar ritual soothing, but today he had an odd sense of unreality, and he felt like he watched everything from a distance.

After the sermon, the choir rose to sing the anthem.

Wil tried to give it his best effort, but his voice sounded raspy and he felt out of synch. His disgust grew as he made more and more silly mistakes, getting the words jumbled, running out of breath before the ends of phrases, and even singing wrong notes.

He hated singing so poorly, but he smiled ruefully as he remembered Norbert Black, a bumbling old gentleman who had died two years earlier. Norbert once told Wil he loved singing so much he sometimes just bellowed out the highest note he could hit. The man's voice wasn't strong enough to make a huge difference in the sound, but Wil believed Norbert's passionate expression had a certain noble grandeur, even if it would horrify a music critic.

Wil had heard many performances that seemed dead, even though they were technically flawless, while others seemed radiant, bursting with vibrant life, despite obvious mistakes in the playing and singing.

Many times, Wil's deepest feelings of authenticity in church services came at totally unexpected moments. He would be moved during a baptism when a grandmother's eyes filled with tears, or as the children gathered around the minister for a story time, and one of them spoke a naïve truth as profound as any bishop at the lectern.

Music often created the most significant parts of the experience for Wil. Sometimes the sermon might seem a bit esoteric, or a certain reading might feel like a drudge, but a sublime musical passage could be a thoroughly transcendent experience for him.

In those moments he felt deep contact with a presence much larger and purer than himself, the infinite God of the universe, who somehow managed to be in intimate contact with human beings. He felt those fleeting glimpses helped him begin to understand, in some small way, the nature of a being he could never fully comprehend.

Today, though, he felt weirdly cut off from everything around him. He wanted to be on his way, and he barely heard a word as the minister pronounced the Benediction.

When Wil stepped back into the choir room, he found it full of people taking off their robes and chatting noisily. Choir membership certainly had an important social dimension. Wil wondered how many people would even be part of a choir if it didn't offer such a good opportunity to visit with friends.

He pushed his folder into its regular storage slot and walked over to the cabinet where the choir robes hung between services.

His friend Doug Butler waved as he slipped his robe sloppily onto a hanger and stashed it in its accustomed place.

"Hi Wil."

"Hi Doug. How's it going?"

"It's going fine with me, Wil. How's it goin' with you?"

"Okay, I guess."

"That was quite an article in the paper this morning."

"What?"

Wil hadn't seen the newspaper in days.

"What'd it say?"

"It talks all about you and this murder. It says you've been charged with it and you're going to stand trial."

"Oh my God."

"I'm afraid it was pretty detailed."

Wil suddenly wanted to run from the room. His blood felt like ice in his veins.

"You don't think I could do something like that, do you, Doug?"

"No way! We're your friends here, Wil. We know better."

Wil looked around and saw most of the people in the room standing at a distance or keeping their backs to him.

The place seemed to be emptying much more quickly than usual.

Wil blurted out the only thing that came into his head.

"I didn't do it, Doug!"

Doug clamped a huge hand on Wil's shoulder.

"Don't worry. You'll come through this, Wil."

"I can't help worrying."

"Yeah, I guess not. Is there anything you need?"

"Just some proof about what really happened. You can't help me there, can you?"

Wil choked out a strained laugh, and Doug smiled with a knowing look.

"Wish I could, Wil, I wish I could. Hang in there buddy."

Doug took his hand away and turned to go.

Wil felt a sudden surge of emotion, and tears stung his eyes.

"Thank you, Doug."

He turned his attention to arranging his robe on the hanger.

Wil felt utterly alone as he walked out to this truck. Who really cared what happened to him, whether he lived or died?

For the first time, Wil wondered if he should pack what he could into his truck and run for his life.

The idea sounded idiotic, but it also had a undeniable appeal.

As he drove away, he took no notice of the dusty, black Cadillac that pulled away from the curb and merged easily into the light traffic several hundred yards behind him.

CHAPTER FORTY-SIX

Jones rinsed out his coffee mug absentmindedly and set it in the sink.

He could see nothing but darkness through the kitchen window, but the sun would be rising soon.

He'd woken up two hours earlier than he wanted to. Questions about the murder kept popping into his head, so he knew he wouldn't be falling back to sleep. He finally groaned and headed toward the shower.

Going to work got harder with each passing day. He really hadn't minded until his sixtieth birthday, but after that, he felt more and more that he had done his part. Was it wrong to think he deserved some freedom and time to himself? The world's problems would continue to swirl and fester with or without him.

He certainly didn't want to spend the rest of his life in an easy chair, but he knew he could find more enjoyable things to do than sitting at that desk waiting for another call to a crime scene.

As usual, the problems of the day filled his head as he ate his cereal and toast.

He took his time finishing his coffee. Helen's accident - or whatever it had been - perplexed him.

The alcohol poisoning might have been unintentional, but why did she have the Glock with her? Helen certainly doubted Falcano loved her, but did she really feel so lonely and frightened that dying seemed the only way out?

That explanation just didn't make sense.

She felt trapped in St. Cecile, but why? She owned a glorious piece of land. It had to be worth a fortune! She might be a complete pessimist, but it seemed hard to believe her prospects were that grim. Everyone described her as enormously talented. There had to be a lot of ways for her to make a good living.

What else could make her want to kill herself?

Could she have killed Falcano? Could she be riddled with guilt?

Jones didn't think so. She might be capable of killing someone, but if she ever did, Jones thought it would be in a moment of white-hot passion. She wouldn't plan a cold-blooded ambush and assemble a bunch of high-tech gear.

There had to be more to this bizarre situation.

Jones pulled on his beige all-weather coat and started toward the door. He cursed when he realized he'd forgotten his keys. He checked his pockets and the countertop and huffed in mild irritation when he realized he'd have to look further.

He really didn't need all the space in this big old house. He'd just never gotten around to selling it. He'd lived alone since his daughter Julie had left for college about a decade earlier. She lived in Oregon now, with her husband and a child of her own.

Jones often wished Julie lived closer, but her husband had a thriving practice as a heart surgeon and wasn't about to relocate. She had a wonderful life there, and Jones wouldn't disrupt that for the world.

Jones' wife Emily had died just after Julie's seventeenth birthday.

The cancer appeared suddenly and progressed with alarming speed. Having a teenage daughter in the house had been a life-saving grace for Jones.

He and Julie helped each other through their grief and developed a bond that time or separation could never diminish. They talked on the phone regularly, and when they were together, they made the most of it and enjoyed each other's company enormously.

Jones adored his granddaughter Amanda and relished every chance he got to see her.

The keys weren't turning up in the kitchen. Jones checked his watch impatiently and tried to recall where he might have put them last night.

Little had changed in the house since Julie moved out, and the place still had a distinctly feminine quality from the frilly cushions and lacy curtains Emily had loved.

Jones spent most of his down time in the informal living room. His favorite recliner gave him an excellent view of the tall maple trees in his neglected back yard. The large television and overstuffed couch reminded him of much happier days when Emily and Julie filled the place with warmth and laughter.

The large oak table in the dining room had seen many wonderful dinner gatherings over the years. Now piles of books and papers covered most of it. Jones only used one of the eight chairs, the one closest to the kitchen.

He wondered if he'd ever be willing to sell the house, even when he did retire, but then he realized he cared most about his memories, not the house.

He could probably move quite happily to his place on Torch Lake and never look back.

Jones didn't see the keys on the table or in the living room, so he walked up the stairs.

He habitually made his bed shortly after he got up, but his tidy bedroom had enough comfortable clutter to look lived in.

Jones found the keys on the nightstand, slid them into his pocket, and took a last, quick look around. He liked being at home in the quiet, familiar surroundings he knew so well. His social life had dwindled almost to nothing, and that suited him just fine too.

He would be more than ready for a new chapter when he could retire, but for now, this place suited him well.

He exhaled softly and turned back toward the stairs, bracing himself to reenter the world in which he had a little matter of a dead conductor to solve.

As he drove toward the station his thoughts turned back to Helen.

What had driven her to the brink of suicide? And what did that have to do with Falcano's murder?

There had to be some connection.

He pulled out his cell phone and punched in the number for the hospital.

The nurse told him Helen was out of danger, but she wouldn't be able to talk anytime soon.

Jones breathed a sigh of relief, but he remained thoughtful as he stashed the phone in his pocket. He had to get to the bottom of this, but how? No one seemed to know much about Helen's relationship with Falcano, thanks to his obsessive secrecy.

What about the partners in the land deal? The mayor obviously wouldn't be much help.

That left Winston Nicholas.

Jones decided to make a stop at *Le Bon Temps* as the light ahead of him turned green. He let three cars pull through the intersection, then crossed two lanes to turn left.

He found Nicholas standing near the urns of flavored coffee, barking instructions at two servers he called Musette and Ariel. Jones recognized one of them as a kid named Annie.

Nicholas didn't seem to notice the looks of disbelief on the faces of the customers nearby. He did stop speaking in mid-sentence when he saw Jones. His eyes narrowed, but he recovered quickly and smiled as if nothing had happened.

"Oh, hello Detective. I'll be right with you."

He turned back to his embarrassed employees.

"Okay, get back to work. There are lots of people begging for your jobs if you can't be bothered to do things the right way."

They bolted quickly, and Jones wondered how often Nicholas had to hire new workers. Somehow he doubted people were waiting in line for the opportunity to work here.

"Well, Mr. Jones. What can I do for you?"

Nicholas appeared to be all smiles, but Jones could sense the tension just below the surface.

"I wondered if we could talk for a few more minutes."

"Sure, give me just a second."

Nicholas made a show of attending to more details in the restaurant before they retraced their steps to his office.

"Sit down, Detective. What's on your mind?"

"I'm wondering about that land development proposal we were discussing."

Nicholas smiled expansively.

"I told you, there's nothing to tell."

Too smooth. He's thought through what he wants to say.

"Maybe so, but I'd like to ask a few more questions. Maybe I can jog your memory. Something that seems like nothing to you may turn out to be important."

"Go ahead, but you're wasting your time."

"What were you planning to build out there?"

Nicholas made a show of furrowing his brow.

"Oh, a hotel, a golf course, some home sites, pretty standard stuff."

"Did you ever see the plans?"

"I'm not sure it ever got that far. If Falcano had some plans, that's news to me."

Nicholas' smile looked too wide, and his eyes hadn't left Jones' face.

Might as well get right to it.

"Why didn't you go ahead with it? Did you run into any problems? Was there some kind of snag that threatened to mess up the whole project."

Nicholas flushed ever so slightly as he pulled his cigarette to his lips.

Paydirt!

He blew the smoke toward the ceiling, and his composure returned.

"What? What kind of snag? I told you I didn't know that much about it, but I can't imagine what you could be talking about."

"You're sure?"

"Of course I'm sure! What could it be?"

Nicholas looked utterly earnest. Jones made a mental note never to play poker with him.

"I don't know, an outstanding debt, a construction problem, you tell me."

"Like I said, Detective, things never got that far. I think you're barking up the wrong tree."

"Ok, I thought it might be worth a try. If you think of something, give me a call, okay?"

"Yeah, sure."

Fat chance.

"Anything else I can do for you, Mr. Jones."

"I'll be in touch."

Jones scowled at the thought of Nicholas' smug look as he walked back to his car.

Don't be too happy mister. As far as I'm concerned, you just confirmed there's something rotten to the core about this deal.

I just have to find out what it is!

Wil scanned the newspaper article for what had to be the fiftieth time.

The first half dozen times he felt a giant fist squeezing his guts. He couldn't breathe and his eyes stung with humiliation and frustration.

This couldn't be happening!

The intensity of his initial reaction gradually subsided, but the feeling of disbelief and outrage only intensified.

The headline trumpeted "Local Musician Arrested on Murder Charge." The rest of the story sounded so matter of fact, so cut and dried. It made everything sound so simple, so damning.

It described him as a "forty-two year old free-lance musician with no apparent steady income."

Why wouldn't he just go ahead and kill somebody? He had no life!

The reporter had a surprisingly thorough rundown of what the police knew. Wil wondered who had been responsible for leaking that.

He had a pretty good idea!

Vivid descriptions of the murder weapon and triggering device led into wildly erroneous claims about his ability to build that kind of a trap.

Unfortunately, the bogus 'facts' sounded very convincing in print.

The *coup de grâce,* the credit card receipt, sounded like the ultimate clue in a Sherlock Holmes story.

The whole article made him sound like a desperate, envious hanger-on who had everything to gain by Henri's death and nothing much to lose.

A galling sense of unreality burned in his stomach. Every time he started to reread the vile story, he willed it to change and become more truthful, more evenhanded, but the same clinical, hard words remained fixed on the page.

The words that made him sound like a cold blooded killer.

Wil's fury surged, and he crumpled up the paper and tossed it against the wall.

Actually, he'd crushed it into a ball and straightened it out several times already. He could barely read it now, but he knew every disgusting word by heart.

He flopped into a chair, rubbed his forehead with the fingers of his right hand and told himself to calm down.

It's just an article in the newspaper. Nothing's really changed!

But as soon as Wil thought that, he knew the publicity changed everything.

People would see him as guilty. Presumption of innocence. Hah! They would consider him one of those oddball killers that nobody really noticed until they committed a brutal crime.

'He seemed nice enough. I never dreamed he could be a murderer.'

Arrgghhh!

Even his friends, what would they think?

They'd all doubt him now, wouldn't they? Just like Pru. It hadn't taken her long to decide he had to go as the interim music director.

How could he ever get his good name back? Even if he got acquitted, no one would ever look at him the same way again.

He just couldn't wait here. He knew he had to do something, but what?

How could he even begin to prove his innocence?

He sat back down in the chair and held his head in his hands, trying desperately to think. There had to be a way. He couldn't just let this happen.

How could he fight back?

Just then he thought he heard a noise behind him.

As he started to turn, something hit him very hard, just behind his right ear.

The sharp, searing pain and the suddenness of the blow shocked him, but only for a fraction of a second.

Then he lost consciousness.

CHAPTER FORTY-SEVEN

Jones walked into the police station warily. He wasn't in any mood to lock horns with the chief.

Fortunately, he didn't see Manning anywhere.

Jones noticed the guys in the station avoiding eye contact with him as he worked his way over to his desk.

He tried to shrug off the slight, but it rankled.

Everybody knew about his conflict with Manning, and after that hatchet job in the paper, they would all think he had been wrong.

Well, so be it. This job wasn't supposed to be a popularity contest!

He only saw one way out of this mess. He had to find out what really happened, and he'd better hurry. The pressure would get much worse, much faster, now that the story had come out in the open.

Manning would probably try to make him leave the case alone and let the district attorney take over. If the chief gave him a direct order to stop, he'd be on very thin ice to keep pursuing it. He certainly wouldn't get any help from his colleagues.

Time to get crackin'!

His gut still told him Falcano's death, the development deal and Helen's breakdown were all related. Jones had clearly touched a very sensitive nerve when he asked the mayor about the plans, and Nicholas' defenses were on high alert.

Jones had no doubt Helen knew more than she had told him, but talking with her was like taking apart a set of those wooden Russian dolls. Whenever you opened one, you found a smaller one inside, and another one inside that. It went on and on.

He knew he could peel through all the layers, eventually, but how long would it take?

Wait a minute!

Jones flipped open his address book, found the number he was looking for, and pressed the numbers on his phone.

"Hullo?"

"Vern? This is Peter Jones."

"Hi Peter. How are you? I read about you in the paper yesterday."

"Well, that's kinda what I'm calling about. I think the kid's innocent."

"What?"

"It's a long story. Look could we get together for a few minutes? I need to pick your brains about something."

"Yeah, meet me at the coffee shop next to the college. Say, twenty minutes?"

"That'll be great. Are you sure you have time?"

"Sure, I don't have a class until 11:00. You're buying, you know. And I'm feeling hungry for one of those three egg omelets."

"You got it."

A few minutes later Jones walked into The Pewter Spoon. He'd arrived early, partly for time to think, but mostly to get out of the office.

Jones savored the unpretentious atmosphere as he claimed a table and ordered a cup of coffee. A goofy collection of knick knacks hung on the walls, nondescript tables and comfortable chairs filled every available space, and the carpeting looked as old as time.

The customers today included an older couple that could be anyone's grandpa and grandma, four construction workers in dusty flannel shirts, and a group of feisty codgers nursing cups of decaf while they pontificated about the world's problems.

Jones loved the place.

He couldn't wait to see his old friend Vern Webster.

Vern taught geology and chemistry at St. Cecile Community College and directed a highly regarded pre-engineering program there.

Jones always appreciated his common sense and his ability to explain difficult scientific concepts in terms anyone could understand. He had always heard him described as a very popular teacher, and he didn't doubt that for a second.

Webster breezed in after a few minutes, and they bantered back and forth until they ordered some breakfast.

Vern gave Jones a quizzical look as he tucked his menu behind the condiment tray.

"Ok, Pete, tell me what's goin' on."

Jones stared back intently.

"He didn't do it, Vern."

"It sounded like he did in the paper."

"Yeah it did, didn't it?"

Jones arched his eyebrows to emphasize the sarcasm in his voice.

"What about that receipt? That seems clear as crystal."

"It's too pat, Vern. It has to be a setup. I know it all sounds bad, but I've gotten to know this kid, and there's no way he could have done it."

"Well, who did then?"

"That's what I'd like to know!"

"And that's where I come in?"

"Maybe"

"I knew you weren't just buying me breakfast out of the goodness of your heart."

"Well enjoy it. I'm gonna make you earn it."

Their food came, and Webster dug into his cheesy omelet with obvious enthusiasm.

He laughed as he savored his first mouthful.

"What can I do?"

Jones took equal pleasure in his plate of eggs, potatoes and bacon. He could hear his doctor telling him to have oatmeal instead, but he was in no mood to worry about extending his lifespan fifteen minutes by denying himself.

The delicious, salty combination of egg and potato probably added twice as much time by the joy it brought him!

"A big part of this whole thing is a land development Falcano wanted to build over by Lake Michigan. I don't know if it was a motive for the murder, but I know in my gut it connects somehow. Something went wrong and I've got to figure out what it was."

"Tell me more."

"They wanted to put in a big hotel, two golf courses, upscale houses, the works. It was all hush hush, and I can't get the other partners to tell me a thing about it."

"Who were they?"

"I can't get into that right now. Suffice it to say some very important people are involved"

"Ohhhh-kay."

"Nobody else seems to have a clue the whole thing was even in the works. The secrecy is mind boggling."

"So how can I help?"

"What kinds of things could create a fatal flaw in a project like that? The planning seemed to be going great guns, then the bottom fell out. I'm trying to figure out why. I think they must have hit some kind of snag they couldn't get around."

"Hmmm, that makes sense.

Concentration knit Webster's brow as he took another enormous bite of eggs, cheese and veggies.

"Let's see, what would happen on a big project like that? There would have to be a slew of permits and stuff. Local officials can be a pain in the butt.

Jones voice oozed sarcasm again.

"They may have had an inside track on that."

Webster gave him a questioning look but didn't press the point.

"The neighbors might put up a stink. Sometimes people don't want a big development next door, especially if their backyard happens to look out over Lake Michigan."

"It's a pretty rural spot. I don't think that's the problem. Besides, the whole thing got stuck in the mud before anybody else knew about it. It must be something else. I wondered if there could be some kind of problem with the land or the underlying rock, something like that."

"Oh, ok. Where was it supposed to be?"

Jones told him and described the lay of the land.

"Yeah, I know that area. There's no marshland or other special habitat they'd have to worry about. The state can be real touchy about that kind of stuff. That stretch is based on solid bedrock, and the land slopes right down to the lake at a nice gentle angle. It sounds like an ideal spot."

"It looks perfect. So what could be the problem?"

"I'm thinking toxic waste."

"What?"

"Maybe it could be contaminated."

"I don't think so. It's out in the middle of nowhere."

"You don't have to be in a city to have a toxic waste problem. There are brownfields all over the state."

"Brownfields?"

"Yeah. That's what they call contaminated areas."

"But wouldn't that mean there was some kind of factory there?"

"Nah, maybe there was an old gas station there with leaky tanks. Or other things could have caused it. It's hard to say, but a lot of brownfields are in small towns or villages. Once the old buildings are torn down, you'd never guess anything had ever been there."

"Wow, that might explain a lot. Would something like that stop a development in its tracks?"

"It might. The land would have to be clean as a whistle before you could open it up for tourists and children. The standards are a lot lower if you want to build an industrial site where the potential risks aren't as great."

Jones thought about Helen.

"Would someone who owned a brownfield be liable for the cleanup costs?"

"It used to be that way. A few years ago, anyone who bought property with a waste problem became the new owner of the liability. Sweet, huh? But in 1995 they passed a law saying only the person who caused the contamination could be held liable for the cleanup."

"But someone trying to sell a piece of land like that could have a hard time, right?"

"Well, yeah. The law requires you to do a baseline environmental assessment, and you have to disclose the results to the state and any potential buyers."

"That might fit. The woman who owns the land just had a very bad breakdown. I think she might have tried to kill herself. What if she found out she has a toxic waste spill and can't clean it up. No one would buy the place, right? And the cleanup could cost more than the land is worth. She loses either way."

"Well, not necessarily. The state has an excellent grant program to fund cleanups for brownfields."

"Oh, really? Well, so much for that theory."

"I wonder. She may *think* she's stuck. Not everyone knows about the law, and private individuals can't apply for a cleanup anyway."

"What do you mean?"

"The grants are given to local units of government, a city, county, something like that."

Jones felt a riveting thrill of excitement as pieces fell into place.

"You mean an elected official would have to be involved?"

"Yeah, usually."

Webster looked up from his breakfast and noticed the intense look on his friends face.

"Why, what'd I say?"

"Oh, nothing. Don't worry about it. One more question. Could an elected official get a grant without a lot of people knowing about it?"

"I'm not sure. I suppose a few people would have to know. There'd be a lot of paperwork involved. The right person might be able to pull it off without too much hassle."

Webster laughed.

"You've got that gleam in your eye, Pete. Just who are you fixin' to go after all of a sudden."

"Never mind. Let's just say if this works out I'll buy you breakfast every day for a month."

"Great, I'll start starving myself now so I can really eat hearty."

"Keep this to yourself, at least for now, will you?"

"My lips are sealed, except of course when it comes to taking nourishment. You watch your back, though, if you're going to go tangling with some bigwigs."

"Don't you worry about me, Vern. I can take care of myself. Besides, if they want to fire me I'll just go live on Torch Lake. I'm more than ready to do that anyway."

"Yeah, but not this week, right."

Jones just laughed.

CHAPTER FORTY-EIGHT

Wil struggled to shake off his familiar nightmare of smothering in hot tar.

Then, with a jolt of panic, he realized he wasn't dreaming!

He really couldn't move or see, and he tried not to choke as he struggled to catch his breath. Some kind of thick, opaque hood held his head in a suffocating, claustrophobic grip, and bindings that felt like heavy straps encased his legs, arms and neck in a painful straightjacket.

A wild rush of desperation coursed through his body as he fought to get free.

He couldn't budge! No fly in a spider's web could be trapped any more completely.

Wil tried to shout for help, but the dense material over his mouth muffled the sound into a weird, strangled howl.

Then he heard a gruff whisper, very close to his right ear.

"Take it easy golden boy. Nobody can hear you."

Icy sweat drenched his body as an entirely different kind of fear surged through him.

"What's going on?"

Wil's voice sounded frantic and screechy in his own ears, even through the thick cloth of the hood. His body shuddered as a throbbing pain shot through his scalp.

"Don't you worry. It'll all be over in a few minutes."

This can't be happening!

"Who are you?"

"You don't need to know that either."

The man put a lot of effort into disguising his voice, but it sounded oddly familiar. Wil couldn't quite make out who it might be.

"Can you at least take this hood off, I can't breathe!"

"You wanna see who I am? You'd like that wouldn't you? Well it ain't gonna happen! But I'll do one thing for ya. I need to get this out of my way anyway."

Strong hands rolled up the bottom of the hood far enough to uncover Wil's mouth and nose.

Wil felt an absurd flash of relief as he drank in cooler air. He could see just a glimmer of light in his peripheral vision.

The fresh air seemed to clear his senses a bit, but a deeper sense of dread filled him as he thought about what would come next.

"What are you going to do?"

"Like I said, you'll see soon enough. Now why don't you just shut up? You're not doing yourself any good."

Frustrated rage mixed with Wil's other emotions as he tried one more time to pull free of the restraints.

"Save it. You're not gonna get loose."

Wil could hear the amusement behind the words, and that fueled his aggravation even more.

"Ok, the joke's over. Let me go."

"It's no joke! Here, let's try this on for size."

A hand like a vise pulled open his mouth.

Wil gagged as his assailant jammed a large plastic funnel into his throat and forced his jaws painfully apart.

"Now don't puke on me, kid. This won't take long."

Wil smelled the pungent aroma of bourbon, then thick liquid surged down his throat, searing his esophagus.

His body went rigid with terror and the smothering sensation of drowning.

What the hell?!!

"Don't want you to choke, do we?"

The cruel voice laughed dryly.

"A little at a time is all it takes."

Wil felt violently ill as more of the liquor seared his gullet, and he tried desperately to wiggle his head away.

"Don't make a mess now. You're just making this harder Wil. We don't want to start over, do we?"

Wil struggled with all his might to answer, but he could only manage a strangled, whimpering sound.

"Breathe through your nose and settle down."

His captor squeezed Wil's mouth tightly against the funnel, and Wil had no choice but to take in air through his nostrils.

"Here, let's get some of these in there."

Wil heard a sound like small pellets and felt a new sensation in the back of his throat.

Pills!

"We'll wash those down and try a few more."

A caustic mouthful of the booze carried the pills down his throat. Then a fresh handful of pills dropped through the funnel, followed by another flood of whiskey.

Wil's tormenter gave him a short break to catch his breath, then resumed the process with an even larger handful of pills and a bigger gush of the bourbon.

The vicious cycle repeated again and again.

"They'll think it was all so tragic. The up and coming composer commits a murder and can't live with himself. Took a bunch of drugs and booze to end it all, just like his good friend Helen tried to do. It was great of her to give me the idea, don't you think? That's the beauty of the way I tied you up. It won't leave a trace."

The smugness in the man's voice pushed Wil's rage to the boiling point. He gave everything he had to one last struggle against the restraints, but his fight proved hopeless.

His head started to swim, and he could feel himself losing consciousness. He started to feel a bizarre detachment, as if he watched the whole scene from a place outside his body.

What a strange way to die.

The last thing he ever heard would be this bastard's triumphant crowing!

"Just a little more ought to do it ..."

Wil had to agree as blackness closed in around him.

Jones sat down at the computer and fired up his search engine.

A search for "State of Michigan" quickly led him to ***Michigan.gov***, a colorful website filled with fresh-looking blues and greens. A gorgeous photo of a sunset on Lake Michigan dominated the cover page.

Jones couldn't help noticing the picture could have been taken from the beach at Helen's place.

An impressive menu of links led to boatloads of information about everything from governmental departments to planning a vacation in Michigan.

Jones typed 'toxic waste' in the search box, but that led to several pages of information about landfills and waste facilities.

He clicked back to the home page and tried his search with 'brownfields.'

Bingo!

Page after page of detailed information explained how grants and loans for brownfield redevelopment worked. Applications could be filed by "Michigan local units of government, brownfield redevelopment authorities, or other public bodies created pursuant to state law, including state funded schools and universities."

Jones thought ruefully everything had to be written by lawyers nowadays!

He quickly found a listing of four coordinators for the state redevelopment program. A colorful map told him Sally Purcell in the Cadillac District Office worked with St. Cecile's region.

He jotted down her contact information and punched in the numbers to make the call.

Several questions took shape in his mind before he realized he'd been connected to an answering machine.

Dammit!

After the beep he identified himself as a detective with the St. Cecile Police Department and asked for a return call. He hesitated, then emphasized the urgency of his call and repeated his number one more time.

He hung up the phone thoughtfully.

The possibility of a cleanup grant explained a lot. The mayor would know exactly how to get the funding, and he wouldn't be fazed at all by little niceties like a whopping conflict of interest! Making a huge personal profit from his official actions would probably suit him just fine.

This information made the strange trio of partners much more logical.

Falcano had the land, or he would soon, Nicholas might be providing some up-front money, and the mayor could quietly come up with a redevelopment grant to eliminate whatever kind of toxic cesspool stood in the way.

Jones wondered if Falcano had taken advantage of Helen, or if he really loved her and wanted her to benefit from the project too.

Maybe he'd never know, but first things first.

What if he got through to the grant coordinator and he wasn't able to learn anything important. What if the mayor hadn't even begun the process of applying for a grant?

Even if he had, what if Sally Purcell didn't know about it or wasn't able to release the information?

He knew he'd have a very hard time getting a subpoena without the chief's cooperation, and at this point, he doubted very seriously that Manning would help him.

Suddenly the phone in front of him bleated.

Well, that was quick.

He picked up the handset eagerly.

"This is Detective Jones."

"Mr. Jones, thank God I got you! I think you'd better get over here right away."

"What? ... Where? Who is this?"

"It's Ted Mason. I'm at Wil's."

Ted's voice sounded frantic.

"I think he tried to kill himself. O my God!"

"What?!!"

"I found him unconscious! I've already called 911, they're on their way. Thank God I remembered how you saved Helen. If I hadn't broken into the house, he'd have died before anyone found him."

"Slow down a minute. What happened?"

"I stopped by to check on him. His car was in the driveway, just like Helen's, but no one answered the door. After what happened to her, I couldn't leave without checking on him. Then I saw his legs and feet. He was lying on the floor in the kitchen, white as a sheet. I think I'm going to throw up!"

"What makes you think he tried to kill himself?"

"There's an empty fifth of bourbon and some pill bottles. Here come the paramedics. Detective, you have to come. Wil's innocent. The press and everybody else will act like this is the last straw! You have to help him."

"I'll get there as quickly as I can."

Jones hung up the phone and started toward his car.

Maybe it was the last straw!

Why would an innocent man pull a bonehead stunt like this?

CHAPTER FORTY-NINE

Jones thanked the doctor and hung up his phone with a shake of his head.

They had pumped almost a fifth of whiskey out of Wil's stomach, and the fluid had been laced with Vicodin. The worst danger had passed, but he would probably need to be hospitalized for several days.

One of the empty pill bottles on Wil's kitchen floor had been a prescription for Vicodin with his name on it.

Jones certainly hoped Wil had a good explanation for of all this!

He stood up to go to the hospital just as Chief Manning strode out of his office.

Jones thrust his hand into his pocket and jangled his change in irritation. Hopefully, Manning wanted to talk about something else.

"Well hello, Peter. You still think he's innocent?"

No such luck.

"Hello Walter."

"I think we need to get this guy's bail revoked and pop him back into a cell. If he pulls out of this, he's a definite flight risk."

"I want to talk to him first."

"Talk about what?"

"About what happened."

The chief gave a sound somewhere between a laugh and a sputter.

"What happened?! He tried to kill himself. A child could see it!"

"That's my point, Walter. This so called suicide attempt is just like all the rest of the evidence in this case. It's way too cute to be true. The last time I talked to Wil he was frantic to clear his name."

"What would you expect him to say? His guilt couldn't be more obvious!"

"Chief, when I think it's clear he did it, I'll be the first one to testify against him, but I don't think it's clear at all."

"What do you need, a picture of him setting the booby trap? That's not the way things usually work, Peter."

Jones lost his battle to stay cool.

"Don't tell me how things usually work, Walter. I've been doing this all my life! I'm giving this thing everything I've got, and I need you to back off!"

The color rose just as quickly in Manning's face, and he leaned toward Jones and jabbed with a beefy finger to emphasize his point.

"I think you're making it way too hard, Peter! The answer is as simple as day, and you're trying to make it something complicated!"

"If you think it's so simple take him into custody yourself. I'll wash my hands of it."

"I'll just do that!"

Manning set his jaw at a defiant angle.

"You're going to be sorry you made me do this, Peter."

Jones stared in disbelief as Manning started to turn toward the duty officer.

The chief's interference had really gone too far this time!

Jones struggled to rein in his temper and finally, with a supreme effort of will, he swallowed his pride.

"No, wait a minute. C'mon Walter. We've worked together too long to let this happen. Let me talk to Wil and see what he says."

Manning glowered at him without saying a word.

Jones hurried to take advantage of the chief's hesitation.

"If I feel like Wil is covering up, we'll put a guard on him and take him back to the jail as soon as he can leave the hospital. I'm working hard on some other angles in this case. I really believe there's more to it."

"Like what?"

"Like that land development for one thing. I have some important new information about that."

"So what are you saying? You think the mayor killed him? Or Winston Nicholas?"

"I don't know! I can't figure out just what did happen, but until I do I'm going to keep after it. Wil is not going anywhere. He probably can't even get out of bed. Let me talk to him."

Manning looked like he had just swallowed a slice of lemon.

"Peter, I've given you slack all along on this case because we've worked together a long time, but don't make me regret it."

Jones disagreed strenuously, but he held his tongue as Manning stood back with a smug look of victory.

"Talk with Walker, figure out what happened, and let's get this case into court. Hey, we're on the same team, right? Let's get this taken care of."

The chief smiled tightly and slapped Jones on the back in an unwelcome show of camaraderie.

Jones knew he'd only been given a very short length of rope. He'd better make the best of it! Manning wanted everything to go smoothly. One big happy police force.

Jones thought they could all get along perfectly if the chief would only see things his way, but he decided not to push his luck by saying so.

"I'll give you a call as soon as I've talked with him, Walter. You've always trusted me. Stay with me on this."

"It's too big a case to piddle around with, Peter. We need to get it wrapped up. You can see that, can't you?"

"Sure, I know that. I'll give you a call."

CHAPTER FIFTY

When Jones arrived on the fifth floor, he found Wil walking in the hallway with a massive orderly who could have been a football lineman.

An IV bag hung from a rolling stand at Wil's side, and a clear plastic tube led to a needle in his arm.

Wil looked up with puffy red eyes full of anguish. His gaunt face looked shockingly white above his ludicrous, flowery hospital gown.

He didn't say a word as Jones approached.

"How you feelin' Wil?"

"Lousy."

"The doctor said you're out of danger."

"Hah! That's pretty funny."

Jones hesitated, wishing he had worded that differently.

"What are you doing out of bed?"

"They said I needed to keep walking to fight off the effects of the drug. If I lie down I'll just go to sleep, and they want me to stay awake."

Jones fell in step with Wil's baby steps, and their strange procession crept down the hallway.

"What happened, Wil?"

"What happened? You're never gonna believe it. There's no point in me even telling you."

"Give it a shot."

"Somebody hit me and knocked me out, ok? Look at this bruise on my head."

Jones didn't want to state the obvious.

"The D.A. will argue you hit your head falling to the floor."

Wil looked back at him sourly.

"Is that what you think?"

"Never mind what I think, tell me what happened."

Wil scowled.

"When I came to I was tied to a chair with a big hood over my head. The guy jammed a funnel down my throat and started pouring in booze and pills. I figured I was dead for sure."

"Who was it?"

"I couldn't tell. I never got a look at him, and he disguised his voice."

"What about more subtle clues? How big a person was it?"

"I was tied in a chair with my eyes covered. All I could feel was the funnel being jammed into my mouth. It could've been anybody."

Jones watched a heartbreaking look of utter desolation cross Wil's face.

"He was trying to kill me! He laughed when he said it would look like a suicide. He was proud of himself for tying me up with some kind of straps that wouldn't leave a trace."

They had come to the end of the hallway, so the trio turned and started back the way they had come.

"It's evil, Mr. Jones, monstrous! I have to do something to protect myself. What can I do?"

"You need to let us handle this, Wil."

"I'm not waiting around for your people to save me, Mr. Jones."

Jones couldn't blame him, but he didn't say so.

"So you have no idea who it was?"

Wil looked up incredulously.

"What do you mean? You believe me?"

"I honestly don't know what to think at the moment. I want to hear what you have to say."

Wil peered at him warily, then seemed to decide that was good enough, at least for now.

"I thought I could hear something familiar, but I couldn't place it. I just don't know detective. It's driving me crazy!"

"Well, it was a man anyway. Something may come to you as time goes on. If it does, give me a call as soon as you can."

Wil nodded as they plodded by his room.

"I'm telling the truth, Mr. Jones! I know it sounds crazy."

Suddenly his voice sounded stronger.

"But I'm just so damn frustrated! Someone is trying to get away with murder by making me look like the killer! He tried to kill me and make it look like I committed suicide out of guilt."

"That makes sense, but we need proof."

"If I go on like this I'm going to die, Mr. Jones."

"What?"

"I'm completely helpless in here. If I don't do something I'm going to be killed in my sleep … or die in the electric chair."

"Michigan doesn't have the electric chair."

"Well, die in prison then. What's the difference?! I can't just wait around for something to happen. If I do, I'll be dead, and someone will get away with this horrible crime."

"You're not in any position to do anything, Wil. You concentrate on getting your strength back and let me worry about finding the killer."

"You believe me then?"

"I've always believed you, Wil. I've wondered what the hell was going on a few times, but I just don't think you're a killer. I don't think you could do it if you wanted to."

"I appreciate that Mr. Jones, honestly, but I can't count on you or anybody else. I have to save my own hide."

Jones' gut burned as he watched Wil's creeping gait. He wished desperately he had some concrete help to offer.

"How are you going to do that? You can barely walk"

"I don't know, but I have to try."

"Don't be crazy. You're in a hospital with a tube sticking out of your arm. You just stay here and get your strength back. What could happen here? There are people everywhere."

Wil looked away.

"Maybe you're right."

"I'll go back to your house and see if I can find any evidence to help us track down this guy."

"Take me with you."

"Forget it Wil. Is there a way I can get into the house?"

Wil stared wearily at the floor.

"There's a key under the doormat."

"Thanks. I'll talk to you soon, okay?"

"Yeah, sure."

When Jones footsteps died away, Wil told the attendant he felt better and could keep walking by himself.

The guy looked unsure, but his boredom quickly won out. He said he'd check back in a few minutes and sauntered off toward the coffeepot.

Wil felt like a trapped animal.

His tormenter would come back and finish him off if he didn't leave here now!

He always thought it looked laughable when someone in the movies got dressed and staggered away from a hospital, but that was exactly what he had to do.

It wouldn't be easy. Wil felt like a limp dishrag, and getting away undetected would be almost impossible in the seemingly quiet hospital.

People came and went in totally unpredictable patterns. Elevators dinged constantly in the distance, employees with large carts made regular trips through the hallways, and the nurse's station at the end of the hall never seemed to be empty.

Wil shuffled to his room, trying desperately to look casual.

He found his clothes in a white plastic bag and stuffed it under his gown. The bundle wasn't too obvious, but he certainly didn't want to give anyone a good look at it.

His wallet and keys weren't here. They must be at his house.

Damn it!

He wobbled over to the door and peeked down the hallway.

He felt like a silly five-year-old sneaking around after bedtime, but he wasn't about to turn back now.

Things seemed to be quieter than usual, so he stepped back into the hallway and resumed his snail-paced walking.

He felt surprisingly calm now that he had made up his mind to leave.

There was only one nurse at the desk, so Wil headed toward the exit sign at the far end of the short hallway.

Maybe the movies weren't as ludicrous as he thought.

He waited until the nurse made a phone call and watched gratefully as she leaned back in her chair, turned away from him and began talking intently.

Now!

He picked up his pace ever so slightly and hurried toward the exit, giving a quick glance to be sure the nurse hadn't turned his way.

When he got to the door, he pulled it open and stepped through as quickly as he could, pulling the IV stand in behind him.

His heart pounded and his head swam as he leaned against the wall and fought for control.

He thought for a minute he would faint.

When he felt a little better, he pulled up the tape on his arm and tugged out the IV needle. Blood oozed from the hole in his skin, so he bunched up part of his gown and pressed it against the wound, squeezing his forearm against the bicep to hold the makeshift compress in place.

He fought a powerful urge to panic as he pulled on his clothes. Rushing too fast could give him away and ruin everything, but he had to get out of here before someone checked his room and realized he had bolted.

His stomach flip flopped when he stood up too quickly after tying his shoes, and his head throbbed in violent protest of the entire venture.

Take it easy!

He didn't see any place to hide the IV stand, so he pushed it into the corner. That would have to do.

He told himself he could make it and started down the stairs.

If someone caught him now, he'd be back in jail for sure.

He had to make sure that didn't happen.

CHAPTER FIFTY-ONE

Helen barely heard her tiny steps as she floated into the kitchen like a ghost.

The heels of her slippers scarcely left the floor, and her body seemed weightless.

She walked across to the table and settled into her regular chair, wondering vaguely what she would see if she looked into a mirror.

Greta had dropped her off the evening before, promising to check back soon.

Pru and Greta wanted her to stay with one of them, but she numbly insisted on going home and made them leave her alone.

They did their best to talk her out of it, but she wouldn't listen.

Eventually they gave in.

She wondered what time it was and guessed mid-afternoon. She must have slept around the clock.

With a quivering hand, she reached into the grimy pocket of her robe and pulled out a cheap plastic lighter. She flicked it three times before it caught, but she finally lit a cigarette and inhaled as deeply as she could.

She watched impassively as the smoke rose in delicate patterns through the stale air and dissipated near the ceiling.

Bright shafts of sunlight poured in through the large windows, making the contents of the neglected room stand out in stark relief.

The grim darkness in the closed-up house made the light seem like an intruder.

Helen looked at the invading brightness incredulously.

As a child she had loved the sunshine, always begging to stay outside until the last rays faded into the night.

Poignant memories of blissful days rushed unbidden into her mind. She could almost see her mother's kind smile and the infinite blue depth of the cloudless sky. She felt again the perfect security of her father's strong embrace as he hoisted her onto his shoulders.

Suddenly, an intense feeling of terror shot through her body. She struggled to catch a breath as cold sweat bathed her skin.

What in God's name had she done?

Had she really tried to kill herself? She could only recall a muddled fog of impressions.

She did remember feeling terrible, thinking everything was hopeless.

Well it was hopeless, wasn't it?! What could she do?

A vivid memory of the terrible, nauseating sensation filled her mind. She felt the pungent liquor filling her stomach as clearly as if it just happened.

A horrifying sensation of drowning in a sticky, amber flood washed over her.

She closed her eyes and ran a fluttering hand over her forehead.

She had carried the gun up there too. Would she have used it?

Could she have?

A violent tremor shook her body. Her quaking abdomen felt utterly empty, as if her internal organs had been cut away.

Helen looked back at the cigarette in her hand. The acrid tendril of smoke curling up from it suddenly seemed like the last remnant of an all-consuming fire.

Had her entire life burned down to ashes?

The thick, yellow skin on her fingers didn't even look like part of her own body.

An overwhelming flood of revulsion surged into her soul.

She stabbed the cigarette violently into the overflowing ashtray and looked with deep yearning toward the brilliant shaft of light flooding into the room.

An almost-forgotten ache pierced the core of her spirit.

When had she forgotten the dreams of her childhood? When had she lost the ability to play, to hope?

She ran and stood in the center of the cleansing shower of light, tossing back her head and running her fingers through her hair, as if the radiance could rinse it clean and flush out the darkness and neglect that filled her soul, just as it did this decaying old house.

She threw open her robe and let the warmth caress her skin through her sheer gown.

Tears filled her eyes, but for the first time in an eternity, they weren't tears of fear or self-pity.

She wept with an overwhelming feeling of release.

She knew she stood at a crossroads. One road led toward life, the other inexorably toward death.

Her heart chose life.

She looked around the room as if she'd never seen it before.

How had she let things get so foul and filthy? She reached for her pack of cigarettes and threw them into the trash.

She felt an incredible, unfamiliar sensation as a joyous laugh burst from her mouth.

Her mind felt clearer than it had in ages.

Something fundamental had shifted in her spirit and the change was permanent, life-giving. By some gentle miracle, she had escaped from the black despair that had taken over her soul, and she knew she would never slip back into its depths.

She also understood this moment wasn't some kind of magical, fairy-tale ending. The powerful feeling of transcendence would fade, and none of her problems would just vanish, but she had slipped out of the trap of believing they held her destiny in an iron grip.

She might lose the house, and she had to grieve Henri's loss and move on. She might have to start over without a penny to her name, but others had done that and more, and so could she.

Her body would crave the nicotine and would struggle mightily before giving it up.

She would need help, but she knew she could count on Greta and some of the others to provide the unflagging support she would need, and she felt ready to accept their gifts without suspicion and resentment.

She practically danced into the large dining room, tossing back the heavy drapes and letting sunlight fill the room.

A thick film of dust covered everything, making the scene look for all the world like some kind of antique photograph.

Helen abruptly realized she was making a mental checklist for how she would clean and scrub and polish.

It would take a long time, but the work would be a healing penance. She would be mending and cleansing her soul as she purged the grime and decay from the house.

She remembered vividly how proud she felt when she helped her mother as a little girl, how they would admire a table filled with dazzling silver or the gleaming wood of a freshly-polished floor.

A delicious sensation of new freedom filled her heart as she ran from room to room, pulling back curtains, opening windows and letting fresh air flush out the staleness that made the house feel like a huge tomb.

Her eyes fell on her violin as she walked into her bedroom, and her heart longed to make music again.

She remembered how intensely she used to love holding the violin near her body and coaxing out glorious melody. She savored the memory of little things about playing, the delicate, antique smell of the wood and the sticky sensation of rosin on her fingers.

When she was younger she would practice for hours, hardly noticing the time passing. The grueling scales and technical exercises never seemed like a burden to her. They were servants to help her learn how to play thrilling cascades of sound and make them sound effortless, magical.

She remembered the joyous day her tireless practice came to fruition and she played her debut recital in St. Petersburg. The sound had truly soared as her hands danced above the fingerboard and guided the bow across the strings.

Americans said her Russian soul made her a great artist.

She knew how much work it took to make the music sound that simple, that pure.

It had been so long since she felt that keen desire to practice.

Suddenly she could hardly wait.

It didn't matter if her career was struggling. The deep abiding love for music had rekindled in her soul. That would be enough to sustain her.

Her eyes filled with tears once more, and she breathed a prayer of thanks.

As she opened the last curtains in the living room, she saw a large black Cadillac turning into her driveway.

When it pulled up near the house, a man got out and started walking toward the front porch.

Oh, it was only him.

CHAPTER FIFTY-TWO

Wil tried to look inconspicuous as he staggered across the hospital lobby.

His crazy hopes for a safe getaway took a nosedive when he surveyed the sprawling lawn and huge parking lot of the hospital grounds.

Nice plan, genius! Now what are you going to do?

Someone would spot him for sure if he tried to walk away, and he wasn't at all sure he could walk that far anyway. The three mile drive to St. Cecile hadn't even entered his mind. How could he even dream of getting all the way to his house?

He could probably find some way to make a phone call. But who could he trust?

Jones? No! Jones would arrest him in a heartbeat.

Pru? No way!

Then, miraculously, Ted walked through the door carrying a ridiculous, bright-orange planter full of greenery and white flowers.

Good old Ted!

Wil hesitated. Could he take his old friend into his confidence?

He had no choice!

He walked over, trying to look casual, and tapped Ted on the shoulder.

"Hi Ted."

"Hey, Wil! What the … did they let you out?"

"Not exactly."

"What?!"

"I'll tell you later. Do have your car here?"

"Sure, why?"

"I need a ride, and a big favor."

"What's that?"

"I'll tell you on the way."

Ted's eyes widened with skepticism.

"Are you sure about this? What's going on?"

"Everything's fine. C'mon, let's go."

Ted knit his brows and scanned the lobby.

Wil almost panicked, thinking Ted might call a security guard, but his friend's genial nature won out.

"Ok, if you say so."

"Um, would you mind picking me up here? I'm not feeling too great."

Ted looked at him with hurt and serious questions in his eyes, but he mumbled his assent and left at a brisk trot to get his car.

Cold sweat trickled down Wil's back as he sat outside the door, wishing he could make himself invisible.

Finally, Ted pulled up in his old Datsun, and Wil sank into the seat with a sigh of exhaustion.

"Thanks Ted, you're the best."

Ted's face gave ample evidence of the alarm bells going off in his head.

"Now are you going to tell me what this is all about?"

"Let's get going first."

Ted maneuvered the car out of the parking lot, waited until the light turned green and turned right toward St. Cecile.

"Where to, Wil."

"Can you take me to my house?"

"Sure.

As usual, Ted settled in near the right edge of the pavement at ten miles an hour below the speed limit. Three cars passed them before they got half a mile.

Wil squirmed down into the seat and shifted his gaze constantly, trying to see everything at once.

"Can't you move it along a little bit, Ted? I'm afraid someone will recognize me!"

"Ok, Ok."

He pressed his foot on the gas pedal and the car sped up almost imperceptibly.

"All right, now spill, buddy. Why are you leaving the hospital looking like death warmed over? How come you're standing in the lobby with no ride, no luggage, nothing?"

"I had to get out of there, okay? Someone tried to kill me, Ted! It was a miracle he didn't succeed."

"What?! We thought you tried to kill yourself. That's what everyone said."

"Do you think I would do that, Ted?"

A look of intense distress crossed Ted's face.

"Well, I don't know. No, I guess not … but it all seemed so obvious. What do you mean someone tried to kill you?"

Wil's self-control snapped.

"What do you think? Someone broke into my house and bashed me over the head. He tied me up in a chair and poured booze and pills down my throat."

Ted wilted as Wil vented his fury.

"Couldn't you just spit the stuff out?"

"He crammed a funnel in my mouth. You think I just sat there asking for it? C'mon, Ted!"

"No, that's not what I meant. It just seems so bizarre, that's all."

Wil regretted snapping at Ted, but he was in no mood to apologize.

"It was unbelievable."

Ted checked the rear view mirror nervously as he turned onto the rougher pavement of the road to Wil's house.

They'd only been in the car a few minutes, but it seemed to Wil like an eternity.

Ted looked a him hopefully.

"Could you tell who it was?"

"No, but he's going to try again when he realizes I didn't die. If the police take me back to the hospital, I'll be helpless. I have to get away from here."

"Wil, the police are trying to solve this thing. You have to give them a chance."

"Most of the police think I'm guilty as hell! I have to try to take care of this myself."

Ted finally bristled.

"Yeah, right. How can you do that?"

"Spare me the sarcasm, ok? If you can't help, at least don't turn me in."

"I think you're making a big mistake, Wil. If you run it just makes you look guilty."

Wil's emotions flashed to the boiling point.

"If I stay here, I'm dead, one way or another! Don't you get it?"

Wil saw panic along with the hurt in Ted's eyes.

Then Ted seemed to realize Wil was deadly serious, and his expression softened.

"Aw-right, I won't say anything, but you be careful Wil. You're scaring me."

"You're not as scared as I am, old buddy."

Wil stared into the distance fiercely. He could feel Ted studying his face.

"What else can I do to help?"

"Sorry, there's nothing. I have to do this by myself."

"Where can you go?"

"I don't know yet. But even if I did, I couldn't tell you. If you don't know you can't tell anyone."

Ted sputtered.

"Do you think I'd rat you out?"

"Who knows? Maybe not intentionally. Maybe you'd decide you were doing it for my own good. I just can't take the chance. I'm sorry, Ted."

Ted gripped the wheel with both hands and stared straight ahead.

"I understand."

They pulled into the driveway and Wil looked around cautiously.

"There doesn't seem to be anyone around. Thanks Ted. I owe you a big one."

"You don't owe me anything. But you be careful. I mean it."

"Ok, I appreciate it. And I mean that."

They parted awkwardly, and Ted drove away.

Wil unlocked the door and went inside with all of his senses on high alert. He threw some clothes and toiletries into an old duffel bag, locked up, and hurried over to his old pickup, scanning nervously in all directions.

He would have to stay on the back roads for a while. He wondered if the police would be looking for him yet.

As he left the driveway, he breathed a small sigh of relief.

He'd gotten away. Now what?

As Wil's truck disappeared in the distance, the black Cadillac crept out of a wooded lane. Without the slightest hesitation, the big car lumbered onto the pavement and sped off in the same direction.

CHAPTER FIFTY-THREE

Jones exhaled loudly as he slouched into the overstuffed chair in Jeanette Field's office.

He'd hardly seen a soul as he walked through the Daily News Building, and he wondered how long the paper could stay afloat.

Jeanette's wry expression made her seem completely unconcerned.

She laughed lightly as Jones loosened his tie and flopped his elbows onto the broad leather armrests.

"You look like you could use a breather."

"I'm thrilled to be anywhere that's not the police station."

"I can understand that. Wil's taking off makes your life a lot more complicated, doesn't it, Peter?"

"You better believe it."

"Why do you think he ran?"

Jones made a sound halfway between a breath and a snort.

"Why? The article you published in the paper didn't help!"

"I'm not a censor, Mr. Jones, and my reporters do what they think is best. None of our confidential conversations played a role in that."

"I know. It was just unfortunate. Wil claims someone attacked him. He figured we couldn't protect him, and he probably thought we'd throw him back in jail in a heartbeat when he checked out of the hospital."

"And you disagree?"

"No, I think he had it right. I'd have probably done the same thing in his shoes."

"But you wish he hadn't done it?"

"Running makes him look guilty as sin. This'll clinch things as far as Manning and the mayor are concerned."

"And you think they're wrong?"

He looked up wearily and almost smiled.

"What is this, twenty questions? Yeah, I think they're wrong. I don't think he's a murderer, and right now I think he's scared to death."

"If you catch him, will they press you to take him to trial?"

"Oh, we'll catch him. He's not exactly John Dillinger. And they'll try to lock him up and throw away the key. There's no doubt about that either."

"So what are you going to do?"

"I have to find out what's behind this development scam. The mayor and Winston Nicholas stink to high heaven as far as I'm concerned. This all ties together somehow. I just have to find out how."

"And you're stumped?"

"You might say that. And thanks so much for pointing it out."

Another dry laugh bubbled from her lips.

"You're more than welcome, Detective. Well, I do have a friend at City Hall that might be able to help."

"I'm starting to think you have friends everywhere."

Her eyes sparkled.

"I have my share. You can't be too rich or have too many friends. Her name is Doris Blank. If there's anything buried in the records she'll know how to find it. I'll give her a call and tell her you'll be stopping by."

"I appreciate this, Mrs. Fields."

"Jeanette! And don't you forget it. I'm looking forward to that story, young man."

"And I like that 'young man' business, too."

"You think I don't know that?"

Her laugh was a bit stronger this time, but it didn't begin to ruffle her elegant demeanor. She settled back into her chair and suddenly became very serious.

"Good luck, Peter. I have a distinct feeling you're going to need it."

Doris Blank turned out to be the City Clerk.

A buzz of activity greeted Jones as he stepped into her office, but everything seemed to be under perfect control. It appeared to be a place where you could ask almost anything and get your answer in a flash with a friendly 'Will there be anything else, sir?'

A smiling assistant ushered Jones into Blank's tidy inner office.

The comfortable room managed to look both modest and vibrant at the same time. Splashes of rich color embellished the sparse furnishings to create a feeling of inviting warmth, and nothing seemed out of place.

"Hello, Mr. Jones. How nice to meet you. Jeanette told me you would be coming."

"It's my pleasure, Mrs. Blank. Thanks for seeing me."

"Please, call me Doris."

Doris's tall frame and erect posture made her look almost regal, but her calm smile and bright eyes kept her from seeming pretentious. Jones couldn't see a loose strand anywhere in the elegant arrangement of her hair. She smoothed the dark fabric of her modest dress as she settled behind her desk.

Jones admired the tastefully upholstered chair as he took a seat across from her.

"And you call me Peter, ok? You have an impressive operation here, Doris."

"Thank you. We do our best. What can I do for you?"

Somehow it seemed like the only thing she could possibly have said.

"I'm looking for some information, but I'm not sure where to look. What kinds of records are kept here?"

"All kinds, birth and death certificates, land transactions, you name it. But that's not what you came to see me about, is it?"

"Well, this may sound kind of strange. I need to know if there's been any talk about asking for a brownfield redevelopment grant from the state."

"A brownfield redevelopment grant?"

"Yeah, it's a cleanup program for toxic waste sites. Only governmental units can apply."

"Why don't you ask the mayor?"

"I'd rather not get into that if you don't mind."

"Oh, I see."

Jones had the distinct feeling she understood completely.

He wondered if his desire to avoid Fitzhugh might put a quick end to their conversation, but she quickly turned to her computer, moved the mouse swiftly, and began to study the screen intently.

"It's spelled as one word?"

"Yes."

"Are there any other pertinent facts you can tell me?"

"I'd rather just go with this, at least for now, if that's ok."

She gave him searching look.

"OK, let's try the City Council minutes."

"It must be like looking for the old needle in the haystack, huh?"

"Oh no, we index all the minutes. I just have to find the right reference."

"You index all the minutes?"

"Of course. You just can't rifle through all the old minutes every time you need to look something up."

"That makes sense. I never thought about it."

"It's our job, Mr. Jones."

Her smile was good-natured, but Jones felt a little foolish.

It wasn't long before she spoke again.

"Well, this is interesting. Eldon Fitzhugh asked the City Council to authorize an inquiry about brownfields right at the end of their meeting two months ago.

"What kind of inquiry?"

"That's the strange part. He asked for a council resolution, but this entry makes it sound like nothing but a formality."

"So you're saying he had the resolution all drawn up and acted like it was nothing."

"Exactly, and apparently, the county commission had already acted on the matter."

"Wouldn't something like that normally involve a lot more discussion?"

"Absolutely. Sometimes people will do almost anything at the end of a long meeting when they're tired and want to go home."

It all made sense. Fitzhugh must have asked the council members to approve the document, giving them a vague idea it was just a preliminary step, then gone ahead with a full blown grant proposal.

Suddenly the door burst open. and the mayor stormed in with Chief Manning close behind.

"Mrs. Blank. What the hell do you think you're doing?"

She looked up calmly.

Jones found her obvious lack of concern enormously entertaining.

"These are public records, Mr. Mayor. Every citizen has a perfect right to see them."

"Well, what's he been snooping into?"

"I'm afraid that's not your concern, sir. Besides, we just got started."

Jones resisted the urge to look at her and smile.

Fitzhugh turned to the detective and shook a bony finger very close to his face.

"Why aren't you out chasing that murderer, instead of sitting here making mischief?"

The mayor twisted his upper body around to face the police chief.

"How much longer are you going to put up with this nonsense, Walter?"

Jones thought the stiff, awkward movement looked painful.

He hoped it was!

Manning opened his mouth and shook his head, but he couldn't seem to say anything.

Jones spoke with a quiet, intense voice that even surprised himself. He apparently found Doris's composure inspiring.

"The whole state police force is looking for Wil Walker, Mr. Mayor. What do you think I could do to help?"

He might as well have poured gasoline onto a fire.

Fitzhugh's face turned beet red, and his body stiffened into a rigid line. He leaned menacingly toward Jones' face and waved a crooked finger near his eyes.

"What good do you think you're doing in here? I can't for the life of me imagine what you think you're going to accomplish."

Jones returned the mayor's icy stare without flinching.

"I think you have a very good idea what I'm trying to do, Mr. Fitzhugh, and I think that's why you're so upset."

The mayor stood even taller and glared at Jones with a look of complete shock and utter contempt. Then, incredibly, he laughed, and his whole demeanor made an abrupt and astonishing transformation.

His forced humor could hardly have been more incongruous.

"I have no idea what you're talking about."

He turned to the others with a condescending smile.

"I just want to see this murderer put behind bars, and it bothers me when someone in my employ is running off like a loose cannon."

The mayor turned toward the door, and suddenly his movements were almost graceful. He had become the picture of decorum.

"Now Walter, you see that he keeps on track will you? Thank you for your good work Mrs. Blank."

He raised his hand in a small, stiff wave and walked out.

Jones couldn't believe what he had just seen. Fitzhugh had thrown a terrible temper tantrum, then completely reversed himself. It was probably the most incriminating scene he had ever witnessed.

Walter seemed completely oblivious.

Jones looked over at Doris Blank, and she raised an eyebrow.

Manning finally spoke.

"Peter, I don't know what you're poking into over here, but I've told you over and over again to avoid provoking the mayor."

It was Jones' turn to be speechless.

The chief held his hands behind his back and shook his head slowly.

"Look Peter, Wil Walker is our prime suspect, and he's on the run. That has to be our main concern at the moment. If you think you're onto something else, we can talk about it when we have Walker in custody. I don't know why the mayor gets so upset, it's just part of his personality, I guess, but he's our boss and we have to get along. Is that so hard to understand?"

"No, you look, Walter. This business with the land…"

Manning pointed his hand at Peter's face like a cop stopping traffic.

"Do you have one shred of evidence linking anyone else to the murder?"

"Well, no, but …"

"Then you concentrate on catching Walker. We'll talk about this other matter later."

He turned quickly and breezed out, following in the mayor's footsteps.

Jones turned to Doris Blank.

"Can you believe that?"

Her placid face betrayed no emotion, but Jones sensed her sympathy.

"Good luck, Mr. Jones. I think you're going to need it."

"You're the second person who's told me exactly that."

Jones' cell phone buzzed in his pocket.

"Do you mind if I take this?"

"No, please, go ahead."

"Jones"

"Hi Peter."

Jones recognized the voice of Stan Devins, the desk sergeant at the station.

"We just had a call. A neighbor found Winston Nicholas dead on his front porch."

"What?"

"The caller heard a loud gunshot and went out to investigate, but it was too late."

"How did it happen?"

"Apparently, the perp used a high-powered rifle from a long ways off. Nobody saw a thing."

Jones took down the address and hastily excused himself.

A dozen conflicting thoughts swirled through his head as he hurried toward his car.

CHAPTER FIFTY-FOUR

Wil tried to ignore the violent protests from his aching body as he turned his pickup onto another narrow lane. The sharp pain in his gut worried him most. He tried not to think about possibilities like hemorrhage or permanent damage.

Without really thinking, he had started traveling south. He chose his route, if you could call it that, by dead reckoning on the checkerboard of old farm roads. A few dead ends had ratcheted up his nervous frustration, but he felt very fortunate about the distance he had been able to cover and his luck avoiding major highways.

He nervously scanned for traffic on the road ahead and checked the rear view mirror for the thousandth time. Several trucks and cars had passed him going the other way, and he'd seen a car or two far behind, but the traffic had been mercifully sparse.

He hoped desperately it would stay that way.

His frazzled nervous system wouldn't let him keep a steady pace. Several times he caught the speedometer inching up to seventy or down to forty, but that didn't really matter. He turned off the road if he saw any car that even remotely resembled a police cruiser.

The police had to be looking for him by now, and he knew they could spot his old pickup in a heartbeat.

A different vehicle would be a big help, but how could he get one? He couldn't just stop in somewhere and buy a car. He wanted to stay as far as possible from places with large crowds of people, and how could he pay for it? His maxed out credit card wouldn't even cover the cheapest clunker on the lot.

He knew better than to use a credit card anyway, except as a very last resort. If he did, the police would know about it before he got out the door.

Dismal, nagging worries about his fragile freedom kept intruding into his mind. He'd gotten away, but what if that had been a terrible mistake?

What could he do to clear his name out here in the boondocks?

He couldn't run forever. The police would find him sooner or later, and his exit would probably convince everyone he was guilty.

He remembered Jones saying the murder weapon had been stolen from a gun shop in Texas, near Denton. Maybe he could go there and find out more about that.

It seemed like a very slender thread, but what else could he do?

Deciding on a course of action gave him an unexpected burst of energy, but problems with the plan crowded into his brain and squelched his new-found enthusiasm.

Could he really get there before the cops caught up with him? And what would he do if he did find something?

How could he even find the place? He couldn't remember the name.

He angrily forced the doubts out of his mind. Doing something, almost anything, beat the hell out of wandering around with nowhere to go.

He was going to Texas!

His relief at making a decision eroded in a flash as a wave of dizziness washed over him. He realized he needed some nourishment desperately, and once he allowed himself to think about food, his ravenous hunger overwhelmed him.

Fortunately, a few minutes later, the road approached a busier two-lane highway where bright lights marked the location of a convenience store.

Wil scanned the highway nervously, drove around to the back of the store and parked in the darkest place he could find.

Jones picked up the phone absent-mindedly, but his attitude changed abruptly when he heard the voice on the line.

"Peter Jones."

"Mr. Jones, it's Wil Walker."

Jones' mind raced as he grasped desperately for words that would convince Wil to come in.

"Where are you, Wil?

"I can't tell you that."

Jones fought to keep his voice even.

"You have to. What do you think you can accomplish out there by yourself?"

"I don't know, but I can't wait there until Henri's killer comes to finish me off."

"I know that. We can protect you."

"Yeah, sure."

"Look, Wil, someone shot Winston Nicholas. He's dead."

Wil didn't respond for a moment, and Jones listened intently, hoping he hadn't made a terrible miscalculation.

"So it looks like I'm guilty of another murder, huh?"

"No, this could help clear you. It happened just about the time you were leaving the hospital. Houdini couldn't have gotten a rifle, shot Nicholas, and gotten away clean."

"But you can't prove that, can you?"

Jones knew Wil wouldn't fall for a lie.

"Give us a chance, Wil. You have no hope out there."

"Everyone but you thinks I'm guilty, don't they, Detective?"

"Not everyone."

"Everyone that matters, right?"

Jones' heart sank, and he hesitated, wondering what he could say.

"I thought so."

"That's not the point Wil. Running away just plays into their hand. You have to work with me while I try to solve this thing."

"I'm sorry Mr. Jones, I can't. Look, I called to ask you a question, but I've changed my mind."

"What is it, Wil? Ask me!"

"No, I can't. It was a stupid idea. Don't worry, I'll be ok."

"Wil!"

Jones shouted at the receiver, wishing he could pull Wil in through the phone cord.

The line buzzed as the connection cut off.

CHAPTER FIFTY-FIVE

Wil stared at the pay phone in disbelief. What had he almost done?

He couldn't be thinking clearly!

If he asked Jones about the gun shop, Texas cops would be swarming in the parking lot when he got there.

With a sudden rush of panic he wondered if Jones could trace his call.

No, it was St. Cecile, not the NYPD, and Jones hadn't expected him to call. Wil thought the police could have traced his cell, but not the pay phone.

Just to be sure, he decided to get moving as quickly as he could.

He walked into the store, scanning for other customers and trying to look casual.

An unnaturally skinny cashier sat inert on a wooden stool behind the register. He seemed to take no notice when Wil came in. The man's dense growth of stubble, faded plaid shirt and stiff-looking blue jeans made him look ancient, but Wil guessed he was only about thirty.

Wil spotted some hamburgers in the refrigerator case, set two of them in the small grimy microwave and turned the dial. While the burgers were heating up, he gathered some Hershey bars, chewing gum, Doritos and pretzels.

When the microwave dinged, he gathered all of his purchases into a pile on the counter and added a two liter Coke and several bottles of water.

The clerk tallied the prices without saying a word and waited impassively, apparently expecting Wil to read the total for himself and pay up.

Wil wasn't in a mood for small talk anyway.

He pulled out his wallet and handed over two twenties.

The man gave him his change, settled back onto his stool, and reverted to his stiff, sightless stare.

Wil saw no way to carry all of his food, so he asked for a bag.

The clerk seemed puzzled by the intrusion, but he reached below the counter and came up with a sack barely larger than a lunch bag.

Wil shoved what he could inside it, cradled the rest in his arms, and hurried out the door. That guy didn't seem likely to remember him, but Wil had no interest in doing anything to make himself more memorable.

The old truck started up with a loud rumble.

Wil backed around and pulled out of the parking lot, spinning his tires on the gravel as he stepped on the gas with a jerk. He cursed again, but a quick look reassured him no one had come into the parking lot to notice.

Accelerating away from the highway helped him relax a little bit, but he felt lots of rigid tension in his body, and it magnified all of his aches and pains. He swiveled his head and shook his arms to try to let some of it out.

The smell of the food filled the small cab, and Wil's repressed hunger hit him like a physical force. He wolfed down both sandwiches, with several long gulps of the Coke, and reached for the Doritos.

After several fruitless attempts to open the large bag one-handed, he steadied the steering wheel with his knees and grasped the balky plastic with both hands. The seal gave way suddenly, and Wil cursed again as chips flew in all directions. He set what was left of the ruptured bag on the seat, pulled out an absurdly large handful, held it up to his face and grazed greedily.

After two of the candy bars and several sips of water, he began to feel a little less shaky.

Could he make it to Texas? Certainly not without getting on the expressway, and the thought of doing that terrified him. The police had to be looking for his truck, and even if he could stay away from them, there were so many other problems to overcome.

A sharp pain throbbed in his temple. He just couldn't think about all of that right now.

Fatigue gradually took control of his body. It would be impossible to keep going much longer without some sleep, and as much as he hated the thought, he knew he'd have to to pull over for the night.

His adrenaline, with its illusion of strength, had drained from his bloodstream long ago.

He found himself relaxing in spite of everything. His mind gradually cleared and began to focus on the minutiae of driving

Steer slightly to the right, now to the left. Straight ahead. Push on the gas a little bit. A curve to the right, ease the wheel in that direction.

He began to hum idly, not so much out loud as in his mind.

Suddenly, in a flash of astonishing insight, music flooded into his brain.

With perfect clarity he heard the glorious, rich sound of cascading brass, soaring strings and electrifying bursts of percussion in a powerful orchestral *fortissimo.*

He recognized the magnificent music immediately as the powerful culminating passage he needed for his symphony. It captured perfectly the purest distillation of the melodies he'd been working with, the fiery essence of the rhythms, and the most profound richness of the harmonies.

The powerful sounds flowed into his mind with wondrous inevitability and settled indelibly into his memory. He knew he could write the music down tonight, or two months from now. It wouldn't matter.

He also knew it was just right, that there was no way he could ever improve on it. The challenge was simply to capture it as faithfully as he could on the pages of his manuscript.

Awestruck chills coursed through his body and goosebumps erupted on his arms.

Of all the crazy things to happen! And why now?

No one would ever believe the music came to him this way, but he had experienced similar revelations before on memorable and rare occasions, and those wonderful serendipities always resulted in his best musical creations, the centerpieces of his finest work.

The miracles always seemed to happen in moments of fatigue or during the hazy time between sleep and wakefulness. Somehow, in those moments, his subconscious mind could show him the perfected form of the ideas he'd been trying to shape.

His eyes filled with tears. He couldn't have said whether they were tears of joy or of sorrow. They were a cathartic release from his deathly fatigue and all the tension he had been feeling.

But more than that, for a few fleeting moments, nothing on earth mattered as much as this music. The ecstatic spirit of this moment eclipsed Henri's death, his own fears, the terrible problems all around him, even the attempt on his life.

The music and his soul joined in a delirious joy that pushed everything else aside.

He had finished his symphony! He just had to work out the details and get it all written down.

As the moment of elation faded, the cumulative effect of his emotional roller coaster hit him like a physical wall of weariness. Another kind of chill coursed through his body, sweat soaked his clothing, his muscles felt rubbery, and he fought to keep from trembling.

A stand of trees came into view, and he gratefully pulled the truck into a small gravel drive leading back into the woods. At the end of the lane he had another wonderful surprise. He had unknowingly worked his way westward to Lake Michigan.

He pulled off the road, stopped the truck and peered through the gathering darkness. The expanse of water, as beautiful as ever, stretched before him as far as he could see in the moonlight.

It's good to see you old friend!

The ground ahead of him dropped off so dramatically he could see the tops of trees far below.

He climbed back in the truck and let his head sink back against the seat.

Far in the distance, he could hear the wonderfully soothing sound of waves splashing against the shore.

Before he knew it, he had fallen into an almost comatose sleep.

The dusty black Cadillac, nearly invisible with its lights off, crept up slowly behind Wil's truck. When the vehicles touched, the Cadillac's engine roared.

A shower of gravel flew up behind the car's spinning tires as the pickup rolled toward the precipice. For a brief instant the smaller vehicle hung on the edge. Then the inexorable laws of gravity took hold.

The truck rolled down the steep grade until it flipped over an unseen obstacle and started tumbling.

A series of sickening crunches led to the violent sounds of metal hitting wood.

After a distant splash, everything became quiet.

A dark figure emerged from the car, walked over to the edge of the bluff and peered down into the darkness.

There was no sound for several moments.

Then boots crunched on the gravel, and the car door opened and shut.

The Cadillac's lights flickered on as it drove away.

There was no longer any reason to keep them off.

CHAPTER FIFTY-SIX

Wil lay face down in the dew-soaked grass, shaking and afraid to lift his head.

Had he been unconscious? He couldn't be sure.

The shocking sensation of the truck lurching toward the steep incline had woken him, despite his overwhelming fatigue. A fresh jolt of panic filled his body as he heard the grinding sound of the car pushing his pickup toward the edge.

A surreal sense of unreality filled his senses as the truck dropped onto the slope and began to roll down the hill. Terror took its place as the truck picked up speed and rushed headlong down the grassy bank.

In a fog of desperate necessity, he put his legs beneath him and lunged out the open window, just before the truck hit something hard and started to flip.

He listened in horror as the truck crashed through the trees into the water far below.

He clutched enormous handfuls of the grass and wished he could force himself through the sod into the soft soil beneath it. Then he lay as still as he could, hoping desperately he couldn't be seen from the hilltop in the darkness.

When he heard footsteps, he crouched even lower and tried frantically to quiet his heaving breath. He waited in overpowering dread for the sound of someone running down the bank, or even gunshots, absolutely certain he would be dead in moments.

Incredibly, those sounds never came.

It seemed like an eternity until he heard the heavy car turn and drive away.

He trembled violently as he realized he had been followed ever since he left St. Cecile. He felt more alone and vulnerable than he ever imagined he could.

Another terrible shock ripped through him when he realized he'd left his wallet stuffed next to the console in his truck. He checked frantically and breathed a small sigh of relief when he found his cell phone still in his pocket.

As he rose to his hands and knees, the remains of his hasty meal surged up from his stomach, and he vomited violently into the darkness.

His gut had never felt so abused. It had been aching ever since the assault, and the paltry meal he had gulped down had only made it feel marginally better. Now an even sharper pain cut at the inside of his belly. He thought he must be bleeding internally.

He crawled a few steps to get away from the horrible smell of his bile and collapsed on his side. Perhaps he should be happy he had survived, but the realization the killer had been right behind him since he left St. Cecile filled him with dread.

His feelings of escape and anonymity had been a complete illusion. He felt like a gnat caught on a giant spider's web, waiting helplessly for the moment when the terrible fangs sank deep into his flesh.

The dew had soaked him completely, and he began to shiver again. The cold seemed to drain his body of what little strength he had left.

A black torrent of fear and bitterness filled his mind.

What have I ever done to deserve this?!

Some part of his mind knew that the question was pointless, but his frustration at least propelled him to get up and start moving.

He had to see if he could get back his wallet. Without his money and credit cards he'd be truly powerless.

It seemed to take him forever to scramble down the steep bank. He slipped and fell several times, and each time his rage grew stronger.

The blinding darkness made him stumble into rocks and bushes again and again, and every shrub seemed to assault him with stinging thorns and whiplike branches.

The going got especially tough in the thick growth of the treeline near the water.

When he finally got to the lake, he couldn't see any sign of his truck.

He thought he recalled flatter terrain and shallow water along this part of the lake, but this spot seemed to be an exception. The sound of the waves lapping against the bank gave a distinct impression of discouragingly deep water.

He stuck his foot into the dark water and didn't feel the bottom.

Wil fought a powerful urge to give up. If he called Jones on his cell phone, he would probably be picked up in minutes. He'd go straight to jail, but at least he'd be warm and have enough to eat. This crazy carousel ride could calm down for a while.

But the killer probably thought he had done him in. If he got away now, he wouldn't be followed.

He couldn't bring himself to turn back now. He made up his mind to at least go down fighting. But first things first. He had to find the truck and get his wallet.

Wil found a place where the shore sloped a little more gently into the water and lowered himself in. The icy water squeezed his body like a giant fist, and the paltry body heat he'd built up in his exertions fled instantly.

Wil remembered happier times when the sudden shock of cool water had been a delicious thrill against his warm skin, how wonderfully blue the lake water could look in bright sunlight.

The blackness all around him seemed all the more menacing in comparison.

He gritted his teeth and forced himself not to think about the deathly cold attacking the core of his battered body.

He swam around in the choppy, agitated water for several minutes, trying to feel for the truck with his hands and feet. He found lots of weedy plants, rocks, sand and muck on the uneven bottom, but he couldn't find any sign of the pickup.

His teeth chattered loudly, and he finally admitted he'd have to wait until morning.

He worked his way wearily back to the water's edge. It took several frustrating minutes to find a place where he could make his way up the slippery bank.

Mercifully, he stumbled across a relatively dry pile of old leaves.

He stripped off his soaked clothes, buried himself in the scratchy leaves and curled himself into a tight ball, trying to conserve what little body heat he had left.

As he sank into oblivion, he wondered if he would ever feel warm and safe again.

Jones sank wearily into the chair just as the sun began to appear on the horizon. He'd hardly slept at all, but he hoped to get a head start on the day before the station got busy.

Every instinct told him to stay as far as he could from the chief and the others, but he knew that was unrealistic. He'd just have to keep his head down and forge ahead as best he could.

He plodded through his email and voice messages numbly. Cops all over southern Michigan were supposed to be looking for Walker, but they had found no trace of him so far.

Jones scowled as he imagined Wil hiding out in some shabby motel room. He still couldn't believe Wil panicked and ran. What a boneheaded thing to do!

Manning and the D.A. considered Walker's flight proof positive, the smoking gun. They had no doubt Wil had killed both Falcano and Winston Nicholas, and Jones knew he had to prove otherwise very soon, or Walker would be in prison.

Jones perked up considerably when the next caller identified herself as Sally Purcell, the coordinator for the brownfield redevelopment grants. She sounded eager to provide any information she could.

Jones punched in her number hopefully and leaned back in his chair, drumming his fingers on the top of the desk.

She answered on the third ring.

Hooray for morning people!

"This is Sally Purcell."

"Hello Sally, this is Detective Peter Jones in St. Cecile."

"Hello Detective. That was quick. I just left you a message a few minutes ago."

"I just got into the office. Thanks for calling me back."

"Sure, what can I do for you?"

"Well, I have a few questions about cleaning up brownfields."

"The reclamation grant program? That should be easy. What do you need to know?"

"I looked up the basics on your website, which is very nice, by the way."

"We try."

Her playful laugh couldn't hide her businesslike efficiency.

"First, can a grant be used to clean up property that's owned by a private individual?"

"Sure, as long as the local government requests it."

"Would it be possible for someone to apply for a grant without a lot of people knowing much about it."

"I suppose so. The application requires support from a local governing body, but those groups have lots of paperwork to deal with. Someone might get a proposal through without anyone paying much attention."

"What's the time frame involved?"

"Approval usually takes about three months."

Jones hesitated.

"Can you tell me if you received a grant application from the St. Cecile area?"

"Sure, that's public information. There is a pending application for a cleanup along Lake Michigan in St. Cecile County. I figured your questions would have something to do with it, so I pulled the paperwork."

"Great, thank you. Who filed the proposal?"

"The cover letter is written on stationary from the mayor's office, and it's signed by Eldon Fitzhugh. He's the mayor there, right?"

"Yes."

Jones hoped she couldn't hear the tension in his voice.

"He says he's writing on behalf of the City and the County, who are joint applicants. There's a lot of talk about projected benefits from new economic development, that sort of thing."

Yeah, it's great for everybody, especially Eldon Fitzhugh, if he can buy that land for a song!

"What's the status of the application?"

"Actually it's due to be funded. Mr. Fitzhugh has asked for the approval to be held up for a few weeks."

"He what?!"

"He said the timing wasn't quite right and asked for the announcement to be delayed until the middle of the summer."

I'll bet he did!

"Thank you Sally, you've been a great help."

"I don't see how, it's just basic information."

"Yeah, but the right information at the right time can change everything."

Wil woke with a start as glaring sunlight hit his eyes.

His arms and legs felt wooden after his all-too-brief sleep on the ground, and his head throbbed sharply as he staggered to his feet. He needed hours of sleep in a warm bed, not a fitful night tossing and turning in a damp pile of leaves!

In a sudden panic he looked up to the hilltop, but no one seemed to be watching him, or worse, pointing a rifle this way.

He swiped absent-mindedly at the dirt and leaf fragments coating his body as he began to scan the water in the early morning light. The calmer surface of the lake seemed much more benign.

It didn't take Wil long to find the truck now that he could see.

The momentum from the fall had carried it surprisingly far from the shore, and it was lying on its side, fully submerged in some fairly deep water.

Wil jumped in feet first, ignoring the shock as his skin adjusted to the temperature, and swam easily out to the spot where the truck had come to rest.

The cab seemed to be at the deepest point.

He held his breath, dove, and pushed his body through the open window into the cab.

The weird sensation of being in an enclosed space underwater made a surprising, claustrophobic panic surge through his body. His lungs emptied in a rush, and he fought his way out and rose to the surface, choking and gasping for air.

He forced himself to relax, took several deep breaths to fill his lungs with oxygen, and dove again. Knowing what to expect this time helped him swim into the cab without freaking out.

He ran his hand along the gap next to the seat and cursed inwardly when he didn't find the wallet where he thought he'd left it. The combined effects of the fall and the surging water must have shaken the billfold loose.

He dove again and again, searching every inch the cab, and finally inspected the bottom all around the truck, hoping against hope.

His eyes ached from exposure to the water, and his gut felt like a hollow void, when he finally gave up and swam back to the land. A deep chill had sunk to the core of his shivering body, and he knew he needed to avoid getting hypothermic. He did his best to dry himself with some of the cleaner leaves from his makeshift bed.

His damp clothes felt wonderful after standing naked and soaked in the cold morning air.

He spent several minutes walking back and forth along the water, hoping to find the wallet floating or washed up on the edge.

His heart sank when he had to admit he wasn't going to find it.

He sat on the ground, put his arms around his legs and lowered his face onto his knees.

Now what was he going to do?

He had no money, no vehicle and nowhere to go. If he didn't get something to eat soon, he would be in serious trouble. It wasn't difficult to imagine he could get pneumonia, or even collapse.

He looked around the small inlet and couldn't find any sign of houses or businesses.

Then he noticed a path running in either direction along the shoreline, and he wondered which direction was the most likely to take him toward something useful.

He shrugged and turned to the left.

He wouldn't be getting to Texas any time soon, but a small move in the right direction seemed better than nothing.

CHAPTER FIFTY-SEVEN

Jones fidgeted in Eldon Fitzhugh's outer office as he waited impatiently to be admitted to the mayor's inner sanctum.

He had almost barged through the door when he arrived, but he reluctantly cooled his heels when the receptionist asked him politely to take a seat.

Somehow it didn't seem right to be rude to her.

He was far too nervous to sit, so he stepped over to a low table and pretended to look at the months-old magazines.

Jones savored the righteous indignation in his gut. He would enjoy watching the mayor squirm after all his slights and insults over the past few weeks.

He had the man dead to rights!

Fitzhugh had sneaked through the redevelopment grant, and Jones had no doubt he would try to get control of Helen's property. If Fitzhugh could buy the land cheap, and have the state pay for the cleanup, he'd make a killing.

Jones frowned as he wondered if Fitzhugh's scheming went as far as murder. He had a hard time picturing the mayor shooting Nicholas Winston from ambush or sneaking around to set up a lethal booby trap. But if Fitzhugh hadn't done it, who had? The mayor was up to his eyeballs in this scheme, and his partners had conveniently disappeared.

With Nicholas out of the way, all the profits would be his. He could end up obscenely wealthy. Maybe he paid someone else to do the dirty work. Maybe someone else killed Falcano and Nicholas for another reason entirely.

Suddenly Jones realized Fitzhugh's assistant had been trying to get his attention.

"I said you can go in now, Mr. Jones."

"Uhhh ... oh, ok. Thank you."

Jones gathered his thoughts and strode over to Fitzhugh's office.

The mayor's eyes hardened into a narrow stare as Jones stepped into the room. He cleared his throat roughly and shouted through the door.

"Clara, come in here."

The receptionist came to the entryway and waited meekly for instructions.

"Shut the door, Clara. And call Walter Manning. I want him in here as fast as he can move."

"Yes sir."

She retreated quickly, and the door slammed behind her.

The mayor regarded Jones with a fierce stare.

"Well, what is it?"

"I found out about your brownfield redevelopment grant, Mr. Mayor."

Jones didn't even try to stifle the triumph in his voice.

"Yeah, so what?"

Jones stared in astonishment. The mayor didn't seem to be bothered in the least.

His actions bordered on fraud, and he had taken great pains to keep the whole thing quiet. At the very least he had abused his office for personal gain.

And he couldn't care less.

"So what? You're planning a huge development that could make you filthy rich, and you're using your position to get the state to pay for the cleanup? Have you ever heard the word ethics, Mr. Mayor?"

"Don't you lecture me about ethics! You're meddling in matters that are none of your concern. And since when is it wrong to be a shrewd businessman?"

Jones could almost feel the heat from Fitzhugh's malignant frown.

"Shrewd? How about underhanded? How about being a cheater, Mr. Mayor?"

Fitzhugh's eyes bulged outward from their sockets, and his mouth opened and closed like a fish gasping for air. Several seconds passed before he could get anything out.

"How dare you call me that?"

Jones knew Fitzhugh wanted to reach across the desk and punch him in the face.

"What about Helen, Mr. Mayor? How much did you plan to pay her for her land?"

Fitzhugh looked wary all of a sudden.

"We have a signed purchase agreement. Don't you start putting ideas into her head."

"A signed purchase agreement based on a fraudulent premise. I don't think it would hold up very long in a court of law."

Jones wasn't exactly positive about that, but he'd be checking as soon as possible.

The mayor's face tightened into a sour scowl.

"Driving a hard bargain is how you get ahead in this world, Mr. Jones. You're about as naïve as they come."

"Is it naïve to think it's evil to practically steal her property?"

"It's not stealing to pay her a fair price for her land."

"It is if she thinks the land is contaminated, unusable. How much do you think it would be worth if she knew it will be cleaned up at the state's expense."

The mayor's face turned into a crimson steel mask.

"You're an idiot!"

A chill of shock coursed through Jones' body. The mayor had no shame. If his machinations ruined people, it wouldn't faze him in the least.

"What about Henri Falcano? Was he part of this scheme?"

Fitzhugh leaned forward menacingly.

"Falcano wanted to marry her, the damn fool! He was going to tell her all about it just about the time he was killed. We asked him to keep it quiet so …"

"So her price didn't shoot up? And with him out of the way, you just decided to go ahead with the purchase, at rock bottom prices."

"I haven't done anything wrong or illegal. And if you think you can make trouble for me you're badly mistaken, Mr. Jones."

He spat the name out.

"We'll see, Mr. Mayor. I wonder how people will feel when they read all about it in the papers?"

The mayor's face turned ashen.

"You wouldn't dare!"

"Oh, but I would. And it will be a pleasure."

Fitzhugh sank into his chair, but his defiance hadn't left entirely.

"You can't threaten me mister."

Jones stared at Fitzhugh increduloulsy.

It was time to ask the fifty-thousand-dollar question.

"Did you kill Falcano and Nicholas?"

The mayor sputtered with a fresh explosion of rage.

"Of course I didn't! How dare you! You don't have one shred of evidence linking me to any of that!"

"I asked you a simple question, Mr. Mayor."

"Are you accusing me of murder?!"

Jones wondered if the mayor's white-hot rage came from outrage, or bottled up guilt.

"I haven't accused you of anything but swindling ... not yet. But don't even think about leaving town."

The mayor burst into a fresh explosion of fury just as Walter Manning came into the room.

Jones turned to leave.

"I think your old buddy needs you, Walter. And if he tells you again to fire me, you might want to take that with a grain of salt."

Wil stared out warily from his makeshift hiding place.

He couldn't have felt more conspicuous without standing up and shouting 'Here I am!' The puny tree trunk in front of him seemed as thin as a pencil, and the tiny new leaves on the surrounding brush hid nothing.

He had come to a small two-lane highway after trudging along the path for the better part of a mile. Only three cars had passed so far, and the distracted drivers hadn't even looked his way, but he wanted to get out of sight as soon as possible.

He vividly remembered seeing news reports about wanted fugitives, with breathless announcers giving detailed descriptions of height, weight and coloring as grungy pictures of the bad guys stared menacingly from the screen.

That's what he was now, a suspect, a fugitive, a perp.

He hadn't seen his own mug shot. Had it already been plastered all over the media?

Suddenly he was sure it made him look like a monster, someone who needed to be dealt with swiftly, and very, very harshly.

He shook his head morosely. He had no desire to step out in the open, but he couldn't just sit here, either.

The exertion of the walk had warmed him up a little, but he felt a frightening chill overcoming his body after just a few minutes of standing still. He had thrown up most of his hasty meal the night before. His gut ached with hunger and his legs felt watery from the lack of nutrition and the aftereffects of alcohol poisoning.

To his right Wil saw several well-worn buildings, two houses, a country diner, a Mobil station and a pop shop. Things looked more open on the left, where the budding trees gave way to some pastureland and a few fields waiting for the first spring plowing.

An old, overgrown driveway led into some thick brush across the way. He decided to see where it led.

Wil waited until there were no cars coming and scurried out onto the road. His stiff muscles protested the sudden activity, and his feet squished in his soaked shoes.

All too quickly he heard a car approaching, and he started to run. He probably should have just tried to look casual, but he didn't feel up to such a demanding performance at the moment.

He breathed a small sigh of relief as he ducked into the opening. The dense, overgrown brush on either side seemed almost opaque.

The rutted gravel track followed the original contours of the land very closely and disappeared around a bend. No bulldozer had invaded here to carve out a straight, level gash in the earth, and any vehicle with low clearance would have scraped bottom on the rough terrain.

He relaxed a tiny bit as he walked along the lane. Soon the sounds of the highway receded in a very satisfying fashion.

After a few hundred yards the brush gave way to an overgrown yard.

Wil crouched near the last bits of cover and cautiously peeked out at a large, graying house, an ancient barn leaning slightly to one side and a scattering of smaller outbuildings.

The place had obviously seen prosperous times, but not recently.

A small wooden shed not far from Wil had weathered to a dingy, grayish brown. The bottom boards of its siding had rotted unevenly, leaving a jagged edge several inches off the ground. Two thick planks braced at steep angles kept the ancient doors from swinging open.

Wil stood still for several minutes, listening intently for any signs of life, and decided that the house might be deserted.

He walked up behind the shed and knelt in the shadows, carefully keeping the bulk of the building between himself and the old house, just in case.

As he poked his head close to the doors, a pungent smell of soil, rust, mildew and old motor oil rose sharply into his nostrils. The powerful odor brought back vivid memories of similar old buildings at his grandmother's house.

He stood up to move closer to the house, but a glimpse of something white and smooth in the dark recesses of the old shed caught his attention.

After another quick look around, he pulled the wooden brace off the right-hand door and leaned it against the wall. The heavily rusted hasp had no lock and offered little resistance as he pulled it open. The old hinges had loosened long ago. He had to lift the creaking door to clear the ground as he swung it back.

The old shed turned out to be a garage, and his heart leapt when he saw a large, late-model car inside, one of those ordinary, anonymous ones that you hardly noticed as they went by. The car's door could only move a few inches before it hit the wall, but Wil had just enough room to squeeze through and climb in.

He reached for the steering column, more out of habit than anything else, and his chest began to pound as he felt a key in the ignition. Hardly daring to hope, he gave it a turn. The engine started quickly and settled into a wonderful, smooth idle.

What luck! There was nothing he needed more, and here it was for the taking. Hopefully he could get far away before anyone missed it and alerted the police.

Wil's mind raced and his breath felt ragged in his bone-dry throat. Was he really ready to commit a felony? The charges against him were much worse, but this felt different. He would be guilty, not just legally, but in his own mind.

With a sharp lurch in his gut he remembered a recurring nightmare from his childhood that always made him wake up in a cold sweat.

In the dream, he would be running frantically from a horde of faceless police. If he could only explain, everything would be sorted out, but the cops kept after him relentlessly until some kind of terrible accident happened. Someone would be killed, or something very valuable would be destroyed. His pursuers flew into a terrible rage and finally, in desperation, he lashed out and killed the first shadowy figure behind him.

That was the line. When that happened he knew he had allowed an implacable evil to take hold of him. Misunderstanding had driven the chase until then, but suddenly, it all became a matter of decision. His choice felt like kill or be killed, but that didn't matter.

He had chosen murder.

As the dream continued, the second crime came easily, and the third even more so, and soon he was filled with an overwhelming sense of guilt and corruption.

A harrowing sense of remorse and loss often gripped him long after he woke up. He told himself not to take a silly nightmare so seriously, and even in the dream logic, he had been compelled to protect himself, but the sorrowful feeling of regret had always affected him deeply.

He shuddered involuntarily and squeezed the steering wheel.

The thought of stealing the car paralyzed him. Why should he feel guilty about taking it? He needed it desperately, and who would he be hurting? It probably just sat here unused most of the time.

But how would it make him look? He had to convince everyone of his innocence. Could he just explain away stealing a car? Would he go to jail for this even if Jones proved someone else committed the murder?

Abruptly he decided he didn't care. He had no choice!

He'd make some kind of restitution, but he had to have the car, and that was all there was to it. It was only an object, a piece of property with a certain value. He was fighting for his life, and he had a right to survive and to fight back.

He squirmed out of the car, set aside the second plank, and started to lift the other door on its sagging hinges to swing it open.

Suddenly he heard a voice.

“Just what the hell do you think you’re playing at?”

He spun around to see the twin barrels of a huge shotgun hovering about three inches from his face and pointing directly at his nose.

CHAPTER FIFTY-EIGHT

Jones saw instantly something had changed in Helen.

The glow in her eyes and the dancing lightness in her movements made her look like a different person. She had pulled her hair back into a neat French braid, and the crisp blouse tucked carefully into the waist of her jeans made her look years younger.

Jones had always seen her in makeup, and he thought she looked fresh and beautiful without it.

The house had changed too. The unmistakable smells of furniture polish and piney detergent had replaced the claustrophobic odors of dust and mold. The place seemed infinitely brighter with the drapes drawn back. A delicious cool breeze flowed through the open windows, purging out the old stagnant air.

Jones couldn't contain his approving smile.

Helen ushered him back to the dining room, and they took seats facing each other across one corner of the massive table.

"Would you like some coffee or something Mr. Jones?"

"No thanks, Helen."

He hesitated.

"Look, I have to say it. Something about you has changed … rather dramatically, actually."

She smiled, almost shyly.

"I guess I hit bottom, you know? If I didn't make some changes I knew I was going to die. All of a sudden everything looked different. You might say I decided to step into the sun instead of cringing in the darkness. Does that make sense?"

"Perfect sense. Congratulations."

"What do you mean?"

"I think you've made one of the most important discoveries you could ever make. You've found out that there are certain things you have to do for yourself. No one else can do them for you, no matter how desperately they may want to."

Jones could see the gratitude in her eyes.

"I quit smoking cold turkey, too. It wasn't easy, but I just couldn't bear it anymore."

"Good for you! It's great to see you looking so confident. You look really alive for the first time since I've known you."

"Thank you. I feel that way too."

Her warm genuine smile lit up the room.

"The reason I'm here is to ask you about your property."

"What about it?"

"Is there some kind of contamination on it?"

The smile melted from her face.

"How did you find out about that?"

"So there is a problem?"

"Yes."

She looked down at her knuckles.

"There used to be lots of cherry orchards here. It turns out processing the fruit leaves some terrible chemicals in the ground, and the original owners disappeared. You can't sell without a report being filed, and there's no way I can get enough for the land to cover the cleanup. I'm screwed!"

Jones could see the old worry cross her face as her brow knit with frustration.

"And Mayor Fitzhugh offered to take the land off your hands?"

She looked up sharply.

"You know about that, too?"

He just nodded.

Her hands started trembling and she squeezed them together under her chin.

"He said he'd offer me what he could for it, but it's basically worthless."

Jones wished he could send a few quotes to Jeanette Fields for the *Daily News*.

"Maybe not. Have you ever heard of a brownfield redevelopment grant?"

"Brownfield? No, what is it?"

"The grants are part of a state program to fund cleanups for toxic waste sites."

"Fitzhugh had me sign a paper, some kind of consent for state business, but he said it was just routine. Are you saying I might be able to get a grant to clean up the place?"

"Not by yourself. It has to be requested by a governing authority."

"But it might be possible?"

"It's not only possible, there's one in the works."

"What?!"

Jones saw her body tighten with shock.

"Fitzhugh applied for the whole thing quietly and bought up property all around here for as little as he could pay."

"That's, that's … it's horrifying!"

Jones thought she might burst into tears.

"Yes it is. It's evil. But don't worry. Your contract with him won't be binding under the circumstances."

And he won't be in any position to enforce it with the publicity he's about to get!

"When the grant goes through you'll be able to sell your property for what it's really worth, if that's what you still want to do."

"You have no idea what difference that would make, Mr. Jones!"

She looked at him intensely as another thought seemed to cross her mind.

"But what about Henri? You said they were partners! Are you saying he was part of this whole thing?"

"No, the mayor told me he wanted to marry you, Helen. He's the second person who's told me that, and in my business that kind of confirmation counts for a lot."

"But why all the secrecy?"

Her eyes showed how deeply that hurt.

"His life was a complicated mess, but he had plans to straighten things out. The others made him promise not to tell you about the land, but he was going to anyway. That was just about the time he was killed. I'm terribly sorry Helen."

She looked down at her hands.

"Was he really planning to marry me?"

Jones found her vulnerability incredibly touching.

"Henri wanted to be part of your life Helen, and to make life better for you. That's very different from what Fitzhugh wanted to do. You know, some guys have a very hard time finding the courage to pop the question."

"Maybe you're right. I have a lot to think about, Mr. Jones."

Jones didn't know what to say.

She looked out the large window toward the lake.

"This place really isn't worthless, even if it is contaminated."

She turned back and spoke in a firmer voice.

"This is a beautiful spot, Mr. Jones. That's what really makes it worth something, isn't it?"

"Yes it is."

They talked a little longer, but her buoyant mood had darkened.

She rose with strength in her eyes as Jones stood to go.

"Thank you for being straight with me, Mr. Jones."

It was Jones' turn to be grateful.

As he left he thought she'd come through fine, one way or another.

CHAPTER FIFTY-NINE

Wil stared at the sixteen gauge in horror and jerked his arms stiffly over his head.

From this perspective the cylinders of bluish steel looked absolutely enormous.

A violent wave of nausea knotted his badly abused belly. He never realized how terrifying it would be to stare into the business end of a loaded weapon.

What would it feel like to be shot, especially at such close quarters? What if the gun went off by accident?

He struggled to focus his vision.

The gun rested, unwavering, in the grip of a woman who looked about eighty. She couldn't have been more than five feet tall. Her soft flowery dress almost hid the big brown boots on her feet, and her old-fashioned white apron seemed wildly out of place next to the menacing shotgun.

Wil had no doubt she would squeeze the trigger if he provoked her. He could clearly see the indomitable will in the set of her round, wrinkled face.

Her narrowed eyes stared at him unflinchingly.

He suddenly felt completely foolish and tried desperately to think of something to say.

"I, I … uh…"

"You just thought you'd take off in my car?"

She clipped the words like a drill sergeant.

"No, I … uh … well, yes."

What was the use of lying about it?

"I was desperate. I didn't think anyone was here."

"So you just thought you'd help yourself to an old woman's car, huh?"

She lowered the gun about half an inch and squinted up at him.

"You don't look like a car thief, sonny. You look like something the dogs dragged in. Where'd you sleep last night, in the barn?"

Wil started lowering his arms, and she poked the shotgun back up to his face.

"Let's just keep things they way they are, at least for now, eh Buster?"

"Ok, ok!"

Wil pushed his arms back up. Tears of shame and embarrassment stung his eyes as he did his best to stand up straight.

She looked at him with a quizzical expression.

"So what's going on with you, young fella?

"Well, it's … um …"

Suddenly, his throat constricted and hot tears filled his eyes. He couldn't choke out a word as all the emotion of the past few days flooded into his mind.

She lowered the gun and shook her head.

"Ok, kid, let's go inside. I can see you got a story to tell, and something tells me it's a good 'un, but first I bet you could use somethin' to eat."

Wil couldn't believe it. She'd caught him trying to steal her car, and now she was going to feed him?

She turned and began marching toward the house.

"Well, c'mon, you just gonna stand there?"

Her strides were long for a woman her size. She had already gone several yards before Wil lowered his arms and started walking, quite a bit more slowly, toward the old farmhouse.

He caught up with her in a small, cluttered mudroom as she pulled off her almost comical boots.

Wil saw the shotgun leaning against the wall. She looked at it and chuckled.

"I reckon you ain't gonna take that and try to turn the tables on me. C'mon in young fella. I ain't got much, but I'll share some of it with ya."

She stepped into some white slip-on sneakers, climbed two small steps that led to the kitchen and opened the inner door.

Wil followed sheepishly.

The air in the house smelled stale and musty, but Wil found the effect more homey than unpleasant.

Toenails clattered on the hard linoleum as two ancient dogs waddled into the kitchen, made straight for Wil, and started sniffing him with unabashed curiosity. Their long shaggy coats had clearly been brushed with great care.

She bent over and gave each of the dogs a hearty, two-handed ruffling around the ears, cooing affectionately the whole time.

"Some watch dogs you two cowards are. I had to chase down this car thief all by myself."

Their tails wagged furiously and their tongues lolled out as they smiled up at her.

When she stood up, the dogs retreated and curled up in the corner. Their eyes followed every move as she turned toward her huge, old refrigerator.

"How about some eggs and bacon, Sonny? You do look like you could use a bite."

Wil had no idea what to say.

"That's for sure. Look, I uh ..."

"You can tell me all about it in a few minutes. For now, just sit down."

She bustled around the kitchen with an air of long familiarity.

Her generosity made no sense, but Wil felt incredibly grateful. The very thought of food made him weak with hunger. It was still only a matter of hours since he'd run from the hospital, and he knew he could easily pass out if he let down his guard.

"You want some coffee? It's a fresh pot."

"Uh, sure."

"What do you take in it?"

"Just a little milk, thanks."

"All I got is whole cream, how 'bout that? No sense worryin' about cholesterol at my age."

She chuckled wryly as she poured a large mugful of coffee and set it in front of him, along with a half-pint carton of cream.

"Help yourself."

Wil grabbed a spoon from the bowlful propped up on the table, poured thick cream into the mug and stirred the heavenly liquid with a shaking hand.

He took a couple of quick sips with absurdly-intense appreciation and stared into the cup as warmth radiated through his body.

"My name is Georgia Steadman, what's yours? And how do you like your eggs?"

She hummed a little tune as she puttered with the pans and food at the stove.

Wil suddenly felt too ashamed to speak.

She turned around and looked at him gently with her hands on her hips.

"I guess I'll just scramble some."

She returned to her work, and a divine smell soon flooded the room.

"Ok son. You might as well tell me who you are, and then start your story at the beginning."

Wil took a deeper drink of the coffee and felt the small child inside him decide to trust her.

"My name's Wil Walker, and you might as well know the truth. The police are after me. They think I killed someone."

Her eyes widened.

"What?!"

"Well, not all of them, but enough, and I had to get away. To make it all worse, someone is trying to kill me."

He expected her to think he was completely crazy, or to recoil in horror and kick him out. He wilted as she stared at him intensely, but her eyes still held both compassion and curiosity.

She cleared her throat and rubbed her hands on her apron.

"You gotta be kidding. It sounds like a Hollywood movie."

"I know. I can't believe it myself."

She seemed to collect herself and turned back to her cooking.

"What do you mean, tryin' to kill you? And how come you're all the way out here with no car?"

Once he started talking, the whole story gushed out.

Georgia set a plate heaped with eggs, bacon, potatoes and toast in front of him, sat down at the table, and listened attentively as she watched him eat.

She asked a few questions, but gave away none of her own thoughts.

Wil finished the last scraps of food as he told her how he lost everything when someone pushed his truck over the bluff.

Her searching gaze found his eyes again.

"That's quite a yarn, Wil, but I reckon it rings true. What are you gonna do?"

"I don't know. I just know I have to do something."

He put his head in his hands and closed his eyes.

"One of the cops told me something, the only one who believes me. I wanted to go to Texas to check it out."

"Well, you can't do much until you get some sleep. Let's get you outta those filthy clothes and into a bed."

Wil looked up incredulously.

"Why are you doing this? I *was* trying to steal your car, you know."

"I know that."

She gently put a hand on his arm.

"I had a son once. He'd have been just about your age, but he died in a car wreck. Damn drunk driver hit 'im. Let's just say I hope someone woulda done him a good turn if he needed it. And for what it's worth, I believe your story. It's too crazy not to be true."

Wil felt his throat tightening again.

"I don't know how to thank you."

"You'll figure somethin' out. But for now, you take a bath and get some sleep. I'll clean up those clothes. Tomorrow you can take the car and get on your way."

"What?"

This couldn't be happening.

"I don't drive it much, and I got friends who can cart me anywhere I might need to go. We'll call it a loan. Get it back to me when you can."

He stared, dumbfounded, down at the table.

"I don't know what to say."

She chuckled dryly.

"Don't say nothin'. But you get your name cleared, you hear me? That'll be all the thanks I need."

CHAPTER SIXTY

Jeanette Fields' eyes shone with anticipation and she leaned in toward her desk.

"Tell me more, Mr. Jones. I want to hear everything."

Jones tried to be matter of fact.

"Who knows how they got together. Maybe Falcano came up with the idea and asked Nicholas to arrange for financing. They might have pulled in the mayor for some political clout. It's all just guesswork. Fitzhugh won't talk about it and Nicholas is dead, but whatever happened, I think the mayor soon became the driving force."

"Did they plan to cheat Helen from the start?"

"I don't know. I certainly don't believe Falcano did, but I'm quite a bit more skeptical about Nicholas and Fitzhugh."

"So what changed?"

"They hit one big snag. Helen's property is contaminated with toxic waste. A very expensive cleanup had to happen before anything like a hotel could be built on it."

"And that stopped them in their tracks?"

"It could have. But Fitzhugh used his position to get a grant from state funds. That's where everything got messy."

"That's not illegal, is it?"

"No, but the way he did it stinks. He planned to pay Helen peanuts for the land. She knew about the problem, and he let her believe the place was worthless. He asked the state folks to keep the grant quiet. He said he wanted to make the announcement at a special time, but the truth was, the secrecy gave him more time to close the deal."

"That *does* sound like fraud!"

"Yes it does, doesn't it?"

"And you think all of this is connected with the murder?"

"I don't know. There's certainly a lot of money involved, and many murders have been committed for less. It's the only thing I've found that even resembles a motive so far.

"You don't sound convinced."

"I'm not. Even if Fitzhugh and Nicholas did decide to murder Falcano, why would they make it so splashy? It seems like they'd try to fake an accident, or make it look like suicide."

"Then who did kill Falcano?"

"I don't know. The only thing I do know for sure is that someone planted most or all of the evidence implicating Wil Walker. Whoever did that is bound to be the murderer."

"So what can we print, Mr. Jones."

"I guess you better leave the murder out of it, but I think the voters have a right to know how the mayor was planning to line his pockets, don't you?"

"I certainly do."

Her smile broadened.

"Eldon has been a manipulative, mean-spirited bastard for way too long, and his high-handed attitude is insufferable. It will be a pleasure to see him get some comeuppance."

"Amen to that."

"Let me get one of my best reporters in here to start getting this all down."

Jones' cell rang as she started to reach for her phone.

"Yes?"

Jones frowned.

"Ok, I'm on my way."

He stood up and started toward the door.

"Can your reporters get started without me?"

"Sure! What's up?"

"They've found Wil Walkers pickup. It's under water in Lake Michigan about fifty miles south of here."

"Oh my! Is Walker dead?"

"There's no sign of him. I need to go check this out."

"Of course detective, we'll talk when you get back."

"I'll look forward to it."

"Not as much as I will, Mr. Jones! Not as much as I will!"

The cream-colored Buick cruised effortlessly along the smooth pavement of the interstate.

Wil felt strange driving ten miles under the limit in the right hand lane, but even at that pace, the miles melted away quickly.

Driving a car the police wouldn't recognize gave him a wonderfully reassuring sense of anonymity, but just to be safe, he had on dark sunglasses, some old clothes and a farmer's cap Georgia had given him to wear.

What a great lady!

She had no reason to help him at all. By rights, she should have given him to the police, or at least chased him off her property with that big shotgun. Instead she had fed him, let him take the car, and even given him some money.

He resolved to make it up to her someday, and he hoped desperately he would have a chance to make good on the pledge.

A sign swung into view confirming he was on I-55 headed south, and another one said Springfield, Illinois was ninety-nine miles ahead. At this rate he could get to northern Texas by tomorrow afternoon, even allowing some time for sleep.

The gun shop seemed like his only hope for finding some useful information, but what would he do when he got there?

He didn't know how to find it, and there could be a lot of gun shops near Grapevine Texas. He decided he'd look in the yellow pages, and if he didn't recognize the name, he'd just start with the first one and work his way through the list. He had nothing but time.

He gradually worked out a plan to pose as a reporter investigating Henri's murder. That would make his questions about the missing rifle make sense. He could even mention some names to see if anyone from St. Cecile had been in the area.

The plan seemed crazy.

He wasn't sure he could fool anyone, and he almost lost his nerve several times, but he resolved to give it a try. If the scheme bombed he'd just have to try something else.

The car crested a small rise and a large expanse of lush green grass came into view on his right.

A golf course!

Wil felt a powerful stab of emotion as he thought about how dramatically his life had changed. On a normal day he might be meeting some friends for nine holes, or just practicing.

God he missed it!

He would give anything to be standing on a manicured fairway in the twilight, filling his lungs with the cool air and savoring the sounds of the breeze in the trees, pausing for a moment to listen to fluting birdcalls or watching a grazing deer clinging close to the shelter of the trees. How he'd love to have nothing more to worry about than how good his lie was, how far it was to the green and what club he might need for his approach shot.

Instead he was on a desperate fool's errand, charged with murder and trying to keep away from the police. He had almost stolen a car, and who knows what other crimes he might have committed to get gasoline and food.

He had no idea what lay ahead of him. What would he do when his money ran out? What kind of desperate things was he capable of if push really came to shove?

He thought ruefully about his old attitudes toward people who committed crimes. Maybe they weren't always trying to wreak havoc or get something for nothing. Maybe some of them were just in desperate circumstances with no idea where to turn.

Why couldn't he be quietly working in his studio, poring over the pages of his manuscript, refining the patterns in his head and assembling the tone colors into sweet, rich tapestries of sound?

He summoned back the climactic passage for his symphony and let the music play in his head like a tape. He could still hear it with perfect clarity, as if an orchestra played it right in front of him.

Could it just have been a couple of days since it came to him like a miraculous dream?

Someone had tried to kill him since then and damn near succeeded!

Why couldn't he be sitting at his piano, playing the newly crafted theme over and over again, letting it sing to him, and beginning to imagine the chords and counterpoint he would weave around it to create the perfect flow of music and emotion?

Maybe it wouldn't matter anyway.

If he spent the rest of his life in prison he'd never get his symphony performed. Getting symphonic music played these days was hard enough. The challenge would be hopeless for a convicted murderer!

Wil stared somberly at the road ahead.

The speedometer had crept up to almost seventy miles an hour. He pressed the brakes gently and eased back to just above sixty.

Feeling sorry for himself wouldn't solve anything. He had to deal with reality and keep pushing forward.

CHAPTER SIXTY-ONE

Jones' emotions boiled as he surveyed the crime scene.

Any fool could see what happened.

The pickup lay submerged in about twenty feet of water. Large gashes in the ground and a ragged swath of damaged vegetation marked the truck's path down the steep grade.

Spin marks in the gravel at the top of the hill clearly showed the place where some other vehicle had pushed the truck over the edge.

A small army of forensic workers swarmed over the area like worker bees. They had come up with good plaster casts of some tire tracks, but those would be useless unless Jones found a match.

The mayor would be apoplectic when officers showed up at his door with a search warrant and checked the wheels on his car, but Jones didn't think he would be crude enough to do something like this anyway.

Fitzhugh would sneak around to take advantage in a land deal, but Jones couldn't picture him pushing a truck with a man inside it over a cliff, and he still didn't think the mayor had the stomach to shoot Winston Nicholas from ambush.

Somebody else had to be behind all this. Someone he had missed completely.

Jones grimaced in frustration as he watched the divers combing the pickup for evidence.

What was he missing?

Meanwhile, where was Walker?

Could he be dead? The strong currents here could easily carry his body away.

The techs had found some evidence of activity on the shore. Could Wil have survived and left here on foot?

Jones wanted to believe he had.

Did the fact he'd come this way mean he was heading south? Or was he just looking for a place to hide out?

Jones scratched his head in frustration.

Damn it Wil, if you're out there, you're not helping yourself!

Deep exhaustion took hold as Wil found a large park and started searching for a secluded spot where he could stop the car and get some sleep.

He had turned from I-55 onto I-44 in St. Louis and had almost reached the border between Missouri and Oklahoma. He thought it would take him about four or five more hours to get to Grapevine.

He began to feel dangerously weak and numb as the adrenaline and nervous tension drained from his body. He really didn't think he'd gained any strength since he left the hospital. He felt chilled to the core despite the mild weather, and he had the heat turned up so high it scorched his face. An ominous trembling had begun in his abdomen, and now he felt it spreading through his torso and into his limbs.

He clamped his jaw shut to keep his teeth from chattering.

He finally found a deserted corner of the park and gratefully turned off the ignition.

With a deep sigh, he pulled the coat Georgia had given him tightly around his body and covered himself with a blanket she had tossed in the car.

The cushy seats in the car had been great as he drove, but he struggled to find a halfway-comfortable position for sleeping despite his numbing fatigue.

Every time he saw a set of headlights he felt a wild sense of panic. When the vehicle had gone by, he told himself no one could still be following him, but he couldn't quite convince himself of that.

After what seemed like an eternity, he accumulated enough warmth in his little nest to stop shaking, and the cacophony of fears and worries gradually subsided in his tortured mind.

He thought one more time he had to make this insane scheme work before he dropped off into a fitful sleep.

CHAPTER SIXTY-TWO

Wil guided the Buick down a small incline and backed into a parking space.

A faded sign over the modest, one-story building in front of him identified the place as Mort's Quality Firearms. Wil hadn't expected the shop to be so busy. Peeling dark brown paint and a stained metal roof made the place look a little dowdy, but the steady stream of customers didn't seem to mind a bit.

He had a small list of places to check and this was the first.

His cheap cell phone didn't have a GPS, but finding the addresses had been easy.

When he got to Grapevine he went to a nondescript convenience store called E Z Stop and asked the woman behind the cash register to lend him a telephone book. She grudgingly complied and watched him warily as he sat down at a tiny table next to the machines offering coffee, instant cappuccino and fountain drinks.

Wil tried to smile at her and she looked away quickly. He wondered if she was afraid he might steal it.

He flipped to "firearms" in the yellow pages, and his heart sank when he saw the long list of possibilities. He counted sixteen, but as he looked closer it turned out most of them were in Fort Worth or other outlying cities.

Mort's seemed to be the only gun store in Grapevine. Three other places in town, including a pawn shop, carried guns along with other merchandise.

Mort's certainly seemed like the best bet.

Wil sat in the car eyeing the gun shop for several minutes. He hadn't expected to be so nervous, and it took him a while to build up the courage to go in and start asking questions.

As he watched, two men came out of the store and stood on the small porch talking.

The taller man wore a crisp suit, a wide brimmed hat and cowboy boots made of exotic, patterned leather. Dust covered his companion's jeans and checked shirt, and dark stains ringed his well-worn hat. A large wad of chewing tobacco poked out the second man's stubbly cheek, and before long he bent over and spit a hefty jet of brown liquid onto the ground.

The two men soon parted and drove away, and Wil climbed out of the car and made his way into the store.

Wil hadn't realized guns came in such an amazing variety of styles and shapes. Racks of shotguns and rifles covered the back wall, and a long glass case filled with handguns and ammunition stretched from one side of the store to the other. The narrow shelves in the front part of the store bulged with hunting equipment, camouflage clothing, fishing gear, camping supplies and targets for practice shooting.

Wil decided the gun business must be pretty lucrative.

He stopped under a large sign that said 'Have You Tried Paintball Yet?' and stared at the incredible variety of protective clothing, helmets and goggles. Large plastic bags held hundreds of brightly colored balls that looked enough like bubble gum to make his mouth water. The impressive array of paintball guns ranged from pistols to fancy combat-rifle styles with barrels like overgrown metal drinking straws.

Wil had heard of paintball. He stifled an incongruous urge to laugh as he remembered one of his friends, a former cop, saying "You mean I can run around in the woods shooting people and not get arrested?"

His stomach lurched as he remembered the task at hand.

He pretended to study some of the stuff on the shelves as he checked out the five guys dealing with customers behind the glass case and the frazzled teenager manning the cash register.

The most striking figure in the store, a skinny older man, sat on a tall stool in the back corner, stroking his grizzled beard with thick-knuckled fingers and holding court for a small knot of hangers on. The thumb and index finger of his right hand held a cigarette at an oddly prissy angle.

Wil felt an eerie sense of revulsion as the guy took a deep drag, ground out the butt in an overflowing ashtray, put a fresh smoke immediately into his mouth and flicked open a huge, golden lighter. His cheeks caved inward when he filled his lungs, and they puffed out like a balloon as he exhaled a cloud of acrid fumes that engulfed the men huddled around him.

His wary eyes seemed to take in everything in the store as he snapped the lighter shut.

He had to be the owner.

Wil tried to wait until the others left, but they didn't seem to be going anywhere soon. Finally, he gave up and walked over.

The man never looked directly at him, but Wil could tell he sensed his approach.

Wil cleared his throat.

"Excuse me, are you Mort?"

The owner answered in a thick drawl.

"I'm Jeter. Mort's been dead quite a while."

Jeter took another long pull on his cigarette as he finished his last word.

"Then you're the one I'd like to talk with."

Wil couldn't believe his voice sounded so pathetic.

"One of these other boys can hep ya. I'm on a break."

The man standing closest to Wil stifled a laugh.

Most of the others acted like he didn't exist, but a short, wiry guy with a thick growth of black stubble stared right at him. The man's slack-jawed look of scorn made Wil feel like a bug on the sidewalk. After an awkward silence the guy spoke in a guttural voice.

"You ain't from around here, are ya?"

Wil swallowed nervously.

"No. Look, I just want to ask a couple of questions."

Jeter's eyes continued their perpetual scan of the shop. He hadn't looked at Wil once.

"Go for it."

"I wanted to ask about a rifle that was reported stolen from here. It was used in a shooting in Michigan."

Wil wanted to kick himself. He'd forgotten all about his ruse of being a reporter.

Jeter's eyes narrowed as a fresh billow of smoke drifted in front of him.

"Someone broke in and took it. What would I know about it?"

He turned his attention to the heaping ashtray and flicked a half-inch length of burned tobacco on top of its mounded contents.

Wil tried to swallow the choking cotton in his mouth. He did notice the man hadn't shown the slightest surprise when he asked the question.

"Well, when did it happen? Do you have any idea who might have done it?"

"Why would that be any business of yours?"

Wil hesitated.

"Uh … a friend of mine was charged with the murder. I'm looking for any information that might help him."

Wil felt the glaring eyes of Jeter's cronies, who were all staring at him now.

Jeter frowned at something in the back of the store and sucked in another huge lungful of smoke.

"A friend, huh? I told the police all about it. It was just a robbery."

"Well, sure. I'm not questioning that. I just wondered if there were any other details you hadn't told the police, something else you remembered."

Wil cursed himself for sounding so tentative and intimidated. All of a sudden, all the questions he'd rehearsed in his head seemed completely ridiculous.

The man turned and looked right at him for the first time.

"You're pretty curious, aren't ya? You know, I just might have some more information for you. Why don't you come back here to my office?"

He turned to the man with the black growth of whiskers and gestured with a small sideways nod.

"You come too, Frankie."

"Sure Jeter."

Frankie grinned with a mouthful of crooked brownish teeth.

Wil shuddered and tried to stifle his powerful desire to bolt for the door. He hadn't come all this way to quit now. He absolutely had to learn what he could.

He told himself his fears just came from fatigue and being a long way from home.

At least he hoped they did!

Jeter held open a small section of the countertop and Wil walked through before he had a chance to think about it anymore.

What else was he going to do?

The men walked through a short passageway half filled with boxes and junk.

Jeter reached for the jammed key ring on his belt and opened a plain door labeled 'Private' in black capital letters. When they stepped into the small, cluttered office, Jeter sat behind an enormous desk and leaned back in his creaking, overstuffed chair.

Wil stood awkwardly. He didn't see any place to sit, and Jeter made no pretense of offering one.

A huge elk's head with enormous antlers dominated the wall, and uneven stacks of catalogs and magazines covered the floor. The only illumination came from a dim bulb in a dangling ceramic fixture several inches off center in the ceiling.

Wil noticed a thick coating of dust and at least a dozen dead flies on Jeter's desk. A burning knot in his gut told him he had walked into a lion's den.

Suddenly, everything he wanted to ask seemed pointless. He had to get out of this room, but how?

He looked behind him where Frankie stood impassively.

The dark man shrugged without changing his facial expression and continued staring at him.

Wil turned back to see Jeter studying him intently for a change.

"So, just what is it you really wanna know?"

Wil made a huge effort to speak with more strength in his voice.

"I want to know if you have any idea who stole that rifle."

"How would I know?"

"I don't know. Maybe you suspected someone and couldn't prove anything. I just need to know if there's any more to the story."

"Why's that?"

"I told you, the police think a friend of mine did it."

"Yeah, that's what you said."

He nodded at Frankie.

Suddenly an incredibly strong pair of hands grasped Wil's arms above the elbows and pulled them toward the center of his back.

Pain shot through Wil's spine and shoulder blades. He struggled to escape, but he couldn't budge.

"Hey, what the ..."

"You just keep quiet, kid. Frankie, keep him quiet."

"You bet, Jeter."

Wil didn't want to find out what Frankie might do to shut him up. He felt too stunned to say anything anyway.

Jeter picked up the phone, punched a few numbers, and regarded Wil coolly while the call went through.

"Hey, I got someone here I think you might like to see … yeah, that's right … well, he don't look dead to me … sure, we can hang onto 'im, you just get down here … hey, no problem."

He hung up the phone and lit up a fresh cigarette, leaning back again in his chair.

"You seem to be causing some people big problems, fella."

He nodded at Frankie again.

Wil felt the grip on his arms release and gratefully started loosening up his stiff limbs.

Then something very hard hit him on the back of the head.

He sank quickly into darkness.

CHAPTER SIXTY-THREE

Helen answered the door and found Jim Pearce standing on her porch.

What was he doing here? She thought she'd made it abundantly clear the other day he should leave her alone! But then again, what would it hurt to be nice to him for a few minutes?

She stifled her irritation and did her best to smile warmly.

"Oh, hi Jim. C'mon in."

"Hiya Helen."

Pearce closed the door and followed her back toward the living room.

"I like that nice bright dress and the way you've pulled your hair back. You look different, what's come over you?"

Helen didn't want to encourage him, but she didn't want to be rude either.

"Quite a lot has changed around here, Jim."

"Hey don't get me wrong. You look great. You always have."

Helen blushed slightly and decided to change the subject.

"Would you like something to drink?"

"No thanks, I'm good."

Helen tidied up a bowl of flowers on the table and settled into a chair near the window. She didn't appreciate his intense gaze and tried to look very proper.

"How have you been, Jim?

Pearce sat across from her and leaned forward intently.

"Look, Helen, there's something I need to tell you. It's about Wil."

Helen's heart jumped in her chest.

"What is it? They're saying on the news he might be dead. I've been worried sick."

"Nah, he's ok, but he needs your help. He called and asked me to bring you to him."

She studied Pearce's face. Something didn't seem quite right.

"He called you? Why would he call you instead of me, or somebody like Ted or Greta?"

Pearce looked almost hurt.

"I'm his friend too, Helen. Why wouldn't he ask me to help?"

Helen had never seen Wil and Pearce talking, much less spending time together.

"But what help can he need from me?"

"He wouldn't go into it. He said something about trying to figure out who killed Henri."

Something tightened in her chest.

"How can he do that?"

"I have no idea. All I can tell you is he wants you to come."

"Can't I just talk to him on the phone?"

Pearce glowered.

"He said that wouldn't work, Helen. Maybe he needs to show you something. I know it seems weird, but he sounded frantic."

Loud alarm bells in her head told Helen to send him packing. But what if Wil really needed her?

"I don't know. I think we should call the police."

"No, no cops. Wil was very strong on that point."

Pearce leaned back and folded his arms.

"Wil begged me not to tell anyone else about this. He needs us to come and that's all there is to it. Are you gonna say no?"

Every instinct told her to refuse. What Jim said didn't seem right, but why would he lie about it? If Wil needed their help she'd have to go. What else could she do?.

"No, I'll come. Where is he?"

"He's in Texas of all places. You better bring some things."

"OK, give me a few minutes."

With her mind made up Helen went up to her bedroom, stuffed a few clothes and toiletries into a small backpack, locked up the house and went out to Jim's car.

Pearce stood by the passenger side and held the door open for her.

She threw her bag in the back and settled into her seat.

"When are you going to get rid of this old Cadillac Jim? It's like a big, black hearse."

"Hey what are you talkin' about? This is a great car."

"If you say so. It must drink gas like crazy."

"Naw it gets great mileage. You just get in and don't worry about a thing."

Jones felt a turbulent mix of emotions as he turned into Helen's driveway.

The unspoiled beach and gleaming blue water called to his spirit as always, but he really couldn't bear the thought of Fitzhugh getting his hands on this glorious place.

He would do anything, anything at all, to prevent that from happening!

And where was Wil?

Jones refused to believe Wil's would-be killer had succeeded. Wil had to be alive! But where had he gone? And how had he gotten away? His wallet had been found about 100 yards up the beach, so he had no money, no credit cards and no car.

Jones shuddered as he imagined Wil hitchhiking through southern Michigan in damp dingy clothes with no resources and no hope. He knew Wil hadn't killed anyone, and he berated himself for doing such a shabby job of protecting him.

If something terrible happened, Jones knew he would have a very hard time living with himself.

Call me Wil!

And he hadn't made one iota of progress toward finding the real killer.

Could the mayor really have killed Falcano to keep him quiet? Greed did funny things to people's brains, but that scenario just didn't ring true.

But if he didn't do it, who did?

Jones scowled. He had nothing!

But first things first. He had to find Wil, and the sooner the better.

Jones savored one more glance at the water as he parked his car and walked up to the house.

He couldn't wait to tell Helen that Fitzhugh would soon be exposed in the Daily News. Giving her that good news would be a welcome relief from all these frustrations.

Helen's car stood in its usual place in the driveway, but the house looked empty.

Jones didn't find that overly alarming. He heard Helen had been spending a lot of time with Greta and some of the other symphony players, and that seemed like a very promising development.

Jones knocked on the door and waited patiently. When there was no answer, he tried again, then again.

Oh well, he'd come back later. The drive had been worth it anyway, if only to keep him away from the excruciating atmosphere at the office.

Jones walked back toward his car, but he froze when he saw a clear set of fresh tire tracks in the soft earth next to the driveway.

What in the world?

The prints weren't from Helen's small BMW. They looked just like the tracks from the vehicle that pushed Wil's pickup into the lake!

Jones felt a chill of dread race through his body.

He studied the impressions in growing alarm as he grabbed his cell phone to summon the forensic team.

Things had gone from bad to worse.

He had to figure all this out, and soon.

Very soon!

CHAPTER SIXTY-FOUR

Wil couldn't see a thing, and the oppressive darkness multiplied all his fears.

The loose dirt of the floor and the room's musty smell made him assume his captors had him locked up in a cellar.

He could stand or lie down, but the handcuff binding his right wrist to an extremely solid vertical pipe severely restricted his range of motion. He had stretched his left arm as far as he could in every direction, but he hadn't found anything within reach to tell him more about his prison.

How long had he been here? The total lack of light robbed him of any sense of time, but he'd fallen into an uncomfortable sleep several times, despite his anxiety and frustration. He could have been there two days, three days, or even longer.

Hunger and thirst gnawed at his insides like a vicious beast.

Wil couldn't believe what a miserable mess he'd made of things! He cursed himself for walking right into this trap and quaked with dread as he wondered what would happen next. He realized, finally, how badly he had underestimated the situation, and he imagined every kind of horrible scenario.

Henri's murderer would kill him in a heartbeat, and probably make him suffer terribly in the process. The man had tried twice already, once with pills and liquor, and once by pushing his pickup over a bluff into Lake Michigan.

Wil knew his enemy would finish the job this time. He tried to face the prospect calmly, but the tremor in his guts kept betraying him.

Suddenly a door opened. Wil shielded his eyes as a blinding flood of light streamed into the room and heavy boots stomped down a rough set of stairs.

Wil recognized Frankie's brutish touch as rough hands released the handcuffs from the pipe, pulled his arms together behind his back, and relocked the cuffs with both wrists bound.

Then Frankie put his mouth near Wil's ear.

"C'mon, you. Jeter wants to see you again."

Wil recoiled from the smell of sour breath.

"What are you going to do? You just can't keep me prisoner like this."

Frankie laughed dryly and pushed Wil toward the stairs.

"Suppose you just shut up. It don't look like you're in any position to make the rules."

When they reached the main floor, Frankie herded Wil unceremoniously down the narrow hallway to Jeter's office.

Wil had a chilling shock of insight and revulsion when he saw Jim Pearce standing near the desk.

"Hello Jim. I didn't expect to see you here."

Jim stared at him matter of factly.

"Shut him up, will ya?"

Frankie punched Wil hard in the kidney with his right hand.

Pain shot through Wil's body and mingled with the burning frustration in his chest.

He had a lot to say, but he decided to keep quiet.

Jeter smirked in obvious amusement and blew a cloud of smoke toward the ceiling as he turned to Pearce.

"Well, cousin, you said he might show up and here he is, pokin' around and asking questions about that rifle."

"Yeah, it's a good thing you called me."

"I never wanna hear from this punk again, you got that?"

"No problem, that was the deal. Let's go Wil."

Pearce took hold of Wil's arm and guided him into the passageway and out through a back door. On the way he showed Wil the butt of a huge handgun in his belt.

"Don't even think about foolin' around Wil."

A big black Cadillac waited in the gravel drive behind the store. Pearce opened the passenger door, and nodded for Wil to climb in.

Wil wondered how it would feel to die as he meekly climbed into the car. He would never have guessed Pearce could be so monstrous, but that hardly mattered now. He had fallen into his trap like a complete fool.

Pearce got into the driver's seat, pulled the gun out of his belt and laid it on his right thigh.

He looked toward his passenger with a leering grin as he started to drive away.

"Now Wil, you just keep your hands down where no one can see those cuffs. I don't want to shoot you ... at least not yet!"

Wil cringed as Pearce seemed to find his own joke terribly funny.

He stared at the gun in disbelief.

"So now you're just going to kill me, huh? What a fool I've been! What about those guys back there in the gun shop. Aren't they worried about being accomplices?"

Pearce laughed dryly.

"As far as they're concerned, you're just a busybody. They think I can keep you quiet by roughing you up a little bit."

"What about Henri's murder? They don't mind helping you get away with that?"

"They don't know that much about it. You're a long ways from Michigan, buddy boy, and those birds don't spend a lot of time reading the papers."

"But they know you had the murder weapon!"

Pearce turned toward him with an infuriatingly smug grin.

"Jeter let me borrow the rifle for a while. I told him someone stole the gun from my house and used it to kill somebody. We agreed it was best to act like somebody ripped it off from here. Nothin' to it."

"So you're just going to kill me and bury me out here somewhere?"

"Don't be so melodramatic, Wil! Don't you worry about what's going to happen? *Que sera, sera*, you know?"

Wil shrank down into the seat. How could he have been such easy prey?

They drove for several minutes before Pearce turned into the driveway of a nondescript ranch and stopped the Cadillac in front of a weathered old barn.

The barren landscape and the gathering darkness made Wil's wretched mood sink even further.

Pearce jerked Wil roughly out of the car, shoved him through the sliding metal door of the barn, and led him through a maze of rusted pickup trucks, farm implements and piles of junk.

When they got to a dark corner in the back, Pearce banged his fist against a large post.

"Pretty solid, don't you think?"

Wil found he couldn't utter a word.

Pearce undid one side of the handcuffs, pushed Wil up against the beam with his hands behind his back, and tightened the cuffs until Wil could barely keep from crying out in pain.

Pearce laughed as he walked away.

"Now you just relax, amigo. I'll be back for you soon. Oh, and by the way, you can yell all you want to. There's no one to hear you."

CHAPTER SIXTY-FIVE

Jones walked briskly toward the old farm house, too distracted to notice the vintage buildings or the handsome lay of the land.

A UPS driver had told the state police he'd seen Wil walking up the lane to this farm. The owner admitted she'd seen Wil, but wouldn't say any more.

Jones felt a critical need to give it another try.

He knocked hard on one side of the wooden screen door and shifted his weight impatiently as he waited for a reply. He was just about to knock again when the inner door popped open.

"Just a minute, I'm coming. Can't move as fast as I used to, you know."

A stocky, grandmotherly woman bustled into view and froze abruptly when she saw his face.

"Oh, who are you?"

"I'm a police officer, ma'am. Can I come in?"

"What if I say no?"

She pushed open the screen.

"Just kiddin'. C'mon on in, but it won't do you no good. I told those other fellas all I got to say."

She sounded casual, but Jones could see bright red flags of caution behind her friendly demeanor as he climbed the short flight of stairs into the kitchen.

Two big, shaggy dogs ran to his side, sniffed his clothes with unbridled enthusiasm, and begged for attention with their wagging tails.

The old woman did the barking.

"Shep, Bonnie, you two lie down. You're the worst watchdogs a body's ever had."

The dogs immediately backed off and curled up in the corner.

Jones almost smiled. On another occasion, he'd relish the chance to visit with this kindly lady and enjoy her homey kitchen. Today he had no time to waste.

The woman settled into an ancient wooden chair and waved Jones toward an empty seat across the table.

"What can I do for ya, mister. I'd offer you a cup a coffee, but I don't think you'll be here long."

Jones stayed on his feet.

"Look … Mrs. Steadman?"

"That's me."

"I'm Detective Peter Jones. I have to find Wil Walker, and I think you might know where he is. It's vital that you tell me what you know."

"What makes you think I know anything at all?"

"I know you do, and I know you want to protect him, but he's in serious danger. I have a terrible feeling we're running out of time."

"He seems to think he's in worse danger if you catch up with him."

"I know. But you have to trust me. I have to find him, and soon."

Her deep searching gaze seemed to penetrate to his core.

"He didn't do what you think he did."

Jones looked at her in amazement.

"He told you the whole story?"

"Yes he did, and he's innocent. I've been around a long time, Mr. Jones, and I'm a pretty good judge of people. He couldn't kill anybody. He says he didn't do it, and I'm sure he didn't."

Jones felt his body start to relax. She would tell him what she knew, if he could be patient enough to earn her trust.

"I know that too, and I'm on his side, but I have to find him as soon as possible. Someone tried to kill him twice already, and if we don't get to him first, I'm afraid we'll be too late."

Jones fought an almost overwhelming urge to look at his watch. He had to let her do this her own way and in her own time.

She looked up coyly.

"Maybe that slimeball won't find him. Wil might be more resourceful than you think!"

"I agree, but can you be sure of that?"

Jones thought about the tire tracks in Helen's driveway and wondered if the killer already knew a lot more than he did.

Georgia stared at him intently, then looked down at her hands.

"If I tell you, what's going to happen to him?"

Jones tried mightily to look calm, but he could feel his façade slipping. Every fiber of his being longed to be making calls and speeding down the highway to wherever Wil had gone.

"I can't be sure. If I catch him he still may have to stand trial, but the truth has a far better chance of coming out if we can protect him."

"Ok, but you have to promise me you'll be on his side."

"You have my word, Mrs. Steadman."

C'mon, please! Out with it!

"Call me Georgia. I ain't that old yet. Well, actually I am, but age has its privileges, don't you think?"

"I do. Please Georgia, every second counts."

She threw up her hands.

"Ok, ok! Wil said something about a gun shop in Texas. He's trying to find out more about the rifle used in the killing. That's all I know. I let him borrow my car and gave him a little money. Then he left. That's it."

Gun shop in Texas! What is he up to?

Jones swirled and hurried toward the door.

"Thank you very much, Georgia. You've been a huge help."

Georgia shouted at his retreating back.

"Now don't you forget, Mr. Jones, you promised to be on his side!"

"I won't forget."

The dogs jumped up and ran to the screen door as it slammed behind him.

Wil burned with determination as he struggled against his restraints.

He had no intention of dying in this wretched place, at least not without putting up all the fight he could muster. He just couldn't let Pearce beat him this way!

Wil whacked his fist against the post in frustration.

Pearce had chosen well.

The six-by-six beam rose up from a solid concrete floor and stretched high into the rafters overhead. Wil tried to shake it, but he might as well have saved his strength. He couldn't budge it even a fraction of an inch.

He surveyed his surroundings in disgust. The small, dirty windows let in enough light to reveal a lower, flatter structure than Wil had usually seen in Michigan. The barn might have been used for cattle at one time, but now it seemed to be a neglected storage area.

A thick coat of dust blanketed everything in sight.

Wil shuddered as the light faded. He dreaded what might happen when the sun went down.

He looked desperately for some kind of tool or weapon, but Pearce had either selected a clear space or created one by pushing things out of the way.

Blazing fury built in his chest until, suddenly, he shouted as loud as he could, struggling against his restraints like a wild animal caught in a trap. The rough wood dug into his flesh as he lunged frantically from side to side, but he scarcely felt it. He had to break free! The pain meant nothing.

His primal cry of outrage left him almost spent, and he felt blood running down his left arm as he sagged limply back against the unyielding post. He must have cut himself on a sharp edge or an old nail.

The blood seeped onto his hand, and he felt his wrist slip ever so slightly against the handcuffs.

A jolt of hope shot through his body!

He squeezed his hand as tightly as he could and pulled against the cuffs again and again, trying to ignore the searing pain. Finally, in total desperation, he pulled with all his might.

He felt certain his bones were about to break, but he decided that would be a fair trade and kept pulling.

Suddenly, with a blinding stab of agony, his hand popped free.

Thank God!

He sank to the floor, panting and covered with sweat from his exertions. Very quickly he realized he had to get out of there. Pearce might be back any second.

Wil crept over to the door and slid it open just enough to peer out into the dusky twilight.

The black Cadillac sat exactly where Pearce had left it.

The strains of some oddly-distorted music drifted through the air from the squat ranch house across the yard. The music had to be extremely loud to carry this far. Wil could see some faint lights, but all the windows seemed to be closed.

Wil shoved the barn door open as quietly as he could, stepped through, and hastily pulled it back shut.

His breath came in ragged bursts, but he held it for a few seconds to listen for any signs of trouble. When he heard nothing, he started walking cautiously along the driveway toward the road. He could barely resist the overwhelming urge to break into a mindless run, but the only opening in the fence lay very close to one end of the house, and he had to get away without being seen or heard.

He crouched close to the ground as he approached the house. He considered edging farther away, but decided he had a better chance of staying out of sight this way.

Then a horrifying sight caught his eye through the window.

Pearce had a frantic woman bound to a large wooden chair. Thick coils of rope bound her abdomen, her arms, and worst of all, her neck.

Oh my God!

It was Helen!!

Wil felt his insides twist as if he'd been stabbed.

She looked incredibly small and vulnerable in the oversized chair, and the thicket of ropes binding her looked painful beyond words. The wide swath of duct tape over her mouth and nose had to make breathing almost impossible.

The terror in her wild eyes ripped at his heart.

He had to get her out of there!

CHAPTER SIXTY-SIX

Jones punched in the number for Mort's Quality Firearms and scratched his scalp impatiently as the call went through. A guttural voice answered after the fifth ring, and Jones heard a grunt that he interpreted as a rough translation of 'Hello.'

"Hello, my name is Peter Jones, I'm a police detective in St. Cecile, Michigan."

"Michigan?"

Jones heard an interesting mix of surprise and distaste in the man's voice.

"Yes, Michigan. Could I speak with the owner please?"

"That'd be Jeter. I'll git 'im."

"Thank you."

Jones drummed his fingertips nervously on his desk as the silence on the line stretched on and on. He had almost decided Jeter had no intention of answering his call when he heard someone pick up the headset.

"This is Jeter."

"Hello Mr. Jeter …"

"It's just Jeter. It ain't my last name."

"Oh, Ok … look, I'm sorry to bother you, but I need to know if anyone has come to your store asking about a rifle that was used in a crime here in St. Cecile."

"I remember the rifle. I told you fellas it was stolen and that's all I know about it. Ain't been no one here asking about it but the cops."

"You're sure?"

"O' course I'm sure. We got a lot a work to do around here, mister. We can't spend all our time telling you boys the same thing over and over again."

"Could you ask your employees if anyone asked them about it?"

"Ain't been no one here, mister. That's all there is to it."

A little touchy!

"Well, if someone does come will you call me?"

"I suppose I could."

Jones read out his number, but he didn't hear Jeter writing it down.

The call ended unceremoniously, and Jones stared at the phone thoughtfully.

That was strange!

Wil stared at the scene in front of him in disbelief.

Blinding red and orange spotlights glared onto Pearce as he gyrated violently in a frenzied caricature of conducting atop a tall wooden platform. A huge photo montage of an orchestra filled the opposite wall.

At close quarters, the wildly-distorted music in the room sounded like a demonic orgy. The bizarre arrangement twisted the familiar strains of Wagner's *Ride of the Valkyries* into a hideous caricature, with a screaming electronic guitar playing the melody and a chaotic background of electronic shrieks and moans.

The deafening music sounded menacing through the closed windows. It had to be terrifying inside that room.

Wil felt a bitter pang of rage as he saw Helen staring at Pearce in absolute horror.

Suddenly, she struggled with all her might, trying to break out of the brutal restraints.

Beads of feverish sweat stood out clearly on her flushed skin, and her tousled hair proved that her painful struggle had been going on for a long time.

Every instinct told Wil to rush in there and try to free her, but he knew that would be incredibly stupid and would probably doom them both.

He needed to get away and get some help!

A horrific shock lanced through Wil's gut as he looked back to the garish, oversized podium.

Pearce had disappeared!

Wil jumped up, all caution forgotten, ready to run as fast as he could in mindless, terrified flight.

He froze, with his heart pounding in his chest, when he turned to see Pearce standing right next to him with the enormous handgun braced in both hands.

Pearce grinned with an odd twist of his lips as he raised the gun and pointed it directly at Wil's forehead.

“Very cute, buddy boy. I don’t know how you got loose, but it’s about time for you to come inside anyway.”

CHAPTER SIXTY-SEVEN

Jones decided it was time to call in a favor from his old friend in the Texas Rangers.

He looked up the number hastily, made the call, and tried to stifle his impatience as the phone rang once, then a second time, then a third.

C'mon, c'mon!

The line finally clicked and a formal voice intoned "Texas Rangers, Company B."

"Perry Christian, please."

"I'll see if he's available."

"Wait! ..."

The operator put him on hold before he could say another word.

Jones fumed through another interminable wait.

Absurd relief washed over him when he heard a familiar voice.

"This is Detective Christian."

"Perry! Hi, it's Peter Jones."

"Hey Peter, how ya doin'?"

"Well, not so good! We'll have to catch up later Perry, I've got a problem in your neck of the woods and I need some help bigtime."

"What's up?"

"We've got a fugitive, Wil Walker, headed your way. He's up on murder charges, but he's not the bad guy. Trouble is, the real killer wants him dead and may know where he is. If he finds Walker before I do, he won't be planning a tea party."

"Gotcha. What can I do?"

"Are you familiar with a place called Mort's Quality Firearms in Grapevine?"

"Mort's?! There are lots of good gun shops down here, Pete, but that's not one of them. It's a pretty slimy operation."

"Tell me more."

"It's run by a guy named Jeffrey Jones. Hey, any relation of yours?"

"Very funny. I talked to him, but we didn't seem to hit it off real well."

Christian laughed quietly.

"I can imagine. They call him Jeter. He's never been a boy scout. We have to check on the place all the time, but he usually steers clear of any real trouble, or at least covers his tracks."

"I got a tip that Walker was headed there. When I called Jeter to ask about it, I got the distinct impression he gave me the runaround."

"You want me to shake his tree a little bit?"

"That'd be great."

"No sweat. What do you want me to find out?"

"The most important thing is finding Walker. Call me as soon as you can about that, but there is one other thing. The rifle used in that murder came from Mort's, and Jeter says somebody stole it. Why don't you hold his feet to the fire about that while you're at it?"

"Sounds good. You want me to call you back at your office?"

"No, try me on my cell. I'm gonna come down there as quick as I can get a flight."

"Grapevine's right next to the airport. Give me a call when you get in if we haven't talked already."

"Will do."

Jones fought back a wave of emotion.

"Hey, Perry, just so you know … I've gotten to know this kid Walker, and I like him. I don't want to see him coming home in a body bag."

"Me either, old buddy. He's on my turf now."

Wil's fury mounted as he stumbled into the bizarre room.

Pearce jabbed the gun into his back again and again, prodding him to hurry with a weird cackling laugh that proved he took sadistic pleasure in taunting his prey.

A look of utter desolation filled Helen's eyes when she saw Wil. Seeing him seemed to dash her last hopes.

Her frantic, terrified look cut Wil to the heart. He had to focus the chaotic jumble in his head and find some way out of this, if only for her sake!

Pearce shoved Wil into a second chair next to Helen's and bound his wrists with a fresh pair of handcuffs. Then, with an air of cowboy bravado, he picked up a large coil of rope and started winding it tightly around Wil's belly.

After every loop he pulled in the slack with a rough jerk.

Wil had never felt anything like the fury building in his gut. His anger turned white hot as his chances of escape seemed to disappear forever.

Pearce grunted with satisfaction as he finished binding Wil's body, grabbed a handful of his hair, pulled his head back against the chair, and began circling the rope around his neck.

Claustrophobic panic coursed through Wil's body as the thick rope wound tighter and tighter and seemed to squeeze all the air out of his body.

Pearce finished his work with a last, cruel yank on the rope, put his hands on Wil's knees and bent close to his helpless victim's face.

"How does that feel, smart ass?"

Pearce's hot breath against his ear made Wil shudder in spite of his searing anger.

"You just relax, punk! I got you tied up tighter than a heifer. You ain't goin' nowhere."

Pearce laughed coldly as he stood up to admire what he'd done.

"I've never seen you two look better! So glad you could come over."

Wil couldn't see Helen with his head bound. He could only imagine what she must be feeling.

"What are you planning to do?"

He choked out the words.

"Oh, I forgot to shut you up didn't I? We ain't here for chit chat. At least not yet."

Pearce reached behind the chair for a large bandana, forced it into Wil's mouth and wound a double layer of duct tape over the gag.

"That's better. Now you can just listen for a while."

Wil fought for breath and tried to focus all of his mind and strength, hoping against hope for one last chance to fight back.

Pearce thrust his arms exultingly into the air and lifted his face toward the ceiling.

"Isn't this music fabulous? It's so gutsy and stimulating!"

Then he looked back with mock sincerity, pulled the gun from his belt and pointed it at Wil's crotch.

"Gets you right here, doesn't it?"

Wil's body recoiled in horror inside the infuriating restraints. He felt like an insect bound inexorably in a spider's deadly trap.

Pearce grinned fiercely.

"I know. I'll put on a little concert for the two of you!"

Another sickening jolt surged through Wil's body as he saw the insanity in Pearce's eyes. He didn't just want them dead to keep them quiet. He had some kind of a sick agenda. What kind of horrors would they have to endure before they died?

Pearce mounted the podium and set the gun on one of the booming speakers.

With a look of triumph, he picked up a gleaming piece of metal at least three feet long and held it up like a conductor's baton.

The lance's razor sharp tip made it look much more like a sword than anything a musician would carry.

Pearce pushed a button on the stereo and the hideous *Valkyries* music shrieked out again from the beginning. As the sound surged all around him he gesticulated wildly, ripping the air with vicious strokes of his ghastly weapon.

Wil struggled with all his strength against the stifling cocoon of ropes binding him, but he couldn't move them a single millimeter. His body shook with frustration and rage as the cacophonous screeching assaulted his senses like a physical force. The sick spectacle went on and on, and the thought of Helen suffering the same humiliation made Wil even more frantic.

When the piece finally ended Pearce stood panting on the high dais, then he turned and looked at Wil with a cold stare.

He walked over and held the tip of his weird baton very close to Wil's face.

"You hate me, don't you Wil?"

He paused as if waiting for an answer.

"You always have!"

Suddenly he shouted, in a violent shriek.

"All of you have!"

He whirled to face Helen.

Wil saw enough in his peripheral vision to know Pearce brandished the cruel instrument in her face the same way.

"You're just like all the others. Both of you think you're so high and mighty, better than me."

His voice choked with rage and rose to a scream.

"I'm ten times the musician either of you will ever be! Don't you understand that?!"

Pearce whirled abruptly and ran across the room to a side wall painted jet black. He thrust the tip of his sword fiercely into the drywall, leaving a white gash, and turned his attention to something lying on the floor.

"I have something to show you. Look at this."

CHAPTER SIXTY-EIGHT

Pearce gazed back at them with odd detachment.

"Oh, you can't see too well, can you?"

He seemed eerily calm as he came over to them and turned their chairs toward the spot where he'd been standing.

"There, that's better."

Wil found the weird, cheery tone in his voice more menacing, and in its own way, more terrifying, than the rage had been.

Pearce went back to the dark wall and picked up a rumpled stack of large papers.

"These are some of the important people in my life. I want you to see them."

He held up the pile of crinkly sheets to show them a blurry, life-sized picture of an older man in a formal pose.

"I've made a lot of copies of these pictures. They mean a lot to me."

He paused, as if deep in thought.

"This is Mr. Jacobs. He was our elementary principal. Doesn't he look like a fine gentleman?"

The withering sarcasm in Pearce's voice only heightened Wil's feeling of dread.

Pearce gathered up some long spikes from a nearby table and mounted Jacobs' likeness on the wall by stabbing one of the long nails into each corner.

He bent down to get the next image and put it up the same way.

"This is his wife, Mrs. Jacobs … Myrtle!"

He practically spat out the name.

"The two of them ran our school. Don't they just look like the ideal couple, bringing book learning to us poor, ignorant little kids?"

Suddenly Pearce seized his rapier-like plaything and sliced the pictures in two with a single, vicious swing of his arm. Then he erupted into a frenzy, slashing wildly at their faces and reducing the papers to ragged shreds.

Wil recoiled at the sight of Pearce's taut, bunched muscles flexing through his sweat-soaked shirt. The remnants of the photos fell away, but Pearce hacked viciously at the wall until he started to carve out a hollow in the sheetrock.

Dust and slivers of paper swirled in the air like a snowstorm when he finally stopped.

His body heaved as he fought for breath.

Then he turned, very slowly, and addressed his captive audience with a demonic leer.

"They look better now, don't you think?"

He bent down, picked up the remaining pictures almost tenderly, and stood up holding an image of a girl who looked about seventeen.

"This is Veronica. She was my high school sweetheart."

The word 'sweetheart' sounded like a curse.

He mounted her picture on the wall next to the spot where the Jacobs had been.

"And I'd like you to meet Paige. She was my fiancé."

Paige, an attractive blond of about twenty-five, filled the spot next to Veronica.

Then Pearce held up a foldout from a soft-porn magazine.

"This is Miss Nude Texas Teen of 1984. I just always thought she was cute."

A weird cackle oozed from Pearce's throat, but his eyes remained hard.

He tacked up the latest picture without hurrying, then burst once again into a maniacal blur of motion with his macabre perversion of a baton.

His voice rose hysterically.

"Take that you filthy whores!"

He thrust at the private parts of the centerfold repeatedly like a crazed sword fighter, then shredded what was left of the images with savage swipes of his arm.

"You bitches have no idea what a man wants or needs, and even if you did, you couldn't care less!!"

Wil's desolate spirits sank even lower when he heard Helen fighting back sobs.

Pearce paused long enough to hold up a familiar representation of Jesus, staring at it oddly.

"I promised you everything."

He sounded like he could burst into tears.

"When were you ever on my side?"

Pearce set the picture on the wall with gentle reverence before he began to rip into it, slowly at first, then faster and faster, harder and harder.

Wil squeezed his eyes shut as tightly as he could, but the sound of his tormentor's brutal strokes and grunts of exertion filled his senses with revulsion.

Even Jesus was supposed to see things Pearce's way!

A dark certainty lanced through Wil's body, chilling him despite his boiling blood. He and Helen would never get out of this room alive unless they somehow got the upper hand on Pearce.

Wil fought the restraints again with a fresh surge of desperation, knowing he couldn't budge them. Hot tears of frustration stung his eyes.

Pearce turned back toward them with his chest heaving, ripping off his sweat-stained shirt and using it like a towel to dry his streaming face.

"And now for the reason we're all here, the big finale."

He reached down, picked up the top picture from the pile and pressed it to his chest.

"Here you are, sweet thing."

He turned the page around and showed it to them.

Even the gag in Helen's mouth couldn't stifle the scream that burst from her throat.

A horrifying smile filled Pearce's face as he held up a picture of her.

CHAPTER SIXTY-NINE

Jones pulled his cell phone from his jacket and pressed the button to answer the call.

Damn these little things!

He had taken a helicopter to the airline hub at Chicago O'Hare, but a voice on the intercom had just announced a delay for his flight to Dallas.

He felt like breaking something!

Jones pressed the phone to his ear, hoping desperately to hear some good news.

"Hello?"

"Peter?"

"Hi Perry. What's happening?"

"I've got some good news for you. We told Jeter his friend was probably a killer, and he got friendlier in a hurry."

"Good! What'd he tell ya?"

"He said he gave the gun to a guy named Jim Pearce from up your way."

"Pearce?!"

Jones wanted to kick himself as he remembered the tall trumpet player from the orchestra. He'd never really paid much attention to him.

"Ok, we've finally got a name. What about Walker?"

"Jeter said Pearce and Walker met up at the gun shop. He didn't seem interested in discussing the details. We're still working on him."

"Did he tell you how we could find them?!"

"He did tell us Pearce grew up near here and gave us an address in Ponder, up near Denton. We've got patrol units heading there now."

"Great work, Perry! When we get this mess cleared up I'm gonna buy you dinner!"

"The thickest steak you ever saw, my friend. I know just the place."

"Let me know what you find out."

"You got it."

"Perry, I've got a terrible feeling time is running out. Get there as fast as you can!"

Jones emptied his lungs with a ragged whoosh as he cut the connection.

He'd give anything to be riding in that car!

Pearce put Helen's picture up where the others had been.

"Well lookey here!"

Pearce lifted up the next sheet with a flourish.

"Here's a picture of you Wil! Wonder how that got in there?"

He mounted Wil's likeness on the wall and cut it from corner to corner with a vicious swipe.

"How do you like that, fancy Dan? Can't you just FEEL it?"

Wil actually could feel it, and he quaked as he imagined the cruel weapon cutting into his flesh.

Pearce ripped through the picture twice more with violent swings. His playful demeanor belied the brutal force in his sword strokes, the vicious power that made his deadly menace unmistakable.

Suddenly he whirled, sauntered across the room and held the tip of his sword near Wil's nose, waving it gently back and forth.

Rage, fear and nausea surged through Will as the fearsome tip of the rapier swirled within millimeters of his eyes. He struggled again to break free, knowing with sickening certainty he had no chance.

Pearce just laughed.

"Give it up Wil! I've tied up broncs three times your size, and none of them ever got away. You won't either."

A wild look passed over Pearce's face as he raised his weapon swiftly into the air and pointed it at Wil's throat.

Terror of a totally new kind lanced through Wil and he waited helplessly for the death blow.

Pearce laughed hysterically as he lowered his arm.

"That look on your face is priceless Wil. Your eyes look like saucers."

The mockery in Pearce's voice cut through Wil like acid.

Pearce stood back, studied Wil as if he were a laboratory specimen, and clucked his tongue in mocking disapproval.

"You dare to call yourself a composer. Beethoven and Wagner were composers. Recognize those names? Tchaikovsky was a composer. Bach was a composer."

Abruptly, his rage exploded and his voice thundered.

"You're nothing!! You're nobody! You've always been a nobody and you always will be a nobody. You and all the others think you're so damn fancy! You never paid attention to the music I wrote, did you?"

Wil tried to assimilate this latest shock. He'd never even known Pearce wanted to write music.

"Oh yeah, I wrote a piece. It was damn good too! I gave it to Falcano and he said he'd get back to me, but he never said a word. He was such a conceited bastard!"

Pearce's anger seemed to evaporate as quickly as it had risen, and he turned his attention to Helen.

"Don't cry, darlin.' Here. Let me wipe those tears for you."

Wil heard a strangled groan, and he could picture Helen shrinking from Pearce's touch. He wished desperately he could at least see her!

Pearce bent even closer.

"I've got something special in mind for you. Don't you worry about a thing."

Wil tried to picture what was happening as she gave a choking squeal of protest.

The sound of a sloppy kiss answered his question.

Good God!

Pearce walked back to his exhibition wall with maddening slowness.

"Oh, yes, there's one more."

He picked up another picture and studied it with exaggerated care.

"Maestro Falcano!"

Wil hadn't thought Pearce could sound any more sardonic, but he'd been wrong. The palpable hatred in his voice made him sound almost demonic.

"Henri, Henri, Henri."

Pearce hung the picture on the battered drywall like the others, grunting with force each time he thrust one of the nails through the paper.

"You pompous, arrogant, scheming, deceitful son of a bitch!! You thought you could force me out of the orchestra didn't you? You thought you had a better player lined up. Ha! You had no idea who you were dealing with, did you?"

Pearce took the rapier back with both hands and thrust it into Henri's face like a medieval swordsman delivering a death blow. The weapon sank deep into the crumbling plaster, but Pearce pulled it out quickly and struck again and again.

A cry of primal fury erupted from his mouth as he stabbed harder and harder.

The attack peppered the conductor's face with holes, then obliterated it, as Pearce's malevolent tantrum went on and on.

Jones cell phone rang again.

"Hello?"

"Peter?"

"Tell me you've got him, Perry!"

Jones had boarded the aircraft for his flight, but the agonizing, slow pace of everything had him jumping out of his skin. He couldn't stand doing nothing while the hunt was on so far away!

"I'm afraid not. The house was deserted. It turns out Pearce's parents died about a year ago in a car crash."

"So it's a dead end."

"Maybe not. A neighbor said the family owned some farmland west of here. Everybody knows everybody in these small towns."

"And?!"

"And we've got some units on the way. It's a pretty isolated spot. It'll take 'em a while to get out there."

"Ok, keep me posted, will ya?"

"Count on it."

Arrgggh!!!

Jones almost threw his phone down the aisle!

Why hadn't he seen this coming?!!

CHAPTER SEVENTY

Pearce's anger seemed to be spent. He walked slowly to his weird podium and set the gleaming piece of metal on the carpet. Then he took a deep breath and seemed to gather himself.

He came over to Helen and Wil, stood in front of them with his hands on his hips and spoke in a voice full of menace.

"OK guys, it's time to find out who wants to live and who has to die."

Pearce turned the chairs so Wil and Helen could see each other, ripped the gag from Wil's mouth, and pointed a finger roughly at his face.

"You just sit there and keep quiet, you hear? Or maybe I'll just shoot you now."

Wil hated himself, but he obeyed and pulled ragged breaths of blessedly cool air into his lungs. His eyes burned with outrage as he stared at Pearce.

Pearce bent close to Helen and ripped the duct tape from her mouth with a vicious jerk.

Her crimson face erupted in an almost incoherent shriek of disgust and fury.

"You bastard, let me out of here! Let me go, now!!"

Pearce calmly stroked her cheek and she shrank in horror from his touch.

"Let's talk about that beautiful piece of land, shall we, Helen."

A new quality, oily and wheedling, had appeared in his voice.

"The question is, do you want to live there like a queen, with me, or do you want to die … here and now!"

A thick, choking cry burst from her throat.

"That's monstrous, how could you even think … how could I ever live with you?"

Then a puzzled look crossed her face as she realized what he'd said.

"Why would you be interested in my land?"

"Your place is going to be worth millions! That's what this is all about. Don't you see?"

"The land is worthless, contaminated!"

"Oh, the mayor's got a plan to take care of that And the state of Michigan is going to pay the bill!"

Pearce chuckled with malevolent glee, and the cold laugh made Wil's skin crawl.

"The land will be good as new. And it's mine now. Are you in or out?"

Helen seemed truly baffled.

"What do you mean? I own that land!"

"Fitzhugh fixed that, too! There's a new deed on file. He and I are the proud new owners, and as soon as I finish with you two, he's going to be in a terrible accident. It will all be mine!"

Helen looked utterly stricken by this latest outrage.

When she finally spoke, her voice came out in a strangled sob.

"A new deed? That can't be legal! It'll be thrown out."

"It's a pretty good forgery, but you're right. It wouldn't stand up if somebody took a really good look at it."

He bent close and put his face next to hers.

"But nobody is going to do that. If you're dead, why would they? And if you're smart, and decide to come with me, there's no reason to."

"But how ... why …?"

The tears streaming down Helen's face made Wil's frustration boil with white-hot intensity. Terrible pain shot up his arms as he fought against the crushing ropes one more time with all his strength.

"It's a perfect place for a world-class resort, Helen, a glittering destination for the high and mighty."

Pearce's face darkened as fresh rage filled his voice.

"It was all my idea, and the sons-of-bitches stole it from me! Henri and I were having a drink, just talking, you know? But when I told him what I could picture on that land, he took the idea and ran with it!"

His hands balled into fists at his sides.

"Henri roped in Fitzhugh and Winston Nicholas, and they were going to build it without giving me the time of day! I thought of it. Me! And they just TOOK IT! They had no idea who they were dealing with!"

Helen looked spent, utterly desolate.

"I knew Henri didn't love me! It was all a game! He was just using me!"

A strange quiver crossed Pearce's face.

"Oh no! That was the problem. The sentimental fool wanted to marry you. He thought if Fitzhugh could get the cleanup approved by the state, you could all live happily ever after."

Helen's last vestige of self-control melted, and her body shook with sobs.

Wil couldn't hold his tongue any longer.

"So why wouldn't he keep the place for Helen and himself. Why would he get Fizthugh and Nicholas involved?

Pearce's eyes became slits of rage as he turned to stare at him.

"Falcano and Nicholas were already partners. They asked the mayor to lend them a ton of money on a sure thing, a racehorse that was supposed to make them millions! But the mayor was greedy, he wanted in. The three of them bought the horse together, mostly with the mayor's money."

Pearce laughed with withering scorn.

"The horse turned out to be worthless, sterile! Trouble was, the mayor poached the money from the city. They had to get a loan approved so he could pay it back before the audit, or he was screwed."

"How do you know all this?"

Pearce's fury exploded as he lunged toward Wil and grabbed the arms of the chair.

"Because I KNOW things, okay! You all underestimated me, over and over and over! I should be running things, don't you see? I should be the man in charge."

Then his face softened, almost imperceptibly, and he chuckled dryly.

"Besides, that's when Fitzhugh got smart and teamed up with me. Falcano wasn't moving fast enough, so Fitzhugh decided to get rid of him and take control of the situation. He needed someone who had the brains and stomach to make it happen."

Helen's voice burst out like a shriek.

"So you just killed him, just like that! That's so evil. He was your friend!"

Pearce glided toward her like a lion moving in for the kill.

"That was the fun part! The look on everyone's face was priceless."

He turned back to Wil with a triumphant smile.

"And making them all think YOU did it, that was a riot too! They all fell for it, hook line and sinker!"

Wil's rage turned to ice in his veins.

"So now you're going to kill us like animals. You'll never get away with it!"

"Oh, but I will, smart ass!"

Pearce's face lit up with smug arrogance.

"Your bodies will be found in the ashes after your house burns to the ground! Everyone will know it was a murder suicide. What else could it be? The guilt finally got to you, so you killed Helen, lit the house on fire and put a bullet in your own head."

Wil squirmed violently as Pearce leaned close to him.

"But don't worry, asshole, I'll take care of the bullet for you."

The rank smell of his Pearce's breath made Wil retch.

A cackling laugh burst from Pearce's throat, and Wil heard the madness in the sound.

CHAPTER SEVENTY-ONE

Wil knew the final moments had come when Pearce rose with a strange, stilted formality, turned their chairs toward his make-believe orchestra, and mounted his massive podium like a man in a dream.

When he reached the middle of the dais, Pearce stripped off his boots and jeans, threw them aside and rose to his full height, naked and unnervingly still, staring straight at Helen.

Angry red splotches on his face and chest provided the only clue to his inner agitation.

Pearce started the *Valkyrie* piece again and raised the volume until the sound pounded in the room like a physical presence. The hideous music tortured Wil's raw emotions like salt in an open wound, but Pearce looked toward the ceiling and flailed his arms with an expression of total rapture on his face.

After several minutes of the horrifying concert, Pearce walked slowly over to Helen's chair, untied her Gordian knot of restraints and pulled her over toward the podium.

The sight of her, sobbing and limp with fear, made Wil frantic to get his hands on Pearce's throat.

Pearce led Helen up the steps, placed her in a kneeling position at his feet and shouted loud enough to be heard above the screeching din.

"It's time for us to be together, Helen. I love you and I know you feel the same way about me."

He smiled with wildly incongruous tenderness.

"Take off your clothes."

Helen stared at him in total disbelief, and Pearce took offense when she didn't respond immediately.

"Now! Take your clothes off, now!"

She raised her arms over her head as if to shield herself.

"No! That's so horrible, how could you even think …"

Pearce's face hardened as he bent over her and grasped her by the shoulders.

"You have a choice, Helen, you can stay with me and live, or you can die, right now, with Wil."

He looked over at Wil with a leering grin that spoke volumes.

"And if you're *very* good to me, maybe I can let him live ... but I doubt it!"

Helen shook her head with a look of deep sorrow.

"You've lost your mind Jim. Let us help you."

Pearce slapped her with what appeared to be his full strength.

She shrieked in terror and tried to creep farther away.

Pearce drew his arm back again, balled his fingers into a fist and punched her full in the face.

Wil grimaced with rage as he saw blood begin to seep from her mouth.

Pearce hit Helen again and she collapsed onto the carpet.

"You ungrateful bitch!"

Pearce's voice choked with rage as he towered over her.

"I could have given you everything, but you scorned me, just like the others. It's going to be a pleasure to kill you, but there's something I want first."

He reached down and ripped open her blouse with a violent twist of his arm.

Helen screamed as the fabric tore.

Pearce hit her very hard on the side of the head. His face turned purple with fury as he ripped off her bra and threw it fiercely behind him.

"Turn over, you filthy whore!"

Helen buried her face in her arms and tried to curl into a ball.

Pearce stamped his foot with terrible force on her back, and she cried out in pain.

"I said turn over!"

He kicked her again, and Wil thought he heard her ribs crack, even over the wild cacophony of the music.

"Turn over!"

Pearce bent down to flip her by force.

Helen suddenly swirled and came up with the gruesome baton in her hands.

A desperate cry ripped from her throat as she struck upward with the weapon, summoning all the strength she could find.

A look of profound amazement came over Pearce's face as the sharpened steel sank into his solar plexus.

He stood up and bellowed with pain, tugging at the dull end of the sword in a vain attempt to pull it out. He looked at Helen stupidly and gasped as he tried to take a breath.

Helen pressed the remnants of her clothing against her chest and edged as far as she could toward the side of the platform.

Pearce picked up the gun with a groan of agony, swung back around and took dead aim at the center of Helen's face.

His face twisted into a mask of total hatred as he cocked the gun with a shaking hand.

Wil's body burned with anguish and frustration as he watched the scene helplessly.

Pearce took a step toward Helen and grasped her by the throat, pressing the gun against her forehead.

Helen stared back at him with an unflinching look of utter defiance.

Time seemed to be frozen for a moment as the hideous music swirled through the room like a demon from hell.

Wil's heart felt ready to burst. He couldn't bear watching Helen wait helplessly for the fatal shot.

Then a look of complete surprise replaced Pearce's grimace of rage.

He took a step backwards, staring at Helen. His eyes widened, and his mouth worked as if he wanted to say something.

He struggled to keep the gun pointed between Helen's eyes, but his arm started to sink.

Then he collapsed, falling to the floor in an unnatural swan dive and landing in an awkward heap.

He didn't move again.

Wil felt a euphoric thrill of relief at the sight of Pearce's lifeless body.

Helen looked down in amazement. She didn't seem to believe he could really be dead.

The fact Pearce couldn't hurt them anymore gradually became real for both of them.

Wil felt thoroughly spent and tried to catch his breath in spite of the suffocating restraints.

Helen got up, walked numbly over to the stereo and seized the power cord in both hands. A primal, cathartic cry of pain and triumph burst from her throat as she jerked the plug from the wall with an emphatic thrust of her body.

She stood still for a moment in the sudden silence, then slowly turned her attention toward Wil.

It took a long time to untie him. Helen had to use one of Pearce's brutal spikes to pry apart the rock hard knots and release Wil from the straightjacket of thick ropes.

When Wil got free, he took Helen in his arms.

She burst into tears, and they held each other for a very long time.

CHAPTER SEVENTY-TWO

Jones thought he would enjoy every moment of Fitzhugh's arrest, but he didn't.

The mayor clearly underestimated what Jones had learned. He tried to plead ignorance, claiming the missing money had just been a loan and insisting he planned to pay it back immediately. He almost collapsed when Jones pointed out an accessory to murder faced a much stiffer penalty than an embezzler.

Jones had waited a long time to see that look of abject defeat on the mayor's face, but now he found he couldn't take pleasure in Fitzhugh's demise.

The man looked very small and insignificant as the uniformed officers lead him away.

Jones felt older, and not much wiser, as he drove back to the station to finish moving into his new office. He had almost let a man and woman get killed! But he had also stepped in as interim police chief when Manning resigned

A quick look at Fitzhugh's bank records showed several large and unexplained payments to his police chief. Apparently Manning had a few thousand good reasons to stick up for the mayor.

In his arrogance, Fitzhugh hadn't even tried to cover his tracks.

Jones didn't covet the job as chief, but he thought the city council might ask him to stay on, and he felt an obligation to stick around and help pick up the pieces.

Torch Lake would have to wait a little longer!

Helen opened her front door to see a tall, elegant woman standing in the bright June sunshine.

"Hello Helen. I'm Eleanor Falcano. I know you may not want to see me, but please, may I come in?"

Helen looked at her guest uncertainly, but her manners won out and she stepped aside.

In the living room, both women settled cautiously onto the front of their seats. They both sat primly upright with their ankles close together.

Eleanor spoke first.

"I'm sure you know I'm Henri's mother."

Helen looked down at the folded hands on her lap.

"Yes."

"This has all been so difficult! I just want you to know Henri told me all about you the day before he died."

Helen looked up expectantly, and Eleanor took a turn looking down.

"Henri knew I had a bitter hatred for Russians since Soviet soldiers killed my husband. That isn't like me, and I know it isn't rational. I just couldn't help myself."

Helen held her tongue.

"He told me all about you, about your love for music, your beautiful violin playing. I was terrible to him, ghastly. I wouldn't listen! I was furious when he left. I said if he married you it would put me in my grave."

An awkward silence filled the air until she spoke again.

"He said he loved you with all his heart and wanted to spend the rest of his life with you. How could I be so cruel to my own son?"

Eleanor buried her face in her hands and wept bitter tears.

Helen waited patiently until she composed herself.

"Do you feel differently now?"

Eleanor looked up with deep hurt in her eyes.

"I'd give anything to ask him to forgive me, but I can't. He's gone."

"I know he loved you, Mrs. Falcano."

"Yes, he did. I never doubted that. But he loved you too!"

Now Helen felt close to tears.

"I wish things could have turned out differently, Mrs. Falcano, for all of us."

"So do I, dear, so do I."

Eleanor's voice broke as she spoke again.

"I know I have no right, but I have to ask you something."

She seemed unable to go on for a moment.

"Can you ever forgive me?"

Helen felt gratitude and compassion well up in her heart.

Her bruised spirit would need time to let this woman into her life, but Eleanor had swallowed her pride and come to her. Helen knew how hard it could be to ask for forgiveness.

She smiled as she stood and walked across the room.

When they embraced, Eleanor trembled in her arms.

CHAPTER SEVENTY-THREE

On a crisp Saturday in October, Wil drove to the concert hall in his 'new' ten-year-old Volvo. He would conduct his first concert as music director of the orchestra in about three hours.

After the performance, he would pay for all his nervous energy by sinking into an exhausted funk, but for now, that thought scarcely entered his mind. He intended to savor every moment of the evening to come.

The highlight, at least for him, would be the world premiere of his new symphony.

Wil walked in through the plain back door with his mind buzzing. He needed to do many things in the coming hours to ensure the evening's success. He knew he couldn't sit still, so he put his scores and tux in his dressing room and went out to the stage to check on details he had already checked again and again.

An hour before concert time, the orchestra assembled for a short warm-up rehearsal.

Wil hesitated before he mounted the podium to the spot where Henri had died. A hushed silence in the room let him know the musicians shared his reverence for the moment.

The beginning of the rehearsal broke the ice, and Wil relaxed as the orchestral sound began to flow with precision, warmth and sensitivity. He tried his best to project an air of quiet confidence as he rehearsed key passages in the music and answered last minute questions.

The musicians had worked hard to master their individual parts, and Wil could feel their intense desire to play his symphony perfectly. They were professionals and always wanted to play well, but more than that, he knew they wanted their performance to be exceptional for his sake.

Wil stopped the rehearsal fifteen minutes early when he sensed they might start trying too hard.

"Well, I think we're more than ready. Are there any more questions?"

Several of the players looked up at him expectantly.

He stared at his hands for a moment.

"Look, I just want to say something for all of you who never doubted me … and even for those of you who did. We've been through a terrible time, and I'm just happy we can be together again making music."

His voice began to choke, and he took a few seconds to regain his composure.

"I guess this piece of music was born in fire, but maybe now we all have a deeper sense of what's really important, and what isn't. Just have fun playing tonight. I know that's what I intend to do."

There was a moment of emotional silence as they shared an unspoken, mutual affirmation, then he stepped down from the podium, and the musicians began to chat, fuss with their instruments, and go about their last-minute preparations.

Helen walked over from her place in the violin section. Her face lit up in a wry smile as she lightly touched his arm.

"Knock 'em dead tonight!"

He grinned.

"I just want to keep from making an ass of myself."

Her eyes sparkled as a taunting smile lit up her face.

"It's too late to avoid that!"

"Oh, thanks a lot."

Wil knew they both wondered where the special bond between them might lead.

The cleanup on her land would begin the following spring, and she had enthusiastic plans to establish an artist's colony there. Renting some of the rooms in her house had already improved her finances dramatically.

Wil thought about his new composition as he peeled off his casual clothes and started putting on his formal attire.

Was he crazy to go on writing orchestra music in an age when rock stars and internet videos were the rage? Probably, but he still took deep satisfaction in writing music he cared about passionately, even if it would never make him rich and famous.

He thought authenticity – being as genuine as possible – mattered more than anything, and he believed fervently he had to write the music closest to his heart if he wanted to create anything that had a chance to matter in the long run.

He finished dressing all too soon, and had nothing to do but pace, so he looked wryly at his reflection in the mirror, trying not to think of all the things that could go wrong during the performance.

There was a quiet knock on the door and Pru McDonough came in.

She looked at him a bit ruefully and offered a slender hand.

"I hope it goes great, Wil."

Their recent conversations had been awkward, but Wil knew the easy confidence of their relationship would return in time.

"Thank you, Pru."

He hesitated.

"Thanks for everything."

"No, you're doing a great job, Wil. There's no doubt you were the right one to take over."

A smile passed between them, and Wil felt one more weight lift gently from his spirit.

As she left, oddly enough, he felt his nerves calming.

After what seemed like an eternity, the time came to take the stage.

Wil stood quietly in the wings as the last of the audience members found their seats.

Then the oboist played a tuning note and the chaotic, strangely-beautiful sound of an orchestra tuning up floated gently in the air. The sound gradually died away, and after a few final toots and plucks, silence filled the hall.

Wil renewed his resolve to enjoy the concert to the fullest and stepped out from behind the curtain.

The strength of the audience's greeting took him completely by surprise. They had all followed his story in the news, and the customary polite applause swelled into a powerful ovation.

Wil's eyes began to sting with tears and he forced himself to blink them back.

No! Concentrate on what you have to do!

He bowed deeply in gratitude, turned with a mixture of tension and anticipation toward the orchestra, and raised his arms to begin the first work on the program, a familiar overture by Mozart.

After the first few measures he felt himself relax, and the joyous collaboration of music making filled his senses.

When the time came to conduct his new symphony, he felt a familiar tingle of nervous anticipation grip his body. He took a ragged breath as he stepped onto the podium, smiled with genuine warmth, and started the great adventure of the performance.

His emotions ran the gamut as the music came to life, flowing just as he had imagined it would. The loudest crashes and the softest slurs felt perfect, and everything meshed beautifully.

The opening movement sounded energetic and taut, with delicate lyricism at just the right moments.

The haunting melody of the second movement spun out with heartbreaking poignancy. For a moment Wil didn't dare look at anyone. His eyes filled with tears as a poignant mix of joy and remembered sorrow filled his soul.

His spirits soared as the third movement danced in playful bursts of rich orchestral color.

The finale began quietly and started a long, slow build to its triumphant ending. Wil thrilled at the miracle of hearing sounds he imagined in his head coming to life as real music, played with passion and skill by superb musicians. At the climax, the brass burst into a triumphant hymn that seemed to fill the room with sunlight and fresh air.

As the final notes echoed through the room, Wil wished the music could go on forever.

He held his hands in the air as stunned silence filled the hall.

Then the applause started and began to build.

Wil held out his arms in thanks to the musicians before he turned and bowed to the audience. He heard shouts of bravo as people all over the audience began rising to their feet.

When he pointed to several orchestra members who had played important solos, asking them to stand for a bow, they shook their heads and stayed in their seats. He gestured for the whole orchestra to stand for a bow, but they also refused.

Then he heard a soft rumble as the musicians pounded their feet against the floor in the ultimate compliment, a special tribute orchestras reserve for those they consider one of their own.

Wil felt strangely self-conscious, but he forgot his awkwardness as the applause went on and on.

He drank in the scene, trying to memorize every detail, and told himself to remember this moment when the inevitable hard times returned.

Today had been a great day!

ABOUT THE AUTHOR

Jonathan Bruce Brown is composer in residence with the Jackson Symphony Orchestra in Jackson, Michigan, and chair of the music department at Spring Arbor University, a private liberal arts school nearby. Bruce's compositions have been performed by orchestras across the United States, and his *Symphony for String Orchestra* was recorded by the Prague Radio Symphony in the Czech Republic. Learn more about his music and writing at jbbrowncomposer.com.

Made in the USA
Columbia, SC
19 September 2018